THE JAZZ

Tor Books by Melissa Scott

BURNING BRIGHT

DREAMING METAL

DREAMSHIPS

THE JAZZ

NIGHT SKY MINE

SHADOW MAN

THE SHAPES OF THEIR HEARTS

TROUBLE AND HER FRIENDS

THE JAZZ

melissa scott

A TOM DOHERTY ASSOCIATES BOOK   TOR®   NEW YORK

THE JAZZ

Copyright © 2000 by Melissa Scott

This book is printed on acid-free paper.

Edited by David G. Hartwell

Design by Jane Adele Regina

A Tor Book
Published by Tom Doherty Associates, LLC
175 Fifth Avenue
New York, NY 10010

www.tor.com

Tor® is a registered trademark of Tom Doherty Associates, LLC.

Library of Congress Cataloging-in Publication Data

Scott, Melissa.
      The jazz / Melissa Scott.—1st ed.
          p. cm.
      "A Tom Doherty Associates book."
      ISBN 0-312-86802-2
          1. Internet (Computer network)—Fiction. 2. Motion picture industry—Fiction. 3. Twenty-first century—Fiction. 4. Computer hackers—Fiction. I. Title.

      PS3569.C672 J39 2000
      813'.54—dc21   00-025228

First Edition: June 2000

Printed in the United States of America

0   9   8   7   6   5   4   3   2   1

THE JAZZ

Seth Halford closed the door of his room, let the music wash over him, the molasses-voiced singer urging him to lay down his troubles while the guitar snarled and railed under it and the reinforcing synth, branding its peace a lie. It was the perfect music for his mood, exhilarated and scared all at once, and he closed his eyes for a second, letting the soaring voice pierce him to the heart. Heaven and Hell, they were called; he had both their CDs and half a dozen downloaded bootlegs, complete with club video footage, on his hard drive. But he had work to do, and he opened his eyes reluctantly. He had to make the deal tonight, while jazz on the Santees was still hot, even if his parents were home. At least he had his own account, and they should still be busy with the aftermath of the workday, the supplemental courses they designed for Continuing Education's current best client, RCD Studios, but still, there wasn't any time to waste.

His room was tiny, one of the downers about the current posting, along with the constant Hollywood hassle about avoiding drugs and drink and bad jazz, so small that he'd had to move his computer set-up into the closet, and keep most of his clothes in the blanket chest at the end of the bed. Luckily, he didn't need blankets much here, and all his mother did was shake her head at the perpetually wrinkled shirts and baggy shorts. He pulled his rolling chair over to the machine, and the motion sensor relit the screen, displaying a familiar range of icons, and a clock face, ticking down the last minutes to his appointment. Beside it was the new icon, the gold-and-silver pyramid that he'd labeled with the name of a popular game hack, and he glanced at the clock again before triggering the program. The screen filled with strands of silver like sheeting rain, and he reached quickly for his gloves and helmet, switching the view from the monitor to the helmet's broader display. The monitor screen went blank, and then the helmet's screen darkened, the silver rain filling the space in front of his eyes, drowning the icons of the control spaces. Then the Notes file popped into view—a preference he had to change, he reminded himself, but he scanned the ornate prose anyway, looking for reassurance. This was the ultimate text analysis program, the file proclaimed, analyzing not just text but subtext, and offering the opportunity to revise text according to the generic pattern required. Seth flicked it away, and the silver rain returned to his faceplate. In other words, he thought, the program tells you how to fit your work to whatever the form is. It was a content editor, but a hell of a lot more sophisticated than anything else he'd ever seen. And it would have to be: Testify, Genericon, Nomos, Coffeetalk, Ellsworth Blue—all the big jazz sites had turned him down, most of them without bothering to do more than an anonymous bounceback, except for Nomos, which had refused to take his connection for a week, punishment for submitting work that didn't meet their standards. He winced at the memory, shoved it aside. At least Testify had bothered to tell him what was wrong, show him where the jazz didn't measure up—and Tin Lizzy, who'd sent him the message, was one of the best back-tech people around, one of the people who did the sets, wrote the background code that allowed the jazz to function—but he still wanted to prove she was wrong. Back-tech wasn't content, and he could do content. He just had to show them.

The silver rain stopped falling, the last of it pouring out the bottom of the faceplate, and a new screen appeared, windows tiling on top of each other. The top was a schematic of the finished jazz, each page reduced to quasi-grammatical symbols, the links strongly outlined, the whole thing forming a shape like an exploding firework. The checklights and the three bars at the bottom of the virtual screen all glowed green, and he clicked on the second window to confirm the changes. This was what made it all worthwhile, all the risks he'd taken, borrowing his mother's unrestricted password, persuading Evan to copy his favorite hacking tools, then burrowing into RCD's systems despite all the rumors that the studio prosecuted even the most minor hackers. This one program—Orpha-Toto was its name, for reasons that remained obscure; the parent company was Orpha-Tech, and it didn't exist anymore—was his key to the jazz, would give him the edge he needed to get hosted on the major sites.

A chime sounded, mellow in his ear, and he reached with gloved hands into the control space, closing down the program. It folded in on itself in a final shower of silver, and the icon vanished from the main screen. He kept his jazz files hidden, or at least obscured, innocuous names tucked deep into nested directories—not that he really thought his parents would search his files, despite the PSAs that urged adults everywhere to find out what their kids were doing, but he didn't want to rub their noses in the fact that he was doing jazz. The studios didn't really approve of the genre, and while Continuing Education was under contract, it was probably smarter to be discreet. He touched the connection icon, leaned back in his chair as the sequence started, screens flashing past so quickly he could barely read them. At least things were fast tonight, but it was early still. He held his breath as he spiraled out into the Net, the upper part of the screen morphing to a tunnel filled with flashing lights. He recognized most of them without having to think about it, RCD's subsidized employee services, chat sites, data banks, miscellaneous locals, and brushed them gently aside. His point of view seemed to slide forward into the tunnel, as though he was flying in a midnight snowstorm, and he concentrated on avoiding the advertising dots and the persistent tide-links that wanted to take him to their proprietary services. Most of them weren't worth the money they charged, were good only if you didn't know the Net, and he couldn't repress a sneer as he batted the last one away. And then the tunnel seemed to open out into a spherical cavern—in the squashed interlink screen, the text message read, "open access achieved"—and he reached for Testify's icon floating in the central space. It opened, flowering on a screenful of color that quickly transformed itself into a barroom. Seth took a deep breath and gave his settings a last quick look. Everything was set to suppress his identity, deflect any inquiries, and his mask was in place, substituting a generic image for his usual personas and muting his voice to something equally generic, and he made himself relax in his chair as a table appeared in front of him.

Jazzman08 was waiting for him, as promised—for sure it was Jazzman08's presence that brought him so quickly through the maze of Testify's primary screens, and Seth took another careful breath. The bar looked full, but most of the figures were wallpaper, part of the scenery like the dark walls and the unoccupied stage. Jazzman08 stared at him from across the table, black-goateed under a black beret, and Seth glanced again at his own settings. He was presenting pretty much the same image, the persona set to choose the most common image in a setting and modify it only slightly, and he suppressed a nervous giggle at the thought of the two identical images bargaining across the table.

"So," Jazzman08 said, and Seth swallowed hard, groping for a nonchalant tone.

"Have you reached a verdict?"

"Yeah." Jazzman08 took a sip of his drink, something dark in a tall glass, and Seth wished he'd thought to bring a cup into his bedroom so that he could mimic the gesture. Without a real glass to model the movement, his software tended to slip, fingers fading in and out of the image, and he ignored the shorter glass in front of him. "I mean, don't get me wrong, Keyz, it's not the second coming, but it's a nice idea. We'd be interested in hosting—"

Yes! Seth closed his teeth over the word, trying to damp down his elation. There would be a catch, there always was. . . .

"—assuming we approve the back-tech."

And there it was, the catch. Seth sighed, knowing his own work wasn't going to be good enough to pass, not on Testify—and Evan's probably wouldn't, either, even if Seth had wanted to explain how he'd suddenly come up with content this sophisticated—and Jazzman08 went on.

"In fact, we'd be willing to put you in touch with someone, if you don't have a regular guy for it."

Then they did want it. Seth suppressed a yelp of sheer glee—no way would they offer him back-tech unless they really liked it—and said, "I don't, at the moment."

"Then would you be willing to work with one of our regulars?"

Seth swallowed again—Testify's back-tech was the best on the Net, and maybe, just maybe, he would even get Tin Lizzy. She'd been decent to him when he gave her crap; it would be really nice to give her something good to work with. "Yeah, I guess so." He was trying to sound cool, as though he did this every day, but from the amusement in Jazzman08's voice, he knew he'd failed.

"I'm sure somebody'll be willing to take on the project. It'll cut down on your profit, though—back-tech ain't cheap."

"No," Seth agreed, and over the sigh of the air-conditioning heard footsteps outside his door. *Not now*, he thought, and automatically muted his outgoing vocal. "Yeah?"

"Dinner's almost ready." It was his father's voice, barely muffled by the hollow door. "And we need to talk to you, Seth."

Shit. "I'll be right down," Seth answered, and waited for the footsteps to move off.

"It's important."

Seth suppressed the desire to shout at him to go away. In the helmet, Jazzman08 said, "We don't have to talk about that until I get you somebody."

"I'm on the Net," Seth said. "I'm just getting off." He reached for the mute button, flicked it off again. "Hang on a minute, please, Jazzman."

He flipped it on without waiting for an answer, and heard the door open behind him. The helmet barred his view; he stared into the bar scene, glad the monitor was blanked.

"That's part of what we need to talk to you about," his father said.

"Just let me finish," Seth said, and knew he sounded close to tears.

There was a pause, then his father sighed. "Five minutes. Be there."

"I will," Seth promised, and finally the door closed again. He took a deep breath, flicked the mute button again. "I'm sorry, something—something came up."

"Not a problem," Jazzman08 said, in a tone that made it clear there was.

Jesus, you try doing this with your parents breathing down your neck. Seth killed that answer, said again, "I apologize."

There was another little pause, and Jazzman08 sighed. "It's all right. So we'll let that ride until I have somebody to work with you?"

"That's fine," Seth said.

"Then I'll get back to you," Jazzman08 said.

Seth took a careful breath, not wanting to spoil the deal. "When should I expect you?"

"Give me a week," Jazzman08 answered. "If you haven't heard from me by then, drop me a line."

"I'll do that," Seth said, relieved, and imagined he heard the other smile.

"It's pretty good jazz, Keyz. We're looking forward to hosting it."

"Thanks." Seth hit the Escape, knowing he was being rude, and then triggered the auto-shutdown, watching the icons fold back into themselves as he lifted off the helmet. The monitor lit as he moved, showing the programs shuffling back into their standard order, and he stripped off his gloves, waiting for the final clearance. It came at last, and he toed off the power. He had less than a minute left of the five his father had given him.

It was a lot warmer in the kitchen, partly from the stove and partly from his having let his room get so cold behind the closed door. His father pointed to the cabinet, and he went obediently to fetch the plates, setting them out on the breakfast bar in a neat row. Whatever was cooking smelled good—something spicy, maybe Cal-Mex, or something out of one of the cooking classes his mother was also editing, and he heard his stomach rumble as he poured glasses of the bottled water.

"Smells great," he said, and his mother managed a preoccupied smile, still stirring something in the big frying pan.

"It's almost done."

"Let's eat out on the porch," his father said, and Seth blinked. Normally, he was the one who asked to eat outside, and his parents who protested the heat and the occasional insect.

"Good idea," his mother said, too brightly, and Seth looked from one to the other, wondering what was wrong. Surely they hadn't found out about Orpha-Toto, he'd covered his tracks too well for that. Maybe it was the jazz, they'd found out he was playing, but that didn't seem right, either. They'd never been as paranoid about it as some of the California parents.

"Cool," he said, trying to sound nonchalant, and the ricemaker pinged.

"Serve that, will you, Fred?" his mother said. "Seth, get the shredded cheese and the salsa verde."

Cal-Mex, then. Seth did as he was told, waiting while his mother poured the thick bean-and-onion mixture over the mounds of rice, then topped each plate as she directed. His father slid open the door that led to the deck, and Seth followed him out into the cooling evening. They'd been lucky in the housing lottery, or so everybody said, a nice two-bedroom place with a view of the hills beyond the development's pool; the drawback was that the units to either side were bigger, occupied by studio families with two young children each. Seth glanced through the lattice that formed the shared side of the porch, seeing a scatter of toys and the hobby-truck on its side in the glare of the security lights. At least the Mendes clan seemed to have gone to bed early, and the windows on the other side were dark as well.

"Sit down," his father said, and Seth sat, perching uncomfortably on the bench below the outside rail.

"What's wrong?" he asked, and wondered if he should have pretended not to notice.

"We've been put on warning," his father said, "we as in ContEd, that someone's been using ContEd codes to hack into some of RCD's protected spaces. Anyone with a certain level of code is going to have to talk to the studio police. Both your mother and I have had that clearance."

Shit. Seth took a huge bite of the rice and beans, blinked hard as the steam scalded the roof of his mouth.

"The codes are going to be changed—"

"Are changed," his mother interjected softly.

"—but since we've always given you free run of the house systems, I want to know if you've been getting into things you shouldn't."

"No." Seth shook his head, took another, more cautious, bite of the rice and beans.

"Seth." That was his mother, her own plate untouched.

"You've been spending an awful lot of time on the Nets," his father said. In the bleak light from the security lamps, he looked old and stern. "What's going on?"

"I'm not hacking."

"That's not answering the question," his mother said, with a strained smile.

"It is so. I'm not hacking, I'm not messing with the studio systems, or your codes."

His mother looked at his father, and Seth felt a stab of guilt. "We've never exactly hidden them. Even the cleaners know about computers these days."

"I suppose." His father sighed, prodded the beans with his fork. "Are you involved in the jazz, Seth?"

Seth hesitated, not quite sure what to say. "I read some, sure," he said, and let his voice trail off. Neither of his parents said anything, and he shrugged again. "I mean, I know how to find the sites, some of them—everybody does."

"Are you playing?" his mother asked, and lifted her fork before he could answer. "No, wait, I want you to think about this. It's important what you say. We—your stepfather and I—have been trusted with another company's access codes. If we are in any way involved in this, not only will we personally be liable, but Continuing Education is potentially liable for any damages. If you're involved, or if you know who might be involved in this—"

"Like Evan Terries," his father said, and his mother gave him a withering look.

"Evan's not a hacker," Seth said, and his mother lifted her hand again.

"If you're involved," she said again, "or if you know anyone who might be involved in this, the sooner you tell us, the sooner those damages can be limited."

Seth opened his mouth, wanting to repeat the lie, promise he wasn't involved, but his mother shook her head.

"Wait. I'm not finished. If you're playing the jazz, I—we—want to know that, too. Because while we personally don't have a tremendous problem with that, depending on content, the studio does. And they employ us. They employ the company. Now. Go ahead."

Seth closed his mouth, opened it again, groping for words. It was weird, weird and scary, to hear his parents like this, scarier still to think that he might have gotten them into real trouble. But he'd covered his tracks. Even if RCD had figured out that it was a ContEd code that let him in, they obviously hadn't been able to trace it back to his account, and there were plenty of other people who had those codes. He'd have to move Orpha-Toto to secure storage—tonight, if possible—but otherwise, he was OK. He'd been careful, done everything Evan told him to, and nothing he'd been warned against. He was safe—and besides, he was on the verge of getting his jazz on Testify. Once it was up, once he'd proved he was good, not just some dumb sophomore talking big, then he could tell his parents. Then they'd know it was good jazz, the kind that helped you get into college, nothing that would get them in trouble with RCD—even if the Santees were an RCD act, his satire was kinder, cleaner, even, than a lot of the real news that was out there. But it had to get hosted before he could make that argument, and that meant keeping his mouth shut just a little while longer.

"No," he said, "I don't play the jazz."

[O]ne of the greatest difficulties in rethinking the nature of the place of new information technologies is not people who can't imagine themselves being in two places at once, but rather those who fail to see that they are anywhere at all. . . .

—Michael R. Curry
New Technologies and the Ontology of Places

Presented at the Information Studies Seminar
University of California, Los Angeles
March 4, 1999

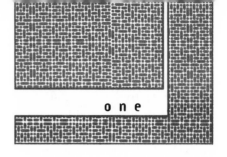

The Dragon Garden was upscale and crowded, black china and linen and chrome trim on the walls, and not a dragon or a flower in sight despite the name. Tin Lizzy paused by the split entrance— lounge to the right, restaurant proper to the left—and heard the dainty euro hostess announce a thirty-minute wait to a trio of suited government types. Lizzy ducked past them into the quiet lounge, dodging a euro waiter with a full tray of appetizers, and slipped into one of the empty seats at the bar. Light sparkled in its black glass depths, resolved to a nicely focused menu as the bartender slid over to take her order. She was Japanese, just about the only Asian visible in the Dragon Garden, and Lizzy matched her smile.

"Here for dinner, or just drinks?"

"Takeout," Lizzy said, and glanced at the menu again. "What's the wait like?"

"About twenty minutes," the bartender answered, the smile widening briefly to a conspiratorial grin, and Lizzy nodded.

"I'll have the special, then, and a side of fried wontons—and a Singapore sling while I wait."

"The special's good tonight," the bartender said, and turned away to key in the order. She brought the drink a moment later, ungarnished except for a chaste black straw, and Lizzy suppressed a sigh, thinking of places she'd been that served mermaids and other dazzling plastic toys with every drink.

"Twenty minutes," the bartender said again, and turned away to deal with a waiter's order.

Lizzy took a sip of her drink, glancing around the dimly lit room. It was almost empty, and even as she thought that, the hostess called a name and a group of four got up from the bar, leaving only her and a business-suited man at the long counter. He seemed oblivious, nursing a bourbon while running something on his smoke—a basketball game, it looked like—and Lizzy started to reach for her own machine. There was an access plate at her seat, but one look at the connection surcharge was enough to stop her. Obviously the Dragon Garden preferred to be a no-smoking restaurant after all.

The trio of suits had followed her into the lounge, were sitting now at a corner table, and the bartender strutted over to take their order, round hips straining the fabric of her short black skirt. Lizzy watched out of the corner of her eye, admiring both the view and the skill with which the bartender managed her silver stiletto heels, and wasn't surprised to see the bartender's professional smile change to something more genuine as she turned away from the table. A performance like that deserved the inflated tip she suspected the bartender had just earned. She could practically see the businessmen's ties curling up in salute, and saw one of them hastily stuff his green temporary pass into the pocket of his jacket. She doubted it would do any good—the rumor was that the bartender was a dyke, too—and wondered if she could turn them to her own advantage. It had been a while since she'd had a date—and tonight wouldn't be one either, she reminded herself. She was due on Testify at nine.

Still, maybe there'd be a chance to get a name, maybe even a phone number, and she took another sip of her drink, rehearsing possible comments. Her left sleeve had ridden up, revealing the edge of her tattoos, one strand of the holographic fiber inserted with the ink catching the light from the bar. She tugged it down, not sure if the bartender would go for something that exotic, and a pair of women burst into the lounge. The one in the lead, dark and softly pretty, looked on the verge of tears, and her tanned friend looked nervously over her shoulder as they came up to the bar.

"Look, Vee, it's not like he's doing it on purpose."

"But he is," the dark woman insisted. She was younger than Lizzy had thought at first, looked barely out of her teens despite the carefully sophisticated makeup. "He knows I'm doing the colors, and what does he do? Brings us to a fucking Chinese restaurant, that's what. He's such an asshole."

Oh, no. Lizzy suppressed a grimace, caught between laughter and guilt. *It's a joke, damn it, it always has been—but some people are just too stupid to get it.* Once upon a time, back when she was first into the jazz, she'd written a page devoted to the color diet: the key was to eat only foods of the same color, and to adjust those colors according to the chakras, to keep yourself in perfect balance internally and externally. She'd shown it to a couple of friends, all bodies and experienced dieters; they'd howled and made suggestions and when it was perfected, she'd posted the thing to a couple of lists. The next thing she knew, there was an entire site devoted to the idea, with recipes and food lists and endless terrifying testimonials to the diet, explaining how the colors had changed their lives and made them happier, saner, richer, sexier. She'd tried talking to the site's owner, an otherwise sane, responsible programmer from Minnesota, but the woman had refused to believe she'd written it. When she'd collected the evidence—original files complete with time stamps, copies of correspondence, everything Lizzy could think of that might convince her it was only jazz—the programmer had waved it away. Whatever the intention had been, she said, the results spoke for themselves.

"Then you got to break up with him," the other woman said.

"I don't want to break up with him," Vee said. "I just want him to stop being a jerk."

"Can I help you ladies?" That was the bartender, her wary look not quite masked by her smile. *No surprise there*, Lizzy thought. *I wouldn't want somebody having hysterics in my bar, either.*

"Two gin and tonics and a couple of beers," the tan woman said, and the bartender nodded, looking at Vee.

"You all right?"

Vee managed a smile, nodded. "Yeah, I guess. My boyfriend's just being a jerk."

"If he's giving you trouble," the bartender began, and Vee laughed shakily.

"Not like that, but thank you. It's just—look, you ever done the colors?"

"Yeah." The bartender's face changed, became newly animated. "Isn't it the greatest?"

"Yeah, except when you're eating Chinese—I mean, no offense, but what's to eat if you're on a white day?"

"Oh, girl." The bartender leaned forward. "Our chef's a genius, he's got it all worked out. Look, you got a smoke?"

Vee fumbled for the purse dangling at the end of its long cord, drew out a small fat smoke in a metallic blue case that matched the fabric of her shirt. She set it on the bar, tugging the built-in minicable to its full fluorescent length, and the bartender reached under the counter to touch a hidden keypad.

"No charge."

Vee smiled back and slipped the cable into the nearest port.

"Now." The bartender tilted the smoke so that they could both see the tiny screen, and the tanned girl stretched onto tiptoe to see over her friend's shoulder. "See, he's figured out how to break down everything, and you can order by the numbers, so your boyfriend won't hassle you."

"This is so cool," Vee said, staring rapt at the screen, and Lizzy drained the last of her drink, rattling the ice. The bartender gave her an including smile, but kept her attention on the screen.

"So for a white day, you can have the special velvet soup, he leaves out the corn and the scallions, and then rice, obviously, and then something like the white cut chicken or maybe puffed shrimp and fava beans."

"What about the jellyfish salad?" Lizzy asked, and all three women turned to look at her. "Sorry. Couldn't help overhearing."

"That would work, too," the bartender agreed, and Vee wrinkled her nose.

"I'm not sure I could handle that. Are you doing the colors, too?"

Hell, no. I just wrote the stupid thing. Lizzy shook her head.

"Oh, you should," Vee said, and blushed. "I mean, not that you need it or anything."

The look on her face said she was less sure. Lizzy sighed, remembering when she was a size six—two sizes smaller than Vee, if she was any judge, for all that she was four or five inches taller—and said, "I thought I read somewhere it was just jazz."

"Definitely not," the bartender said. "There's all kinds of proof."

There was an indignant note to her voice that made Lizzy glad she hadn't tried to get the other woman's phone number. Anyone who believed any jazz as unlikely as the colors was not someone she wanted even for one night.

"I'll have to try it sometime," she said, and was glad to see a waiter emerge from the kitchen carrying one of the restaurant's trademark black bags. She paid for her dinner, ignoring the bartender's veiled disapproval, and headed for her elevator.

The apartment had cooled nicely—the house system had

worked for once, no brownouts to upset the timing—and she left the
bag of food on the breakfast bar and went to open the long blinds,
curious about the day's weather. The lights from the other buildings
made it impossible to tell if it was cloudy—even on a clear night, you
couldn't see anything less than a full moon—but she was startled by
the puddles dotting the courtyard. It had been sunny that morning
when she left for work, though of course she hadn't been outside in
weeks. Or was that a month or more? she wondered. There was no
need to leave CC Underground, not with her job at one end of the
tunnels and her apartment at the other, and plenty of shops in the
mall or willing to deliver. That was one of the advantages of living
here, the way that the whole city seemed to flourish underground,
out of sight of the weather—one of the reasons she'd stayed, even
after Sandy left. For a second she hesitated, feeling faintly guilty,
then shrugged the worry away. The fountain was running, at least,
which usually meant no more rain was expected. If she wanted to go
out, it would at least be dry.

   She started to turn away, drawn by the savory smell of her dinner, but a movement between the buildings caught her eye. She
moved closer to the window instead, to see a man and a woman,
foreshortened by the angle and the height. They paused beside the
fountain, and the woman tossed something into the water; they
embraced, passionately, and Lizzy caught herself looking for the
cameras. They had to be exhibitionists, making out like that in full
view of the towers—and tourists, not to know how unlikely it was
that anybody would be interested.

   She clicked on the television to check her mail, sweeping
smokes aside to scroll through the messages while she unpacked her
dinner. There was nothing of importance, just a note from
Jazzman08 confirming the meeting at nine, and she switched to the
weather channel while she ate. At least her meal was satisfyingly
polychromatic; she grinned and shook her head, thinking of the
women in the bar, and poured herself a glass of wine.

   She finished well before nine, and with nothing to clean up, just
a single black carton of leftovers folded neatly shut and set into the
almost-empty refrigerator. That left time to play, and she moved into
the bedroom, switching on the computer there. Her headpiece and
gloves lay on the bed, where she'd left them that morning, and she

put them on, working her fingers into the stiff metal while she watched her system come to life in the darkened glasses. The gloves warmed rapidly, unfocused feedback tingling against her skin, then the internal menu appeared and the sensations stopped abruptly. She reached for the menu, watching the shadow of her hand slide over the points of light, feedback pulsing from each one, until she found the one that was almost hot and as sharp as a pinprick against her fingertip. She selected it, the pinprick dissolving as her fingers closed on it, and in her glasses a new menu burst into view, bright as a firework. She let the automated routines handle the passwords, presenting the comfortable Tin Lizzy persona she generally used on Testify, and then, quite suddenly, she was falling through the neon night of her own Bourbon Street. It wasn't much like the real thing—no drunks vomiting on their shoes, no skinny addicts lurking in the shadows, no police copters sweeping lights across the alleys. She had kept only the houses, with their wrought-iron gates like lace hiding secret gardens and green parlors, that and the splashing light as a door opened far away, and the music floating almost too faint to be heard. At the moment, she had the scene to herself, except for her own creations: an old man nodded from the doorway of the corner store, a knowing smile creasing his face, and a woman leaned on her balcony, framed in flowers paler than the moon. The music swelled as she passed an open door, and she glanced left to see a woman dancing in a red dress, bright as blood against the dark walls and faces and the glittering steel of a guitar.

A chime sounded in her ear, overriding the music, and an icon bobbed into view, inviting her to a private conference. She started to bat it away, but then the codes registered: Jazzman08 had spotted her already. She sighed, and reached for a pull-down menu, switching herself into Testify's bar.

Bourbon Street dissolved, messily, colors smearing to mud, then slowly reconstituted itself as a reasonable facsimile of a smoky bar. Thrash sounded in her ears, and she turned slowly, to see the band in the corner leaning into the song, the lead guitarist snapping his head back and forth so hard that his long hair sprayed sweat in bright arcs, glittering in the stage lights. She recognized the source of the clip—a two-year-old concert video, one of Leo9's last performances with Aggie Martino on drums—but she had to admire the way it had been integrated into the bar setting. And the way the setting had been subtly altered to match the band: the wallpaper patrons wore the usual leather and denim, but the vivi-tattoos and T-shirts all carried symbols from Leo9's CDs. It wasn't her work, or any hand she recognized, and she made a mental note to look up the person who'd done the back-tech on this one.

Leo9 had always sounded better in the small spaces, where the crowd could get bleary-drunk, but that would make conversation difficult, even with Testify's filters. She sighed, and tugged down a setting menu. It popped to life, offering a dozen different possibilities, and she hesitated for an instant before choosing cabaret. It was a good signal, showed she meant to listen—not as ironic a choice as jazz would have been, but she couldn't stand the music. The images swam around her, long hair and leather morphing to nu-rad suits and expensive casuals, and she glanced down to see that her bottle of beer had become a long-stemmed martini. The air thickened with smoke—every third person held a cigar, a holdover from the Millennium styles of forty years ago—and she glanced over her shoulder to see a cream-skinned diva in a skintight black sheath leaning on a white piano. She was someone Lizzy knew she should recognize, a face in the jazz, a provider rather than a player, but she couldn't remember the name until the woman started to sing. Sierra Skye had been a rising star in RCD's music lineup, but she'd been connected to Njeri Shida somehow, and RCD had dropped her the minute Shida's first suits were filed. Now she was reduced to realworld appearances, and the occasional clip for sites like Testify.

Lizzy looked away, scanning the crowd—all unreal, so far, mere wallpaper—and sat down on the end of her bed. The program slid a table in front of her, complete with ashtray and crumpled bills for a tip, and she took a cautious sip of her drink. The taste of wine startled her, and she glanced under the edge of the display to remind herself that she was really holding a tumbler of cheap chardonnay, not an icy-clear martini. The air smelled faintly of incense, but it took an effort of will not to convert it to the pungent scent of the tobacco that hazed the imaginary air.

A door opened—not quite in the far wall, but close enough—

and a spotlit figure strolled toward her through the crowd. The program drew Jazzman08 as a model-boy, broad shoulders broadened by a padded suit jacket, hands casually in his pockets. Lizzy lifted her glass in greeting, and with her left hand reached to check his choice of setting. To her surprise, he'd chosen haut country, and she caught a quick glimpse of herself in a flippy skirt and mile-high hair, and Jazzman08 in tight jeans and snakeskin boots, before she dismissed the inner screen again.

"Glad you were early," he said, and a chair appeared as he sat down. His drink appeared as well, another martini, but he ignored it, so Lizzy couldn't tell if it was a prop or a representation of something real. "You've looked at the file."

That was Jazzman08, always straight to business. In her earpiece, Sierra Skye began a Judy Garland song, one of the great queer-boy anthems, and the crowd morphed with it, half the women transforming into men. Lizzy ignored the effect—not one of hers—and kept her eyes on Jazzman08. "Yeah, I looked at it."

"And?"

"I think it's good." Lizzy took another sip of her wine, the martini glass sparkling in the display.

"Good enough for us to host?"

Lizzy nodded, reluctantly. "Yeah. Good enough for that."

"So we're all agreed," Jazzman08 said. "It's good enough—personally, I think it's better than good enough, but I'll take y'all's word for it. So what's the problem, Lizzy? Money? You don't hold me up—nobody holds me up—but I could see my way to finding a bonus for working with new talent."

"It's not the money," Lizzy said. "Though if I take this job, I will hold you to that bonus, Jazzman, let me tell you. It's just—" She hesitated, shook her head. "When did Keyz get this good? The last piece we saw, that wasn't five months ago, and it was just OK, nothing like this. And the piece before that was so bad, I banned him for a month for putting up crap like that. I don't trust this kind of sudden improvement—I don't believe in it."

"So maybe he really put his mind to it this time," Jazzman08 said. "For that matter, maybe it's not the same Keyz."

Lizzy lifted an eyebrow behind her glasses, knew he couldn't see the gesture, and took a deep breath, groping for the right words. "If it's not the same person, it's the same public account. And why would anybody pretend to be Keyz?"

"Exactly," Jazzman08 answered. "There's no reason not to take this. What the hell is your problem, Lizzy?"

"I told you. I don't trust sudden spurts of genius." Lizzy paused. "I'm almost certain we're dealing with a kid, or we were—"

"Maybe he's not a kid," Jazzman08 interjected. "Maybe you're wrong, Lizzy."

"Maybe I am," Lizzy said. "But if he's not a kid, I'd really like to know how he got this good this fast. He's got to have had help, Jazzman, and you know it."

There was a little pause, the music sounding in her ears, and then the song ended, the crowd fading back to a mostly straight mix with the applause. Jazzman08 sighed noisily. "The jazz is, he's got some kind of deal—yes, some kind of helper."

"Great. Does this—helper—get credit?"

"Don't start."

Lizzy could almost hear his scowl. "Come on, Jazzman, you know this is important. It could be a sting, for chrissake. Copyright's always after the jazz sites—like I need to tell you that."

"No." Jazzman08 reinforced the word with a shake of his head. "I'm absolutely sure it's not a sting—and, yeah, I know about copyright, probably better than you. Don't try to teach me my job."

She'd hit a nerve. Lizzy made a face behind her glasses. "Sorry. I just don't like silent partners."

"As far as I know, no credit's required," Jazzman08 said. "And I don't even know for sure if there is a partner. There's a lot of whispers, nothing solid."

"What kind of whispers?" Lizzy asked.

"Jesus Christ!" Jazzman08's hand appeared out of nowhere, slammed into the tabletop, disappearing for a second below the fuzzy surface. "What the hell does it matter?"

"I want to know," Lizzy answered, and after a moment Jazzman08 sighed again.

"The jazz is: one, it's somebody who'd been off-line for a long time, wants to get back in the game, but can't hack the regular channels. Russ Conti's name has been mentioned in that connection. Two, it's a program, some kind of expert or even an artificial intelligence, but there's not much chance of that. Three, it's somebody else using Keyz's name—personally, I think that's the most likely, especially if it's some kid."

"Russ Conti," Lizzy said, startled in spite of herself, and Jazzman08 swore under his breath.

"You know it's not going to be Russ. He's out of it, long gone."

Lizzy nodded, acknowledging the truth of that, but said anyway, "If it is Russ, Jazzman, I'm out of here. I want that up front."

"It's not going to be Russ," Jazzman08 said, through clenched teeth.

"If it is."

"Whatever. Fine."

Lizzy nodded again, satisfied, and Jazzman08 went on.

"Or, four, it's one of Njeri Shida's games. And that's why I really want you doing the back-tech, Lizzy, just in case it's him."

That was pure flattery, but Lizzy smiled, appreciating the compliment. Not that this file was Shida's work, the jazz that came out under his name tended to be tighter, flakier, at once more pointed and more off-the-wall. This was truly clever—genuinely funny, a cute idea carried to real absurdity—but it sat squarely in the middle of the jazz tradition, if you could call anything tradition when the whole form had only existed for the last fifteen years. Shida's stuff tended to lie on the edges, the sort of thing that people loved and hated in about equal numbers. Pretty much everybody was going to like this piece, and she doubted that would ever be Shida's style. Not after the man had sued the biggest studio in the country to get control of his own image, not when his films for RCD had been some of the highest grossing—and stupidest—pop hits ever made. "I don't think it's Shida," she said, and Jazzman08 set his glass back on the tabletop.

"Will you do it?"

Lizzy sighed. "Yeah. I'll do it. And I want the bonus."

"You'll get it," Jazzman08 promised. "You got models?"

"Yeah."

"Then let's talk to Keyz."

Before Lizzy could answer, Jazzman08's figure flickered, winking out for an instant before the image was restored. Another door opened, still not quite in the far wall, and a slim man in an expensive suit moved through the wallpaper crowd toward their table. The image was thoroughly enhanced—one of the good commercial masks, she thought, her attention sharpening. Masks, personas, were her other speciality, the other side of the same skills that made back-tech, or, more precisely, those skills turned on a person rather than spread out to create a place. She reached for the right menu, and her probe flashed like a camera, momentarily drowning the bar in a haze of white light. She caught a quick glimpse of a shadowy shape, an extrapolation from the extremely limited input of the goggles-and-glove interface, before the bar reasserted itself, a security icon wagging its finger at her from the bottom of her screen. She saved the resulting file anyway, knowing it was probably pointless, and shifted her hand to check Keyz' choice of interface. The second screen formed, showing her the bar remade by the beat template, transforming Keyz' slightly too-sharp suit to a cardigan and narrow tie, dark glasses hiding the face above the model-perfect jawline. Across the table, Jazzman08's image became angular, the suit shrinking to a black turtleneck and beret. Lizzy nodded to herself and let the screen disappear again. It wasn't anybody's favorite music, but it worked for this situation, let Keyz submerge his personality in a format that had no realworld analog.

"Keyz," Jazzman08 said, and a chair appeared for him to join them. "This is Tin Lizzy—you'll know her work, she's one of the best back-tech guys around. The best around."

"Hi." The voice that went with the mask was enhanced, too, but subtly, a pleasant, undistinguished tenor, and Lizzy wondered for an instant if Keyz were actually a girl. It wasn't like a boy to choose something so unimpressive.

"I think we've met," she said, and Keyz tipped his head in ambiguous acknowledgment.

"Now," Jazzman08 said, and leaned forward. His hands appeared on the tabletop, wrapped in a shimmer of light, and Lizzy dragged her mind back to business.

"As I told you earlier, we're interested in picking up your scenario," Jazzman08 went on, "and I've asked Lizzy to do back-tech and she's agreed. The only thing now is to work out the details."

"Not a problem," Keyz answered, still in the bland false voice that matched the movie-star look. It was going to become annoying after a while, Lizzy thought.

"Let's start with the models," Jazzman08 said. "Lizzy?"

Lizzy reached for the prepared files, hit the upload switch. The images blossomed just above the tabletop, her own expanded versions of Keyz' original images. The scenario was simple enough in outline, an expose site that purported to reveal that Gwayne and DeLoy Santee, RCD's most notorious act, were really quiet, sober men whose only scandal was that they'd been happily married fathers of five for the last ten years. Seth's faked photos were good, compiled, Lizzy guessed, from published shots and retro-90s ads, showing Gwayne Santee barbecuing by the pool while DeLoy played with a grinning, pigtailed toddler. The baby's mother sat drinking iced tea beside them—a particularly nice touch, Lizzy thought, how he'd made her cute rather than pretty, wholesome-looking—while another child paddled in the bright water. She'd taken that lead and run with it, packaging it in acid pinks and pearls, trippy and saccharine all at once, like something by the legendary Martha on a sugar high. The links and side-tech artifacts had a bizarre, handcrafted quality to them, as though they'd been made of gilded chicken bones or some other organic leftovers. She heard Keyz catch his breath and then subdue the reaction, was impressed with the way he waited, studying the files, before he answered.

"I like this look a lot."

"Then you're willing to work with it," Jazzman08 said.

"Yes. Absolutely."

"We—Testify, that is—are prepared to offer you our standard contract," Jazzman08 said. "That's a two-week hosting with an option for week three and a further option for a revised weeks four and five if interest warrants. For that, you get five hundred v-dollars, with a riser of one hundred v-dollars for week three and two hundred-fifty v-dollars for weeks four and five. Plus, of course, a rebate on any connect charges."

That was less than half what Testify would offer a known talent, less even than the deals they usually offered promising novices, and Lizzy hid a smile. *He must think Keyz is a kid, all right—and it'll be very interesting to see if he takes it. And maybe that's what Jazzman is counting on, so he'll find out one way or the other.*

"I heard—I understood that Testify paid double time for revisions," Keyz said.

"Two hundred fifty v-dollars for each week," Jazzman08 said promptly. "Of the revisions, that is."

"And what would you pay in real money?" Keyz asked.

"We don't pay real," Jazzman08 answered. "And you're better off taking virtual anyway."

That was true up to a point, if you came from a country with a dicey currency, and if you were good at judging the money markets—but it was also true that Testify did pay in real currencies sometimes. Lizzy herself was paid in real dollars, and saw the draft cleared through her accounts before she began working.

There was a little pause, then Keyz said, "I'll take virtual. But if I have to do revisions, I want five hundred for them, plus the fees for the week."

"Not possible." Jazzman08 shook his head. "That'd be as much as you got for writing the thing."

"Well, I'd be writing it again, wouldn't I?" Keyz asked, and Jazzman08 sighed.

"All right, we can do it this way. Five hundred for the first two weeks, another hundred for week three, then three hundred up front for the revisions and one-fifty for each subsequent week. After all, you're not starting from scratch."

There was another little pause, and Lizzy wondered suddenly if Keyz' mysterious adviser was with him right now, passing along the right move.

"All right," Keyz said, and despite the enhancement sounded at once nervous and excited.

Or maybe not, Lizzy thought. This wasn't a great deal, especially not in v-dollars—though on the other hand it was probably better to take it and get hosted on Testify, the best known of the jazz sites, than to risk the deal by annoying Jazzman08.

"Great." Jazzman08 laid his hand flat on the tabletop, not quite disturbing the images. "Then let's talk a little about the tech."

Lizzy leaned back, remembered in time that she was sitting on her bed instead of the chair she imagined, and reached to call up a secondary screen to hold the outline of Keyz' scenario. "What did you have in mind, Keyz?"

She could almost hear Jazzman08's scowl. "I think we should start with what you can reasonably provide."

He laid heavy stress on the word "reasonably."

"I'm not seeing anything too tech-heavy," Keyz said quickly. "I'll provide files to be cleaned up. I'm afraid I don't have access to a full-image processor."

"They shouldn't need too many changes," Jazzman08 said. "There's no actual editing, just cleanup."

Lizzy nodded, disappointed, scrolled through her file. "What about micros?"

"I've noted what they should do," Keyz answered.

But you'll have to write them: no wonder the kid sounded embarrassed. Players were supposed to be able to do at least some of the programming—a lot of them prided themselves on being able to do most of it, not just providing the content. *For sure it isn't Russ, if he's got a helper: Russ would never let him get away with it.* Lizzy nodded again, mentally added another five or six hundred to her fee. "I can take care of that."

"Then it's settled?" Jazzman08 said. "At least for preliminaries."

Lizzy suppressed a sigh. "If you get me the files, I'll build you a prototype with all the tech in place, and pass it to you for Keyz' approval."

"To Jazzman—?" Keyz began, and sounded embarrassed again. "Of course. Yeah."

"Privacy's important," Jazzman08 said smoothly.

Not to mention it keeps the talent from ganging up to cheat the host sites. Lizzy said, "You'll have to give me"— she scrolled through the file again, calculating—"say forty-eight hours from when I get the full version."

"We'd like to get this up as soon as possible," Jazzman08 said.

"I'll get it to you as soon as I can," Lizzy answered. "No later then forty-eight, but not a lot sooner."

"All right," Jazzman08 said. "Keyz, you have my drop address. Get me the files as soon as possible, please."

"I will," Keyz said. "Um, as soon as I get the credit, please."

Lizzy laughed in spite of herself—maybe the kid did have somebody cuing him after all—and Jazzman08 nodded. "Of course."

"I'll be waiting for it," Keyz said, and his image abruptly vanished.

"Well," Lizzy began, but Jazzman08 lifted a glowing hand.

"Hang on."

"You don't think that kid's going to try ghosting," Lizzy said.

"Never hurts to check," Jazzman08 answered, and Lizzy swallowed the last of her wine.

"OK, I think we're clear."

"You still think this kid is working on his own?" Lizzy asked, and Jazzman08 rose to his feet, the chair vanishing as he moved.

"I doubt it, but you know what? I don't care. I want this jazz, Lizzy, and I want you to do the tech."

Lizzy tilted her head back. "We haven't talked about my fee. Or that bonus."

"I'll give you your usual rates, plus ten percent for working with a stranger, and another five if you have to do more than one revision," Jazzman08 answered. "And I'll add on an even thousand if you can get it done in twenty-four hours."

Lizzy hesitated. Twenty-four hours probably wasn't nearly enough time—except that the back-tech wasn't all that complicated. If she cut back on sleep, called in sick to her other jobs, she could probably do it. "All right. It's a deal."

"Glad to hear it." Jazzman08's image was already receding toward a new door, though his voice didn't seem to move. "I'll get you the files as soon as I have them. Your clock starts when you get them."

He was gone before she could protest or even agree. Lizzy sighed, found the shutdown switch, and watched the bar dissolve into the darkness of the smoked glass. She set the glasses and gloves on the shelf beside the boxy miniframe, and went out into the kitchen to get herself another glass of wine. She hadn't closed the curtains, and the lights from the apartments in the opposite tower glowed golden, a few dark shapes moving against the brightness. She watched them idly as she refilled her glass, wondering if it was an image she could use—not on this jazz, though. This jazz didn't call for anything that subtle. She reached for the keypad beside the main door, touched the button that slid the shutters into place, wondering if Sandy had been right after all. The jazz wasn't getting any better—*but it isn't getting worse*, she told herself, *and I'm not getting old.* This was just a job, even if Keyz was getting help from somewhere. There was no reason to think it was anything more than just the same old jazz.

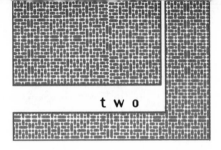

Mail filled her workshop, an explosion of brightly colored squares between her and the wall that held her tools. Lizzy stared at the symbols for a long moment, then, swearing, reached for the nearest square. It was what she'd expected, yet another message querying her about Keyz' site, and she slapped it away with more force than was necessary. One of her new filters had failed, that much was obvious—probably from simple overload, judging by the look of the workspace—and she swore again, dragging crooked hands through the active space to conjure a virtual keyboard. A smaller screen formed in the same instant, offering command-line input, and she typed a string of commands, fingers clumsy in the gloves. The new sort parameters appeared on the screen, blinking for confirmation, and she touched the virtual button, leaning back against her pillows as the squares began to disappear. She should never have let Jazzman08 talk her into being listed as Keyz' back-tech provider—though of course any serious player would have recognized her hand. This was one place her multiple personas didn't help at all: it was Tin Lizzy the players wanted, not any of the dozen or so other people she'd built over the last few years.

She sat up reluctantly as the last square vanished, leaving her with a tidy mail list of no particular importance, and brushed away keyboard and secondary screen. This whole thing was getting seriously out of hand. Maybe it was time to check out the jazz, see what the players were saying—and see what Testify was making off this particular scenario. If it was doing well, maybe she could hit Jazzman08 for a bonus, just for the annoyance value.

She waved her hand through the lower control space, brushing aside her workshop, and reached for the access menu to select her service. She had over a dozen different accounts, set so that each of her personas had a home account, and individual access for their customized smokes, but tonight she chose one of the unenhanced accounts, one she kept for nights like this, when she wanted to lurk without attracting notice. It was low-profile, too, offering only the legally required source number without even a hardware code, and she let it launch, dropping her into a familiar staging area. The main portal rotated in front of her, the icon a spinning torus, revealing a new scene with each turn, but she ignored it, scanning the secondary logos. This was one of the easy ways into the jazz; with any luck, Testify would have a portal up tonight. Another icon slid closer, attracted by her gaze, flashing the familiar cactus logo of the Tijuana Bar and then a cascade of celebrity faces. Lizzy rolled her eyes away and saw Testify in full session, its logos almost drowned by the bright red of its nielsens. The demos flashed beside it, trumpeting a prime eighteen-to-thirty-five catch, and Lizzy's eyebrows rose. No wonder she was getting questions, if Keyz' scenario was drawing this much attention.

She hesitated, then reached for a preset, touching it to drop her into the heart of the scenario. The space behind her glasses turned bright blue, icons tumbling behind the wash of color, her point of view swooping down on and into Testify, and she swallowed hard, dizzied by the movement. The preset slammed her down into the middle of the site, bypassing menus and chat rooms, and she blinked as the bright yellow and red scandal headlines formed around her.

NEW REVELATIONS IN SANTEE SCANDAL!

"THE TRUTH WAS WORSE THAN I THOUGHT," SAYS GRIEVING FAN

RCD Studio Spin Doctors Attempt Damage Control

So far, there was nothing special, nothing she hadn't put there herself, and she reached for the toggle that let her view as much of the underlying code as Testify was willing to reveal. To her surprise, instead of the lines of code, a new text screen appeared.

:: Due to overwhelming interest in this new piece—a twelve
:: share for Testify!—we have set up a special discussion area
:: exclusively for this piece.
:: If you'd like to view sections of the code, or to debate the mer-
:: its of the presentation, just go on in.

Lizzy's eyebrows rose again at that. Jazzman08 should have warned her if he was going to do something like this—it was no wonder her mailboxes had overflowed. She touched the link, already guessing what she was going to see, and blinked hard as the headlines vanished, replaced by a grey background filled with blazing letters.

:: >>>jazz is that somebody's helping him, maybe Russ Conti.
:: >>Bullshit! Conti's dead, or near as makes no difference. This
:: >>Keyz is just good
:: >The jazz I hear is that Keyz is working with a program, some
:: >kind of expert that tells him how to get effects. It does all the
:: >work and Keyz gets the credit.
:: If you're stupid enough to believe that, you're even more of a
:: loser than you look! Nobody's ever written a program that
:: could do that complex an assist.

Below the message, a new icon blinked steadily, offering live chat. Lizzy shook her head, hesitating—the last thing she needed was to be dragged into this—and a new message popped into view.

:: >If you're stupid enough to believe that, you're even more of a
:: >loser than you look! Nobody's ever written a program that
:: >could do that complex an assist.
:: Apparently you're an ignorant asshole. Orfanos's research from
:: '30 on proves that AI complexity is not needed to produce these
:: effects. It's very possible that this Keyz person is using a pro-
:: gram built from that research—if indeed he isn't the program
:: himself.

Lizzy laughed aloud at that, wondering if Keyz would be angry or flattered at having been mistaken for a machine. Flattered, probably; she would have been at his age, always assuming she'd guessed right and he really was a kid. If he was an adult, he'd probably be furious, and she could hardly blame him. But if that was the jazz surrounding the scenario, no wonder Testify was getting the ratings. People were always talking about Ultimate Experts, claiming that some program or other had passed the Turing Test. And if the jazz was this convincing, it would be hard to argue that any program that wrote it hadn't passed.

Except, of course, that she was pretty sure that Keyz was a kid. His helper, and Jazzman08 had been the first to admit he had one, might well be a UE, but that didn't mean the program was capable of playing the jazz on its own. No, if it was a program—and she could believe it was, there was a feel to it that smacked of programming—it was something like the formula that RCD Studios was supposed to use to decide what product to back, a program that predicted success or failure according to its own arcane logic. And there were plenty of people, the studio loudest among them, who denied that any formula existed at all.

She reached for a control point, dismissing the most recent messages, and found another icon that released her into Testify's main lobby. This account's default was invisibility to everyone except the Testify staff, and she reached for the presentation menu to adjust it, adding a name and code that she gave only to a few other players. It would be worth hearing what other people thought about the situation.

Sure enough, a chime sounded within seconds, a new screen appearing to offer a private chat in one of the bars. Miller was always worth talking to, a voice of quiet irony who never let himself be drawn into flames, and she accepted with relief. He did back-tech, too, as well as straight jazz, and wrote his own mini-apps: his opinion was definitely worth hearing.

The bar formed around her, a thrash band in a club whose brick walls were streaked with graffiti as high as anyone could reach. In the wallpaper crowd, men and women alike had long hair and glittering tattoos that matched her own, and the lead singer twisted and posed in the spotlights, cracked voice barely audible over the noise of the guitars. *Who needs to go out*, she thought, *when all this is ready to hand?*

"Lizzy." Miller's voice cut easily through the howl of the band, dropped into their own little pocket of unlikely silence. "It's been a while."

"It has." Lizzy leaned back on her elbows, wishing she had brought in a chair—and a drink, for that matter.

"So what's new?"

Lizzy laughed. "Don't give me that, Miller. You want to know about Keyz just like everybody else."

Miller laughed, too, and Lizzy closed her eyes, letting his imagined image fill her mind. The icon was a biker, bearded, heavy-bodied, and she'd always thought, irrationally, that it had to be close to Miller's real looks. Uglier than the icon, of course, and probably older, but there was something about it that seemed to fit Miller's personality too well for it to be pure jazz.

"You got me."

"If you want to know how to find him," Lizzy said, "I can't help you. If you want to know if he's as good as all that, can't help you. If you want to know if Keyz is a machine, can't help you. If you want to know if I did the back-tech, hey, it's on the credits."

"I want to know why you think he had help."

Lizzy blinked at that, too good a guess, and knew she'd waited too long to answer. "What makes you think I think he had help?"

"Oh, come on, Liz. If you thought he hadn't, you'd've weighed in on the debate. That would've shut everybody up, maybe saved Testify some hassle. But you haven't. So, is the Jazzman pissed?"

"Oh, yeah." Lizzy sat up again, rubbing an elbow that had stiffened. There wasn't any point in denying it, not when it was that obvious—and besides, Miller was generally a reliable guy. "So what's it to you if the kid had some help?"

"Kid?" Miller sounded startled, and Lizzy sighed.

"Well, I think it's a kid. I'm pretty sure, actually."

"So somebody's helping out a kid," Miller said, thoughtfully. "Doesn't make sense. Anybody wrote a piece that goes this big, they'd take credit."

"Unless they couldn't," Lizzy said. That had been Jazzman08's suggestion, and she was suddenly curious to see how Miller would take it.

"Nobody's that bad off," Miller said.

"Russ Conti," Lizzy said, and couldn't keep the bitterness out of her voice.

"What's your problem with Russ?" Miller said. "He was an all-right guy. It wasn't his fault the cops fucked up."

"He should never have given up the data." Lizzy took a deep breath, got herself under control. "Besides, it's not Russ. Russ would have made him do the links better."

She could almost hear Miller nodding in agreement. "So who?"

"That's the thing," Lizzy said. "I'm not sure it's a who."

There was a little pause. "Yeah? So you subscribe to the machine theory?"

"It's not as unlikely as it sounds." Lizzy hesitated again, but the desire to talk to someone was overwhelming. Sandy would have told her to keep her mouth shut, that it was stupid and maybe even dangerous to tell too much to anyone, but then, Sandy was long gone. "When I was working with him, I know he was getting help from somewhere—and if you repeat this, Miller, I'll deny it—but whatever it was, it wasn't a person who knew anything about anything except the actual content. I mean, Jazzman08 got the kid to take v-cash, and nobody in their right mind is going to tell a protégé that's OK."

"But a program writing jazz?"

"The program's not writing it," Lizzy said. "At least, I'm pretty sure it's not. It's more like Keyz is using it as, oh, a spellcheck or something." There was a silence, barely filled by the drone of the band, and Lizzy took a deep breath, trying to articulate something she hadn't really thought about. "I know it sounds stupid. But I would swear that was what he was doing when we went over the final proof. He got the files, linked them up, and then I swear he was stalling me until he could get a final readout from—whatever it is."

"You know, Liz," Miller said. "There's—I think I heard about a program like this. And I'm not talking formula, either, this was something real. There was a project at one of the big schools, Mellon, maybe, that was supposed to be able to read what they called cultural grammar. Thing was, it could tell you what was going to work in a given genre if it had a big enough sample of that genre to work with."

"Sounds like a studio formula to me," Lizzy said. She paused then, a memory tugging at her, something Sandy had said, or done. "Actually, yeah, that does sound vaguely familiar. Something about deep . . . ?" Her voice trailed off, and she shook her head behind the glasses. "I can't place it. But, yeah, that was kind of what it felt like, working with him. Like I said, it was like he was running it through a spellcheck or something."

"Jazz is, Njeri Shida's interested in things like that."

Miller's voice was very casual—too casual, Lizzy thought. Her interest sharpened, and she did her best to match his tone. "Shida? I wonder why?"

"God knows," Miller said. "That's just the jazz. It's not a bad piece, by the way—kind of cute."

Lizzy laughed, accepting the change of subject. "Not a bad word, but I won't tell Keyz. If he's as young as I think he is, he won't appreciate it."

"Pity he didn't push it a little harder."

"I guess." Lizzy sighed. "No, you're right, it's just I'm sick of the whole thing. My mailbox was jammed tonight."

"Got you," Miller said. "Sorry to add to the hassle."

"I wouldn't have talked to you if you did," Lizzy answered, automatically. She watched Miller's icon waver against the wallpaper as the band behind him morphed into someone else. "So you think this might be a program?"

"You know everything I do," Miller answered. "It's what I heard, that's all."

"I wonder why Njeri Shida would be interested?" Lizzy asked again, and tipped her head to one side, waiting for the response.

"Not a clue," Miller said. "It's just jazz."

Yeah, Lizzy thought. *Just jazz. But it's jazz you wanted me to hear.* She said, "Whatever. Thanks for letting me know."

"Thanks for talking to me," Miller answered, and his icon vanished from the bar.

Lizzy shook her head and reached for a control point, releasing herself from the private setting. With the same gesture, she drew down another menu, reselecting her invisibility, and let herself drift back through Testify's main lobby. At this level, she was little more than another unmarked disk. Testify's search daemons could find her, but they couldn't notify their senders without her consent, and she had no intention of talking to anyone, at least not until she'd sorted out Miller's news. She hadn't expected to hear from him—

Miller, of all people, usually had contempt for the easy jazz—but then, everybody was getting drawn into this controversy.

A search daemon yapped at her feet, and then another, but she ignored their beeping. The main thing, she thought, was that Miller generally didn't lie. If he said he'd heard jazz that Njeri Shida was looking for this program, the odds were good that he'd heard just that—and he'd had enough confidence in his source to make a special effort to pass the word along. Lizzy tilted her glasses up on her forehead, peering under the edge of the display at the muted television. The night's weather played in its screen, soundless images of rain and wind from somewhere in the Midwest. Of course, not lying left a fair amount of room for not saying, not telling something important, but Miller had always been a pretty straightforward guy. He wasn't that heavily invested in the jazz, either, which cut short a lot of posturing.

That still left the main question unanswered. Why would Njeri Shida, actor and player, be interested in what seemed to be a spellchecker for the jazz? Though of course the program had to be more complex than that . . . Lizzy frowned, the vague memory teasing her again. Sandy had talked about something like this, in the months after he'd finished her tattoos, a program out of some university—that was it, one of the people involved had died, and Sandy had insisted on reading the obituary aloud at breakfast. Lizzy closed her eyes, blotting out the weather, remembering how Sandy had loomed over even the largest smoke, back hunched down to read the small print. Between bites, he'd scrawled in more requests, come up with a ton of articles, all about this guy and the program he'd been associated with. The program had vanished, though, or never been more than vaporware to begin with, but Lizzy couldn't remember the details.

She sat up, annoyed, the icons of the chat lobby bouncing back into position, but couldn't make the memory come clear. Sandy might have left something on the house systems—he hadn't cleaned out his files, which was the only reason Lizzy thought he might come back—and she reached for a remote keypad to initiate a search. It would have to be very general, maybe just for stuff with Sandy's tag—or maybe she'd try a shortcut first, see if the obituary had been saved to hard memory. She routed the display to her glasses, the virtual screen only partly hiding the chat-room icons, and began filling in search parameters.

Something barked at her feet, in the lowest curve of the display, and she looked down to see a new search daemon bounding at the bottom of the chat screen. It glowed virulent orange, priority coding flashing from every facet of the little icon, and she lifted a hand to flick it away, but hesitated as the system belatedly identified the sender. Keyz must have heard about the controversy, she thought, and was coming to ask her what to do. For a second, she contemplated getting rid of it anyway, but that would only delay the inevitable. She'd done Keyz' back-tech; her silence was contributing to the current jazz.

She dismissed the search with a sigh, and reached reluctantly for the daemon, accepting the contact. To her surprise, the display filled with security prompts, moving past commercial levels to government and banking and then beyond, and she lifted her eyebrows behind the masking glasses.

"Aren't you overreacting just a little?"

The murmur was loud in the silent apartment; she made a face, and entered her own passwords, matching Keyz' security with her own. The screen cleared slowly, leaving a fringe of security icons running down the left side of the image. A jerky picture formed, Keyz' face seen through a cheap camera, the kind that doting grandparents mounted on the sides of their children's monitors so that they could get regular updates on the offspring's progress. He was definitely as young as she'd suspected, a shock-haired blond in a skate-logo T-shirt, and she made a face behind her glasses.

"I don't have a camera in place," she said, and in the screen Keyz gave a nervous smile.

"That's OK." He sounded scared, and more than scared, actually terrified, the brown eyes wide under the sun-blasted hair. "Listen, I'm in trouble. I need some help, and Jazzman08 won't talk to me."

"If you mean about your jazz," Lizzy said, "I wouldn't worry too much about it. The worst that can happen is that you'll have to break in a new name." And for some people, she admitted silently, that was hard enough, but not for a real player.

Keyz gave a wincing shrug. "That's pretty bad, too, but that isn't the problem. I mean, I guess it's part of it—" He glanced over his shoulder, the camera dropping frames to keep up, but whatever had frightened him didn't appear, and he turned back to the screen. "Look, I really need to talk to Jazzman08. Can you help?"

Lizzy made a face, hidden behind her glasses, but admitted that Keyz at least showed an understanding of the way Testify worked. She was a freelancer, handling back-tech, had nothing to do with the day-to-day management of the site. "I can see if he'll talk to me," she said, cautiously, and the imperfect audio still carried Keyz' sigh of relief.

"Thanks. I really appreciate it—"

"Don't thank me yet," Lizzy said. "Wait here." She froze that connection with one hand even as she spoke, reached into the control space for another menu with the other. She found the right search daemon, tagged it and set priority, and let it go. Jazzman08 was bound to be on-site, keeping an eye on Keyz' jazz, if nothing else, and she wasn't surprised when a secondary screen opened almost instantly.

"Lizzy?" Jazzman08 sounded genuinely startled. "What are you doing here?"

"Checking out some stuff," she answered. "Look, I'm doing a favor for someone, asking if you'd meet with them—?"

"Keyz?" Jazzman08 asked, his voice suddenly flat, and Lizzy frowned.

"Yeah. Why?"

"I won't talk to him. No dealings, no nothing, and if you have any sense, you'll tell him the same thing."

"What the hell's going on?" Lizzy felt a chill seeping over her that had nothing to do with the air-conditioning. She'd heard that note in Jazzman08's voice before, almost five years ago, when Hasto B. had gotten into libel trouble during the Shida trial. He'd cut Hasto loose then, banned him from the site and then refused to testify for him at his trial. RCD Studios had gotten several million in punitive damages, and Hasto B. had disappeared from the Nets.

"The kid is poison," Jazzman08 said. "That helper of his is something he hacked—stole, Lizzy—and the right owner's going to come looking for it any day now. There's nothing I can do, and nothing I will do. I won't risk the site for him."

"Come on, this is a kid," Lizzy began, and Jazzman08 cut her off.

"The program's value is way over the limit. Kid or not, I can't afford to have anything to do with him."

Lizzy hesitated. It made a depressing sort of sense, and it matched the little Keyz had said, but she asked it anyway, not caring if he thought she was naive. "Where'd you hear about this?"

"Webmasters list," Jazzman08 answered, and Lizzy sighed. The Webmasters were rarely wrong. "They put out an all-systems alert, warning not to host."

And you've already done just that. Lizzy said, "What are you going to do about the jazz that's playing now?"

Jazzman08 sighed. "Keep it up, I guess—it'd look too bad if I yanked it, no explanation—and play stupid."

"Not likely," Lizzy said, in spite of herself, and heard Jazzman08 swear under his breath.

"Yeah, I know, it's thin—and I'd appreciate you backing me on this one, Liz—but it's all I've got right now."

"I'll back you," Lizzy said, and Jazzman08 went on as though she hadn't spoken.

"But I won't meet with him. I won't talk to him, I won't see him, I won't admit the little bastard exists. Is that clear?"

"Couldn't be clearer," Lizzy said.

"Good." Jazzman08 paused. "If you have any sense, you'll do the same."

"Yeah," Lizzy said, and released the connection, grimacing behind the glasses. If this was a prosecuting matter, Keyz was still a juvenile, but already in the grey area where he could be prosecuted as an adult. A lot depended on the value of the program, but mostly it came down to whether or not the program's owner wanted to push for the harder sanctions. Most of them didn't, not with a kid, and not with a simple hack, but there were a few companies who made it policy to prosecute everything at the ultimate levels. They kept it relatively quiet, but anybody who hacked or played the jazz knew who they were. Hopefully Keyz wasn't the kind of hacker who had to prove how tough he was by stealing from any of them. She sighed again, reaching for the return menu. If the program was valuable enough, she might have some issues with it herself: she had two convictions already, was on her third strike. If somebody decided to push it—*but they probably won't*, she told herself, without conviction, and found the correct control that let her back into the maze of security.

Keyz reappeared, pale and strained, leaning forward a little as though that would bring her back faster. "Will he talk to me?"

"No." There wasn't any other way to put it, but Lizzy still winced at the panic in Keyz' face.

"Did you tell him I'm in trouble—?"

"He knows," Lizzy said. "Apparently you're too hot."

"Oh, shit." Keyz glanced over his shoulder again. "Look, I've got a confession. Some of what they're saying is true. I did have help, only it wasn't from any person."

Lizzy nodded. "I had a feeling you had help."

"Thing is," Keyz rushed on, "thing is, it's not my program. I hacked it, and now I'm in major shit. I mean, they're threatening to fire my parents already, and the only thing that's keeping me safe is they think Evan did it, not me—"

"Slow down." Lizzy heard her own voice sharpen. "Who's they— who'd you hack it from, Keyz?"

Even in the jerky image, she could see Keyz take a deep breath. "RCD Studios. My parents work for one of their hire-ins."

"Jesus Christ." Lizzy stared at the display. RCD was one of the worst, a company that always prosecuted, always went for the highest fines and penalties, and if the kid's parents worked for them . . . "Do they know you did it?"

"No." Keyz shook his head, looking genuinely miserable. "The studio cops think it was Evan—Evan's my best friend. They were over here today, looking at my files, trying to get me to say Evan did it. He's out of town, they wanted to get solid evidence before he got back. But when he does get back, he's going to prove it wasn't him, and then they'll know it's me. And they already said I'd end up in juvenile and my parents would get fired, just if I didn't help them."

Which meant at the very least that he'd end up in an adult jail while his parents sweated out some major fines if he admitted to the theft. RCD—*Gardner Gerretty, it's his doing, his policy*—didn't accept excuses. Lizzy took a slow breath, shying from the memory of her own encounter with RCD and Gerretty. "How old are you, Keyz?"

"Sixteen."

Shit. Definitely old enough to be tried as an adult if the crime was serious enough. Lizzy said, "Do you still have the program?"

"Sort of. I stashed it in some off-line space—one of the secure spaces."

"Can you get it back to them? Trash it and deny you ever saw it?"

"I don't think it'll help," Keyz said. "Not with the jazz I did."

Lizzy nodded in reluctant agreement. "Can your folks help?"

"No!" Keyz' voice scaled up, and he swallowed hard. "No, I can't ask them. The only way they're going to come out of this all right is if I keep them absolutely out of it."

That was probably true, too, Lizzy thought, and even if they wanted to help, there wasn't much hire-ins could do to stand up to any studio. She sighed again, remembering when she was sixteen. She'd been in care again, for most of that summer, before her father won back custody for the fourth—or maybe it was the fifth—time. The foster parents had thrown her a nice party for her birthday, cake, ice cream, hot dogs on the grill, her and the five other kids in the house and a couple of girls from the school, but she'd known even as she thanked them for the cheap smoke that the good times wouldn't last. Her father had taken it away as soon as he got custody back, and she'd started working the District underage. She shook the memory away, said, "When does your friend get back?"

"Tomorrow night. Evening, really."

That wasn't enough time. In the display, Keyz' expression held the same knowledge.

"I don't even know why I'm talking to you, I just thought maybe, I don't know, you'd know something."

Lizzy took a deep breath. "Where are you?"

Keyz blinked at him. "Huh?"

"Where are you?" Lizzy repeated. "I'm on the East Coast, US, a place called Crystal City. Technically it's in Virginia, but it's pretty much part of DC."

"Uh, I'm in California." Keyz' voice had the wariness of a kid coached from the day he could use a mouse never to tell anybody anything about his realworld identity.

That made sense, if his folks worked for RCD. "Get on-line. If you haven't spent all your money, get a ticket through to BWI or Reagan or Dulles—there's got to be a flight you can make. Then come look me up. Gabrielle Rhea, Crystal City, area code 7034. I know some people who might be able to help you, but the main thing is not to get busted yet, and getting you out of jurisdiction can only help. I've got some ideas, but once you're here, we can figure out exactly what to do."

"You'll get into trouble, too," Keyz said, and Lizzy grimaced. *More than you know—more than I'm likely to tell you. But I don't want you dealing with RCD.*

"Don't worry about it," she said. "I know what I'm doing."

Keyz opened his mouth, closed it again, offering a tentative smile. "Thank you."

"It's OK. Get on the plane, and I'll see you in the morning."

"I'll be there," Keyz said, and cut the connection. Instantly, the security began to unravel, lights and color spinning in the lenses, and Lizzy pushed the display up onto her forehead, wondering what she was getting herself into.

The system chimed, indicating a successful shutdown, no prowlers, no taps, and Lizzy pulled off the glasses, leaving them on the bed while she went into the galley kitchen. The remains of her dinner were still sitting on the counter—pizza, this time, cheap and greasy—and she picked up the last half-eaten piece and chewed on it while she tried to decide if she wanted a drink. Sandy would have told her no, just like he would have made them cook dinner instead of eating out five nights running, but Sandy was gone. She wiped her hands on her jeans and reached into the cabinet for the bottle of Jack Daniel's.

There was only so much she could do to protect herself and Keyz—first, find out about the program, what it was and why it was important enough to turn full security loose on a sixteen-year-old kid. If studio security was threatening the law, they weren't caring about keeping things quiet, and that wasn't like studio security at all. Second, see what her own connections could turn up—a few of the local Systems cops were supposed to be trustworthy, but she didn't know them. The ice cracked as she dropped it into the glass, and she flinched at the gunshot sound. It would take a cop to get Keyz out of this discreetly, though, and she took a sip of the liquor, letting the harsh sweetness roll over her tongue. Chessie Vara had taught her to drink JD, back when she was getting her own tattoos done, nights at Sandy's studio because she was spending the days at an FBI course. Vara was still a Systems cop out in Lakeview, head of her division, the last Lizzy had heard, so maybe she could help. And she was far enough away that Lizzy's record might not have to come into it.

Lizzy tipped her head to one side, considering, couldn't find a flaw in the idea. She'd be discreet, of course, play up Keyz' age and the studio's overreaction, see if there was anything Vara could do for them. Of course, with Gerretty involved, all bets were off. . . . She shook the thought away, angry at herself for even admitting it. There wasn't any reason to think that Gerretty was taking a personal interest in the case, and the rest of RCD had to be more sane. They'd deal, if she or Vara could figure out something plausible to offer them.

She reached for the bottle, topped up her glass, and went back into the bedroom, leaving the lenses on the bed in favor of keyboard and monitor. She had Vara's address stashed in protected memory, the sector that would trash itself if anybody messed with her passwords. She pulled it out along with her favorite secure mailer and sat for a second staring at the blank screen. Her security was good, the best she could find in the shadows, where the phreaks gave away programs that could beat most government decryption, but you never knew for sure when you'd gotten something with a trapdoor built in. She'd have to be careful what she said. She took another swallow of Jack Daniel's and began to type.

:: Chess—
:: I've got a friend with a potential legal problem, hacker-wise.
:: Some people

She hesitated then, wondering if she should identify at least the fact of studio involvement, and erased the last two words.

:: Apparently some studio types are pissed off and threatening jail
:: time, either juvenile or adult depending on what my friend
:: does as to cooperation. Any words of advice? Time's a little
:: tight.
:: —Tin Lizzy

She reached for the mouse, added her personal key, and only then thought to wonder if Vara had kept her codes on file. Vara had been Sandy's friend, and Sandy's friends had always been wary of her—*not without reason*, she added silently. But then, Vara was also a Systems cop, and they knew the value of connections. She'd never throw away an address that might be useful later.

She took a deep breath and opened her secure connection, watching the standard tracers stream across the screen. Everything showed green and clean, and she clicked the last button to send the message. A new screen appeared, confirming both the successful drop and the on-line charges, and she winced at the rates. To accommodate this level of security, she had to have a full commercial account, and every second cost. She broke the connection, grimacing as another two-second increment clicked onto the screen, and then leaned back in her chair. There was nothing more she could do until Keyz arrived, or until Vara responded; that left Keyz' UE program, and the vague memories it stirred. And that meant she should probably take the time to finish the search she had started: if the two things were connected, the more she knew about it, the better she'd be able to broker a deal.

The first search turned up nothing, but a second, broader search through the files Sandy had left turned up at least some of the articles she remembered. She stared at the first one, the obituary that had started it all, complete with a grainy black-and-white photo from the days when academics were expected to look unsexy and unaware of publicity, trying to tease out the truth beneath the adulatory prose. Paul Orfanos had been a professor emeritus of half a dozen different institutions when he died, from the University of Chicago and the Mellon Institute to EduTech and Continuing Education Inc., but none of them had claimed him on their Web sites or offered links to any scholarly papers created under their auspices. The only highlighted text referred to work for RCD Studios, crediting him with a film translation program, but the link had long expired.

Lizzy frowned at the screen, wishing she'd tested into the upper grades. The RCD link was suggestive, but since she was having trouble telling exactly what Orfanos did, it didn't help as much as she'd hoped. She thought the man was a linguist—a linguist specializing in computer analysis of languages, she amended, reading the screen for a second time, and of metalanguages, whatever they were. *A language used to talk about another language*, her on-screen dictionary said, which didn't help as much as she would have liked—except that it suggested that maybe there was a connection between Miller's jazz and Keyz' program. She filed the thought for later and made herself focus again on the obituary. She might not know what a metalanguage was, or what it was this guy Orfanos actually did, but she did know how to read the jazz. And that was all this obituary was, just more jazz.

She leaned back from the screen, letting her eyes focus on the shape of the article, structure rather than content, and was struck again by the lack of links. With all those credits, the "several important books and dozens of articles," she would have expected the institutions that had bothered to keep him on the letterhead after his retirement to link to the notice, trumpet the work he'd done for them. And—she scrolled back to the top of the article, checking the date of birth. Even allowing for vanity lopping a few years off his age, Orfanos had only been sixty when he died. That was young for retirement, even if he'd been private-sector. The whole thing seemed to hint at a scandal—except that if there had been something, personal or professional, EduTech and Continuing Education and Home-School Resources would have dropped him like a hot potato. Those companies never trafficked in anything at all controversial, or allowed their employees, no matter how famous, to do so.

She could always try lurking on some of the academic lists for linguists, see if the name came up—that was what Sandy would have done, maybe already had done to collect this information, but he would have figured out a way to drop the name without betraying that he wasn't one of them. That was beyond her capability, at least not without spending a week or two picking up the jargon and patterns of speech, and she doubted she had a week to spend on the project, not with Keyz arriving on the red-eye in the morning. *Maybe after he's here*, she thought, and paged quickly through her address book, scanning the list of names. As she'd expected, none of them were really academics—well, there were a few players for whom she'd done back-tech who were also employed by one or another of the Educational Maintenance Organizations, but they were so far in the closet about their jazz that she didn't dare ask them anything. She flipped back to the main screen and the stacked articles from Sandy's files, eyeing them without enthusiasm. It had taken her the better part of two days to read them the first time, even with Sandy prodding her on, and all she'd gotten from them was the vague memory of vaporware that somehow connected with Miller's jazz-check, the cultural grammar program. There would be time to deal with them in the morning, she decided, or maybe Keyz himself would have some of the answers.

She shut down the machine, saving the papers to a folder that she could pick up on any of her smokes, and ran her hands through her hair, wishing she could sleep in tomorrow. And, shit, she was supposed to go to work, too; she'd have to call in sick when she got up. She put that aside along with Orfanos's jazz, wondering why anybody cared enough about this particular posting to be willing to threaten a petty hacker with serious jail time. It didn't seem to make sense, and she was sure she was missing something—but she would cope with that, and Keyz, in the morning. She glanced at the row of smokes lined up on the counter, each one filled with an ID template and the programs that belonged to a different persona, the bright blue case that went with the Helena Carr name, all apparent wealth and deceptive stupidity, the sports-logo case that never left the apartment because she couldn't play Joe Anderson convincingly off-line, eyeing them and half a dozen other possibilities. But with the trouble the kid was in, she'd need a real machine, and she picked up the plain black case with a sigh. The personas were fun, but this smoke had all the tools she needed to rebuild any of them, and more besides. There was a good chance she'd need it all, dealing with Keyz.

three

H allac's smoke buzzed the instant he turned in the studio gate. He frowned, fumbled for it one-handed as he turned the car toward his parking spot, but flipped the lid to see nothing but static. Out of range, he guessed, and looked for a transmitter button even as he backed the car into its place. There were none—no need, in this part of the lot—and he slid it back into his pocket, nodding to the guard on the main door. The smoke buzzed again as soon as he entered the lobby, and this time the screen lit, switching automatically to pager mode. Jeff Ishihara's face looked back at him, the stress lines bracketing his mouth deep as scars, and Hallac silently kissed his evening at home good-bye. If RCD's head of Development Security was looking for him, instead of the studio police having to beg a few minutes of Ishihara's valuable time, something had definitely gone wrong. The fact that he'd just spent most of the day trying to track down a teenage hacker suddenly assumed new significance, and he grimaced in spite of himself. He hated hackers, not so much for what they did but for all the hassle they caused, never proportionate to anything they took, and this was bidding fair to be no exception.

"John, as soon as you get this, please contact me. The president wants to see us."

Hallac whistled soundlessly, checking the time stamp—the message was almost an hour old, which meant whatever it was was too sensitive to post on the outside networks—and reached for his phone. Ishihara's number wasn't on his speed-dial, and he wasted seconds trying to remember it before he gave up and punched for the studio operator. She was clearly expecting the call and transferred him directly to Ishihara's personal extension. The Ultimate Expert voice-mail secretary informed him that Ishihara was on another call, but the instant he spoke his name, Ishihara broke into the line.

"John. Thank God you're back. Gerretty wants to speak to both of us."

This is your problem, Jack, not mine. Hallac killed the words, knowing they were pointless—and they weren't true, either, any security breach was ultimately his problem, fell under the studio police's jurisdiction—and said, "I'm on my way up. Your office?"

"Yeah." He heard Ishihara take a breath. "We can ride up together."

"And you can tell me what's going on," Hallac said.

There was a little pause. "Yeah, all right. As much as I can."

Hallac closed the phone without answering, swallowing his anger as he turned for the elevators. Ishihara was being as fair as he could, maybe as fair as he dared, offering to face Gerretty with him, but it wasn't likely to do either of them much good. What would have made a difference was information, he thought, not for the first time—but Gerretty was a lunatic for security, too.

Ishihara was waiting in the cramped lobby that served R&D—his department liked to be seen to spend its money on things that directly affected their output—and waved from the desk for Hallac to hold the elevator. Hallac pressed the pause button, glad the car was empty, and Ishihara stepped in beside him.

"Sorry. But it's better not to keep him waiting any longer." Ishihara's automatic smile was forced. He was a California boy, Hallac knew, born and bred in the studio-dominated suburbs, though his family had been mostly talent, directors and technicians, rather than executives. But he would know the implications of this summons as well as anyone. "Do you have anything?"

"A solid lead," Hallac said. "A boy at the high school. We thought it was the best friend, but he fingered a kid named Seth Halford, and I think it's good. We just made application for a warrant. What's the panic, Jeff?"

Ishihara shrugged. "Damned if I know. But all of a sudden, it's a presidential matter."

Shit. Hallac said, carefully, "You told me the formula was mostly jazz. Nothing to do with this."

Ishihara had the grace to look abashed. "That's the jazz we were using with everyone, including most of our own department."

"I would have handled the situation differently if I'd known that." Hallac took a tight grip on his temper, knowing he was on the verge of losing it completely. People had been talking about RCD's formula for the last five years, ever since Gardner Gerretty had become president. At first, he'd thought it was just malicious jazz, a jibe at RCD's top-grossing films and the Interactive Division, but Gerretty's boast that he could improve revenue by thirty percent had made people pay more attention than they might otherwise. And the fact that he had done it . . . That had given an undercurrent of truth to the whispers, or what passed for truth in the jazz. A lot of people—even people in the business, people who he would have thought knew better—had taken it seriously. And now, infuriatingly, it turned out they were right.

Ishihara nodded. "I know. For what it's worth, I told the president that myself. But until now, he felt it—you didn't need to know."

"Goddamn it—" Hallac broke off as the elevator door opened onto the red-and-gold carpet of the top-floor lobby. He'd only been there once before, on the mandatory new-hires tour, and then they'd never gone beyond the inner lobby. Richard Kullen had been president then, had made his welcome speech in a room darkened to show off the cases of Oscars and Emmys and Grammys and Herbies. That had been the year that *All the Seven* and its Interactive had swept the DTV categories, and Kullen had kept his hand on a display cube the entire time, explosions and stunts and actors' faces, Norbert Krakau's craggy good looks alternating with Shida's fey handsomeness and Candida Paul's vivid beauty, the scenes flashing under his fingers as though he'd invented the whole thing. Which, of course, he hadn't, Hallac remembered, and it was because he hadn't managed to keep Krakau under contract that the shareholders had finally eased him out. The whole direct-release project had been Gerretty's idea: his idea, and the reason the shareholders voted him in as president.

The inner lobby was much brighter than he'd remembered, the screening panels folded back to expose the long windows. From this high up, Hallac could see the full width of the company landscaping, a careful mix of native and exotic plants, the latter grown in discrete beds beside the fountains that watered them. Even as he watched, one of the fountains fired, throwing a tower of mist that shone in the spotlights. In the distance, he could see the cars on the freeway, a river of white light against the paler lights of the city beyond. The rest of the decor was subtly different, too: the cases of awards remained, but the framed posters and the display cubes—smaller than in Kullen's day—showed scenes from Gerretty's tenure. The receptionist was also new, a chunky, homely woman in an expensively dowdy suit. Chosen precisely because she was ugly enough to be jealous of everyone around her, Hallac thought, and was instantly ashamed of the stereotype. She met his stare expressionlessly, probably knowing the thought, and tapped a button on her phone.

"Mr. Ishihara and Mr. Hallac are here, sir."

There was no audible answer, but she nodded, and touched another button.

"Please go on in, gentlemen."

"Thank you," Ishihara said, with anxious courtesy, and she nodded again, her attention already on her desktop screen. Hallac glanced back from the doorway and saw the pale wire of an expensive earpiece snaking down from her hairline: no surprise, but it was good to know it was there.

"Gentlemen."

Gardner Gerretty looked very much like his pictures, Hallac thought, and was instantly annoyed by his own naïveté. Gerretty had probably paid good money to create this image, and he and the studio had certainly paid a great deal of money to publicize it; he wasn't going to allow himself to change now. And it was a pretty standard look, Hallac thought, greying at the temples, good-looking but faintly ethnic, nothing that would compete with the talent. The suit was expensively forgettable, something to put on because it showed everyone that the wearer was important, but otherwise it had no style. And then Gerretty rose to his feet, the benign mask vanishing, and Hallac realized he'd been expertly played.

"So, Jeff. I assume you've got a report for me?"

The voice was extraordinary, not exceptionally deep, but resonant, not as trained as a studio voice, but definitely the man's best weapon. Hallac blinked, and Ishihara cleared his throat.

"We came straight here, as you requested. I understand John has a solid lead, but I don't know all the details yet myself."

Gerretty lifted an eyebrow at that, and Ishihara met his stare squarely.

"You did say you were in a hurry, sir."

"I like my people to know what their staff is doing," Gerretty said. "Well, Hallac—it's John, isn't it?"

"Yes, sir."

Gerretty nodded, and Hallac was suddenly sure he'd been neatly filed somewhere in the big man's brain. "Your lead," Gerretty prompted, and Hallac shook himself.

"We think we've tracked the penetration to a high-school kid, son of one of the Continuing Education execs working on the supplemental courses." He gave a controlled shrug. "It doesn't look like he was taking it to sell. He's into the jazz, probably took it as a tool— a pure hacker's job, no more, no less. We've applied for a juvenile warrant. I was on my way back from the hearing when I got Jeff's message."

"He's an employee—the child of an employee," Gerretty said. "What the hell do you need a warrant for?"

"If you want the case to go to court," Hallac began, and Gerretty swore under his breath.

"I want this contained, damn it. I want to be sure—absolutely certain—this doesn't get any further than this kid."

"My brief was to prosecute," Hallac said, and saw Ishihara swallow.

"That was my understanding, too, sir."

"You understood wrong." Gerretty fixed the younger man with a fulminating stare, and Hallac winced, knowing he was seeing the end of a promising career. He braced himself for the explosion, but to his surprise, Gerretty controlled his temper. "Right. Let's salvage something. When do you expect this warrant to come through?"

Hallac glanced at his watch. "By seven. We're pulling in favors to get it today, too."

"All right. This boy's had long enough to sell Orpha-Toto"— Gerretty gave a thin smile—"which is our program's proper name—so I suppose we'd better keep it court-worthy. Get the warrant, get over there, and make sure he doesn't have any more copies in his home system. And see if you can get him to tell you where he's sold it."

"I don't think he's taken it for sale," Hallac said. "We haven't heard anything, and Cady Corbitt—she's my systems specialist— thinks we would have by now if he'd tried to market it."

Gerretty rolled his eyes. "Orpha-Toto is worth a couple mil on the open market. Maybe more. He'll sell it."

"Only if he finds out that it's worth that much," Ishihara said.

"Do you really think he won't?" Gerretty snapped.

"He might not," Hallac said. "He's not a studio kid; he wouldn't necessarily recognize the formula. That was entertainment jazz—"

"Then why the hell would he take it?" Gerretty asked, and Hallac shook his head again.

"He's a kid. He wants to play the jazz."

"But he's not a hacker," Gerretty said. "Or so you said."

"No. Not as far as we know." Hallac fixed his eyes on the line of trees that bisected the window behind Gerretty's desk. Beyond it, he could see a line of darker violet that might be mountains or distant sea, barely distinguishable from the bruised-looking sky.

"Then make damn sure he doesn't sell it."

"To do that, sir," Hallac said, carefully, "I'll need to know who might want to buy it."

For a second, he thought Gerretty was going to explode, but to his surprise, the man laughed instead. "Any other studio, for starters. Orpha-Toto, John, is a predictor of sure things—of real, quantifiable hits, product we can take to market and know what kind of profit we're going to make. With that in our pocket, we have a significant edge over all the other studios, and all the other entertainment providers, for that matter. And we become a much more attractive investment all around. Which, right now, is a matter of some importance."

Hallac nodded slowly, wishing he'd known this from the start. If he had, he would have handled the investigation differently—been harder on the Halfords, for one thing. . . . He shook that thought away, focusing on what he'd been told. The merger with FireFish Studios had absorbed operating capital, everyone knew that, the money siphoned to pay off FireFish's debts. This was not the time to have to pull a buyout, particularly if there were other studios desperate to get the same edge Gerretty already had. It was also a bad time to make investors nervous, and there was nothing like a hacker incident to make fund managers wary. He nodded again, said, slowly, "Is there anyone in particular who's shown interest?"

"Everyone and no one," Gerretty said.

"You couldn't expect to keep it secret forever," Hallac said.

"Of course not." Gerretty glared again. "But as long as we can keep it just jazz, we can control it."

"Sir." Hallac hesitated, not wanting to anger Gerretty any further. *But you must know it's impossible to keep something like this secret once a copy's loose.* He said, "Once the word gets out—and there's every chance something will—we're going to see some serious hacking, and I'm afraid even the best-defended system is vulnerable somewhere."

"I'll fire the first bastard who sells out," Gerretty said. "And I'll see them jailed for theft."

Well, at least he took my point, Hallac thought. *Employees are always the weakest link. So our best bet is to catch the kid. Find him before he finds out that he has something to sell, because otherwise we're going to have to come up with cash for a buyout. And buyouts rarely work.* "I'll get on it," he said. "If we find the kid—"

"When you find the kid," Gerretty corrected, "I'm going to see him put away for a long time. How old did you say he was?"

"Sixteen," Hallac said warily.

Gerretty's gaze was fixed on the wall behind them, looking at something only he could see. "That's old enough to be tried as an adult. We'll go for that."

"Technically, yes," Ishihara began, sounding doubtful, and Hallac frowned.

"We may need to offer a deal to get the program back."

"Offer him whatever you have to," Gerretty said. "But I want him to do time."

"Sir," Hallac said, "he may not want to deal with us on those terms."

Gerretty blinked once. "Offer him whatever you have to," he said again. "We can deal with the rest later. But just find him, John. And get that program back."

"Yes, sir," Hallac said, and hoped Gerretty could continue to control his temper. The last thing they needed was for RCD's president to refuse a deal just because he wanted to see someone punished for their troubles. *But you don't get to a presidency without learning when to compromise. It will be all right. The main thing now is to find the boy and the program.*

Ishihara was silent in the elevator until it dropped below the fifteenth floor. Hallac watched him out of the corner of his eye, not knowing what to say—after all, what was there to say to a man who'd in all likelihood just earned himself a scathing quarterly review, if nothing worse? As the car passed the fourteenth floor, Ishihara cleared his throat.

"He's not serious about this, right?"

"About which?" Hallac asked, and Ishihara made a face.

"About trying this kid as an adult. I mean, he can't, can he?"

Hallac shrugged. "It's possible, sure—technically, if you've got a kid between twelve and eighteen, or one that can be construed as having acted in an adult manner, the prosecution or plaintiff can petition to have him or her considered an adult for the purpose of resolving the particular complaint. Something like this, hacking, people generally don't, but, like I said, technically, you can."

"So you think he would?" Ishihara sounded genuinely shocked.

"No—" Hallac started to shake his head, stopped, remembering Gerretty's tone. The man had been in deadly earnest—*not a nice metaphor, when you think about it, either. But it won't happen.*

"I'm not so sure," Ishihara said, and shot the other man a guilty look.

Hallac refused to meet his eyes. "Legal wouldn't let him."

"He is the president."

"It would be stupid," Hallac said, repeated it with more confidence. "Seriously stupid. Juries don't like that kind of thing. And one thing Gerretty isn't, is stupid."

"No," Ishihara said, sounding doubtful, and Hallac heard again Gerretty's determination. *But it is stupid, incredibly stupid, risks losing more than just a conviction, would be the kind of jazz studios don't live down.*

"He's not that stupid," he said, and hoped he sounded more confident than he felt. Still, that wasn't his business; his business was to plug the leak, and leave the rest for Legal. He straightened his spine as the doors opened onto his floor. Gerretty couldn't be that stupid, not and be where he was.

• • •

The warrant arrived on time, but when they reached the Halford house, tucked away on its dead-end circle between the two larger houses, no one was home. Hallac had been ready for that, had an RCD real-estate agent waiting to let them in, and set Corbitt to work on Halford's computer while he waited for the parents to come home. They arrived within the hour, probably called by the neighbors Hallac could see watching from behind their drapes, were ushered into their own living room where Galen Lapenna could question them. Hallac could hear their own inquiries, the worried voices clearer than any words, and the softer murmurs as Lapenna and Jae King deflected the questions and added queries of their own.

The boy's room was pretty typical, small and so crowded with furniture that the computer had been relegated to the closet. Corbitt was already busy at the keyboard, frowning into her own display glasses, and Hallac glanced idly at the stacks of CDs and ROMs, knowing better than to interrupt her. There was nothing significant among them—a typical kid's choices, the Santees, Heaven and Hell, Big Jesus, a handful of RCD Interactives—and he looked back at the screen. It was filled with icons, all ordinary and recognizable, and he bit back a groan, guessing she had barely gotten started.

"John?" That was Jae King, shaking her incongruous braids back out of her face. They were left over from her last assignment, undercover on the Strip, and they went badly with her sober suit. "The parents say Seth is supposed to be home—was supposed to have been home hours ago. We've checked the friends' houses where he hangs out, and he's not there."

Hallac glanced at the clock, saw that it was almost midnight. It was unlikely any of the friends could be hiding him. If nothing else, this was studio territory; any friends the boy had were almost certainly children of employees, either RCD's or Continuing Education's. They would know better than to lie. "He's run, then."

King nodded. "I think so."

"Yeah." Hallac glanced around the room again, looking this time for signs of packing, and his eye fell on the open clothes chest. He had assumed it was just adolescent untidiness, but now he had to wonder. "Get his mother up here, see if she can tell you what he's taken with him."

"John," Corbitt said, and there was a note of urgency in her voice that silenced anything more he would have said. "I've got something. Looks like he bought a plane ticket, headed east."

"Where?" Hallac asked.

King spoke in the same instant. "How? They said he didn't have credit."

"He had e-cash," Corbitt answered.

"Christ," Hallac said, under his breath. If the kid had sold the program already . . . "How much, can you tell?"

Corbitt shrugged, touching keys. "Probably just enough for the ticket, the account's closed out." She worked the keyboard again, and a new window opened on the monitor. "It was a red-eye, headed for Reagan—" Her shoulders drooped. "And it left ten minutes ago."

"Oh, shit," King said.

"Why Reagan?" Hallac asked. That wasn't hacker country, wasn't even the fourth or fifth place he'd expect to find a buyer for Orpha-Toto. Corbitt shook her head, shrugging again, and he reached for his phone. He touched buttons, and watched Gerretty's private number crawl across the little display. It wasn't a call he wanted to make, not after the earlier interview, and he braced himself for the president's anger.

To his surprise, however, after the first explosive curse, Gerretty reined in his temper and restricted himself to the job at hand. "I assume he's already taken off?"

"Yes," Hallac said. "We can get local cooperation at the other end, have officers waiting at the terminal." *Assuming they can find him, of course.* Halford was proving more resourceful than he'd expected. "The best bet's probably to track him to his meeting. We get both parties that way."

"Can you get there yourself?" Gerretty asked. "You and your team?"

Hallac blinked, waved to Corbitt, and she popped a schedule onto her monitor, scaling up the type so that he could read it from a distance. "Yes. There's a flight leaving in an hour, one of the transcontinental jumpers. It'll get us in about half an hour after him."

"Good thing the kid didn't catch one of those," Gerretty said, and Hallac allowed himself a lopsided smile. *Better than you know, sir*, he thought. If the kid had a buyer, they'd probably have financed the faster flight.

"All right," Gerretty went on. "Get on that flight, all of you, and bring him back."

"Sir," Hallac began, and then abandoned the attempt to find a more tactful phrasing. "The locals will have a better chance of stopping him if we tell them what's going on—"

"No," Gerretty said. There was a brief pause, and when he spoke again, his voice was more relaxed. "Look, John, I know you think I'm paranoid, but the main issue here is to protect our interests. I want one of our people—you, specifically—with that kid from the moment he's arrested. That way, there's no chance he could make a deal with some cop, trade the program for a chance to run."

"I don't really think that's likely," Hallac said, but even as he said it, he doubted the words. There were still plenty of dirty cops, and there were even more cops who didn't really believe that programs were property, not the way that cash or drugs were property. It could happen—it still wasn't likely, but the possibility was real enough to make Gerretty's worry legitimate. "All right. We're on our way."

"Good. And good luck." Gerretty cut the connection.

Hallac sighed, folding up his phone, aware of King and Corbitt watching curiously. Unsurprisingly, it was Corbitt who broke their silence.

"So we're off east?"

Hallac nodded. "Get us tickets, please. You can have suitcases shipped to meet us, and we can make the rest of the arrangements from the plane."

King made a face, but Corbitt just nodded, began closing windows on the boy's machine.

"You got somebody you can trust to take over that"? Hallac asked, and she nodded again.

"Oh, yeah, no problem."

"Right." Hallac glanced around the little room again, wondering where the boy had gone, what kinds of friends he'd made who would take him in under these circumstances. Not good ones, he suspected, more like the kind who'd be happy to buy and sell questionable programs, and he made a face, thinking of the mess that would leave. If the formula, this Orpha-Toto program, got loose on the market, there would be hell to pay, and Halford would pay most of it. The only way to stop it was to move faster than Halford's mysterious friends.

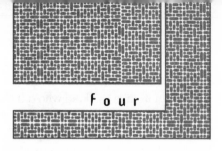

Tin Lizzy leaned one hip against the wall surrounding the stairs that led down into Crystal City, grateful for her sunglasses in the morning glare. The sky behind the towers was already as white as the concrete, and she hoped Keyz had been paying attention when she spoke to him at the airport. He'd been too nervous to take in the directions that would have brought him into the underground, and reluctantly she'd broken her own rule, and agreed to meet him at Crystal Plaza. The Plaza formed the roof of the mostly underground city, but the distinction that seemed so clear to locals tended to confuse strangers. The towers that loomed over the courtyards reflected the heat, bouncing it back to the stone-and-concrete plaza to catch in her throat, and the draft from the stairwell did nothing to help. Keyz was later than she'd expected, even given the morning traffic; another five minutes, she decided, and then I'll go down. But then, if he had come to Crystal City—if he'd taken the subway, say, come into the lower station—he should have realized his mistake and be looking for a Plaza exit: better to stay here, and assume he was at least as bright in real life as he was in the jazz. Not that that was a given, of course, she added, with a quick smile, but she had a right to assume that much. The other possibility, that he had gotten caught, didn't bear thinking about, not with two strikes already on her record.

She pushed back her jacket sleeves, wincing a little in the heat, turned her arm so that the strands of holofiber under her skin caught the light, points of fire and diamond against the black lace. It was probably too much, though, and she sighed and shoved them down again. She had dressed with care, jeans and a black/silk jacket that censored her figure, her mane of hair subdued into a loose knot, picking the uniform that Keyz would recognize as a player's, but you never knew what else he might have found on the Nets. At least she'd been a player long enough that her body had probably vanished even from the free archives. She could feel her hair frizzing loose as it dried and shoved a strand impatiently behind her ear. The biggest problem—the real problem—was that Keyz should have been here by now.

A taxi pulled into the loading arc, and she tensed, then allowed herself a broad smile as she recognized the stocky figure. The camera had made Keyz look taller than he was, almost adult height; from across the plaza, it looked as though he had yet to get his adolescent growth spurts. She started to lift a hand and wave him over, but he hoisted a heavy-looking backpack onto his shoulder and started toward her. She slid her hands into her pockets and waited.

"Keyz?" she said, when she thought he was in earshot, and he nodded.

"Tin Lizzy?" His voice was faintly breathless, the heat, maybe— or maybe fear, she thought, looking at the worried face, and let her glasses slide down her nose so that she could peer over the top of the frame. Keyz was smaller than she'd expected, and utterly ordinary, just another pasty-faced, pale-haired kid in loose shorts and a skater-logo T-shirt. She saw him swallow hard, and lowered her glasses even farther.

"You all right?"

Keyz nodded, still silent, and Lizzy forced herself to smile, swallowing her own impatience, the desire to get back into the underground.

"We can talk here," she said. "It's a lot more private than it looks."

"All right," Keyz said. His voice cracked, and she saw the color rise under his pale skin: a serious player, she thought, to stay so pale in California, the only place in the country where the skin cancer rates were still rising.

"Most everybody's at work," Lizzy said, and tipped her head toward the closest tower, its windows mostly blanked against the sun. "And anybody who isn't is probably watching TalkTV."

"Yeah." He sounded a little more sure of himself, and Lizzy made her voice easy, soothing.

"So tell me about this program."

Keyz took a deep breath. "I told you most of it. It's not mine, I just, like, found it in the server listings. Not even in an active volume: I thought it was something they'd discarded. I didn't know what it was, except that it was supposed to treat texts like they were sentences in a language, break them down to grammatical parts, and from that you can see what they're really saying. That was what I wanted it for, to give me an edge on the jazz." He hesitated, then added, defiantly, "I didn't like getting bounced from Nomos."

Lizzy lifted an eyebrow at that, and Keyz had the grace to look away. "So it is deep structure," she said. "And it does work."

"It got me on Testify, anyway," Keyz said, and Lizzy nodded, acknowledging the truth of that. "You know what it is?"

Lizzy looked over the top of her glasses again. "It's the formula, isn't it? Even I've heard that jazz."

Keyz nodded, the bravado fading as quickly as it had appeared. "I didn't know—didn't realize, when I copied it. I just wanted it for the jazz."

"No wonder they're pissed," Lizzy said. "Why the hell did you hack RCD? You had to know their rep."

"I didn't start out to hack anything," Keyz said. "I just—my folks had codes, they keep open systems, and I was just looking around. I thought it was something nobody was using, a discard, something that didn't work out—it doesn't even look finished, for God's sake."

Lizzy shook her head, and saw the boy scowl, knew he could hear her unspoken criticism.

"So what do I do about it?" Keyz went on, his voice scaling upward in spite of himself. "I mean, they're threatening to put me in jail. My parents, too."

Lizzy pushed her glasses back into place, unable to stop her instinctive answer. "Welcome to the jazz, son."

Keyz glared at her, and she made herself relax, reminding herself why she was doing this. If she didn't help the kid, nobody would. "You could try giving it back," she said. "They might deal, particularly if they can assume you haven't had time to make copies."

"RCD doesn't deal," Keyz said. "You said so yourself."

"Something like this, they'll deal," Lizzy said. The trick would be keeping them from going back on it, particularly if Gerretty was involved.

Keyz was shaking his head. "They can't ever be sure I didn't make copies. Besides, it's not fair to my parents. They didn't have anything to do with this. I don't want to get them into trouble."

Lizzy looked away, knowing her smile was brief and bitter. "I hear you—" She broke off as the first blue light slanted across the paving, and then the police cars slid into the curb. Keyz started to turn, drawn by her stare, and she snapped at him.

"Don't fucking move."

Keyz froze, then scowled. "What do you mean—?"

"Don't turn. Don't look." Lizzy kept her voice soft, conversational, hoped the cops wouldn't be able to see the tension in her body.

"Trouble?" Keyz asked, in a small voice, and Lizzy closed her hands into fists, the nails digging into the palms of her hands. She could taste fear like copper at the back of her throat, swallowed it down.

"It's the fucking cops." There were two more cars now, and she guessed more on the far side of the plaza. "Four cars that I see—you are a badass, Keyz."

"What do we do?"

"The apartment's not in my name," Lizzy said. Her voice was surprisingly calm, and she took a careful breath. "So all they have is my account and probably a phone trace. So they don't have a description— at least not of me—and they may not have a real name, either."

A shard of blue light slanted across the plaza again, and in spite of himself Keyz turned to look. "Oh, shit—"

"Just relax," Lizzy said sharply, moderated her tone with an effort. "It's OK, anybody would have looked. Just breathe."

Obediently, Keyz took a deep breath, and then another, and Lizzy looked past him, focusing on the police cars. There were still just four of them, tucked conspicuously into a no-parking zone, doors still open while uniformed men and women fanned out across the plaza. A man in a civilian suit followed at a walking pace, talking on a cell phone.

"Oh, shit," Keyz said. "Oh, shit, they know what I look like, I've talked to them—"

"The studio cops?" Lizzy asked, and the boy nodded. "Are they there?"

Keyz shook his head. "No. No, I don't see them."

"Breathe," Lizzy said again. "It'll be OK." Her eyes were still on the cops, split into two groups now, one flashing badges at the doorman of her tower, the other heading for the service entrance. "Ah, shit," she said, not quite under her breath, and Keyz gave her a scared look. "No, it's all right, I just hoped—that's where I lived, that's all." She allowed herself a grimace at the instinctive, unintended past tense. "So we have to assume it's for you."

"So what do we do?" Keyz asked again, and Lizzy lifted a hand.

"Wait." She watched the civilian—*plainclothes, more likely*—finish his phone conversation and stroll toward the door. He paused to talk to the doorman and one of the uniformed men, then vanished into the building. Lizzy gave a sigh of relief. "Let's go."

She started down the stairs that led to Crystal City, Keyz following more slowly. The sudden rush of cooler air was dizzying, particularly combined with the orange light, and she reached for the railing to steady herself. She ignored the nearest subway sign, turned left and away from it, brushing past a knot of window shoppers clustered in front of a wire-fronted shop kiosk. Keyz scrambled to keep up with her.

"Where're we going?"

Lizzy paused, but she already knew the best answer, however much she didn't like it. "Out," she said. "Come on." *Don't ask questions now*, she thought. *I don't have any answers.* She hadn't expected the cops to show so quickly, or in such force, was caught with nothing but a couple of money cards and her second-best smoke. *I should have known, though, I should have figured he'd respond like this, knowing it was Gerretty . . .* What she needed first was money, as much cash as she could get before they cut off access to her accounts, and then she needed access, somewhere safe to plug in her smoke and tie into the accounts that even the cops wouldn't be able to link to her legal names. That probably meant the District, the one place she was sure someone would let her use a secure machine, for ready money if not for old times' sake, but she wasn't sure she wanted to face that yet. *Get the money first*, she told herself, *and maybe something will turn up.* It meant leaving the haven of CC Underground, but she couldn't see any other choice.

She brought them down the length of the upper corridor, avoiding the elevators, and brought them out again at another Plaza stair. The renewed heat was like a slap in the face, and she saw Keyz wince as the door closed behind him.

"We're going to have to walk," she said, and made it half an apology.

"Where to?" The boy squinted into the sunlight, and she made a mental note to make sure he bought sunglasses. He looked naked without them.

"Subway station," she said. "It's, oh, three blocks, I guess. But we're going to need cash—at least, I need cash, and I want to get it somewhere a long way from where we're going."

"Where are we going?" Keyz asked, and Lizzy forced a grin, wishing she had a better answer.

"First let's get the money. We get that far, we'll be set."

"All right," Keyz said, sounding dubious, but Lizzy ignored the tone.

They were at the very end of Crystal Plaza. No one came here much, and the white concrete was cracked, patched in places with a slightly darker mortar. There was a new planting, courtesy of the housing committee, a sturdy tangle of evergreens that were designed to serve as a barrier, and Lizzy remembered that they were worried about the possibility of drug sales in the blind corners. To her left, cars filled the six-lane; on its far side, small, neat houses and a few small-town-style stores rose along a low hill, as unreachable as if they'd been on the other side of a river. The signs on the stores were all in Chinese characters, and in front of one an old man was walking a dog. There were no other pedestrians on their side of the street. The sidewalk ran empty along the blank faces of identical apartment buildings, ironwork gates shutting them out of the inner courtyards.

The subway station was on the far side of the highway, and a narrow pedestrian bridge spanned the streaming traffic, its white paint already peeling. Lizzy caught her breath, climbing the long stairs—if there was an elevator, any handicapped access, it was nowhere in sight—and remembered again why she had never used to use this station. On the bridge itself, she paused to wait for Keyz, the heat rolling off the highway along with the seashell noise of the cars, and felt the asphalt tacky underfoot. There were six police cars parked by Crystal Plaza now, and as she watched, a seventh pulled into the curb.

The station was relatively cool, and she stood for a moment in the path of the blowers, pretending to study the fare machine's instructions, before she could make herself move. "You got a five?"

Keyz reached into his pocket, brought out two singles. "This is it. The cab took pretty much everything else."

"It'll do." *But we need cash worse than I thought.* Lizzy took the coins, fed them into the machine, and followed them with two more. The machine spat two flimsy cards and then a brief shower of change. She collected them, and handed one of the cards to Keyz.

"Come on. There should be a train through soon."

It was hot on the platform despite the canopy's shade. Keyz collapsed onto the first empty bench, automatically looking around for a smoking plate. When he didn't find one—*like they'd have them outside, in a subway station, in the middle of the city,* Lizzy thought—he slumped low in his seat, closed his eyes as though he was exhausted. Which he probably was, Lizzy admitted, up all night on the red-eye. Nobody she knew slept well on planes, and he had more to worry about than most of them.

She slipped her hand into her pocket, feeling the familiar shape of her own best smoke. It was a good machine, and she'd filled it with useful programs, a dozen of her favorite masks; if she could just get secure access, they'd be all right. All her old personas would be blown, of course, or would be as soon as the cops read her other smokes, but she would make more, once she had access. She sighed, then, running down the short list of people left who would do her that kind of favor. All of them were in the District, from her former life, a previous name, before Sandy, before the Wilson. Going back wasn't going to be easy—except they'd always known she was a player, even when she'd been a body. Though that probably wasn't going to help much, either: there were plenty of people who'd be glad to see her fail, and all the excuses in the world weren't going to change the fact that she'd had to come back to them for help. For a second, she wished she'd never listened to Keyz, but shoved the thought aside. It was done, and she was committed. There was nothing left but to see it through. She took a deep breath, already feeling herself falling back into the person she'd been—not Gabrielle, never her, never again, but maybe Lindi Ray, or Camelia Knight, or any of the other names she'd called herself after she'd left home, before she'd found the jazz. Or at least on-line jazz: she'd never been able to tell herself that it wasn't all the same game.

• • •

The apartment was neat and ordinary, breakfast dishes in the sink, media remotes piled on the coffee table, the coffeepot itself turned off half-full. Ordinary except for the smokes, Hallac thought. He could count a dozen just lying in plain view in the living room, every kind from cheap sponsored services in logo-bright cases to what looked like a top-of-the-line Arcana model, and he suspected there would be more once they had had a chance to search the place. Seeing them was something of a relief. Corbitt had pulled a nice coup, first pushing Testify to admit that the Halford boy had been in contact with one of their freelance back-tech makers, then connecting the work name to this realworld space, but there'd been no guarantee that the person called Tin Lizzy was really here. This, though, all the smokes . . . the person—people, maybe, there were two names on the lease—who used this space was unmistakably a player.

He glanced around the room again, spotting more smokes—an older Zaradi tucked into the bookshelf beside the answering machine, the most recent Sports Unlimited promotion on the floor by the couch—and stepped aside as Corbitt moved from the media center into the bedroom. The exercise machine in the corner had a towel hanging from one handle, still damp to his cautious touch, and he allowed himself to relax a little. If Tin Lizzy had bothered to exercise this morning, there was a good chance they hadn't realized what they were dealing with. He might still get lucky, catch Lizzy and Keyz—*Halford*—walking in the front door on their way back from breakfast. It had happened before.

But you couldn't count on it, either. Hallac flipped open his phone, touched the three-key code that tied him into the local uniformed channel.

"Anything in the stairwells?"

"Not so far." The sergeant's voice was deferential despite the heat and the exertion. "We'll let you know as soon as we find anything."

"Right." Hallac flipped the phone closed, glancing around the almost compulsively tidy room—tidy except for the smokes strewn everywhere. *Had Lizzy been looking for something?* he wondered, and shook his head. There was no way to tell for sure, unless maybe

Corbitt turned up something in the big computers. You couldn't even judge personality by the cleanliness: an apartment stack like this was bound to have an in-house cleaning company.

"Yo, John." Jae King stuck her head in the main door. "I've got the floor super."

"Great. Bring him in, will you?" Hallac looked toward the bedroom, and as if on cue, Lapenna pushed the door fully open.

"Main computer's in there, John, and another half dozen smokes. I haven't touched any of them."

"Cady can deal once she's looked over the main system." Hallac fingered his jacket pocket where the warrant lay. It explicitly covered virtual materials, but the courts had been inconsistent about material stored on distant servers. "OK, Jae, you said this was the superintendent?"

King wagged her hand back and forth. "Floor super—kind of a landlord's rep. No joy with the landlord so far, it's a firm."

"Really, I just keep forward checks, call the contractors when something breaks," the man said. Beside King's lanky height, he looked even more stooped than he probably was, all the color long gone from his hair and skin. His knitted jacket was the color of button mushrooms. "Things like that. They give me a break on the rent, you know. I've been here since '05."

"Really?" Hallac asked, his attention sharpening. "Then you know the people who live here?"

"Person," the floor super corrected. "It was two of them. But the man moved out, oh, six months ago."

"Let's start with their names, Mr.—" Hallac paused, realizing he didn't know the old man's name, and King supplied it.

"Baggia. Tom Baggia."

"Thanks. Mr. Baggia." Hallac glanced at Lapenna and then at the comfortable-looking couch, and Lapenna nodded. Nothing to be learned from it, then, and Hallac waved the floor super toward it. "Have a seat, please."

"Is this going to take long?" Baggia looked from Hallac to Lapenna, who had already unholstered his databook, and Hallac allowed himself a sympathetic smile, recognizing the real question: not *how long* so much as *how serious*.

"We're investigating a property crime," he said, in his most reassuring voice. "We have leads to this place, but we don't know how, or even if, the person in this apartment is involved. I don't think it'll take more than an hour, probably not that."

This time Baggia did sit, folding his hands on his bony knees.

Hallac nodded. "Now, about the person—people—who live here?"

"The name on the contract was Stone," King said. "Alexander Stone."

Baggia nodded. "That's right. Sandy, he went by—it even said Sandy on his checking account. He was a nice man, I liked him. Not what you'd expect, considering."

"Considering?" Lapenna asked, and Baggia swiveled to look up at him.

"Considering what he did." Baggia blinked, looked back at Hallac. "He tattooed people, you know. I gather he was very famous, in those circles—and he did some painting, too." He nodded toward a trio of drawings hung one above the other on the wall beside the media center. Hallac had assumed they were prints, and marked them now for later examination. "But he moved out. As I said, that was probably six months ago. And Lizzy stayed."

"Lizzy?" Hallac couldn't keep his voice from sharpening a little at the confirmation—*not even bothering to hide the workname*—and Baggia stiffened.

"That isn't her real name, of course, it's a nickname. She's a nice young woman, very quiet."

"They always are," King murmured, not quite under her breath, and Hallac frowned at her.

"What was her real name, Mr. Baggia?"

"Rhea—that was her last name, R-h-e-a. Gabrielle." Baggia smiled very slightly, almost involuntarily fond. "I remember, you see, because of the hair. She always looked rather angelic."

Out of the corner of his eye, Hallac saw King's eyebrows rise in sharp amusement, and spoke before she could say anything. "Did Ms. Rhea pay the rent directly?"

"There's a transfer account," Baggia answered, and Hallac nodded. He hadn't really expected anything else, but sometimes you got lucky when you asked the obvious.

"Jae. You want to get the records, run the disks, anything like that, that Mr. Baggia has for this apartment, see if we can run down any other accounts for this Gabrielle Rhea?"

King nodded. The amusement was still there, but controlled, and Hallac looked back at the floor super. "Do you know why Mr. Stone moved out, where he's gone?"

Baggia shook his head. "I didn't like to ask."

"Was there any trouble, arguments, anything like that?" Lapenna asked, and Baggia tipped his head back again to look at him.

"No, nothing. I just ran into Lizzy one day in the elevator, and I asked her about Sandy, how he was doing, something like that. He used to do me favors, sometimes, you know, pick things up at the discount stores that are hard to bring home on the subway. I don't have a car, you know. And she told me Sandy'd moved out. I'd assumed he was working somewhere on one of his projects—he did that sometimes, be gone for weeks—and then Lizzy seemed so quiet, I didn't like to pry. For some reason, I had it in my head he was overseas?" He stared for a long moment at the window, the glass darkened now as the sun moved over it, but then shook his head again. "I don't remember now why I thought that."

Probably a dead end, Hallac thought. "How about Rhea? Do you know where she works, any family—is there an emergency contact in your files?"

Baggia looked embarrassed. "I know, I was supposed to get a new one. It was Sandy, you see, at his studio number."

Strike one, Hallac thought, but he hadn't really expected anything else. "What about a job—she was working?"

"She works for one of the gossip sites—on the web," Baggia answered. "I'm afraid I don't know the name. I'm not really into that, you know."

"Would it have been Testify?" Lapenna asked, and Baggia spread his hands.

"I don't know. I'm sorry."

Strike two, Hallac thought, and Baggia went on.

"But she also worked a couple of days a week for one of those nonprofit groups over in the Sturggis Building. That's at the other end of the Underground. I think this was one of her days, actually—she used to joke about Tuesdays being her Mondays, you see."

And a solid single into left field, Hallac thought. *Let's see if we can stretch it to extra bases*. "You wouldn't know the name of the group, would you?"

"Citizens for a Clean Bay," Baggia answered. "I'm a member myself—they're very good, very responsible. "I've got their number in my office."

Yes. Hallac looked at Lapenna, who closed his databook with a snap, and King straightened herself in the doorway.

"I'll get on it."

"Thanks." Hallac looked back at Baggia, who had risen warily to his feet. "No need to worry, Mr. Baggia, we just need to talk to her. If you'd go with Mr. Lapenna here, find him the phone number and give him a description, I'd appreciate it."

"A description?" Baggia blinked, looking for an instant very much like a turtle. "But that's her, in that print there. The middle one."

Home run, Hallac thought, and crossed the room in a single stride. Sure enough, the middle print showed a slim young woman—nude, of course, and naturally blond, assuming the artist was accurate in his choice of watercolor washes. The white-blond hair was cut so close it looked like stubble, and the face beneath it was stylized, but definitely recognizable. He lifted it off its hook, and Baggia looked alarmed.

"That's Sandy's—Lizzy's now, I suppose—"

"I'll give you a receipt for it," Hallac said, and Lapenna flipped open the databook again, began working the stylus. "One for you as the landlord's rep, and one for Ms. Rhea when she gets back."

Baggia nodded, not looking fully convinced, and Hallac hoped he wasn't losing the old man's cooperation. The databook's built-in printer whirred, spat two streamers of paper tape, and Lapenna freed them from the slot, glancing at them briefly before handing one to Baggia.

"If you'd just sign here, sir? And here."

The old man took them, fumbled in his pocket, but couldn't find a pen. King took one from the holder by Lizzy's telephone and handed it to him, and Baggia signed in a tremulous hand, frowning over the tops of his glasses.

"Thank you, Mr. Baggia," Hallac said. "Galen, if you'd go with him . . . ?"

Lapenna nodded, touched the old man's shoulder. "This way, please."

Baggia let himself be drawn away, and Hallac reached for his phone again, waiting for the door to close behind them. "Anything, Sergeant?"

The line crackled for a few seconds before the answer came through. "Nothing. For what it's worth, I don't think she left this way."

Hallac looked around the apartment again, at the dishes and the smokes and the remotes, clearly waiting for Lizzy's return. "I think you're probably right, from what we're seeing up here. OK, stand your people down, but keep an eye out for her coming in. There's a chance she doesn't know we're looking for her."

There was another little pause. "Will do, sir, but I don't have a description."

Shit. "Sorry," Hallac said, and lifted the print again, trying to focus on the face rather than the naked body. It was signed and dated in one corner, and he tilted the frame to try to read the year. According to that, the drawing was seven or eight years old. "Caucasian female, blond—very blond, almost white-haired, probably in her mid to late twenties, height I can't tell, weight—" He shook his head again. "I can't tell that either, but thin. No eye color, no distinguishing marks."

At his shoulder, he heard King snort, but ignored her.

"I'll get you a copy of what we have as soon as I can."

"I'd appreciate it," the sergeant answered. "We'll do what we can until then."

"Thanks." Hallac flipped the phone closed, looked at King. "What?"

The woman shook her head, swallowing her grin. "Nothing."

"Right," Hallac said. The phone buzzed, two short and one long, and he snapped it open with relief. "Yeah?"

"Got the phone and address," Lapenna said. "Locals are on their way."

"Great," Hallac answered, and the phone buzzed again. "Hang on, Galen." He touched keys, switching lines. "Yeah?"

"Lieutenant Hallac?"

"Yeah."

"O'Brien, Metro. I'm over at the Sturggis Building, CFCB offices. I'm afraid your suspect isn't in today—she called in sick, the receptionist said."

"Quick work," Hallac said, and could almost hear the woman shrug.

"I was in the area, got the call. You want me to hold people until you get here? It's a small office, there's only six of them here."

"Ask them if they'd stay," Hallac said, and hoped O'Brien could appreciate the distinction. "We won't keep them long."

"Right, Lieutenant." There was a pause, and then O'Brien's voice came back stronger again. "I don't think it'll be a problem."

"Thanks." Hallac killed that line, switched back to Lapenna. "Galen. No joy at the environmental place, but I'd like to talk to them. You finished there?"

"Almost done," Lapenna answered, and Hallac nodded.

"Meet you at the car, then." He closed the phone, reached into his pocket for the warrant, and handed it to King. "You'll need this. I want a full background check, everything you can find out about this Tin Lizzy, Gabrielle Rhea, whatever her name is. We need to find her fast."

"Absolutely," King said, taking the folding paper. "And the hardware?"

Hallac grimaced. "You do the background, leave the hardware to Cady. Make sure Rhea doesn't have this Orpha-Toto thing."

King looked around the apartment. "It's going to take time, John. The smokes'll have windows, but the main machine's going to be a bitch."

I know. I've been doing this at least as long as you have. Hallac curbed the thought, born of frustration rather than real anger, and nodded instead. "Just keep in touch," he said, and let himself out into the hall.

f i v e

The train was surprisingly cool, the air-conditioning working for once, and Lizzy leaned back in her seat, feeling the sweat chill on her skin. So far, so good; they'd made it to the malls and out again with the cash she needed, as much as she could pull from her accounts without triggering alarms, and that should be more than enough to buy them some safe time in the District, the free zone that had grown up between the DC suburbs and Baltimore. She glanced sideways, saw the kid watching her, and forced a smile, grateful that the sunglasses hid her eyes. Keyz managed a weak smile in return. He was looking fried, Lizzy thought, and no wonder. *Kid hacks this program, gets himself hosted on Testify, and then the whole thing blows up in his face, so he fetches up on my doorstep begging for help just before the cops show up. Not your average day, even for a somebody with all the boy's advantages.* But she was being nasty there, not reasonable. At least the kid had had the sense to ask for help, which was more than most of them had, even if he'd been beyond stupid to hack RCD.

Which raised the question of what she should do about the program. She gave Keyz another sideways glance, saw to her relief that the kid was staring at the train yards rushing past outside the window. Keyz was sixteen, and he'd been raised in the corporate enclaves; he didn't know, couldn't know, what this could mean in the right circles. The train swung into a shallow curve, rising up on an overpass so that for a second Lizzy could see down into the walled yards behind a line of battered row houses. They looked like the places where she'd grown up, down to the bare wood and the starred plexi in the first-floor windows, and the laundry hanging on the back porches was the sign of enough money to buy a washer. Otherwise, the yards were empty: smart parents kept their kids inside, away from the gangs and everything else the street had to offer, and the smart kids found their ways out all the same. It was all very well for people like Russ Conti to talk about beating the Tests, using the schools and the GPATs as a way out—though Russ had believed in it, too, had even offered extra classes, teaching what the Test writers were really looking for—but she'd never been able to get it into her head, at least not in a way that she could ever put down on paper. She'd learned on the streets, like everyone else she'd known from that time, first from her tricks, learning to be what they wanted, then as a body, and then from the jazz. She'd taken to it like the proverbial duck to water, and she still thought it was because being a chameleon was already second nature. She'd learned to build her own personas, documents and programs and all the oddments of identity, but they'd just been tools, born from that already well-honed talent. She could still pass as anything from white trash to rich suburbs, even academic if she didn't have to do it for too long, and it was that talent that might save them now.

If it was my program . . . But it wasn't hers, and that was the other side of the problem. If it was hers, she could sell it and then disappear; she had friends and connections and sources that could get her new ID and accounts, let her start over with a new name. But Keyz made it a different game. First, it was harder to make two people disappear together, and she couldn't abandon the kid, he'd never manage on his own. Second . . . She glanced again at the boy leaning against the train window, the backpack wedged between his face and the glass, lost in exhausted sleep. He shouldn't have to disappear, not at his age, with his chances. She'd had nothing to lose, when she first went missing. Keyz was about to lose everything.

The District hadn't changed much in the eight years she'd been away. This early in the evening there wasn't much traffic, just a handful of businessmen and a knot of older women dressed like waiters in white shirts and black trousers. They probably were waiters, too, or bartenders coming on the early shift, just like the heavily muscled man with the shaved head was probably a bouncer. He looked like he was a steroid user, too, and Lizzy made sure they kept well clear of him as they made their way down the stairs to street level.

The neon was already lit, pale in the last hazy sunlight, long lines of it banding the Jamaica, loops and swirls throwing out a line of awkward pink cactus across the face of the Tijuana Bar, gaudy gold-and-red frills draping the front of the Old Orleans and framing the holograms of the featured dancers. Next to that profusion, the unmoving red-and-white glow of the 24/7 looked almost pale—the chain had stores everywhere, even in the District, though the windows were reinforced with steel mesh above the red-checked siding. There were more clubs farther up the street—the Rampart, the Eagle, half a dozen branches of the various private gentlemen's clubs each with their discreet security and keycard entrances—but Lizzy turned down the alley between the Jamaica and the Tijuana Bar. The cleaning crew had been through recently, or it had been a quiet day: there were only a couple of condoms discarded at the blind alley where the Jamaica's kitchen used to be. Farther down, the new kitchen door was half-open, wedged with a fire extinguisher, and Lizzy caught the familiar smell of hot oil. There was no music yet: the legit downstairs shows wouldn't have started yet, and the upstairs rooms were too well insulated for anything to leak out.

"This is cool," Keyz said, and Lizzy looked back at him, almost startled to remember he was there.

The boy's face reddened with more than the reflected neon. "I've never been in a free zone before, OK? So where are we going?"

"There's a place through here, a boardinghouse, kind of. I thought you could stay there."

"Not you?"

Lizzy shook her head. "Under-eighteens only. Besides, I've got work to do."

Keyz' expression was frankly skeptical. "Is this some kind of mission? Like, a rescue house?"

"No." Lizzy grinned in spite of herself, remembering, then reconsidered. "Well, it's not religious, anyway. But the people who run it are OK—they won't turn in runaways, which is the main thing, and they don't let adults in, which should make you feel a little safer."

"I wasn't worried."

"Well, you should be."

Keyz shrugged. "Whatever. I can take care of myself. And anyway, I want to see the District. I mean, here I am, in a free zone—"

"It's just like a porn site, only live people," Lizzy said. "And don't tell me you never hacked any of them." Keyz opened his mouth, to protest or deny, and she overrode him. "Besides, you'll only make it harder for me to get what I need."

"So what's that that's so important?"

Lizzy took a deep breath, controlling her temper. "I need to talk to some people—first, I need access, and then time to talk. Then—" She shrugged. "I need a phone, for sure, maybe a car. Depends on who I can talk to."

"I can do some of that," Keyz said. "I'm good at searching. Let me come with you, help you out. That way I can see some of the District."

Lizzy blinked at him for a second, wondering if he really was as naive as he sounded. Probably, she thought, and shook her head. "If you show up with me, the people I want to talk to are going to think I'm pimping you. And I don't have time to deal with that."

"But I'm not gay," Keyz said.

"You don't have to be," Lizzy said. "All you have to be is available."

"I'm not that, either," Keyz said, and Lizzy gave a bitter smile.

"Anybody your age in the District is available."

"Like hell," Keyz muttered, went on more loudly. "What about people your age? Are they automatically available?"

"No." They were at the end of another alley, where it widened into a turnaround for the delivery trucks. Lizzy stepped over the remains of a smashed crate and turned right down a slightly wider street. There were more neon-ringed doorways here, mostly private specialty clubs, and she saw Keyz' eyes widen as he made sense of the pictures on the display board.

"I can take care of myself," Keyz said again.

"You wouldn't last two minutes," Lizzy said, and knew as she spoke she was making a bad mistake.

"Like you'd do any better." Keyz' voice cracked, mixed fear and embarrassment, and Lizzy glared at him.

"I've done better. And I got myself back off the street, too."

"You were one of them?" Keyz waved vaguely toward another display, naked dancers circling a steel pole. Lizzy glanced at it, looked away.

"Close enough. I did films, too. There isn't much market for players here." That was a sideways lie, she hadn't become a player until later, after she'd met Russ Conti, but maybe it would be enough to keep Keyz in line. "That's why I thought I'd stash you with Bruce."

There was a pause, then Keyz shrugged one shoulder. "Who's Bruce?"

"That's the guy who runs the boardinghouse." Lizzy paused, remembering the big man sitting in the narrow kitchen washing salad greens while his stocky wife—she was foreign, looked Asian—stirred the kettle where the pasta boiled. She'd never known what her real name was, none of them had: she always refused to tell them, said gently that they couldn't pronounce it, though once Lizzy had heard Bruce use it, whispering to her when he thought they were alone. The jazz was, Bruce had been in the army, met her overseas somewhere. "Him and Mrs. Bruce. They're all right."

Keyz made a small skeptical noise, and Lizzy looked at him.

"You want to find your own place to sleep? Plenty of people to take you in."

"Whatever," Keyz said, but followed docilely enough.

They were at the turnoff anyway, where the clubs and bars gave way to cheap apartments and hotels. Lizzy glanced around for landmarks, saw without surprise that the Ukrainian restaurant was gone, replaced by another sex shop. The toys in the window looked as though they'd been there a while, the leather cracking, the vinyl and silicone a little faded from the original bright colors, but she saw Keyz staring back at the open door. The girl on duty—tall, angular, with a dominatrix's straight-backed strut—saw him looking and favored him with a nasty smile, and the boy looked quickly away.

Bruce's house was down the side street, marked only by a hanging sign with the street number. Lizzy pressed the buzzer, not bothering to look for the inevitable securicams, and after a moment the intercom screen lit, displaying a broad familiar face. The woman narrowed her eyes, and Lizzy managed a smile.

"Hi, Miz Bruce."

Her voice had gone Southern on her, and vaguely childish, and the woman looked startled. "Lindi? Is that you?"

"Yes'm."

"We heard you'd left the District."

In spite of what Lizzy was sure was the older woman's best effort, she heard a blend of disapproval and disappointment in her voice, swallowed to hide the sting of it. "I did. I—my friend here's in some trouble, and we need your help."

"You can't stay, Lindi," Mrs. Bruce said. "You're overage, you know that."

"I don't need—it's not what you're thinking," Lizzy answered. She saw Keyz give her a sideways glance and willed him to keep quiet, not ask about the different name. "Keyz just needs a safe place to sleep."

"Ah." Mrs. Bruce didn't apologize, but her face vanished from the screen. A moment later, the door opened a few inches, and she peered out through the crack. "Runaway?"

Keyz nodded, looking subdued.

"Your parents looking for you?"

"The police are, probably," Lizzy said, and the woman narrowed her eyes.

"Let the boy answer, Lindi. He's old enough for that."

Keyz made a face. "Yeah, the police are looking for me."

"What'd you do?"

Lizzy said, "It's a misunderstanding—"

"Shut up, Lindi."

"Yes'm," Lizzy said again. She hadn't felt like this since she was sixteen herself, and she didn't like it, remembering the tension, the perpetual low-grade anxiety that kept you safe, mixing with the present spiking fear.

"Well?" Mrs. Bruce demanded, and Keyz shifted uneasily, both hands closing on the strap of his backpack.

"I—I was hacking, found something I shouldn't. I'm just trying not to get anybody into trouble."

"What about your parents? Can they help?" Mrs. Bruce asked, her expression softening slightly.

"I really—I can't get them involved," Keyz answered. "They'll get fired for sure."

Mrs. Bruce looked from him to Lizzy, shook her head once. "All right. You can stay. Ivan!"

A moment later a figure appeared at her shoulder, a thin boy so pale he looked like a ghost in the dimly lit hall.

"Tell Bruce we have another guest for supper," Mrs. Bruce went on, "and you can take—what's your name, son?"

"Keyz," Lizzy said, quickly, and earned another glare from Mrs. Bruce. Keyz nodded, and the older woman shook her head, visibly disbelieving.

"All right. You can take Keyz up to the fourth floor. He can have Peter's old room."

"Pete's not coming back?" Ivan asked, sounding stricken, and Mrs. Bruce shrugged.

"If he does, he can share. Go on, both of you."

She stepped back, opening the door farther, and Keyz stepped reluctantly over the threshold. He looked back once, his eyes wary in an otherwise expressionless face, and Lizzy wished suddenly she'd thought to warn him about theft. Bruce did his best to keep it under control, but everybody knew you had to watch your things pretty closely.

"What are you doing back here?" Mrs. Bruce asked again. "We heard you'd got a job, even, and here you are back with a kid of your own in tow."

"He's not my kid," Lizzy said.

"Not unless you had one without me knowing it," Mrs. Bruce said. "Which is possible, you kept yourself to yourself. And he's got your coloring."

"He's not mine," Lizzy repeated, and Mrs. Bruce smiled.

"What happened to your job?"

Lizzy sighed. "I've got a job, or I did have until this morning, doing back-tech, settings, you know, for the jazz. Keyz is a player, he picked something up by mistake, and—hell, he's just a kid. I think the situation can be sorted out, if we just talk to the right people, but that means not the cops. Or at least not the cops first, anyway."

Mrs. Bruce's hard face softened into a smile, and she shook her head. "Who'd have thought it? Lindi Ray to the rescue."

"Oh, come on—"

"Russ would be proud of you."

Fuck Russ. Lizzy swallowed the words, knew from the change of expression that Mrs. Bruce had guessed them anyway. "I've got to go. Look, do you know, is JoJo still around?"

"Your old cellmate?" Mrs. Bruce's face was unreadable.

Lizzy nodded.

"She's at Jamaica now. In the kitchen." Mrs. Bruce closed the door, not slamming it, but definitely all the same. Lizzy shivered in spite of the heat and turned away.

She found a phone a few blocks away, opposite the side door of one of the gentlemen's clubs, and made the call from there. The woman who answered the phone was as hostile as Lizzy remembered, but eventually put her through to the kitchen. Whoever answered the phone there wouldn't put JoJo on—dishwashers didn't get phone privileges, apparently—but promised to pass on the message. Lizzy sighed, knowing it was the best she was going to get, and retraced her steps toward Hayes and the Jamaica. She just hoped JoJo was still willing to talk to her.

But JoJo was waiting by the kitchen door, cigarette in her mouth, apparently oblivious to the smell of garbage from the Dumpster at the end of the alley. Lizzy approached carefully, as wary of the other woman's mood as she was of the slimy puddles underfoot, and stopped a couple of yards away, not wanting to be in easy reach. JoJo hadn't changed much, was maybe a little lighter, still with the stocky figure and the hard-won heavy muscles through her upper body. She was dressed for work, stained apron over jeans and a white T-shirt, a white cap hiding her cropped hair. She straightened, moved to meet Lizzy, and her boots were loud on the wet pavement.

"So you've come back. Didn't last too long, did you?"

"Long enough, I guess." Lizzy felt defiance swelling to match the other woman's anger, and took a careful breath, damping down her feelings.

"But you're back. And you're in trouble." JoJo folded her arms over her heavy breasts, and Lizzy made a face.

"Yeah." *And I need your help*: she knew she should say it, but in spite of the years apart she was falling back into their old habits, and they kept her mulishly silent, knowing she should speak.

"And you need my help," JoJo prompted, and Lizzy nodded.

"And I need your help."

"I'm with somebody else now," JoJo said. "A special lady."

She laid heavy emphasis on the word "special." Even though she'd been expecting it, Lizzy flinched, unreasoning loss sour in her stomach. "Congratulations," she said, and JoJo showed teeth in what might have been a grin.

"Besides, I heard you weren't queer no more."

"It wasn't exactly like that—" Lizzy began, but JoJo ignored her.

"Heard you left here with some guy. You finally got a real taste for it, after all those years hooking?"

"I made a deal," Lizzy said. She held out her arm, pushed back the sleeve to show the tattoos, turning her wrist so that the holofibers caught the light from the alley's mouth. "Sandy Stone—you've heard of him?"

JoJo nodded, slowly. Sandy was a name, a presence, someone who'd made the move from the street to respectability—*and nobody's swearing at him for it*, Lizzy thought, bitterly, *except maybe someone who's like Jo to him.*

"He saw me at a shoot, right after I got out," Lizzy said, and swallowed all feeling, kept her voice without expression. The shoot had been a nightmare, a trash film to start with, plus she'd put on weight in prison and was starving to get back to filming shape. And then she discovered she'd lost her knack for it, so that they'd had to dub her face in more than one reaction shot, and the director had told her he'd make sure she never worked again. "Sandy liked my looks, and he was looking for somebody to be a canvas, and I—it seemed like the thing to do. I was looking for a change, after the Wilson." The tattoos had meant she couldn't go back, had to find something else, some other work, and she looked away from that knowledge in JoJo's stare. "I liked the design—it's a half-body glove, ankle to wrist to just under my neck, ink and fiber—and I moved in. You know the jazz, he likes to sleep with his models. It was worth it to get these done."

"That's cold," JoJo said, and Lizzy looked away again, composing the lie, but then stopped herself. She owed JoJo, of all people, better than that.

"It wasn't that simple," she said. "I mean, it started out that way, but it got complicated. He was a decent guy, most of the time, and I liked him, most of the time. It was hard when he left." *And much better, too: Sandy wasn't an easy lover—wasn't an easy anything, and I was somebody in the jazz by then.*

"He left," JoJo repeated, and Lizzy nodded.

"Yeah."

"So you're back here. Damn it, Neff."

"No." The old name and the disapproval that went with it were almost too much to bear. Lizzy heard her voice sharp over the constant surf sound of the traffic, moderated her tone. "I've been playing the jazz, I told you I could, and I've been making a living at it. That's one of the reasons he left, that I got a life. No, I'm here because I did something stupid, tried to help somebody."

"No good deed goes unpunished," JoJo murmured, with a sneer.

"I couldn't—look, there's this kid, a player, hacker, he stole something from RCD, and they're down on him like they always are. I couldn't just leave him."

"RCD," JoJo said. "Fuck, girl."

"I did his back-tech," Lizzy said. "I couldn't stand back and see him busted."

"I bet the rest of your players did," JoJo said, bitterly, and Lizzy grimaced. "I thought so. Who is this kid?"

Lizzy hesitated. "Just a kid."

"Not one of us," JoJo said, with certainty.

Lizzy nodded.

"So why're you helping him? You've got two strikes already, you get busted again—particularly if they can make this a major felony— you're looking at some hard time. I wouldn't do it, not for some dumb rich kid."

Lizzy opened her mouth to protest, to say Keyz wasn't just a dumb rich kid, but she'd been thinking the same thing all afternoon.

JoJo went on, heedless. "Nobody took any chances for you."

"Yeah. I know." Lizzy took a deep breath. "That's why I've got to do it, Jo. If I'm going to say that, then I can't turn him down now."

"Fuck." JoJo shook her head slowly, the old faint smile finally back on her lips. "You always were a hard-ass, Neff."

"Can you help me?"

JoJo sighed. "Depends on what you need."

"I need access." Lizzy jammed her hands into her pockets, shaking now that it was going to work after all. "That's the main thing. Then a phone. The cops showed up before I was expecting them."

"I can't help with that," JoJo said. "All I got's the home phone, and everybody taps it." She shrugged. "Goes with parole."

Lizzy nodded, disappointed, but not surprised. "Does Kim Algadi still work at Jamaica?"

JoJo shook her head. "She's at the Tijuana now."

She sounded faintly disapproving, and Lizzy gave her a wary look. "Is there a problem?"

"I guess not." JoJo sounded reluctant. "I guess she's all right."

"Jo, if there's something I should know—"

"No." JoJo shook her head again, decisively. "She'll see you, I expect."

She ought to, Lizzy thought. *I did enough favors for her back in the old days.* She said, "You wouldn't know if she's around tonight?"

"Yeah, she's around." JoJo gave another of her mirthless grins. "Every night's a play night at the Tijuana, and she handles their video feed."

That explained the attitude: JoJo had never much liked the film industry. Lizzy wondered briefly if Jo's current lady was a body, too.

"Look, tell you what." JoJo straightened again, glancing at the heavy watch banding her wrist. "I'm off in about an hour. You want I should meet you? Just in case there's a problem?"

Lizzy stared for a second, mouth open. She hadn't expected that, not from JoJo, not after all this time—but then, JoJo'd always been a generous friend. *Loyal and true*, she thought, the catch line from the soap that had occupied their entire cellblock, helped make the time bearable, and shook herself back to the present. "I think it'll be all right. Kim ought to be willing to help." She paused, added awkwardly, "Look, I—my best to you and your lady, OK?"

JoJo accepted the words with a nod, face stern again. "Look, don't be surprised if I show up anyway. Kim's been a little weird lately."

"How do you mean, weird?"

JoJo shrugged. "Just—weird. If I could put a finger on it, I'd let you know, believe me. You can count on me, Liz."

"Thanks." The word was little more than a whisper, choked by memories, and Lizzy shook her head, driving them back again.

"Got to get back to work," JoJo said, checking her watch again, and pulled herself up to her full height. "See you around."

"Hope so," Lizzy said, and didn't know if she hoped the other woman heard. JoJo lifted a hand and vanished back into the steam and heat of the kitchen.

Lizzy stood for a moment in the shadows, reflections of the neon on Hayes Street flashing in the puddles, wondering if she was making a mistake contacting Algadi. Kim had always been reliable, but if she was getting weird—*whatever that means. If Jo knew what the problem was, she'd've said, she's always up front about that kind of thing.* That was what had made her such a reliable driver, which was probably why parole had her working in kitchens instead of in the garages where she belonged. For a second, she wished she could just use JoJo's phone, trust to her own encryption and multiple accounts to keep the other woman safe, but she knew better: nothing but one hundred percent reliability would do for JoJo, and she could never guarantee that. She took a deep breath and started back toward the neon.

There were a dozen doors into the Tijuana, each ringed in colored neon and labeled according to preferences—life imitating a Web site—but all leading eventually into the main lobby lined with video screens. A pair of private security guards lounged near each entrance, all in Kevlar jackets marked with the Tijuana's cactus-and-woman logo: the District was generally safe, paid enough in taxes and to the illegal elements to keep itself well patrolled, but there was enough money flowing in and out of the major houses to make it sensible to take precautions. She thought one or two of them looked curiously at her, not quite remembering, but she ignored them and the brightly lit doors, made her way around the side of the building to the only unlit doorway. A plain sign above the door buzzer read "stage door"; it had been "employees" at Jamaica. Lizzy pressed the buzzer, waiting for the intercom to answer, but to her surprise the door opened and a woman looked out. She was older, with sternly handsome features—she'd do well in uniform, Lizzy thought, remembering the Tijuana's specialty films, and shook her head at how quickly the old instincts came back.

"Yeah?"

"I'm looking for Kim Algadi," Lizzy said.

"So?"

"I—used to work for her," Lizzy said. "At Jamaica and here. I wondered if I could talk to her, if she was free."

The woman's expression eased slightly. "I don't think she's hiring."

"I just wanted to talk," Lizzy said, and knew the other woman didn't believe it. She knew what the other woman saw, an ex-body too heavy now to film even if the fiber in the tattoos didn't screw up the cameras, and wasn't surprised to see the flicker of something between pity and contempt cross the other's face.

"I'll see if she's available. What's the name?"

"Camelia Knight."

The woman stepped back into the shadows, leaving the door open, spoke softly into an intercom. The answer made her raise her eyebrows, but she beckoned Lizzy inside. "She's upstairs, in the control room. Solitaire will take you."

"Thanks."

The woman who stepped out of the shadows was small and dark, her long hair piled on top of her head in calculated profusion, and her makeup accentuated her theatrical prettiness. She was really too short for the role, but Lizzy couldn't help thinking she'd pass for Dali Evered, assuming the Tijuana was still making most of its money with faked films of media stars. Lizzy herself had once provided the body for a fake of the action star Candida Paul only because she'd had muscles and height; Solitaire at least looked more like Evered than that. She led the way up a narrow stairway, brightly lit like all the employee-only spaces, and paused on the tiny landing to touch an intercom button.

"The girl you sent me for is here."

The answer was garbled, but the door swung open with a heavy hiss that spoke of serious soundproofing.

"There you go," Solitaire said, and vanished back down the stairs.

Lizzy stepped warily into the control room, letting the door close again behind her. Console miniframes and server towers lined the walls, a dozen monitors and keyboards wedged in seemingly at random, most showing pages of text and control characters, others displaying versions of what looked like the Tijuana's Web site. Another bank of monitors filled the end wall, this one showing video from at least twenty cameras. Supposedly they came from hidden cameras in the various playrooms, but most of them were staged or even created out of nothing: the Tijuana's management understood where lawsuits came from. Kim Algadi swung away from her console, leaving a clip playing half-finished on her screen.

"Cam. It's been a while."

"It has." Over Algadi's shoulder, Lizzy could see the clip reach its end, a reasonable facsimile of Njeri Shida reverting abruptly to a much paler man.

"I heard you were out of the business," Algadi went on. There was a faint note of satisfaction in her voice.

"I was," Lizzy said, and corrected herself instantly. "I am."

"Too bad." Algadi's grey eyes flickered over the other woman's body, and Lizzy repressed a scowl. She knew she was too heavy to work in film anymore, except maybe in "amateur" productions. "There was a job came in, you'd've been perfect for it, especially with the tattoos, but now . . . If you were going to let yourself go, why couldn't you go all the way? There's money in fat."

"I'm not working," Lizzy said again. She thought about adding something more, something about not starving for a living, but she still needed Algadi's help.

"So what was it you did want?" Algadi asked.

"I'm looking for access," Lizzy said. "I need a secure site, and of course I thought of you."

"Are you in trouble?" Algadi's voice sharpened, all hint of gloating vanished. "Because I don't need any of that here."

Lizzy took a deep breath, hesitated. *Might as well give her what she expects*, she thought, and tried to look convincingly embarrassed. "Just—personal trouble. The guy I was with, he moved out, and, well, I need to get in touch with some people. That's all." For a second, she thought Algadi wouldn't believe her, that she'd recognize it for the jazz it was, but there was no reason for Algadi to have connected her with the Tin Lizzy who did back-tech for Testify. The other woman shook her head.

"You are in trouble, aren't you?"

"It shouldn't bounce back on you," Lizzy said. Algadi didn't know, she realized, hadn't made the connection, and relieved as she knew she should be, she had to swallow sudden rage.

"That's not what I wanted to hear." Algadi turned back to her console, touched keys to banish the unfinished clip, and replaced it with what looked like a scheduling screen. "They hired me here because I don't attract trouble."

"It's not your kind of trouble," Lizzy said. "I just need access, that's all. I'm locked out of my regular accounts."

"Pissed off your boyfriend good," Algadi said, and Lizzy shrugged. "For free, too, right?"

"Yeah. If possible."

There was a moment of silence, the images flickering the background, and then Algadi sighed noisily. "This is so typical. All right, you're in luck, nobody's using the business centers. I'll log you in—give me a password."

"Global." Lizzy pulled the word out of thin air, not wanting to give any of her regular passwords, and hoped she'd remember it later.

Algadi typed it in. "You're in the system for the next twelve hours. You can have a room until somebody wants it—you remember where they are?"

Lizzy nodded. "Thanks, Kim. I really appreciate this."

"Just remember to keep me out of it," Algadi answered. She glanced over her shoulder. "I mean that, Camelia."

"I'm not likely to forget," Lizzy answered, and let herself back out into the hall.

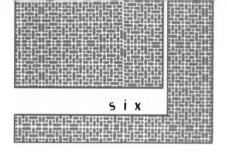

s i x

The business center was larger than she'd expected, and nicer, fitted out with a short couch and expensive-looking chairs as well as the autodesk that held the monitor. There was a pay bar in the corner, too. She closed the main door gently, the click of the lock drowned in the distant mumble of voices from the lobby below, and went to the bar, crouched on the carpet, and fed coins into the slot until the door slid open. She searched the shelves until she found the racked bourbons, pulled out two plus ice before the racks locked up again. It was probably stupid, it was always stupid to face the Nets even slightly impaired, but being back in the District, back in her old skin, with her old selves breathing down her neck, was unsettling, and a drink would only help.

There were glasses on the bar top, real glass, not plastic, and she poured herself a double, took a long drink before she turned to the desk. It was an expensive model, had been top-of-the-line as recently as two years ago, and she ran a hand over the polished surface, guiltily brushing away a drop of water. There were no coasters; she found a notepad instead, set the glass on it before pulling up a rolling chair. She punched in her password and leaned back as icons blossomed on the screen. She didn't recognize the interface, touched keys to dismiss it, and nodded to herself as the familiar defaults popped into place. There was good encryption and a privacy shield that would—in theory, anyway—keep anyone from tracing her current location. All things considered, she guessed it would work: any of the Tijuana's clients who would use the business center would want that layer of protection.

The connection manager offered a dozen presets, most of them national providers who advertised full security and monitoring— exactly what she didn't need—but there were a couple of looser locals, and she hesitated only for an instant before choosing MetroNet. It was the cheapest and most popular of the local services, and always crowded; for once, the traffic would work for her,

making it harder to sort out her activity from everything else that
was going on. She clicked the preset and opened the smaller of the
desk's two mail-retrieval programs. It was set to leave all messages
on the server, and she set it to shred its trash instead. The connection came up quickly, for once, and she launched GoodDog,
waited while it found her first account, asked for a password, and
opened a secondary screen to read the file. This was her private
account, Tin Lizzy's, the one she'd used to contact Vara, and she
was startled to find an empty screen. *Where the hell is she—why
isn't she getting back to me? Surely this isn't too hot for her: she's
supposed to be one tough cop* . . . She shut off that train of thought
as too likely, sent GoodDog after a second account and then a second name.

These were the jazz accounts, and there were plenty of messages, all from players wanting her opinion or her work, but nothing
she was looking for. She hesitated then, wondering if she should risk
tapping her household accounts, but that was one address she knew
Vara had. She was working through a shield, and on MetroNet: even
if the cops were monitoring, even if they made a lucky hit, it would
take six or seven hours to sort out her physical location. She took
another swallow of the bourbon, and launched the final inquiry.

It seemed to take even longer for this screen to appear, and
Lizzy felt a thread of real fear worming through her gut. If she'd mis-
calculated, if the Tijuana's security wasn't as good as it should be—*if
Kim blew you in*, a voice whispered, and she shoved that aside—if
Systems was going all out, the cops could be here within the hour.
Then at last the screen appeared, and she leaned forward to scan the
list of names. Still nothing from Vara, and she started to pound her
fist on the desktop, changed the gesture at the last moment to a
caress. Instead, there was the usual list of bills and notices, imperfectly sorted as usual, general mail from the people at CFCB, and a
short note from someone she didn't recognize. She frowned at it for
a second, ready to dismiss it as spam, but then memory kicked in and
she placed the name. Tom Baggia was the landlord's agent for their
floor—*and why the hell would he be sending me mail?* Lizzy touched
the button to open it, stared for a moment at the message spreading
across the screen.

:: Ms. Rhea

That was definitely Baggia, about the only person in the world who called her by her proper name. Lizzy grinned, remembering the man—thin, stooped, fussy, beyond everything *old*, but always willing to help if there was a problem anywhere—and then her smile faded as she read the rest of the message.

:: I'm writing to inform you that the police have been to your
:: apartment and have taken away the portrait drawing Mr. Stone
:: did of you. They left a receipt, but I thought you should be
:: notified by me as well. I do not know what the police wanted,
:: although they assured me it was nothing important.
::
:: I hope you are well.

There was no signature line, just the man's name, Thomas Baggia, at the bottom of the message.

Lizzy stared a moment longer, then took another sip of her bourbon, wondering exactly what it meant. She appreciated the warning, the news that the police had at least one version of her face to match at least two of her names—and a part of her wanted to cry for the loss, one more thing of Sandy's that was gone—but she wondered why Baggia would have bothered. Had the cops put him up to it, she wondered, hands busy on the keyboard, closing screens and connections. *No, probably not. Baggia's the kind of guy who'd worry about a receipt, want to make sure everything was kosher—but still, it's a bit of a risk. He can't have believed the jazz about it being nothing serious.* . . . And then she remembered the one time she'd been in Baggia's apartment. She'd gone down to thank him for something, help with the chronically unreliable trash service, she thought, and there had been pictures on the wall, pictures of a younger Baggia in an unfashionably shapeless suit, always with other suited people, and a plaque honoring him for work with some watchdog agency. Maybe he trusted the police as little as she did.

She shook the thought away, finished closing screens until only her most private Tin Lizzy account remained. It was set to go through an anonymous remailer—though Russ Conti had proved that those were only as secure as their owners—and she typed in Vara's work address from memory, hoping that maybe she was on-line and checking her mail. She could be, Lizzy thought; Systems tended to work late, given the nature of their job. Even if Vara wasn't in work, there was still the other message: one of them was bound to reach her, and then she would get in touch. If she didn't . . . Lizzy killed that thought. She would deal with it only if she had to.

She reached for the keyboard again, typed the message— *Chessie, meet me in the bar at Testify at 2100 EDT. I'll have a private room, and I'll be there for at least an hour. It's IMPORTANT*—and sent it before she could change her mind. With any luck, Vara would show, and she could ask her what to do about helping Keyz.

In the meantime, there was the jazz to review, half a dozen sites, gossip and serious news, to check for word of this mysterious program, and of any word that RCD wanted to make a deal. Somebody was bound to have thought of a buyback, which was all well and good, except she wouldn't trust Gardner Gerretty even if he had a gun to his head—

The door opened behind her, and she spun in her chair, drink sloshing over her free hand, to see Algadi in the doorway, accompanied by a big man in one of the logo jackets.

"You lied to me, Cam," Algadi said. "You're in some serious shit, and you told me you were clean."

"It's not like that," Lizzy began, but Algadi ignored her.

"Boyfriend problems, my ass. Metro cops are looking for you, and I'm half-tempted to tell them where to find you." She took a deep breath, went on in a bright controlled voice. "In other words, you have five minutes to get yourself out of here, and I don't want to see you again unless and until this is cleared up. Understood?"

Please, I need more time . . . The words died unspoken as Lizzy looked from Algadi to the bouncer at her back. "Mind if I take the drink?" she asked, and knew it was useless bravado.

Algadi shook her head, and Lizzy stuffed the remaining bottle into the pocket of her jacket.

"Right," Algadi said. "Steve will show you out."

There was clearly no appeal. Lizzy nodded, made no protest when Steve caught her by the elbow, steering her toward the side stairs and the nearest exit. At the bottom of the stairs she looked back, but Algadi had already vanished, was probably watching them, only on one of her screens. *But I need to stay*, Lizzy thought, *I need access, I need to be on-line, on Testify, at 2100, I've got to talk to Vara*—She opened her mouth to say something, anything, and Steve pushed the door open in front of her.

"You're out of here."

And you're a hell of a lot bigger than me, and probably armed, too. Lizzy stepped past him into the neon-streaked night, wondering where else in the District she could find access. A hotel, maybe, but around here they were basically for turning tricks, not overnights, which meant they wouldn't have much more than a basic phone line. The other clubs, maybe, but if Algadi knew she was in trouble, so would they—and that made leaving the District even more risky.

"Don't come back," the big man said, and closed the door gently in her face.

Lizzy stood for a second staring at the door—painted to match the brickwork to either side—unable to think of a next move. Vara would be looking for her on Testify in less than an hour, assuming she got the message, and if she didn't find her waiting there—She cut off the thought as useless, at least until she could find someplace where she could plug in—run it through her smoke if she had to, no matter how insecure that connection was. Maybe JoJo, she thought, and rejected the idea as soon as it formed. Now more than ever, she couldn't use JoJo's account.

"Neff."

She swung on her heel, just managing to damp the movement down to something almost polite, saw JoJo standing on the edge of the sidewalk, hands jammed in her pockets. She'd changed out of her work clothes, looked respectably tough in dark jeans and a leather jacket with a peeling picture of a flame-haired demon crawling up one arm.

"I heard you ran into some trouble."

"Yeah." Lizzy felt the knot in her stomach ease, irrationally, as she looked at the other woman. "Look, I need to get on-line, right away. Somebody's waiting for me that I got to talk to—"

"I can't help with that," JoJo said. "You know me, girl, I don't know shit about that stuff."

"Isn't there anyplace, a cybercafe, something?"

JoJo shook her head. "Who wants to go on-line when it's all real right here?"

"Shit." Lizzy barely stopped herself from kicking the pavement, aware that people were starting to notice them. JoJo saw them looking, too, and smiled thinly.

"Let's walk."

Lizzy fell into step beside her, matching the other woman's easy amble. "I need a phone—" A phone number was ID, access, identity, all rolled into one; once she had a phone, she could get what she needed. After that—well, ideally, if she and Keyz had to run, a car would be nice, but the first thing, the main thing, was the phone.

JoJo made a noise that was almost laughter. "You know where to go for that."

"There's got to be somebody else," Lizzy said.

"You think Boomer'd let anybody horn in on his business?" JoJo asked, and Lizzy sighed.

"Not likely, no." She'd always had a prickly relationship with Boomer Murfree, mostly because Murfree scared the shit out of her, but there was no denying that he controlled most of the street trades in the District. "You still known to him?"

"Oh, yeah." This time JoJo did smile, showing all her teeth. "As a matter of fact—" She stopped, looked thoughtfully at the other woman. "You're looking pretty classy these days."

"Thanks—"

"And I know Boomer's looking for high-class white girls right now."

"I'm done with that," Lizzy said, heard her voice flatten.

JoJo shook her head. "Not hooking. Something else of his. You know."

"No, I don't know." Lizzy stopped herself, shook her head. "Sorry."

"His other lines," JoJo said, vaguely. "The jazz is, he's offering a fair amount of cash. Maybe you can get a phone out of it."

Lizzy hesitated. On the one hand, she didn't like Murfree; on the other, he had a generally good reputation. And he was smart, there was no denying that. "All right," she said, and JoJo nodded.

"Let's go." Without waiting for an answer, she lengthened her stride, started south down Hayes.

Beyond the Eagle, the street changed, the neon dropping off, replaced by discreetly lit brass plates and dark awnings stretched over broad steps that led to the sidewalks. They were designed so that cars could pull up and discharge their passengers into that shadow without being seen. Lizzy rolled her eyes, passing the line of cars waiting outside the venerable Playboy Club, and JoJo smiled back, careful not to draw the drivers' attention. Limos waited all along this end of the street, armed and armored drivers smoking and chatting while their bosses played indoors. The one public venue was new, a restaurant whose menu proclaimed an S&M theme—a chain out of New York, Lizzy vaguely remembered—but its dull black paint was overwhelmed by the lights from next door. Of all the halls at this end of Hayes, only the Lodge boasted even a hint of neon, bands of pale gold outlining the frieze of athletes, football, basketball, baseball, soccer, tennis, tack, even a jockey and horse running across the face of the building. Beneath that, a plain sign spelled out the name: Murfree's Sports Lodge.

It was good jazz, too, Lizzy thought, and maybe that was the problem. She'd checked out the Lodge's virtual counterpart as soon as it opened, still couldn't believe Boomer was getting away with it all. According to the bio pages, Joseph T. "Boomer" Murfree had been an aspiring basketball player—"like every other young man in the 'hood"—until he was sidelined by a middle-school injury that pulled him out of the sports track. He'd never lost his love of the game, however—at least according to the bio—and used his vocational training in kitchen services to build the Lodge from a neighborhood bar into the multimillion-dollar business it was today. The focus on sports and sports gambling was an obvious choice, given Murfree's still passionate interest in the game.

Lizzy snorted, and JoJo gave her a sidelong glance.

"What?"

Lizzy made a face, but they were out of earshot of the Kevlar-jacketed drivers. "Just thinking about Boomer, that's all. Serious jazz."

"Yeah." This time, JoJo did grin, and Lizzy blinked. It wasn't like JoJo to appreciate that level of pure bullshit.

"I mean, hell, when I knew him, he said his real name was Embaye, and everybody knew he started out in street drugs, designer and not. I don't know how he got away with it."

JoJo's grin widened. "Yeah, that's what he told everybody, that and the story about that old guy, the numbers guy, taking him into the business—supposed to be how he got the old Border Inn, right? Turns out his mother was a dentist, out in Fairlawn. That was where the money came from—I guess it was drug money if you stretch a point, but not nothing like he made out."

"How do you know?" Lizzy asked. It was possible, she supposed, anything was possible, but that didn't change the fact that Boomer was the street trade in the District. Whatever you wanted, drugs, freelance sex, gambling over the legal limits, it all came from Boomer Murfree—discreetly and with deniability, and his lawyers were more than willing to point out that the Lodge was the only black-owned business on Hayes Street anytime somebody wanted to close him down, but there was still no mistaking the fact that Murfree was the real power.

"Last lawyer I had, lady who handled my parole," JoJo said.

"Oh, come on," Lizzy said.

"No, she was all right, a sharp lady, no bullshit," JoJo said. "She said she grew up with him in Fairlawn, said he put together that first jazz because the white kids from the suburbs thought they'd get better stuff from a boy from the 'hood."

"Shit," Lizzy said, as much in admiration as disbelief. It could be true—any of the versions she had seen and heard could be true, that was the trouble, and it only made Murfree more dangerous that he could play them all, play the jazz in the real world better than most people could on the Net.

"Yeah," JoJo said. "Beats reality all to hell, doesn't it?"

They were at the bottom of the staircase that led up to the Lodge's main door. Lizzy put her foot on the first step, looked back when JoJo didn't follow. "Aren't you coming?"

JoJo gestured to her body, the heavy, well-worn jacket and sturdy boots. "I'm not dressed for it. Tell the doorman I passed the word."

Boomer had asked for JoJo's current lady, Lizzy realized suddenly and certainly, and this was JoJo's way out, her way of keeping Boomer happy and her lady safe. For a second, she was tempted to turn around, abandon the whole thing, but stopped herself. This was her best chance, maybe her only chance; nothing less was going to help her.

"Thanks," she said, and JoJo nodded.

"No problem."

She turned away, her boots loud on the damp sidewalk, and Lizzy started up the stairs. The doorman was waiting, a tall man in a sharp suit, and Lizzy gave him her best player's smile. He didn't return it, merely nodded.

"Good evening, miss."

"Evening." Lizzy could hear her vowels lengthen, the cracker voice of her childhood slipping out unbidden, sounding worse than ever against the other man's perfect diction.

"This is a members' club, miss."

"JoJo Tam said she'd heard that Boomer was looking for someone for a particular job," Lizzy said, and wished she dared cross her fingers. "She recommended me."

The doorman looked her over, visibly assessing the clothes, the hair, the look, then nodded. "Go on through to the gaming room, please. Just past the dining rooms. Someone will meet you there. And what name do I give?"

"Tin Lizzy. Lizzy Ray." Murfree would remember at least the second one.

The doorman nodded again, unblinking, and swung the door back with a sweep of his arm. "They'll be expecting you."

"Thanks," Lizzy said again, and started down a hallway lined with videos of sports stars. She recognized a couple of them, mostly from jazz she'd written, emerged with relief into the brighter main lobby.

The main floor was crowded with TVG kiosks, chairs and tables arranged around a central display pillar. Each one showed a game in progress, a dozen sports she recognized and more she didn't, and waitresses and bet runners shuttled back and forth between the kiosks and the main bar. Most of the tables were occupied by well-dressed people with intent, serious faces: here, at least, the sports jazz was taken very seriously indeed. Beyond the lobby, the twin dining rooms were just as crowded, one with ceiling-mounted multi-screens offering a dozen different channels, the other with banquettes, each with a private display set focused on the tables. Expensive, Lizzy thought, and from the smell of it the food was just as expensive. Boomer was working this jazz for all it was worth. A hallway led away from the dining rooms, past rest rooms and toward the kitchen, and she hesitated for a second, wondering if she'd misunderstood the directions. But then the door that she'd thought led to the kitchen opened, and a light-skinned man waved her over.

"Tin Lizzy." His face held only polite disbelief at the on-line name. "Mr. Murfree wants to see you."

That's what I'm here for. She bit off the words, knowing they were born of fear, and stepped past him into the hidden room. It was cool and dimly lit, all the light concentrated over an empty table with a green-felt top. The door closed behind her with a soft hiss that cut off the noise from the main room, but she kept herself from looking back, instead let her eyes move across the empty chairs until she found Boomer. Murfree was sitting in the far corner, the lamp on the table beside him casting more shadow than light. There were two more men in sharp suits—bigger and more sharply dressed than Murfree himself—between her and Murfree, but at his gesture, they moved aside. Lizzy stepped closer, a part of her mind trying to remember where she'd seen this scene before. It wasn't jazz, or maybe it was, jazz on a film, some big shot in his office holding court—*trust Boomer to try to pull this off, too,* she thought, but didn't feel much better.

"You've changed, Miss Ray," Murfree said, and Lizzy nodded.

More than you know. "So have you," she said, and allowed her look to take in the surroundings.

"I heard you went straight after you got out of the Wilson," Murfree said. "I'm surprised JoJo's recommending you for anything."

Lizzy forced a shrug, hiding the sting of the words. Despite all their promises, both she and JoJo had known there wasn't any future for them, not once they were both out of the Wilson. "She knows I'm looking for some things. She thought it might be a good match."

"Could happen." Murfree gestured to one of the waiting men. "You want a drink?"

It was definitely something out of a film, Lizzy thought. "Jack

Daniel's on the rocks," she said, and one of the men in suits moved to get it. This one did look like an ex-athlete, a football player, probably—not like Murfree, who had never been nearly tall enough to play basketball, and Lizzy wondered again how he was getting away with his current jazz. She made herself meet the man's eyes as she took the drink, and was startled at the absence of hostility.

"Sit down," Murfree said, and Lizzy did as she was told, wary of the massive chair's too-soft cushions. "What was it you were looking for? Looking to buy?"

Lizzy nodded. "A phone."

"And everything that goes with it," Murfree said.

"Yeah." Lizzy took a sip of her drink, and suddenly remembered the bottle in her pocket, felt stupid all over again. That was a kid's trick—ever since she'd come back to the District, she'd been acting like the kid she had been, like the bimbos she'd played in bad films. It was time she stopped.

"That's not cheap."

"I have money," Lizzy said, and hoped it would be enough.

"I heard you'd gotten out of the business," Murfree said. "Gotten out of the District. Got some rich white guy to keep you. Why isn't Daddy taking care of you?"

"You got two out of three," Lizzy said. "I'm out of the business, I'm out of the District. For the rest—" She shrugged again, controlling the automatic anger that Murfree raised. "I've been keeping myself. I've been playing the jazz for the last eight years."

"So Russ was right," Murfree said, and grinned.

"No—" Lizzy stopped, recognizing an attempt to provoke. "Not exactly."

Murfree waited, and Lizzy took another sip of her drink, barely tasting the harsh sweetness. Then, as abruptly as it had appeared, Murfree's grin vanished, and Lizzy tensed, hand tightening on her glass so that it almost slid through her damp fingers.

"Let me tell you a little story," Murfree said. "Seems that me and my man Paul there were in the market for a new car. A nice new car, nothing flashy, nothing that he couldn't drive anywhere in this city. And I thought, hell, buy American, support the brothers out in Detroit, and hell, let's buy local, too, so I told Paul, go over to Bart's, test drive that new Excelsior I've been seeing in *Fortune* and all that.

Man on the floor says fine, but Paul has to leave his phone. Paul looks around, sees all kinds of people taking their test drives and not leaving their phones, so he asks why he has to. And the man on the floor, he's got no good answer, because his only answer is that Paul's a black man and black men steal cars. So Paul says no thank you and he comes back to me and tells me what happened. So I wait a week, ten days, and I go over there myself, in my suit, and I give the man on the floor my card and I tell him I want to buy a car. And the man on the floor is all smiles, until I tell him I want to take a test drive, and I don't want to leave my phone. And he gets all nervous and gets his boss and they whisper in the corner and they finally decide that's OK with them. And while this is going on, I watch two young ladies get into two cars, take their drives and come back with nobody asking them for any phone, all before those two men made up their mind."

Murfree stopped, collected a smile. "I didn't buy the car."

Lizzy held her breath. She could almost see what he had in mind—*typical Boomer, too, never holds a grudge unless he can work it*—but she wanted to hear it spelled out, find out exactly what Murfree wanted, before she even thought about an answer. Her glass was almost empty, though she couldn't remember drinking. She set it carefully on the glass-topped table, wiped her hand on the chair arm.

"Now," Murfree said. "Now you come walking in here saying you're in the jazz."

"And wanting to buy a phone." That was another man, moving up out of the shadows, a tall man built like a basketball player, his hair in a cluster of long braids, incongruous over his conservative suit. There was a note of warning in his voice that made Lizzy wonder if he'd spoken to Algadi.

Murfree stopped him with a look. "So maybe we can make a deal."

"What did you have in mind?"

Murfree laughed, not without humor. "Don't tell me you can't guess."

"Spell it out for me anyway," Lizzy said.

"I want you to go over to that dealership, take a test drive—make it something nice—and don't bring it back. When you turn it over to Tyree"—Murfree nodded to the man in braids—"he'll give you the best phone I can get you, with a thousand in credit on the account."

Pretty much what I expected. Lizzy nodded, her mind racing. She could probably do it—pull the hair back, roll the shirtsleeves down, borrow a pretty pin for her expensive silk jacket. If she talked like a college girl, they'd probably let her take the car as long as they didn't get a look at the tattoos. Murfree would keep his word about the phone—*and maybe I can even leverage this into a car. Not the stolen one, obviously, but a trade from wherever he takes it.*

"I still think you should send your lawyer over there with me," Tyree said. "Bust his sorry ass in court. Makes you look better than ever, Boomer."

Murfree shook his head. "No. I don't have time or money to waste suing him. That'd tie me up in court for the next decade, and I don't need that. You just do what I said."

"All right." Tyree sounded dubious, and Murfree grinned.

"Don't worry, man, it'll be fine. Better than fine."

Sure, Lizzy thought, *because if anybody gets caught, it'll be me, and there's not a person in the whole metro area stupid enough to try to cut a deal that sells out Boomer Murfree. Certainly not me.* But it would work, that was the thing, and that was why Murfree was doing it this way: elegant, pointed, and only incidentally illegal. It fit the jazz that had built the Sports Lodge. "I've got two questions," she said aloud, and drew a frown from Tyree. "First, I'll need somebody else's driver's license to leave—I assume they'll at least ask for that."

"I understood new names and papers were your specialty," Murfree said, and Lizzy lifted an eyebrow in spite of herself. So Murfree had taken the time to check her out after all.

"I can give you a name, and plausible details, but I can't make a license out of nothing."

"Fair enough." Murfree nodded. "Give me a name, address, we'll print it up."

"Second. Have you run this play before, or is this the first time?" Lizzy felt a touch of pride at the sports metaphor, saw from Murfree's face that he'd heard and appreciated it, too.

"You're the first," Murfree answered.

And probably not the last. "And the phone," Lizzy said. "Tell me about the accounts."

"You said two questions," Murfree said.

"This is negotiating," Lizzy answered, and this time Tyree smiled as well.

Murfree reached into his pocket, pulled out a minismoke, and flipped back the cover. "Bell North Jumpgate with pager, couple gigs flash RAM, regular and smoke ports, Bell's Gold Star National service paid up through the end of August, one thousand dollars credit in the cash account. It's a blank, you pick the name."

It was a better deal than she'd expected, and they both knew it. Lizzy didn't bother pretending to consider, but nodded. "All right. When?"

Murfree glanced at the minismoke. "Tomorrow morning, I think. No point in hanging around." He flipped the minismoke closed, restored it to his pocket. "There's usually a bit of a rush right before noon, I'd suggest you go then."

You've been planning this for a long time. Lizzy swallowed the words, knowing it was none of her business, and nodded again, wondering where she was going to sleep. She didn't want to beg a bed from Murfree, but JoJo's would be equally awkward.

"Now." Murfree rose easily to his feet, and Lizzy copied him, levering herself out of the too-soft cushions. "Under the circumstances, I think it'd be better if you stayed the night. On the house, of course, Lizzy. You can work up your names in comfort."

"Of course," Lizzy echoed. That solved one problem, but she wasn't sure it made her feel much better.

"You understand." Murfree favored her with a smile that reminded her of the sharks in the Aquarium.

"Whatever." Lizzy met the act with her own blank stare. *I understand perfectly well—you don't trust me any more than you trust anybody who isn't yours—but I'll be damned if I let you know it bothers me.*

"Curtis'll show you upstairs," Murfree went on. "Feel free to order from room service. They'll take care of you. Buzz when you've got your name—but just be sure you tell me which one's which."

"Thanks," Lizzy said, with a sour smile, and followed the former football player out into the hall.

The upstairs rooms were not quite as nice as the rooms on the main floor, or else, Lizzy thought, she'd been given a trick room. Probably the latter, she decided, checking the furniture. It was all solid, comfortable, even nice, but the media well didn't have a smoking port, much less a regular datajack or a dataphone that could be stolen. Murfree wasn't taking any chances. She ordered dinner anyway—not the most expensive meal, but the full five courses—and then pushed the curtain aside to stare out into the night. She was looking down on Hayes and the line of limos, their black roofs reflecting the distant neon, and she rested her forehead against the warm glass. This was going to be interesting jazz—she'd never really played the jazz in the real world before. And she still had everything working for her: age, race, and looks. She slipped out of her jacket, grateful now that she'd grabbed the good silk when she went out to meet Keyz eighteen hours ago, and hung it up carefully in the narrow closet. It would carry her through the morning, and after that . . . After that, she'd have the phone—she already knew the name she'd use for that, Jaen Sanders, a persona she'd only just begun drafting—and she could collect Keyz and find a place to hole up so that they could finally contact Vara. But first she had to set up Murfree's jazz.

She reached for her smoke, flipped it open, scrolled through the shortform personas stored in its memory. None of them would do, of course—for one thing, there was a good chance the cops had them already, and for another, she wanted to keep them clean, but there might be some bits and pieces she could use. She needed a good name, something nicely white-bread, and a better address, so that she would look like the kind of woman who would—who could—buy an expensive car on a whim. She couldn't do much with the physical details, not in the real world or at least not on this short notice, but a Virginia address, something or other Farms, suggesting horses and money, would probably help. Her Hollis Jones persona lived in Little Difficult Farms; she could borrow that, she decided, use another number in the classy and oh-so-pricey condo development, and go from there. She reached for the stylus, calling up a starter form, and began filling in the blanks. Most of it was irrelevant, much more than Murfree would need to get her a driver's license, but they were things she would need to know to carry off the jazz. A girl on the verge of getting married, she decided, with wedding-present money to burn, and a touch of uncertainty. That would let her go for the flashy cars, one last touch of rebellion before she settled down.

She scanned her notes a final time, then reached for the pad of paper by the phone and copied down the details for the driver's license. Another polite, well-dressed man answered her call and collected the paper, with the promise that the license would be ready in the morning. The door slid shut behind him, and she closed her eyes, letting unexpected exhaustion sweep over her. JoJo had done her a huge favor, bringing her to Murfree, and then she'd done the right thing, handling him the way she had. She wasn't the kid she'd been—neither was Boomer, for that matter—and it was time she remembered that.

And maybe I should start thinking about Gerretty the same way. A light flashed outside, the bright red-to-orange flash of an emergency vehicle, and she looked automatically to see an ambulance making its way up the street. Gerretty had been her private nightmare for a long time, from the day she'd been stupid enough to steal his smoke—no, that had been normal enough, the kind of thing that hadn't usually mattered, not when most of her tricks would rather lose a cheap smoke than admit they'd been paying for sex at a place like the Tijuana. The nightmare had begun when the police had showed up on her doorstep to arrest her for it, with Gerretty willing to testify just to see her go to jail. He'd been obnoxious, ordering her around—treating her like street meat when she'd been a body for almost a year. It had seemed a fair exchange, her pride redeemed with the smoke, just an ordinary, low-security model, the kind of thing you bought for under a hundred at any of the chain stores, something theoretically you could afford to lose. She closed her eyes, wishing she could avoid the memory, the sour taste of the fear once she'd understood how serious he was. Even the cops had been surprised, though they'd been more than willing to back him up. She'd been in the Wilson almost a year, half her sentence, before she'd understood what had been going on.

Understood was maybe too strong a word, she thought, and to her surprise realized she was smiling faintly. That had been the year Gerretty was elected to run RCD, ousting Richard Kullen, and she had assumed that Gerretty had been willing to prosecute because he was afraid of what she might have seen in the smoke. It would have been the perfect place to hide data that he didn't want any of his colleagues to see, the kind of cheap machine executives carried as a spare or for family photos—so cheap and ordinary, in fact, that she hadn't bothered looking at the contents. No one would have looked, and that, she was fairly sure, was where he'd hidden all his preparations for the takeover. She'd let the story spread in the Wilson, carefully not claiming too much, and that had raised her status a little, made life a little easier.

And now here she was facing him again. She turned away from the window, rubbing her eyes, wondering how best to handle this. If it was anyone else, she would have encouraged Keyz to cut a deal, return Orpha-Toto in exchange for a promise of immunity, but with Gerretty involved . . . Keyz would need more protection than just RCD's word. She glanced at the darkened media wall, wishing it had a smoking port. What she really needed now was a few hours on the Net, sampling the jazz, maybe even giving a little direction to the inevitable rumors. That was the only thing she had going for her now that she hadn't had then, and it didn't feel like much. But at least it would be something practical, something useful to do even if she couldn't contact Vara: the smoke's security wasn't good enough for that, was deliberately crippled to allow government access.

She shook the thought away. There was nothing she could do until she had real access again, and she wouldn't have that until she earned her phone. Murfree's plan would work—*has* to work, a voice whispered, *or that's your third strike right there.* She pushed that knowledge away, too, concentrating on the job itself. There was nothing else she could do.

The whole thing went easier than she'd expected. The dealership was pretty much exactly what Murfree had described, more showroom than lot, the sales staff in suits that were a knockoff of Brooks Brothers' second most conservative line. Tyree dropped her off in a high-end Beemer—Lizzy leaned in the window for a few extra seconds, talking to make sure it was seen and noted—then made her way across the narrow lot into the showroom. Even that short walk was enough to raise a sweat, and she was grateful for the expensive soap that Murfree provided for his guests.

The air in the showroom was almost chill. Two of the half dozen display units were occupied, one by a young couple who almost certainly couldn't afford the sedan showing on the screen, the other by a suited woman and a solemn man who probably belonged to the dealership. Lizzy moved toward the nearest open terminal, touched the screen to activate the displays. The first screen was a fulsome description of the dealership, touting its range of offerings and the professionalism of its staff, and she touched the interrupt to skip directly to the list of cars and models currently available. It was a long list, and from the look of the lot, most of them had to be ordered from the maker; she glanced out the window, checking the cars in sight, and touched the screen again to select the Firefly.

"Very nice car, ma'am." That was one of the sales assistants, moving up at her right shoulder.

"Yes." Lizzy chose voice and words with care. "Not really—practical, though." She put just the right note of regret into her voice, and saw the assistant's eyes narrow slightly, trying to figure out if that was a genuine objection or a way of saying the price was too high.

"Were you looking for anything in particular?"

"Sort of." Lizzy gave him her best confiding smile. "I'm getting married in the fall, my father wants me to get something—appropriate."

"The Firefly's not really a family car," the assistant agreed. "Have you considered the new Solida?"

Lizzy shook her head, allowing herself to look dubious. This girl—for a panicked second she couldn't remember the name on the license in her pocket, then retrieved it—would have heard the name, the ads were ubiquitous, but she wouldn't have paid enough attention to something that far outside her demographics to be sure.

"If you don't mind—?" The assistant gestured to the terminal— no hard sell here—and Lizzy shook her head again, stepping back to give the man access to the keyboard.

"There's the graphic," the assistant said, "and those are the specs."

Lizzy allowed herself an inner grin, studying the boxy, practical car rotating in the central display. It was a car for a person about to settle down, raise a family in the suburbs, safe, conventional, exactly what she'd implied her father wanted. "It's OK. But I was looking for—oh, I don't know, something a little . . ." She let her voice trail off, tried the smile again. "I mean, we're not planning to have kids for a while yet. We don't need a minivan."

The assistant's mouth twitched at that slander—the Solida was nothing like a minivan—but he held on to his smile with an effort. "Something a little more sporty, perhaps?"

"Yes. But, you know. With trunk space." Lizzy kept smiling, as though she didn't know she'd asked the near impossible.

To his credit, the assistant didn't flinch. "Maybe the Bolivar, then." He touched keys again, summoning image and text, and Lizzy pretended to study them. Out of the corner of her eye, she could see that the showroom was getting more crowded, more than half the terminals in use, and more sales assistants were edging discreetly out of the back rooms to handle the flow.

"Well, that's all right," she said. "It's just not, you know, cool."

She let the assistant display half a dozen more models, all in the same price range, all the sort of car that a young woman might want to impress her friends and spouse, at the same time letting more and more facts slip about the groom and her father and the plan for purchasing the car. The first thirty thousand was a wedding present— her father didn't know why girls shouldn't get cars for a wedding, gave them something to think about besides dresses—but she had money of her own, from the sale of her condo, and since she was moving into Tad's place, she thought she'd put it into something that was her own. By then, she was Carri to the assistant's Brian, and there was a line for the display terminals.

Brian glanced over his shoulder—carefully, but Lizzy saw the movement, and hid a grin—and touched the keyboard again. "I think I understand what you're looking for," he said.

He ought to, Lizzy thought. She'd pretty much done everything but tell him she was settling for second or third best, with the mythical Tad, and that she needed a car that would make her feel sexy again. She gave a diffident smile, setting the hook. "I know I'm taking up your time."

"No problem at all," Brian assured her. This time, the smile did widen just a little: a woman who worried about taking up a car salesman's time was going to have a hard time saying no to extras. He turned back to the screen. "I've been thinking. This is a little more expensive than the models you've been looking at, but it's a significantly better car. And it's probably more along the lines of what you're thinking."

Lizzy looked at the image coming up on the screen, carefully hid her elation. This was the car she'd been waiting to see, the Firefly's sober cousin, its base price almost twenty thousand more than the figure she'd "accidentally" mentioned. It was displayed in red and champagne—*One for the midlife-crisis buyers*, Lizzy thought, *and one for the genuinely young*. It was the perfect compromise car, four doors, but with the sexy lines of the Firefly, a boxy rear to leave room for the trunk, but a cockpit-style front seat to make the driver feel as though he'd bought something totally impractical.

"That's really nice," she said, and for a second almost meant it.

"It's the same engine as the Firefly," Brian said. "And the same driver's package."

"Yeah?" Lizzy pretended to study the specs. "Wow, you've even got one on the lot."

"Two, actually," Brian said. He gave a self-deprecatory smile. "It's a popular model."

"I bet," Lizzy said, her eyes still on the screen. Out of the corner of her eye, she could see an older man waiting for the terminal, and a senior sales assistant frowning at Brian from behind the man's shoulder. "It's a little more than I was thinking of spending."

She made the words halfhearted, and Brian cleared his throat. "Look, we do have a couple on the lot. Maybe you should take a test drive, see how you like it."

Yes. Lizzy looked back at the screen, deliberately spinning it out. "I don't know . . ."

"I think you'll like it," Brian said. "Frankly, it's a heck of a value."

"Well," Lizzy said again, and looked up from the screen. "Oh, jeez, look at the time."

She could almost hear Brian's groan and the thought that went with it: *all this time, and the bimbo backs out now . . . ?* The assistant kept quiet, though, and Lizzy looked back at the screen.

"Well, I guess I'm late enough already. Yeah, why not?"

"Great." There was genuine relief in Brian's voice. "Let's get you set up."

The car was hot even though the windows had been left down to let the air in. Lizzy handed over her driver's license, then leaned on the doorframe, watching as a sweating Brian switched off the security system and ran through the various components. She smiled and nodded at the fancy stereo, scanning the dash for the antihijack package. Sure enough, there was a tiny green pinpoint, almost buried among the rows of lights and dials, and she made a note to remind Tyree it was there. Brian slid out of the car, gestured for Lizzy to take his place.

"Why don't you take a look, see if there's anything else you need to know about."

Lizzy nodded, feeling the sweat running on her back, not just the heat now, but the knowledge that they were at the sharp end at last. She slid into the leather seat, shivered once as the padding molded itself against her, put her hands on the wheel, and looked at Brian with a self-conscious grin. "It's really nice."

"It's a great car," Brian said again.

"Yeah."

"Ready to take her out?" Brian took a step toward the passenger door, and Lizzy caught her breath, trying to think of a way to keep him from coming along. She'd been counting on the lunchtime crowd to keep him busy answering questions—and then the showroom door opened, and one of the older sales assistants stood silhouetted against the dark. Brian straightened, answering that unspoken call, looked down at her. "You all set."

"Yeah, I think so." Lizzy looked at the dashboard's range of displays, the fancy, theft proof ignition system. "I mean, am I going to be all right without my license? Suppose the police pull me over?"

"Don't break the speed limit." Brian grinned to take the sting out of it. "Though you're going to be tempted, I guarantee it. Seriously, you've got dealer's plates. Just tell them you're taking it for a test drive, they'll understand."

"OK." Lizzy triggered the ignition, and Brian stepped back out of her way.

"Enjoy!"

Lizzy lifted a hand in answer and edged the car out of the lot. It was every bit as good as Brian had said—and a lot more powerful than the Honda she'd left in the condo's garage, so that she had to step very lightly on the pedals to keep from racing the engine. At the corner, she glanced in the rearview mirror, saw the lot empty behind her, and allowed herself a slow breath of relief. She'd done it, after all.

Tyree was waiting six blocks away, across the invisible line that divided the nice neighborhoods from the edges of the District, leaning against the side of a different, older car than the Beemer he'd been driving earlier. As Lizzy pulled in behind him, the back doors opened, and two more men got out. Lizzy snapped the car into reverse, heart pounding, but Tyree waved them back, came over to the Firebrand's door.

"Any problems?"

Lizzy shook her head, tried to sound casual. Stealing cars was JoJo's business, or it had been—not that JoJo could ever have gotten away with this method. "There's major antitheft on it, though. It was one of the selling points."

Tyree snorted. "I bet. All right." He held out a leather satchel. "Here's the phone."

Lizzy took it, set it on her lap in front of the steering wheel, balancing it awkwardly while keeping her foot on the brake, and pawed through the contents. The phone was there, as promised, a base unit and a satellite, plus adapters, batteries, and the matching Connect-Card.

"It's in the name you gave us," Tyree said. "And everything's activated."

"Since when?"

"The accounts have been open since three years ago," Tyree answered, and Lizzy nodded. That was good, meant she'd be less conspicuous, exactly what she'd have done if she'd set up the account herself. She wished suddenly that there was some way she could check them, make sure they worked as promised, but she suspected she was already pushing Tyree's patience. JoJo had been clear about these things: the sooner a hot car was out of sight, the better.

"All right," she said, and clicked the car back into park. Tyree stepped back, still holding the door's edge, and Lizzy slid awkwardly out of the deep cockpit.

"That's it, then," Tyree said, and nodded to one of the men.

Lizzy tensed, but the man brushed past him, slipped easily behind the wheel.

"I'd advise you to get out of town," Tyree went on. "Nobody wants any fallout from this."

"Absolutely," Lizzy agreed, and felt herself flush. She hadn't meant to sound so fervent, but Tyree's smile was almost sympathetic.

"We won't be seeing you, then," he said, and stepped back to his own car. Lizzy watched them pull away, turning in opposite directions at the next corner, then lifted the satchel onto her shoulder, ready for the long walk back to Bruce's place.

She rang the doorbell, and was answered by the soft whine of an unoiled mounting as a security camera swiveled to accommodate her image. A moment later, the door opened, and Mrs. Bruce looked out at her, round face without expression.

"I've come to pick up Keyz," Lizzy said.

"You should leave him here." Mrs. Bruce's face didn't change, but her tone was absolute.

"I can't," Lizzy answered, and the older woman shook her head.

"You can. You just don't want to. Think, Lindi. We can protect him, you know that. He's better off here than on the street."

"He's not on the street," Lizzy said, and took a deep breath, swallowing her own automatic defensiveness. She wasn't an under-age hooker anymore, and this time she did know better than Mrs. Bruce. "Look, I'm not dissing you, I know what you do, what you did for me. But—look, can you keep him safe from the cops? Not turn him in if they show up with felony warrants?"

Mrs. Bruce glanced automatically toward the cameras and stepped back from the doorway. "Come in. But just the hall."

Lizzy nodded, stepped into the refreshingly cool dark, and let the other woman close the door again behind her. Mrs. Bruce adjusted something—a security touchpad, Lizzy guessed—and turned to face her again.

"He talked to me last night, told me more about what was going on. I can't imagine a studio would go to that much effort for one teenage hacker."

"It's RCD," Lizzy said. Her heart sank as Mrs. Bruce shook her head.

"So?"

"They have a reputation—an earned reputation, no jazz. They don't let anybody get away with anything."

"I can't believe they'd prosecute him," Mrs. Bruce said. "He's well underage, and any half-good lawyer could argue he didn't know what he was doing."

"They'll offer a deal," Lizzy said, and heard herself bitter, "and then they'll break it."

Mrs. Bruce looked at her, unconvinced, unspeaking, and Lizzy sighed.

"Look, I wouldn't drag him out of here if I didn't believe it."

"Yes, but believing doesn't make it true," Mrs. Bruce answered.

"I know." Lizzy took a deep breath. "You remember what happened to me?"

Mrs. Bruce hesitated. "You were arrested and convicted of stealing a smoke from one of your tricks." Her voice was once again without expression. "The jazz was you were guilty."

Lizzy nodded. "Yeah."

"Such a stupid thing to do," Mrs. Bruce said, with a flash of real anger. "You knew better. We could never get you off the street, but I know you knew the law."

Lizzy winced, but made herself meet the other woman's eyes.

"Yeah. It was stupid. I know it was stupid. But did you ever wonder why I got two years in the Wilson?"

Mrs. Bruce's angry stare flickered, and she nodded. "It seemed—disproportionate."

"The trick—" Lizzy stopped herself, angry at the ease with which the old words came back. "The guy I stole it from, he pushed the prosecution. He got them to put in every charge they could think of, and then he got his lawyers to argue for maximum sentencing—I heard he arranged for us to get a hard-line judge, too, but that might be jazz." She was sure of it, needed no more proof than prison rumor, and knew her flat tone made her belief clear. "But I do know that he stood up in court and argued for the sentence on the grounds that he'd lost face in his career, and the judge bought it all the way. Eight months later, Mrs. Bruce, he was running RCD. It's the same guy who's going for Keyz."

There was a long silence. Lizzy blinked, trying to force her eyes to adjust to the relative darkness, wishing she could read Mrs. Bruce's expression. Then, finally, the other woman nodded.

"All right," she said, softly. "I believe you. I'll call him."

"Thanks," Lizzy said, and felt a wave of dizziness wash over her. *Too soon for relief*, she thought, and the other woman disappeared for a moment into the interior of the house. Lizzy heard heavy footsteps on the floor overhead, and a minute later, Keyz appeared in the doorway. He didn't look as though he'd slept much the night before, and she wondered guiltily if she should have warned him about theft. Bruce tried to keep it under control, but it was inevitable.

"Hey," she said, and hoped she sounded normal.

"Hey." Keyz looked over his shoulder, and Mrs. Bruce appeared behind him.

"You can still stay," she said, softly, "but I think you'd be better off with Lindi."

Lizzy blinked at that—unexpected support—and Keyz nodded.

"Thanks for everything," he said, sounding almost shy, and Mrs. Bruce nodded.

"Be careful. Both of you."

"We'll try," Lizzy said, and pushed open the main door. The white heat slammed into her, and she grimaced, wishing she'd been able to keep the car. "Come on, Keyz."

They caught the commuter train out of the District, heading west, away from the cities, and then a series of trolleys and buses, arriving finally at a street so whitewashed as to be almost blinding in the early-afternoon light. Keyz stared openmouthed as the trolley inched along the tracks, slowed not by traffic—there were only a handful of cars in sight—but by a constant stream of pedestrians getting on and off. All of the men were wearing suits and hats, like Orthodox Jews except for the subtle, summer colors, and all the women had dresses or skirts and neat, old-fashioned blouses. Their children, toddlers in strollers and older kids walking on their own, were as tidily dressed, shorts and shirts for the boys, little dresses or pastel sunsuits for the girls. One mother and daughter, waiting to cross the street, wore identical flowered dresses, and, looking closer, Lizzy saw that the doll clutched in the girl's arm wore a third version of the dress. Out of the corner of her eye, she saw Keyz' mouth open in disbelief as the trolley slowed for a trio of boys in baseball uniforms. It reached the stop well ahead of them, but the driver waited for them, nodding as they found their passes and showed them one by one. They moved on to the back of the trolley, and it lurched into motion again, rocking Keyz backward in his seat.

"Where is this?" he hissed, leaning toward Lizzy, and she couldn't suppress a grin.

"This is Americana."

"I know that," Keyz said. "I mean where are we?"

"That's the name," Lizzy answered. "Americana, Virginia. It's a township, I think. A covenanted community, anyway. There's a place just outside town where we can get some lunch and talk in private."

Keyz made a face, but subsided into his seat again. Lizzy leaned forward slightly, looking for their stop, relaxed again as she realized they hadn't even reached the town green. Americana had always fascinated her, from the first time her father had brought her through on the trolley—the streets and the people so different from where she lived, none of the familiar chain stores, no 24/7 or B&N or any of the chain drugstores, the glassed-in storefronts all bright as jazz, innocent of mesh or bars. She'd tried to move there once, the first time she'd run away, but her persona hadn't been good enough, she hadn't known how to create the documents she needed. The town didn't take underage individuals, only families, and no one had been

interested in the contested adoption of a fifteen-year-old with a juvenile record. It was just as well: she doubted she could have followed
the community rules, kept the town covenant, and stayed sane. Still,
it was a good place to break their trail, and a relatively safe space to
stop while she worked out their next move: none of the covenanted
communities, even one as law-abiding as Americana, ever liked dealing with the outside world.

The trolley slid to a bouncing stop at the town park, where a
giant flag flew over a war memorial that showed a tank-helmeted
woman holding an injured Marine. The uniformed boys got off
there, racing across the grass toward a game just getting started, and
several community women got off, too, the younger ones holding
back to let the oldest work her way stiffly down the step. A blue-
uniformed policeman—not even a bulletproof vest covering his
badge—stopped traffic to let her across the street. There was even
an ice-cream truck parked in the distance, a line of kids waiting to
buy under their mothers' benign gaze. Lizzy shook her head, wondering how she had ever thought she could fit in.

Beyond the park, a highway arched over the road, the solid concrete supports like a wall closing in the community. The trolley slid
through the well-lit tunnel—no graffiti on the walls, Americana's
influence reaching out—and Lizzy reached overhead to press the
signal strip, swaying to her feet as the trolley slowed for the stop.
Keyz followed her out, stood gawking on the corner as the trolley
pulled away again. This was a more ordinary neighborhood, typical
suburbs, with a 24/7 on one corner and a coffeehouse opposite
where geometric-haired kids stacked skateboards against the outdoor tables. There were still some of the community around, three
neatly dressed women walking together pulling a wire cart stacked
high with groceries, heading for the pedestrian tunnel, and a pair of
men in pale grey hats talking as they made their way to a car, and
Lizzy sighed, remembering the community rules. Members were
supposed to stick together in the outside world, defend each other
from its malign influences, never let a fellow member be alone
there. At the time, that had seemed like a wonderful thing, perfect
protection.

"So now what?" Keyz said, and she dragged herself back to the
present.

"Lunch," she said, and nodded to the building across the street from the trolley stop. It was the only one that flew an American flag, bright against the glossy white paint, and the words AMERICANA CAFE were painted in red and blue over each of the bay windows.

"I don't think so," Keyz said, and Lizzy lifted an eyebrow. To his credit, the boy blushed. "I mean, they're cultists, that's obvious. And if that's their recruiting center, I'm not going in there."

"It's not that easy to join," Lizzy said, and in spite of knowing better still tasted the bitterness of that rejection. "And the food's good and cheap. Relax. There's no hassle."

Keyz shook his head, but made no further protest when Lizzy brought them across the street. The hostess, handsome, greying—*motherly*, Lizzy thought—brought them to a booth at the back of the room, and a fresh-faced waitress came over almost at once, bringing menus and a pitcher of iced tea. She recited a couple of specials, ham and turkey club, beef stew—*home cooking*, according to the menu, but not the home cooking Lizzy was used to, and she wondered what Keyz thought of it. She looked at him as the waitress moved away to serve an elderly couple, and saw him fidgeting against the cushions, looking for the nearest port.

"Don't bother," Lizzy said. "This place is strictly no smoking."

"You're kidding." Keyz looked around again, as though he couldn't believe what he was hearing.

"No. They don't believe in smokes—in the jazz of the web or anything virtual," Lizzy said. "They say it takes away from real life."

"Wow." Keyz picked up the menu, put it down again. "How did somebody like you ever find out about a place like this?"

Lizzy hesitated, fishing for the respectable part of the truth. "I came here when I was a kid, sometimes. My father brought me here. And then I realized that where there's no smoking, there's no way to trace a player—as long as you stay clear of the Nets and don't use credit, that is. It breaks the trail, stopping here."

Keyz nodded, thoughtfully, then glanced at the menu. "OK. But, no credit . . . I don't have a lot of cash left."

"Don't worry," Lizzy said. "Get what you want. I've got enough."

"I thought you said we needed a lot more," Keyz said.

Lizzy nodded. "We did. It's taken care of." She touched the phone in its bag, and Keyz's eyes narrowed.

"What'd you do?"

Lizzy shook her head. "Don't ask."

"Oh, come on."

"I mean it," Lizzy said, and heard her voice sharpen. The last thing the kid needed was to be implicated in a car theft. "You don't need to know, so don't ask. As far as you know, I've always had this phone."

Keyz paused, and in the fluorescent light Lizzy thought she saw him blush. Well, maybe that wasn't such a bad thing, she thought. Let him think she got it from a trick, that would maybe insulate him from Murfree and the stolen car. The waitress appeared then, bright and cheerful, and Lizzy glanced down at the menu. Keyz ordered a hamburger, waited impatiently until she'd ordered and the waitress was out of earshot.

"So what are we going to do now?" he asked.

Lizzy dragged herself back to the present. Tyree had told her to get out of town, and all in all, it was probably a good idea. The only question was where to go. She'd been thinking Virginia, but now, with the car hanging over them, farther might be better. "Lakeview," she said, and hoped she was making the right choice. "I've got a friend there, I mentioned her, she's a town cop. She should be able to help us." *And if she can't, or won't, there's always plenty of privacy in a casino town.*

"Lakeview." Keyz's eyes were wide. "Oh, man, I wish there was a port here."

Lizzy stared at him, hearing a player's fervor suddenly in his voice. "Why?"

"I saw something, last night—oh, man, it could work!"

"Go on." Lizzy kept her own voice quiet, and Keyz shook himself, moderated his tone.

"See, I was smoking last night, checking out some sites for some guys at Bruce's, you know? And when they got bored, I thought I'd check some things on my own, so I did a big search on Njeri Shida— that was the other person you said could help us, right?"

Lizzy nodded.

"So there's a whole bunch of jazz on him and Lakeview, saying that he's been seen there, or at least been playing in those virtual casinos that they do—you know, sites pushing to look for him on-line, showing icons he uses, stuff like that. And I think it's real. So if we go there, even if your friend can't help us, maybe he can."

Lizzy nodded again, suppressing a stab of pure jealousy. She was supposed to be the player, she was the one who knew how to read the jazz—but if he'd seen it, she could trust it at least that far. "You really think he's there?"

"I don't know." Keyz shrugged again, but his grin belied the gesture. "I mean, I know better than to believe the jazz. But I think there's a chance it's real."

"What exactly did the sites say—what sites were they, anyway?"

"Movie Jock, Testify, Modality, JPC/Celebrity, Beckworth, a couple of others." Keyz took a breath, gave the last name with the air of someone playing an ace. "And Celeb Watch had a piece on it."

That was something—Celeb Watch was realworld reliable, meaning that it was usually thirty hours behind on any jazz, but if a story made it to them, it had had time to gel. "What'd they say?"

Keyz closed his eyes, visibly trying to remember. "It was just a little piece, on the Rumors page—just a box that said people were looking for him in Lakeview."

That was less good—a mere sidebar, a report of a persistent rumor more than anything else—but it was more than she'd expected. Lizzy leaned back in the booth as the waitress appeared with two enormous platters, waiting while she set them down and fussed over condiments. If Shida really was there, it would be the first stroke of luck they'd had—but in any case, they'd be safer there than in Virginia. There was no way the RCD cops could anticipate this move; even if Vara refused to help them, there were other options she could try.

"Lakeview it is," she said, and Keyz grinned.

"You think he'll help us?"

"Not a clue," Lizzy answered. "But who's going to look for you there?"

The loan of the office was grudging, but Hallac accepted it with thanks, having been on the other end of the situation more than once. He had never liked having strangers in his department, working on, moving in on, his turf, and he had no desire to antagonize the Metro cops, especially when they were the ones who would have to make any arrest he could create. He leaned back in the wobbling chair—salvaged from someone's yard sale, by the feel of it—and stared down the length of the narrow room, lit uncomfortably by fluorescents and Corbitt's computers. Not that he was anywhere near making an arrest: for all the Metro had been able to find out, Tin Lizzy—or Gabrielle Rhea, or Lizzy Rhea—seemed to have vanished from the face of the earth, and Halford and the program had vanished with her. He was reduced to searching old records, for all the good that was likely to do him, and he let the chair drop again, frowning unhappily at his desktop. The computer screen was littered with files, one for Gabrielle Rhea, one for Alexander Stone, one for Tin Lizzy, plus the few files Corbitt had liberated from supposedly secure databases—not much there, certainly not enough to risk pushing the Privacy Acts and possibly having the case thrown out, and he'd told her to concentrate on the machines they'd taken from the apartment.

He lifted his head, peering over the top of his own display, to see Corbitt frowning over yet another smoke. They were all insecure, all fitted with the legally required back doors that let law enforcement read their contents; she'd been unable to break the security on Rhea's main machine on the first try, and was now scanning the smokes in the hope that Rhea would have left some hint on one of them that would help break her security system. Privately, Hallac had his doubts—Lizzy didn't seem like the kind of player who would make that mistake—but Corbitt claimed she was looking for more subtle indications, hints of the way Rhea thought, the way she worked, not actual passwords. Corbitt was the Systems specialist,

Hallac told himself again. She had to choose her own path, and he had every reason to be confident in her skill.

He made himself look back at the files on his screen. There wasn't much on Rhea, either under her real name or under her alias—more under the Net name, actually, though it was hard to tell how much of that was jazz. According to that file, a lot of people thought the Tin Lizzy who did back-tech for Testify was an older man, somebody who'd grown up along with the jazz; another group swore she, or he, had come out of the Caltech or MIT design programs. The Metro's Systems people had conscientiously marked all the contradictions, and the few things that they knew for sure were jazz, and Hallac shook his head again. Testify swore that their Tin Lizzy was Lizzy Rhea, legally Gabrielle Rhea, and they should know . . . except that someone else might be paying for the use of that identity, that cash drop. He grimaced, still staring at the screen. That was the problem with the jazz. Once you admitted the possibility of a lie, started questioning what you were told, you couldn't stop, but had to go on assuming that everything was not merely false but infinitely falsifiable.

Still, despite the Metro's questions, it seemed a safe bet to assume that Gabrielle Rhea was Tin Lizzy. She went by the name off-line, at least according to the old man at the condos, and Testify claimed her: that ought to be enough. From the look of the Metro's file, most of the Tin Lizzy information had been compiled in the context of a libel investigation, collected on the off chance that there was something the Metro could use to pressure Lizzy into giving up the real name of the player who'd actually written the questionable jazz. Lizzy hadn't caved, and that didn't sound like the person who lived in that cluttered, weirdly impersonal condo. Rhea seemed more ephemeral than that, not somebody who'd stand up to serious pressure from the Metro. But then, with a player, you could never tell.

Alexander Stone had a handful of tickets, most for parking, one for speeding, and an arrest in Massachusetts for illegal tattoos. Hallac blinked at that, then realized that Stone had been arrested for tattooing someone, not for being tattooed. All of them were old, the most recent ticket issued almost three years ago, and he closed the file, accepting that the old man had told the truth when he said Stone was long gone. Hallac sighed, and clicked open the even smaller file on Gabrielle Rhea. After she turned twenty-two, there was nothing of significance and nothing of use, just a better-than-average driver's record—no tickets, not even for parking, a minor miracle in this city—and the note that Rhea had reported a theft once, in her capacity as technical manager of Citizens for a Clean Bay. The office had suffered a break-in, real, not virtual; they had lost petty cash and the office copy cards, but the CPUs and peripherals had been too old to be worth anything on the resale market. Remarkably, Rhea had actually had records of the card numbers— Hallac could still hear the staff at CFCB, each one saying, over and over, how efficient Lizzy had been, and how quiet, how unlikely it seemed she could be involved in a realworld theft—but nothing had ever been recovered. But from eighteen to twenty-two . . . Her file had been transferred from Juvenile after a conviction as an adult, which had resulted in a two-year sentence to the F. T. Wilson Center. That was unexpected: the Wilson was usually reserved for serious offenders, and he glanced involuntarily at the bulky paper file that held Rhea's juvenile record. This time, the victim's name had been suppressed, unusually, and the stolen item was well under the usual serious-felony value, with no hint as to why the prosecution had decided to try her as an adult and push for the "serious offense" designation.

That left Rhea's juvenile records, and Hallac shifted his chair so that he was facing the untidy paper file, filled with red-stickered sheets where information had been removed when the subject turned twenty-one. This one started when Rhea was nine, caught shoplifting, and went on until she turned eighteen, ending with the notation that the current record had been transferred to an adult file in accordance with the judge's ruling. Interspered with the arrests and the red-marked pages where arrest reports had been removed were pages of social service notes. No surprise there, Hallac thought, but always too bad. The first report followed hard on the shoplifting arrest: the school caseworker thought that Rhea's father had beaten his daughter for getting caught, though father and daughter both agreed that the girl had just gotten caught up in a rough game of soccer. There were more after that, and a few pages where those reports had been removed with the arrests, but what was left was a depressing listing of injuries, home removals, foster parents' reports, and court orders returning her to her father. No mention of a mother, Hallac saw, or any other relatives to take the child. He flipped back to the first caseworker's report, curious, and saw that the father claimed to have sole custody. He had come to the city looking for work, or so he said, but from the progression of addresses—all in the fringe, always apartments, never a house—it looked as though he hadn't found any. Hallac paused, wondering if it would be worth his while to check the older Rhea's record, check out his last-known addresses, but he couldn't see Lizzy returning to her father, not after all the times she'd run away.

He flipped back to the arrests, seeing without surprise a string of arrests for prostitution mixed with a couple petty thefts—all smokes, he saw, and remembered in spite of himself the apartment crowded with the little machines. All of them were strictly legal, according to Corbitt, despite a multitude of accounts, but it was hard not to wonder what was going on there. Rhea had been a body as well, working in the porn films that came out of the District, had been cited twice for working underage, but there was nothing, nothing at all, that explained why she'd been sent to the Wilson. He frowned, checked the computer screen again for the name of the arresting officer. As he'd hoped, Peter Lennox was still with the department, assigned now to Burglary, but he professed himself willing to talk. Probably because it got him away from his desk, Hallac thought, but bought coffee for both of them without comment. Lennox took it as though it was his due and leaned back in the flimsy cafeteria chair, rocking onto its back legs.

"So what do you want to know about Lizzy?"

Does anybody call this girl by her right name? Hallac nodded.

"That kid." Lennox shook his head. He was a big man, brown-skinned and greying, sweating a little even in the relative cool of the cafeteria, the kind of man who suffered in the damp heat. "Lizzy Ray—Camelia Knight, she went by, when she was making films, and I think she had a couple more names. A pain in the ass under every one of them."

"You arrested her a bunch of times," Hallac answered. "Including the last time. What I don't get is why it was pursued as a serious offense."

"Oh, yeah." Lennox nodded, took a swallow of coffee. "That was when I was working Vice."

"I wondered if there was a Drugs connection," Hallac said.

"No." Lennox reached for the sugar, added another healthy slug to the milk-pale liquid. "Lizzy was never into that."

Hallac nodded, though the admission surprised him. On the way down to the cafeteria, he had almost convinced himself that that had to be it, that Lizzy or somebody had to have been dealing drugs, and that was why the prosecution had come down so hard. "So why the Wilson?"

To his surprise, Lennox hesitated. "That was for stealing the smoke—she did that when she was pissed at somebody, typical dumb kid thing to do. This guy, the john, he pulled some strings. Seemed fair enough, considering he was facing a serious reprimand of his own."

"Was that why the name was suppressed?" Hallac asked, and again there was that fractional hesitation before Lennox answered.

"I guess so. It was a while back."

"Who was the guy? Off the record."

"I don't remember," Lennox said, and Hallac was suddenly sure he was lying. "Just some guy."

"Political? Educator?" Hallac asked, and Lennox shrugged. "Oh, come on, he had to be something special, or he wouldn't have earned a reprimand."

"I told you, I don't remember," Lennox said again.

Hallac waited, and, after a moment, the big man frowned.

"Studio, actually—like you. Administrator, not talent, so they couldn't put a spin on it. But that wasn't my part of the case."

And that was a lie, too, Hallac thought, but he let it go. "Was she into the jazz then? Or did she pick it up after the Wilson?"

Lennox laughed, a short and angry sound. "Oh, she knew the jazz, she just didn't want to work at it." He took a breath, went on in a more controlled voice. "We know what the District's like, we try to get those kids out of there when we can—hell, we turn a blind eye to a lot of things when we think it might help a kid, and Lizzy, she hooked up with at least two of the people that I personally know did more for more kids than almost anybody in this city. She had a place to stay—she was one of Bruce Halska's strays, and Bruce and An-Dong, they will go to the wall for those kids. Plus she had a chance to get a real job. There was this guy, Russ Conti, he was a computer tech and a programmer, he taught at the high school and then he set up an after-school program, got a lot of kids to come in, work on good machines, learn some programming skills. Lizzy was one of the bright ones, and not just with the jazz; she could have kept up with it, could have gotten work—but it didn't pay as much as the films, as much as hooking, so she walked." Lennox snorted. "And now you tell me she's playing the jazz. That figures—she's still not doing an honest day's work when she can make a crooked buck." He shook his head. "But let me tell you, that girl had chances. She's just too much of a loser to do anything about them—and that's one thing that won't have changed."

Hallac lifted a hand in surrender, feeling more depressed than ever. "There are kids like that," he said, knowing it was true, and took a swallow of his own coffee. It was good, even lukewarm, and he allowed himself a second to savor it.

"So you all are after her," Lennox said. "What's the complaint?"

"We've had a theft," Hallac answered. "Out of our R&D main files. We think—Rhea isn't the primary thief, but she may be involved in fencing it."

Lennox nodded. "Figures. That's her style all the way."

"Any idea where she might go, if she's in trouble?" Hallac asked, and felt instantly stupid. Given Lennox's attitude so far, he was swinging on a 3-and-0 pitch, deserved the strike that was sure to come, but to his surprise, Lennox pursed his lips, visibly considering.

"My bet would be the District," he said at last. "She used to work the big clubs, the Rampart, the Tijuana, the Jamaica. My guess is, she'd go back there, try to make a deal from there. Assuming she wants to sell whatever it was she stole."

Hallac felt a chill at the thought. Corbitt said she would know as soon as Lizzy made a move, tried to contact a buyer, but if Rhea decided to operate in the real world, all Corbitt's connections would be useless. "Can we find her?"

"We will." Lennox stressed the first word, smiling again. "We've already put the word out, nobody down there will give her house room."

Hallac nodded, recognizing quick action. "I appreciate it. And I appreciate the information about Rhea."

Lennox pushed his chair back, not smiling anymore. "Just wanted you to know what you were dealing with."

Hallac nodded again, and tossed his empty cup into the trash before heading back upstairs to his borrowed office. He was tired, his body still on California time, and talking to Lennox had done nothing to improve his mood. And maybe he was being unreasonable, he thought, flattening himself against the wall as a pair of armored cops wheeled a lie detector down the hallway. The story Lennox had told was depressingly familiar, just another bright poor kid who wouldn't wait or work for money that was easier to get illegally, and the stint in the Wilson was just a nasty closer, except for the fact that the victim had pulled strings to make sure Rhea ended up doing hard time. And maybe Lennox wasn't as comfortable with that as he pretended: he'd been lying, Hallac was sure, when he claimed to remember none of the details. Not that it mattered, that case was long over—except that kids who screwed up that badly, who cut corners and lost and never learned from their mistakes, didn't end up living in expensive condos, or if they did, they didn't keep them for more than six weeks after their protectors moved on, never mind six months. There was more to Lizzy—under either name—than Lennox was willing to admit.

Corbitt had dimmed the lights over her desk, was working now on a different screen. Hallac glanced at it, and stopped abruptly, staring at the image filling the display. An island floated in brown-toned space, brown sky, gold stars, planets ringed in amber and agate. A diffuse light reflected from its surface, offering here a flash of color, there the glimpse of a face or a scene. It was disorienting, the solidity of the picture dissolving as soon as he looked closely at it, and he shook his head.

"What the hell is that?"

Corbitt looked back at him, teeth flashing as she smiled. "That is what I just pulled out of Tin Lizzy's mainspace—the one that wasn't networked, otherwise, I think she'd have had better security on it. But that's some of her work."

"What is it?" Hallac leaned closer, trying to make out the details. It looked almost as though the island resolved into an inverted pyramid made up of soap bubbles, except that the bubbles were opaque and multicolored.

"It's a funhouse," Corbitt said. "I don't know who the client is, but it's really nice work."

Hallac nodded, leaning closer, and Corbitt obligingly adjusted the image so that the screen filled suddenly with a vast darkness. Hallac blinked, bracing himself—funhouses were rarely benign, despite the name—and the darkness faded. Walls appeared, and a floor, and then faces in bas-relief covering the walls. Faces and hands, he realized, clawing hands, as though their owners were sealed inside the grey stone—or was it metal? It flowed over the struggling forms as though it had been poured. The fingers barely broke the surface, but the faces were nastily distinct, teeth bared in a scream, vampire fangs bared in a final snarl, there a face visibly without eyes or mouth, another that was nothing more than a skull. Not a room for the claustrophobic, Hallac thought, fighting for distance, definitely the sort of thing that would earn a VG rating, though there really wasn't anything in the scene that you could pick out as specifically objectionable.

"There have to be repeats," Corbitt said, "I mean, this just isn't that big a file, but I can't spot them." Hallac could hear a craftsman's frustration in her voice, looked at her, and then back at the screen as the scene changed again, flickering rapidly through a series of images. "It's a maze-game—all the mechanisms are exposed right now, or I wouldn't be able to do this so fast—but the object is to get here."

Light blazed suddenly from the screen, vivid false sunlight, and the screen divided into planes of blue, one flecked with white, the other unmarked. Sea and sky, Hallac realized, reflected, refracted through the facets of a giant crystal, or the massive lens of a lighthouse. Corbitt rotated the point of view, turning away from empty ocean to focus on a distant, golden beach, and the bright tower of a second lighthouse. Even after only a single room, the impression of light and air was almost overwhelming; what would it be like, Hallac wondered, to win this view after traversing the entire dark maze?

"Impressive," he said, and Corbitt looked back at him.

"It's one of the best I've seen. Every one of the rooms is as developed as the first one, and the paths—well, she's built some neat connections between them, between the imagery, so you have to pay attention to what you're seeing, not dodge monsters, to get through it. She's got serious talent."

Hallac nodded, still staring at the screen. "So what do you think about this, Cady?"

"About what?"

"About what she'll do with this kid."

"I'm not paid to make assumptions." Corbitt's face and voice were wary, and Hallac gave a wry smile.

"Off the record."

Corbitt hesitated, then waved her hand at the pile of smokes. "That's the flip side. On the one hand, she's one of the best VRcitects I've seen. On the other—John, every single one of those smokes has a different ID configuration, she's got a different name for each day of the week and then some. And she sells them. She's got masks for sale under at least two of those names, and probably some more I haven't found. About a third of her mail is people wanting either a new mask or an update."

"I thought masks were illegal," Hallac said. They were expert programs, he remembered, tailored to help a player maintain each of his multiple selves. Some of them were just shortcuts, a way of storing all the necessary details about the persona, but the most sophisticated were pushing UE status, could maintain a persona's low-level activity for months without input from a human player.

Corbitt shook her head. "Only when you use them to defraud. Anybody can be anybody they want, as long as they—whichever version—don't break the law."

"Great." Hallac scowled at the glittering seascape, a single bird now floating against the cloudless sky. It didn't look quite as appealing as it had a minute before. "So you're telling me we're looking for somebody who's used to changing identity—changing shape, that's the Net slang, right?—just for the hell of it. That doesn't make me feel real good about this, Cady."

Corbitt's mouth twitched, and Hallac guessed she was biting

back a smile. "Oh, it's not that bad. I think—I've got enough of her work here, I think I can pick up some patterns. Plus I've probably got most of her names on file."

"You really think that'll help?" Hallac asked, and this time Corbitt did smile.

"She probably won't use any of the ones I have, but I've got enough information to work out how she works, build an analysand that'll make it easier to spot her. Yeah, I think it'll help."

Hallac nodded, accepting arcane knowledge. "You still didn't answer my question."

Corbitt looked wary again. "Question?"

"Yeah. About Lizzy. What do you think she's going to do with this kid, or with his program?"

Corbitt didn't say anything for a long moment, and Hallac sighed.

"I said off the record."

She looked at him for a long moment. "Off the record? I hope you've got more on her than you're telling me, because it's not making sense. We should be offering a deal."

That was the answer he'd been afraid of getting, and he sighed. "We've got instructions," he said, and pointed to the liter bottle of Coke on her desk, dangerously close to the keyboard. "I thought we weren't supposed to have food and drink in here."

Corbitt's mouth thinned, anger this time, but she accepted the change of subject. "You ever know a cop shop that meant it? Besides, the duty sergeant sent one of the aides to ask if we wanted anything."

Hallac nodded, mollified—if it was Metro's idea, they couldn't really complain—and Corbitt went on.

"I got you a water and some cookies."

They were oatmeal, the Goody Doyle brand that advertised themselves as good for you. Hallac suppressed a sigh, wishing his staff didn't think he always wanted healthful food. "So what else have you got?"

Corbitt shrugged. "No joy on the bank so far, of course—I mean, I know where the account is, but I haven't been able to get into the transaction records, and I want to be very careful how I do it, so it'll maybe stand up in court. It'd be easier if you'd get me a warrant."

"No warrants," Hallac said. Gerretty's instructions had been explicit, no matter how much he disagreed with them. And now, knowing Rhea was a mask-maker, he disagreed even more. *What we should be doing*, he thought, *is exactly what Cady wants, get a couple of warrants, financial and virtual, then put the word out that anyone who deals with Rhea is taking poison. And then find a way to make a deal, because there wasn't a player stupid enough to refuse to negotiate with RCD. Except, of course, that the reason people will negotiate with us is that we generally keep our word, and Gerretty's already made that impossible.* He dragged his thoughts away from that too-familiar problem, made himself focus on what Lennox had told him. The story didn't match the work he'd seen on Corbitt's screen—sure, artists were human, skill didn't imply morals, ethics, or even manners, but it was hard to imagine that the person who would go to the effort to make that funhouse wasn't willing to work. She might have wanted more money, faster money, than Conti's job could have provided, but Rhea wasn't the kind of loser Lennox had described. He frowned then, a memory teasing him, and said aloud, "Cady, why is the name Russ Conti familiar to me?"

She swung around to face him, leaving another of Tin Lizzy's images unfolding like a flower on the screen behind her. "You don't remember?"

Would I be asking if I did? Hallac shook his head, swallowing the words, and Corbitt made an apologetic face.

"Sorry, boss, I guess it was mostly a Systems thing. People are still fighting about it."

That sounded vaguely familiar, too, and Hallac's eyes narrowed. "Wait a minute. Something about protecting information, or protected information, something like that. . . ."

Corbitt was nodding. "Yeah. Russ Conti ran an anonymous remailer—oh, legally, it complied with all the Federal regs, et cetera—I think it was here in the District, actually. He was kind of a funky guy, programmer, did some jazz back when it was cool to do tech, you know, into the problem more than the paycheck. But then there was a murder in one of those gated communities—or maybe it was a covenanted community, I'm not real sure about that part—and there was reason to think the killer was getting at his victims through this remailer. But the main thing is, the police seized his servers and said they'd throw him in jail if he didn't give up the key codes. He did, and the cops caught the guy, but in the process, they spilled a lot of the information they got off the servers and there was a whole lot of bad fallout. One guy ended up committing suicide over it, and there were a lot of people on the Net, in the jazz, who said Conti should've gone to jail instead."

"They caught the killer," Hallac said.

Corbitt shrugged again. "One way I heard it, the cops could have caught the guy if they'd paid a little more attention to what was going on in the community. But that might be bad jazz."

"What happened to Conti?" Hallac settled himself in his chair, unwrapped the six-pack of cookies. For supposedly healthy snacks, they had a heavy dose of sugar and fat, and he bit into one with relish. If Conti was still around, he might be a useful go-between, or at least a resource—

"He disappeared," Corbitt said, and Hallac sighed again, resigning himself to another strike. "Dropped off the face of the Net." She tossed the remains of the candy bar toward the trash bin, made a face as it bounced off the rim. "Why?"

"From what Peter Lennox told me, Russ Conti also ran a program teaching computer skills to the underprivileged," Hallac answered. Corbitt's screen seemed to be bleeding, the upper half solid vermilion, with great viscous streaks spreading down from it. At the center was something that looked like the stamens of a flower— the whole design was a flower, bleeding off the screen. He deliberately looked away. "Rhea was one of his students. I guess she wasn't exactly one of his successes, though."

"I don't know about that." Corbitt turned back to her screen, grimaced at the bloody flower, and touched keys to dismiss it. "That might explain where Lizzy learned the jazz—probably does. You know, it might also explain why so many people think she's an older guy. From what I heard, Conti was a real stickler for aesthetics, and that'll make a program look old-fashioned. Could come in handy."

"Oh," Hallac said. It would probably be useful for tracking Rhea, at least on the Nets, but he doubted it would do much for them in the real world. And that was where they had to keep Rhea, at least until Metro could catch up with her and the Halford boy. Before he could go on, the telephone rang at his elbow. He picked it up out of reflex, was scowling at the mistake as he gave his name.

"Please hold for Mr. Gardner Gerretty."

The voice was sweet and mechanical, offering no option to refuse, and Hallac grimaced, wishing he'd let anyone else answer. "Holding."

There was a silence, the emptiness of dead air, and then Gerretty's voice growled in his ear. "So they're not giving you a photophone?"

"No, sir." Hallac saw Corbitt turn to look at him, waved her back to her computer. "These are hopefully temporary quarters."

"Whatever. I want to talk to you about the investigation. Any sign of this Rhea person? Or the boy?"

Hallac took a careful breath, controlling both anger and fear, and was pleased that he didn't sound conciliatory. "Not so far. We have several leads on Rhea, assuming she has the boy, but there's nothing on him after he left the cab this morning."

"I understand Rhea has a criminal record," Gerretty said, and Hallac damned him under his breath. Why couldn't the man let him conduct his investigation, without sniffing around in the public crime databases?

"Primarily a juvenile record," he said, "and one adult conviction. She's been clean since then."

"The arrests were for?"

"Petty theft, working in adult film without a permit." Hallac took another breath, wondering why he was defending Rhea. "Also prostitution."

"Ha."

There was another little silence, and Hallac imagined he could hear the other man's breathing. His own mouth was dry, and he wished he dared take a drink of the water, but knew he couldn't swallow without making too much noise.

"You know," Gerretty said, "we've got some worried parents here. No matter what this kid has done—not that I'm condoning theft—it's not safe for him to be off on his own. Especially in the company of an ex-hooker. Not at sixteen."

Great, Hallac thought. *That jazz always goes down well in the suburbs.* "I don't have any reason to think that this is a sexual matter," he said, deliberately obtuse, and heard Gerretty sigh.

"The parents are concerned."

As well they might be, Hallac agreed, *but mostly for their own jobs. They'd go along with whatever the president wanted to stay employed—and, to be fair, it would protect their son.*

"Is there any reason to think Rhea might have known the boy before this, might have lured him into a relationship in order to set up the theft?" Gerretty continued.

"No." Hallac knew he sounded too definite, moderated his tone. "Everything we have suggests the opposite. Halford contacted Rhea, first to set up this jazz piece, and then when he needed help."

"Still. It's an unstable situation," Gerretty said. "This Rhea—Tin Lizzy—could well pose a threat to the boy. I think it's something you have to consider."

It was not a suggestion—not even a comment. Hallac hid a sigh, knowing that Gerretty would spread the jazz as soon as he came up with anything resembling evidence, said, "I'll bear that in mind."

"Please. For the parents' sake."

Hallac could imagine Gerretty's smile. "Yes, sir."

"Keep me informed," Gerretty said, and cut the connection.

Hallac put the handpiece gently back in its cradle, took a final slow, deep breath. He didn't like this game at all.

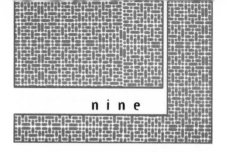

nine

They caught a flight from the new charter field, where sleek jump-jets ferried passengers to places like Lakeview and Atlantic City and the offshore resorts like the Isle Rialto. Lizzy was still feeling her way into the new persona, not sure who this Sanders woman was, and kept herself as inconspicuous as possible as she settled into her seat, leaving Keyz the window. She had paid for the tickets with the new phone-card, a risk, but less memorable than paying cash, and she reached for her smoke, plugging into the plane's databank as soon as the smoking lamp flashed on. The screen lit, offering a series of menus—casino ads, tutorials for various games, a chamber of commerce history of Lakeview, YENN and a couple of ISOO news sites—and she pretended to study them, wondering what Jaen Sanders would choose. Not the tutorials, she decided, this woman already knew how to play, though if there was a simulation, she might play a few hands or bet on the dice just to get her hand in, and probably not any of the news sites, though she probably had a custom feed from YENN if she followed sports or celebrities. Probably Sanders would go for the casino ads, she thought, but she herself couldn't face the too-loud colors and the constant hard sell. She tapped the screen, triggering the history file, relaxed into her seat as the muted images appeared.

Lakeview was one of the extraterritorial towns, entertainment gone wild, descendant of the Indian casinos and bingo halls, though the file, while stressing the parallel, glossed over the fact that Lakeview itself didn't claim to support any disadvantaged group. It practically boasted about the lake, though, pointing out that Lake Calo had been dug specifically to accommodate the floating casinos housed in the decommissioned cruise liners, and the Chamber even included helpful maps showing how the Lake Michigan canal and the layout of the lake itself had been constructed to allow the government to count it as international waters. Lizzy smiled to herself, tapping the controls to return to the main menu. It seemed that nobody was above using a little creative jazz now and then.

She studied the menu again, tapped the screen to choose YENN. If Jaen Sanders would have a personalized feed, it was time she set one up, and she scrolled past the breaking-news splash screens to edit a new profile. She'd done this hundreds of times before, for herself and for the masks she sold, but this time she couldn't seem to concentrate, found herself staring at the prompts without any idea how Sanders would respond. Usually this was the easy part, a simple game that helped her build the persona in her own mind until she could slip into that other skin simply by calling its name. That was the real trick to it, of course, the trick that her masks tried to automate: you had become that person in order to make it real. But this time, nothing was working.

Maybe it was being on the plane, she thought, and flipped back to the main YENN feed. It would be easier once they'd landed. Out of the corner of her eye, she saw Keyz fully occupied with one of the teaching games—dice, she thought, not the worst way to lose his money—and looked back at her own screen, guiltily grateful for the break from his company. She wasn't used to having someone around full-time anymore, had been glad when Sandy left to have her own space back. . . . She shook that thought away, tapped on the screen again to call a general studio feed. Maybe Sanders was a video junkie, she thought. That would be easy enough to play, and it would justify keeping tabs on RCD. The little screen filled with logos, three of the six flashing to indicate breaking news, and she caught her breath, spotting RCD among them. She touched the icon, and watched another breaking-news icon appear. She waited while it cycled and vanished, slowly replaced by a split image, the Santee brothers in one-half of the screen, caught in an unflattering moment of rage, and an all-too-familiar white face in the other. Both offered story links, and she didn't hesitate, tapping Gerretty's image. His face faded to form a faint background, and then heavy text appeared beneath a second image, this one of Gerretty standing in the lobby of the main studio building, beneath the massive stained-glass dome that was a map of the night sky. The jazz was that it had originally been a map of the world, but that someone had persuaded Gerretty that a single world limited RCD's ambitions unduly. It was easy enough to believe, remembering the man, and she grimaced, watching as the man stepped up onto a temporary platform between two huge pillars that looked as though they should have come from one of RCD's shooting stages. He mimed a speech to a crowd that was mostly grey-suited backs, and Lizzy wondered if they were real or merely wallpaper. The text crawling along the bottom of the page was a summary rather than a true transcription, but the message was clear enough. *Studio insiders report that Gardner Gerretty, CEO of RCD Studios, spoke today to a mass meeting of department heads. Although no details were released, and RCD refused comment, sources say that Gerretty referred to "certain recent events"— believed by sources to be theft of intellectual property—and informed his managers that the situation had been "appropriately dealt with." RCD stock remained steady today in heavy trading.*

"Hey," Keyz said. "Did you see this?"

Lizzy looked up, saw the boy tilting his own smoke toward her, the same image filling his screen. "Yeah. I just got it."

"So what the hell does that mean?" Keyz asked, and in spite of his best efforts, Lizzy could hear the fear in his voice. "I mean, we haven't been dealt with yet."

Lizzy looked back at her screen, touched a button to rerun the clip. "I think it's one of two things," she said, and lowered her voice until she could barely be heard over the whine of the engines. "Either word's gotten out about this program, or he's letting us know he's willing to make a deal."

"Do you think he would?" For a second, Keyz sounded even younger than he was, and Lizzy scowled.

"I think it's more likely that something's leaked." *And the question was what had gotten out, and just how much more difficult it would make their lives.*

"But if he was offering," Keyz said. "Could we do it?"

"It's your program," Lizzy said. "You want to deal, all right, I'll even help you set it up, but I won't be there when it goes down."

She heard Keyz' sigh even over the noise of the plane. "So you think it won't work?"

I know it won't work. Lizzy swallowed the words, not wanting to explain, to admit her own history with Gerretty, said instead, "Look, you said it yourself, it's too late for that. Gerretty can't be sure you didn't copy it, or sell copies, or even just let somebody take a long, hard look at it. He can't afford to trust us. And we can't afford to trust him."

Keyz slumped a little in his seat, scowling, and Lizzy looked back at her screen. Whatever Gerretty was doing, and maybe it was just the most obvious, trying to allay rumors of some word that had gotten out that the formula was missing—She stopped abruptly, wishing she'd been able to spend more time on the Net. Surely, though, if there was enough jazz out there to reach the stockholders, or even the old media, someone would have been in touch with her, especially after the debate about Keyz' mysterious helper? So there was a good chance Gerretty was up to something else, like trying to lure them into a deal he had no intention of keeping—except that she hadn't managed to stay on-line long enough to check out any of the current jazz. And that had been almost twenty-four hours ago: long enough for almost anything to have happened.

She sighed, tapping the screen again to switch into the airline's assortment of canned magazines, and set a technology story unfolding in her screen. Maybe Sanders should be a techie, she thought, that was something she could fake easily enough, but she couldn't muster her usual enthusiasm for the game. It was fear, she realized suddenly, and almost laughed out loud. It had been so long since she'd been in this position that she'd almost forgotten what it felt like. *Not that I've missed it at all*, she added silently, still smiling, *but at least I know where I am.*

They got into Lakeview a little after ten. Just before mandatory shutdown, Lizzy braved the hotel ads and made their reservations at one of the nicer hotels along the lake. She had hesitated over a less-expensive choice, something closer to the middle of town, but knew that she needed to keep Sanders's persona consistent if they weren't to draw attention. They shared the van with a trio of musicians, bound for a three-week stay on one of the party boats, and Lizzy found herself staring out the window, trying to ignore their nervous chatter. Keyz stayed quiet, too, and she was grateful. She rested her head against the night-cool glass, watching the neon flash by outside as the shuttle turned onto the ring road that described Lakeview's boundaries. On the inside of that loop, the lights were brilliant, neon and hologram and the occasional full-scale son et lumière; to the outside, beyond the town line, the fields stretched dark and empty toward the distant glow of the mills at Newtons.

Their hotel was opposite the docks, brightly lit and crowded with water taxis offering variously discounted rides out to the party boats. That meant it was also less than a ten-minute walk to the center of town, and Lizzy studied the city map floating beneath the surface of the counter while the clerk confirmed their reservations and assigned rooms. The place she wanted wasn't marked, of course—it hardly counted as a standard tourist attraction—but she'd downloaded a more detailed map on the plane and was already starting to get a sense of the topography.

Their rooms were in the back wing, on the second floor overlooking tennis courts and a visitors' parking lot. Keyz claimed to be disappointed that they couldn't see the lake, then discovered that by opening his window all the way and leaning out, he could catch a glimpse of the water taxis heading for the *Mediterrania*. Lizzy left him to divide his attention between that and the gambling tutorials, grateful that he'd found something to distract him, and retreated to her own room.

It was small but well laid out, and she switched on the media screen, not really seeing the thinly disguised advertisements that flipped past on the local channel. She couldn't contact Vara from here, not without drawing exactly the kind of attention she wanted to avoid, and she couldn't really check out the current jazz, either: SafeSurf stickers were posted prominently on the screens and the access ports, and their filters would cut out most of the information she needed. She reached for the remote instead, and clicked over to the directory menu, searching for cybercafes. Not too surprisingly, there were none in the tourist database—tourists didn't generally need that kind of random access—but in the "night life" section she found a club called the Border that advertised itself as catering to a sophisticated smoking crowd. That looked like her best bet, access to both the jazz and the unmonitored communications, and she switched off the media wall. She stretched, wishing she had time to sleep, to wait for morning, but slipped her phone into her bag and tapped on the connecting door.

"Keyz."

"Yeah?" The door opened slowly, Keyz peering through the crack.

"I'm going out. I want you to stay here."

"But—" Keyz' voice rose in instant protest, and Lizzy shook her head.

"It'll complicate things too much if you come along. Stay here, order room service, watch a movie, surf, if you want."

"Like I can get anything good here." Keyz scowled.

Lizzy shrugged. "Suit yourself. But stay here."

Keyz made a face, letting the door swing open a little farther. "Oh, come on, if I've got to live with filters, I want to go with you."

"It's not a good idea," Lizzy said.

"Why not?" Keyz' scowl deepened. "I mean, it's not like this is the District."

Lizzy took a deep breath, controlling her temper. "No. This is Lakeview. And the person I'm trying to get hold of is a Lakeview cop, who just might feel obliged to turn you in if you were there in the flesh."

"You're kidding," Keyz said, and Lizzy shook her head. "So what are you going to tell him?"

"I'm going to tell her I knew you from on-line," Lizzy said, and shrugged, the gesture already Sanders's. "I don't think she'll press the issue." *At least, I hope she won't—and I hope she'll let me walk if she can't do anything for us. . . .* She shoved that thought away, not wanting to borrow trouble, and Keyz glared at her.

"I thought you said we couldn't go to the cops."

"I said we couldn't trust, couldn't make a deal with, the ones chasing you," Lizzy said. "Chess—my friend is a local cop, a Lakeview badge. She has some leeway that those guys don't."

"Can she help us?" Keyz asked, and sounded eager again.

Lizzy sighed. "I don't know. That's why I want you out of sight. If there's any problem, I don't want you accessible, all right?"

"Oh." Keyz's eyes widened slightly. "OK."

Lizzy nodded, relieved that he was finally showing some sense, then hesitated. "And if I don't come back—if you don't hear from me by, oh, nine tomorrow, check out of here."

"But where do I go?" Keyz asked, and Lizzy paused for a second, remembering just how young—and how sheltered—he really was.

"Find a no-tel—you know about those?"

"Yeah." Keyz sounded indignant, but Lizzy ignored that.

"There's bound to be plenty of them around—check the local yellows under 'rooms for rent.' Then—" She stopped, stymied. She had no real idea what Keyz could do in that case, ran down the list of her own contacts looking for someone who might help. If she didn't come back, Vara was out, and Testify had already made its position clear. Most of the players were just that, players, they wouldn't risk their reputations to help a kid who wasn't one of them. She heard the echo of JoJo's voice in that, and grimaced. "You've got some choices," she said aloud, and hoped it was true. "You could go back to Bruce's, they'd help you—"

"And how am I supposed to get there?" Keyz demanded. "I haven't got any money."

You could try earning some. Lizzy killed the thought, knowing it was born of her own fear, and said, "I'll transfer some to the hotel account for you. They'll refund the unused part when you check out." *And that isn't a bad idea,* she thought. *Even if he doesn't have to use it, it'll make us look more authentic.*

"OK," Keyz said, sounding a little less nervous, and Lizzy crossed to his media center, leaned over the keyboard to start the transfer. Three hundred would be more than enough, she decided, would get him back to the city and still leave plenty for her, and she touched keys to enter the figures, flicking away the extra options that automatically appeared. The machine asked for her phone account as confirmation, and she tugged the minicable out of its housing and plugged it in, watching as the account screens cycled and finally produced its own approval codes. She copied them to her smoke and nodded to Keyz, who reached for his own machine. She watched him copy the information to his own protected accounts, and nodded.

"If that doesn't work—" She hesitated again, wishing she had more names, more options, but no one she knew was likely to be willing to take on RCD. "There's always Shida. Tell him what you have and ask him why he wants it. He should have enough clout to be able to help you."

"Nobody just goes and finds Shida," Keyz said.

"You said you were good," Lizzy answered, and felt a stab of guilt as the boy visibly drew himself up to the challenge. She didn't trust Shida—she didn't know him at all, so how could she?—but she doubted he'd be willing to help Keyz without exacting a significant price. "If you can't find him, or if you're desperate—" She paused, wishing she had another option. "There's a guy I used to know. His name's Russ Conti, he's not on-line anymore, but you can probably track him off-line, you're good enough. Tell him—just tell him what's going on. Ask him to help you. He's—I think he'll do it."

Keyz nodded, detaching his smoke from the transfer cable, and scribbled down the names.

"But it shouldn't come to that," Lizzy said. "I think Chess—my friend will help us."

"I hope so," Keyz said, and Lizzy forced a smile, trying to make it Sanders's. Keyz gave her a wary look, but moved back to the media wall. After a moment's hesitation, he flipped to on-line gambling, daring her to disapprove.

"Don't lose more than your ticket will cost," Lizzy said, and shut the room door between them. She took a deep breath, paused in the hall to wind her hair into a half-conservative knot, and rode the elevator down to the lobby.

The Boardwalk was bright and crowded, a deliberate echo of the one in Atlantic City, complete with arcade games beaming their lights across the worn flooring, except that it ran parallel to the oily beach rather than out into the water. But there was safety in numbers, and Lizzy moved easily with the crowd, letting the old skills come back, the way that a person could drift with a group, not so much a part of it to make them notice, but close enough that a single gesture, a simple question, could make you part of them in the eyes of any observer. Of course, she was overdressed for the Boardwalk, black jeans and jacket conspicuous among the tourists in their loose shorts and skimpy tops; she would be underdressed once she made it to the players' clubs, a crow among peacocks and panthers, but that could be passed off as affectation—assuming she could find the right streets. She paused in the shadows between two arcades to check her smoke, guessed from the little map that she had another half mile or so to go before she reached the junction with Mills. The smell of the water, fish and oil, rose to greet her, and she wrinkled her nose, wondering if Lakeview ever cleaned its shores. In the middle distance, the party boats glowed white and gold, reflecting streaks of light across the dark water. The rising moon was lost in their brilliance. It was hot, despite the blowers perched on every other building, and when she looked west, she wondered if she saw heat lightning or just the flicker of the distant mills.

Probably mills, she thought, and pushed herself away from the rail to merge again with the slow-moving crowd. There were a few smoking parlors on the Boardwalk, cramped, busy places that catered to the kind of tourist who wanted to send photos home to friends and grandkids, but most of the narrow buildings were given over to game arcades and video gambling and always the ubiquitous slot machines. Their ching and jingle was a constant counterpoint to the smooth roar of voices: Lakeview was old-fashioned that way, it seemed, attracted an old-fashioned crowd who liked to see the dollars pouring out of the machines instead of cashing in a clip of paper. She paused for a moment, pretending to consider the odds on a machine clad in reflective silver, and saw nothing but tourists behind her.

Mills Street met Lakefront Drive and the Boardwalk in a small circle, complete with a sculpted fountain in its center. A slim, slightly curved pylon rose toward the black sky, water shimmering along its sides; there would be a light show at midnight, according to the tourist pages she'd viewed at the hotel, but for now half a dozen teens were wading in the shallow basin, oblivious to the signs that warned them off. No one seemed to notice, especially not the drivers, tucked bumper to bumper as the lanes merged and flowed around the curve, and Lizzy was grateful for the pedestrian overpass that spanned the streets. She made her way down Mills, moving faster now that the pedestrian traffic had gotten lighter, and knew by the way the clothes changed that she was getting closer to the neighborhood she wanted. There were fewer obvious tourists here, and the ones that were visible were yawning, probably on their way back to the cheap hotels after a day on the water. Most of the crowd was younger, tougher, dressed for a night on the town in sharp-cut Euro-style slacks and jackets; a lot of them would be employees of the resorts, she guessed, swimming and tennis and golf instructors, but there would be a decent mix of players among them. They weren't all perfect, none of them truly up to the standard of the beautiful people, but they were trying very hard."

A few blocks farther down the wide street, the crowd thickened again, a mass of people spilling out of a building with PARADISE splashed across its side in bright pink letters. Lizzy eyed them warily, wondering if she'd be better off facing the traffic to get to the other side of the street, but as she came closer, she heard music. *A dance club, then*, she thought, and kept walking, feeling the pulse of bass and drums through the concrete itself. They'd come outside to talk, she guessed, and slipped through the edges of the crowd without haste, idly spotting familiar types. An older man, nicely dressed, was talking to a trio of college-age girls—no, she realized, not just talking. She slowed her steps, watching out of the corner of her eye, and saw without surprise the moment that he passed a tiny packet to the tallest of the girls. *Trippers, probably*, Lizzy thought, *or maybe just candy*: that was pretty common jazz, especially in the tourist towns.

Beyond the Paradise was the club she was looking for, deceptively plain and quiet under a gold sign. Definitely the kind of place any self-respecting Systems officer would check more than once a night, she thought, and felt her spirits lift a little. She could drop a note to Vara's private address, then wait, check out the real jazz on Shida, and let Vara come to her. The doorman gave her a blank stare, but didn't challenge her; Lizzy matched the look and stepped past him in to the club's warm shadows.

It wasn't as dark as she'd thought at first glance, but the lights were dim, orange-toned like safety lamps, and left pools of shadows between the tables. She lifted an eyebrow at the hostess dressed like a dancing girl at a funeral, black-chiffon trousers and cropped top that showed her belly-bangles, and she waved a ringed hand vaguely toward the floor. Lizzy nodded, not quite thanks, that was more than was expected, and found herself a table toward the sidewall. The menus faded to life under the display glass; she keyed in her phone number to start a tab, and ordered a drink and general access. The drink came faster than the port cleared, and Lizzy sipped it cautiously, waiting for the system to acknowledge her account. There was no reason for it to take this long, not when the phone had cleared at the hotel—or maybe it was just some kind of general slowdown, some problem with the Border's servers. That was a reassur-

ing idea, and Lizzy leaned back in her chair, casting a careful look
around the big room. It was hard to tell in the uncertain light, but
the other smokers looked restless and irritable as well.

That was something of a relief, even if it meant that the Border
was probably on its way out as a player's bar, and Lizzy glanced at
the food menu. The smoke pinged then, announcing access at last,
and she tapped the menu aside, hunger forgotten. The screen
flared, colors reflecting through the dark glass of the tabletop, and
she didn't bother to mute them, drinking in the sight of the open
system. This was a jazz host, all right; the gateway was already open,
just a bright gold frame surrounding a sea of familiar icons—even
Testify was there, one of its rare fixed-access nodes. Obviously the
Border rated, Lizzy thought, even with its technical problems. She
scrawled a command on the input screen, sending the message she
had composed on the plane, and then taped another icon to connect
to her favorite search engine. A tiny window popped open, and she
tapped the stylus against her lips for a second, ordering her
thoughts. She needed to track down the full story on Shida, find out
if he really was around, and was interested in Keyz' program, and
then she wanted anything new on RCD and Gardner Gerretty.
Shida first, she decided, and scrawled the parameters on the pad.
The window shrank obediently, taking the inquiry with it, became a
pulsing square in one corner of the screen, and Lizzy nibbled the
tip of her stylus, considering the array of icons. There wasn't any
harm in skimming a little extra jazz while she waited for the engine
to give her its list of links, and she touched the Man on the Moon's
broad face, seeing familiar icons blossom, headlines shimmering
behind them.

"Tin Lizzy?"

She looked up and back, knew instantly that she had made a mistake, lost her persona with no hope of getting it back. There were
two of them, men in suits a little too neat to belong to anybody she
wanted to know, and she could tell from their faces that she'd
responded too quickly to deny the name. She lifted an eyebrow, trying to look rich and innocent, and the bulkier of the two men slid
smoothly into the empty chair at her right.

"Where's your boyfriend?"

"Huh?" The question caught her by surprise, and she knew she

looked genuinely blank, couldn't understand what anybody in those
suits—they looked like bounty-men—would want with Sandy.

"Don't play dumb," the man behind her said, and the first man
shook his head fractionally.

"The kid," he said, to Lizzy. "Halford. Where is he?"

"Kid?" Lizzy repeated. It was probably a stupid game, but
maybe that moment of real incomprehension would get her through.

"You're Tin Lizzy, right?" the man at the table said, with false
patience.

"We know you're Tin Lizzy," the other man said.

"So where's the boy?"

Lizzy looked from one to the other. "A lot of people use this
name. I don't know what you're talking about."

She saw the two men exchange glances, and then suddenly the
man beside her reached across the table to pin her left wrist. It
looked innocuous enough, she guessed, a man making a move on a
woman, but she couldn't pull free. She leaned back in her chair,
froze as something solid touched her back, solid and round right
between her shoulder blades. *Gun barrel?* she thought. Bounty-men
weren't supposed to carry lethal weapons, but most of them did anyway. *Stun stick?* She couldn't tell through the layers of jacket and
shirt.

"Look at that," the seated man said, and reached across with his
free hand to push back Lizzy's sleeve, baring the tattoos.

"Now that's not in the description," the other man said, and
Lizzy felt the pressure point between her shoulders ease a little.

"Check again," the first man said, and looked back at her. "If
you're not our Tin Lizzy, you want to cooperate, right? You don't
want to be helping a child molester, do you?"

"What?" Lizzy knew she looked and sounded stupid—hoped she
sounded a lot stupider than she was, that she could somehow turn
this into a new, plausible persona. The first man gave her a look of
contempt, and looked at his partner again.

"Well?"

"No mention of anything like that."

There was a click, the sound of a smoke closing, and the pressure slithered over the jacket's silk. It was a stun stick, Lizzy thought,

and for a fraction of a second thought she might pass out from sheer relief. Just a stun stick, painful at worst, but she wouldn't be dead.

"And you'd think they would," the standing man went on, and his partner grunted.

"Oh, sure. You know what they're like."

"Well, you would think."

"Yeah." The seated man looked back at Lizzy, still not releasing her wrist. *If I screamed,* she thought, *would the bouncers help?* Places like this had to worry about ex-boyfriends, ex-lovers, all the possibilities—

"All right," the seated man went on, "if you're not our Tin Lizzy, you won't have any objection to proving that fact, will you?"

"Maybe." Lizzy took a careful breath, trying to sound indignantly innocent. She didn't have a persona for this act, fumbled for the right tone and attitude. For a second, she wished passionately she was back on-line, with all her masks cued up and ready to run, and the option of simply dropping out. "What the hell is your problem?"

"It's a simple thing," the standing man said. "You look one hell of a lot like our contractee—we've been hired by the parents of this kid, who's taken off with a known sex offender. You're not her, come into the main station and prove it, and we'll apologize, buy you a drink, whatever. You are her, and you better come along quietly, 'cause, like my partner says, we don't much like child molesters, and we don't mind making a scene. But either way, you're coming with us."

Jesus Christ. Lizzy sat frozen for a second, blinded by the sheer brilliance of this jazz. Whoever had put out this complaint—and she doubted it was Keyz' parents, it felt more like Gerretty's style— whoever did it was a fucking genius, because anybody in the world could find out she had a record, and what it was for. . . . "All right," she said, dry-mouthed, and nodded to her smoke. "Mind if I shut down first?"

The seated man shook his head, and released his hold on her wrist.

"Go ahead," the standing man said.

Lizzy freed her stylus, scrawled a meaningless command on the pad, trying to buy time. The identity she'd gotten from Murfree wasn't designed to stand up to a real investigation, wouldn't last

an hour once they got down to the police station. Of course, if
Vara was there, it wouldn't matter, but that wasn't a risk she wanted
to take. The smoke beeped softly, querying the command, and
she snapped the lid closed as though nothing was wrong. In the
same movement, she yanked the cables loose and stood up, shoving
the table in one direction and the chair in the other, slamming it
and her free elbow into the man behind her. The stun stick fired,
off target, numbing her left arm, and she put her head down and
ran, dodging between tables, toward the nearest exit sign. She heard
the standing man swear, caught a crazy glimpse of the other man
struggling to his feet, fighting the tangle of table and the wires
that had been ripped up when the table fell, and then she banged
down hard on the emergency release. Hard white light flooded
the room with the howl of the Klaxon, and then she was out into an
alley, the smoke still clutched in her locked fingers. She turned right,
away from the street, realized an instant later that this was a dead
end, and turned back too late, to see the bounty-men blocking the
roadway.

"I knew it was her," the bulkier man said, savagely, and the other
nodded.

"We've got her now."

Lizzy froze again, knowing she wasn't going to talk her way out
of this one, wondering what she could trade them, short of Keyz, or
if they'd take Keyz, and let her go—She rejected that thought
instantly—what would be the point, after she'd gone this far?—and
caught her numb elbow in her good hand. The whole arm was numb,
unresponsive fingers curled over the smoke's negligible weight, useless as a club even if she could make her shoulder work. She didn't
dare step back, not wanting to be caught against the wall, knew there
wasn't anything she could do.

"Hold it!" The voice came from the head of the alley, a harsh
deep sound that Lizzy only belatedly recognized as female. "Lakeview Police. Drop your weapons and put your hands against the wall."

"Oh, for Christ's sake," the bulkier man began, but the taller
man raised both hands obediently, crouched to lay the stun stick
carefully on the pavement.

"Hands against the wall," the woman repeated, and the bounty-
men turned reluctantly to obey. "You, too, blondie."

Lizzy blinked, almost recognizing the voice then, but the light was behind the other woman, and she couldn't be sure. She turned slowly, leaned forward into the old position. A man's hand yanked her left arm up, dragging her knuckles over the brick, and she winced at scratches she couldn't yet feel. Someone patted her down impersonally—the man, she thought, smelling aftershave and male sweat—and then pulled her upright again.

"She's clean."

"Yeah." the woman straightened, holding ID tags that flashed their message across the alley. "And I've got a pair of bounty-men."

It was Vara after all, Lizzy realized, light-headed with pain and relief, Chessie Vara large as life, sliding her pistol back beneath the hem of her jacket. She wouldn't have thought anyone could run in that outfit, narrow suit skirt and chunky heels, but the big woman moved then, and Lizzy saw the slit that ran well up her thigh and the runner's tights beneath it.

"We've got a private warrant," one of the bounty-men said.

"Jurisdiction?" That was the man who'd searched her, still with his hand ambiguously on her shoulder, and Lizzy looked sideways to see a tall man in a baggy, rumpled suit. He was a perfect foil to Vara's impeccable grooming, and she wondered crazily if they'd assigned him to Vara for just that reason.

"California," the other bounty-man said, and Vara snorted.

"Private doesn't cut it here. Not out of CA—and not out of any-where without a confirming warrant."

"She's a kidnapper," the first bounty-man said, and Lizzy made herself straighten painfully.

"I don't know what's going on, but these guys—"

"You lying bitch," the bounty-man said, and his partner spoke quickly.

"She admitted it—why else would she have run?"

"That's enough," Vara said, and looked at her partner. "I know her. It doesn't seem likely."

"Better bring them all in," the big man said, peaceably. "Maybe she'll press charges."

Vara nodded, looked back at the bounty-men, still braced pre-cariously against the wall. "We'll check out this warrant when we get there."

Blue lights flashed at the end of the alley, the nose of a cop van sliding into view behind them, and the big man nodded toward it. "Transport's here."

"Then let's get moving." For the first time Vara looked directly at Lizzy, her broad face blank. "You've all got some explaining to do."

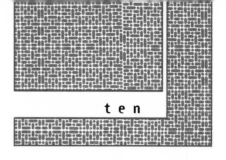

ten

They rode back to the precinct house in silence, Lizzy in the front section with Vara's partner, who seemed even bigger in the cramped space, Vara in the back with a guard and the two bounty-men. At the station, however, they switched off, and Vara's partner led the bounty-men into a bleak side room that Lizzy recognized as an interview room. Vara herself shook her head once, and nodded to the younger woman's hand.

"You need to wash that."

Lizzy looked down, grimaced at the blood and dirt caked on her knuckles. "I still can't feel it."

"Better now than later, then," Vara said, not unkindly, and beckoned a dark girl who didn't look old enough to be wearing a patrol-man's uniform. "Gem'll take care of you."

Lizzy followed the uniformed woman down a long, too brightly lit corridor. The bathroom was cool and empty, and she took her time cleaning the scratches, wondering what the hell she was going to do. Vara wasn't exactly looking friendly, and the bounty-men had a good story—*but Vara knows me*, she told herself. *She won't let them railroad me*. The stun effect was beginning to wear off, a faint tingling in her fingertips that meant worse to come, and she pried them gently away from the smoke casing. She slid the machine into a pocket and held her hand under the water she couldn't feel for a long time, trying to think of a plan, but nothing came. She dried her fingers carefully, wrapping a towel around the skinned knuckles. The bleeding had mostly stopped, but it was going to hurt later on.

The uniformed girl brought her back down the hall and opened the door to another interview room. Lizzy stared for a second at the pale green walls—it looked like the interview rooms in the District, probably like every interview room anywhere—but made herself take a seat, resting her tingling hand on the tabletop.

"Would you like coffee?" the girl asked, her voice faintly accented, and Lizzy nodded, managing a wan smile.

"Please. Whatever you've got, with cream and sugar."

"Sure," the girl answered, sounding for the first time faintly sympathetic, and stepped back into the hall, closing the door gently behind her.

Lizzy leaned back in her chair, knowing she was at least under automatic surveillance, and wondered if someone who'd never been in a police station before would think to look around for the camera holes. Probably not, she decided, not if they were innocent, and knew they were innocent, the way Jaen Sanders did—She stopped abruptly, unable to repress a grimace. That act wasn't going to do her any good here, not when Vara already knew precisely who she was.

The door opened again, and with it came the welcome smell of coffee, but to her surprise, it was Vara herself who brought in the steaming cartons, balancing them carefully in one hand as she closed the door behind her. Lizzy accepted hers gratefully, folding the numbed fingers around it in the hope that the warmth would speed her recovery. Her other hand was trembling a little, and she closed it into a fist, willing herself to stay calm.

"So," Vara said, and dropped into the seat opposite. "You all right?"

"The guy caught me with a stun stick. It's coming out all right."

"You could file a charge on that," Vara said, sounding hopeful, and Lizzy remembered that the other woman hated bounty-men. For a second she hesitated, tempted, then shook her head.

"I don't think so." She had been going to say she didn't think it would be smart, but swallowed the words in time.

Vara made a face and leaned both elbows on the table. "Is this why you wanted to talk to me?"

"Part of it—"

The big woman shook her head. "What the hell have you been up to, Lizzy?"

"Oh, man." Lizzy blinked once, hard, startled by her own sudden fragility, forced a smile that she knew was more like a flinch. "There was this kid, on one of the sites I comp—just starting out, into the jazz but not there yet, you know? I dropped him the word when he wrote some stuff that was half-good, tried to give him a couple of pointers. Then he comes up with this piece that was really something, got him hosted on Testify, only it turns out he didn't

write it, at least not exactly, he had this program that helped him figure it out. And then it turns out he doesn't own the program, he just
hacked it out of RCD, the studio computers, so he's got them on his
tail. His folks work for them, which just makes it worse."

The story came tumbling out, not as ordered as she'd planned it,
but at least comprehensible, and when she'd finished, Vara shook
her head. "So where's this child molester thing coming from?"

"Keyz is sixteen," Lizzy said, and knew she sounded bitter. "And
they've got my record. Sex and scandal is always great jazz in the
suburbs."

"They're playing hardball," Vara said, her voice neutral, and
Lizzy sat up straighter.

"You don't think—" She stopped abruptly, took a breath, controlling her own anger. "You know me, Chessie, good and bad. What
the hell would I be doing with a sixteen-year-old boy?"

"Shit." Vara looked down, rubbing the bridge of her nose as
though she had a headache. "Yeah, I know you. I agree, it's not your
style—weren't you the one who said once she never slept with a guy
who hadn't paid her?" She stopped, shook her head. "Sorry. That
was uncalled for."

Lizzy looked away herself, recognizing old words, an old anger
she'd long abandoned. "That was a long time ago," she said. "I was
just out of the Wilson. I know you were Sandy's friend, but he knew
what he was getting."

"I know." Vara sighed. "He didn't exactly complain."

Except by leaving. Lizzy winced, and Vara shook herself, working her shoulders as though they were stiff.

"Hey, I know it's not my business, but Sandy's a friend. I didn't
think you were real good for him—nothing personal—but I thought
he was a jerk, leaving like that."

"Do you know where he's gone?" Lizzy grimaced, embarrassed
to have blurted out the question, and flexed her stinging fingers, trying to hide the emotion.

Vara blinked. "You'd go back to him?"

"No." Lizzy shook her head for emphasis, was relieved to find it
was true. "But I'd like to know what he thought he was doing."

This time, Vara's smile was genuine. "Wouldn't we all? But
that's Sandy for you."

"Yeah." Lizzy took a sip of her cooling coffee, flexing her fingers again. The joints felt swollen, but she knew that would pass.

"So what are we going to do with you?" Vara said, and Lizzy drew a sharp breath. All this, and she still hadn't said the most important thing.

"There's more."

Vara pinched the bridge of her nose again. "More?"

"Yeah. I've still got the kid."

Vara shook her head, not releasing her nose. "So give."

"He's stashed at a hotel by the taxi docks. I'm suppose to be back by nine tomorrow, or he's going to fade."

"Oh, great," Vara said.

"No, he'll sit tight until then, but I need to get him out of there if we're attracting this kind of trouble."

"You know, they could have my badge for this already," Vara said, and sighed. "I can't just let you walk, Lizzy, you know that."

Lizzy blinked, unable to believe what she was hearing. "I can't stay here—"

"They've got a warrant," Vara said, and there was a knock at the door. She stopped, swiveling in her chair, and the door opened to reveal her partner, a sheaf of printouts in his hand. "Got something, Jack?"

"Yeah." The big man had discarded his jacket somewhere along the line, Lizzy saw, and his shirt was wilted. "You're not going to like it."

"Surprise me," Vara said, sourly, and he reached for the door.

"I don't think we should talk here—"

Vara shook her head. "You can talk in front of Lizzy. I told you, I know her. The charge is jazz, it's a hacker thing."

Lizzy blinked again, startled by the sudden support, and Vara went on, "Lizzy, this is my partner, Jack Iovanni."

"Hi," she said, weakly, and Iovanni gave her an embarrassed nod. "Chessie . . ."

"We can talk here," Vara said again. "Unless there's something you need the computers for."

Iovanni shook his head, capitulating. "It's all here," he said, and held up the stack of paper.

"So tell me."

"First of all, the warrant's good," Iovanni said. "The good news is, it's only just good—the issuer's a private police force, from one of the studios, RCD, not a municipality. The bad news is, the complainant's the kid's parents, people named Halford. They said they'd been advised by friend and by the local authorities that this was a good way to find their son maybe faster than the cops could do it, so they thought they'd try it."

Vara made a face. "Isn't that pretty expensive?"

Iovanni shrugged. "Maybe not so much in California, not with studio connections. And they said something about insurance covering it."

"You talked to them?" Vara asked.

"Hell, yes. I get something like this, I want to hear what the complainant has to say." Iovanni held out a sheet of paper. "This is what came back on the fax query."

Vara took it, scanned the faded printing, and then slid it across the table toward Lizzy. "This is the original warrant?"

For a second, Lizzy thought Iovanni was going to protest, but he just grimaced, and held out a second sheet of paper. "Uh-huh. Issued by Sheriff Toni and signed by Judge John Smith, no less."

Vara looked as though she wanted to spit, and in spite of everything Lizzy grinned. Sheriff Toni was the star one of RCD's LawNet shows, a busty blonde who seemed unable to buy a uniform shirt that fit.

Iovanni went on, "And this is the original application. It took me a while to pry it out of them, too."

"Out of who?" Vara asked, her attention on the new sheet.

Lizzy reached cautiously for the first page, turned it around so that she could read it. It didn't have much, just the same information the bounty-men had already given her, and she pushed it back toward Iovanni, who slid it back into his pile.

"RCD. Their police force. Most of the studios have them, I guess."

Vara dropped the second sheet, nodding, and Lizzy reached for it. There was a lot more information here, not just the parents' names and addresses, but their employer's name and address, as well as notes from the interviewing officer. Those commented on the parents' concerns, suggesting that as far as they knew their son was "sexually inexperienced and potentially confused by sexual attentions." *It's probably true, too*, she thought, *but it doesn't help me at all.* Then what Iovanni said registered, and she looked up sharply.

"The Halfords don't work for RCD. They're with Continuing Education." She swung the form around, pointing to the name under *employer*.

"Apparently they're doing contract work for RCD," Iovanni said. "Some kind of teaching thing, they do tapes and stuff—an enhancement course, I think they said. The Studio police have jurisdiction in any case."

"But it's not like teachers automatically hire out private warrants to find a runaway kid," Vara said. "They don't usually have the resources."

"This is private education," Iovanni said, but his tone was less certain than the words. He looked from one woman to the other. "What are you thinking, Chessie?"

"The same thing you are, or you wouldn't be in here with that," Vara answered. "What else have you got there?"

"The studio has a man on assignment on this one," Iovanni answered. He looked at Lizzy. "He's asking us to hold you until he can get here. He's sent all the right forms."

Lizzy suppressed a shiver. "When does he get here?"

"Tomorrow morning."

"Shit," Vara said, with contempt. "You think the captain will go along with it?"

Iovanni shrugged. "You got a reason he shouldn't?"

Lots of reasons, Lizzy thought. *Like why would RCD take all this trouble over a kid whose parents don't even work for them?* She opened her mouth to speak, and Vara gave her a warning glance.

"You said you talked to the parents, Jack. How'd they sound?"

Iovanni looked away, shaking his head. "All right, you got me. They didn't sound—right, somehow. Not worried enough, maybe?" He shook his head again. "No, they were worried, all right, but not about their kid being off with some woman. Not even when I said we hadn't found him, just her."

"And RCD's sending a cop personally to deal with this," Vara said. "What's his rank, anyway?"

Iovanni sorted through his papers again. "Uh—lieutenant.

We've got an intro from the studio, they ask us to extend all courtesy to him and his team. . . ."

His voice trailed off thoughtfully, and Vara said, "A team? And hire bounty-men? That's their name on the policy, check for yourself. For somebody who doesn't even work for them?"

"I don't know," Iovanni said. "I mean, no, it doesn't make any sense, but—" He stopped, glared at Lizzy. "So what do you say is going on here?"

Lizzy took a careful breath, and Vara spoke first. "I'm being a little careful here, Jack, understand me. You remember I was worried about a hacker problem? This is it."

"Not good enough." Iovanni shook his head.

"Keyz, Seth Halford, acquired something out of RCD's vaults," Lizzy said, "and they want it back really bad."

Iovanni spread his hands, the papers rustling. "Why go to all this trouble? Why not just bust him on straight burglary?"

"How seriously do we take that kind of shit?" Vara asked, and the big man grinned.

"Put a big enough value on it, it's a felony. We have to do something then."

"They don't want people to know it exists," Lizzy said, and Iovanni shook his head.

"I don't know. Look, what's the harm in you staying, meeting with these guys? I can guarantee you the captain won't let them book you with the kind of information we've got here."

Lizzy took a deep breath. "I've already been convicted of a felony, a double-strike offense. I can't afford to be involved in this until I can prove I didn't have anything to do with stealing the program in the first place."

"You should have thought of that before you took up with the kid," Iovanni said.

"When I said I'd help, I thought it was something a lot smaller," Lizzy muttered.

"What was she going to do," Vara said, "drop him as soon as she knew there was a problem? Come on, Jack, there's no point keeping her overnight."

"You think I don't know she's going to fade?" Iovanni glared at his partner, and Vara met the stare firmly.

"You really want to help these guys? When they're pulling jazz like this?"

"Have we got a choice?"

Vara glanced at Lizzy. "Let's talk. Excuse us, Liz."

"Sure," Lizzy answered, faintly, and Vara levered herself to her feet. She motioned Iovanni toward the door, and the big man obeyed with only the slightest hesitation. Vara followed him, pulling the door almost closed behind her.

Lizzy sat for a moment, head cocked to listen, but even holding her breath she couldn't hear more than an indistinct mumble. She eased her chair back, silent on the stiff carpet, and edged toward the door. With any luck, the observation room would be empty—it was bound to be, the way the two of them were talking—and if they caught her, she could always say her hand was hurting, that she'd gotten up to clean it again. That was true enough, and she grimaced, lifting it to her shoulder to slow the returning circulation.

"—you know this is crooked," Vara was saying, and Lizzy froze, still a good yard from the open door.

Iovanni's voice was softer, but still distinctly audible. "Yeah, fine, but what the fuck are you proposing we do about it?"

"I want to ride along." There was a little silence after Vara's answer, and when she spoke again, her voice was urgent. "Look, you're right, she's going to run, and I'd run if I was in her place. If I go with her—go with them—I can maybe find out what's really going on."

"That's fucking crazy," Iovanni said. "You'll lose your badge."

"That's why I'm trying to get permission," Vara answered.

"Jesus!" There was a dull thud, as though Iovanni had slammed his fist into the wall.

"Look," Vara said, "you're sick of this kind of warrant. I'm sick of this kind of warrant, everything stinking to high heaven and nobody willing to stick their necks out to ask questions."

"Plus she's your friend," Iovanni said.

"So? Maybe that makes me just not such a great person, that I'm not doing it for everybody," Vara said. "But this kind of shit—it's got to stop somewhere."

"The captain won't buy it."

"Maybe not from me," Vara said, and Lizzy heard Iovanni sigh.

"You want me to help you destroy your career."

"Or make it," Vara answered. Her voice was moving toward the door again, and Lizzy skipped backward, dropping awkwardly into her chair as the door swung open again. Vara ignored her, still staring at the man beside her. "Well? You willing?"

Iovanni locked eyes with her a moment longer, then finally looked away, swearing under his breath. "All right. If the captain buys it, I'll back you."

"Right." Vara's nod was brisk, but Lizzy could sense the other woman's relief. "Lizzy, we'll be back in a few minutes."

"Don't go anywhere," Iovanni added, and this time pulled the door closed behind them.

It was closer to fifteen minutes before anyone returned, and then it was only the uniformed officer, offering another box of coffee. Lizzy accepted gladly, sat working her fingers and sipping the hot sweet liquid for another half hour before Vara finally reappeared. Iovanni was nowhere in sight, and she hoped that was a good sign. Then Vara smiled, and Lizzy released the breath she hadn't known she was holding.

"You're clear, and I'm your woman, at least in a limited sense. It's just lucky Captain Markham really hates bounty-men, this whole thing's really thin."

"It's not that thin," Lizzy said. "It's just—" She laughed suddenly, unable to stop herself. "It's just lousy jazz, that's all. Nobody believes it because it's not artistic enough."

Vara allowed herself a smile at that, but it faded quickly. "Come on, let's get you out of here. This is likely to get ugly, you know."

"I'll call you in the morning," Lizzy said.

"Just do it discreetly," Vara answered, and held open the door.

Lizzy followed her down the long hall toward the squad room, filled at this hour with mostly empty desks. It was almost quiet, too, just the muted sound of the radio as somebody opened the door to the dispatcher's cubicle, and, distant in the corner, the sound of someone snoring. A tall woman in tight jeans was leaning against the wall beyond the barricade of the duty desk, hugging herself, a tissue against her mouth; another, older woman waited with her, not touching her, not really looking at anything. There was a cat carrier on someone's desk, complete with cat, an orange, spotted thing idly rubbing its head against the mesh while a uniformed officer scribbled notes into his smoke. It had a collar, Lizzy saw, and felt obscure relief.

"You'll want a cab," Vara said, and motioned for the sergeant at the duty desk to buzz them out. Lizzy stepped out into the relative heat of the lobby, working her shoulder against the last of the stiffness, and nodded. It was late to be walking back to the hotel, late to be trying to find another place to go—*and I still haven't had a chance to look at the jazz*, she thought, with sudden despair. *If I don't get access soon, unfiltered access, real access . . .* She shoved the thought away, looked back at Vara as the other woman turned away from a cab call box.

"Look, Chessie, I'm still—I need help."

"Yeah." Vara nodded. "I know. Don't worry, I'll do what I can."

I just hope it's enough. Lizzy killed that thought, knowing it was ungrateful, managed a nod. "Thanks, Chessie," she said, wishing she could say more, say how much she knew, and out of the corner of her eye saw a cab round the corner. Back to the hotel first, she decided, and then a new name, a new persona, and a new plan.

Hallac left his smoke open in his lap for the ride from the airport, wishing he'd been able to snatch more than a couple hours' sleep on the plane. The call had come in too late to do anything except charter a private jet, and he was still cringing at the thought of his expense account, but the Lakeview captain—and then the chief of police, roused from his bed at three in the morning—had been less than cooperative. *Not that I blame them, either*, he added silently, looking at the documents floating in the smoke's narrow screen. *How anybody could think a warrant issued by LawNet—by no less a person than Sheriff Toni herself—and signed by Judge Smith of the syndicated* I, The Jury, *would impress anyone outside the studios. . . .* Except that he'd never thought Gardner Gerretty was a stupid man, and it was obviously Gerretty's hand at work here. Not only was it his charge, statutory rape instead of virtual taking, simple theft, but the whole thing was being paid for out of RCD's employee policy, and only Gerretty could authorize that extra expense. *Probably Judge Smith was the most convenient person they could find to sign the warrant*, Hallac thought, and straightened as the car pulled up to the central police station. It was a big building, relatively new, like everything in Lakeview, the cream stones of the trim still bright against the red brick, and he levered himself carefully out of the backseat.

"Wait for me," he said to the driver, and headed toward the security gate.

The night-shift captain was still on duty—waiting for him, Hallac guessed, and knew that was one more strike against him. He braced himself for hostility, but instead the man ushered him into a cluttered office, offered him a chair and coffee before seating himself behind the big desk. Hallac declined the coffee with thanks, and seated himself carefully opposite the other man. Markham was even bigger than he'd looked in the smoke's screen, a thick-set, fair-haired man who probably had respectable brawler's muscles under the bulk. He looked like someone you'd want working the night shift in a casino town, big enough to handle anything, but not the kind of guy who'd get too smart and try something on his own. And looks were almost certainly deceiving, Hallac told himself, especially in a town like this, where pretty much everybody played the jazz out of habit. This was not the time to let himself be fooled.

"So," Markham said, "you're the guys who couldn't catch up with this bimbo."

That was more what he'd been expecting, and easier at this point to deal with than the incongruous courtesy. "No," Hallac said, "we're the guys who were looking for her in the first place. This was a private warrant, taken out without our consent and against my advice. If they'd asked me for it, that is." He paused, inviting sympathy. "The parents are pretty frantic."

"That's not what my man tells me," Markham said.

So much for sympathy. "And what do you mean by that?" Hallac kept his voice easy, just allowing an edge of annoyance to frost his tone.

"Jack Iovanni called the Halfords last night, let them know we'd found the woman they thought seduced their little boy." Markham leaned forward, folded his hands to rest heavy forearms on the desktop. "You know, under the circumstances, I'd expect them to be flying out here to try to find the kid themselves, to be screaming at us to lock up the bitch, find their kid, all of that. But they didn't even ask about the kid. Iovanni had to tell them we hadn't got him, and even then they weren't that stressed about it."

"They're pretty much in shock," Hallac said. *Damn Gerretty and his jazz. I knew it wouldn't hold up if anybody started talking to the Halfords—they're too worried about their jobs to think of anything else.*

"Yeah. Whatever." Markham's expression didn't change. "I don't like bounty-men, Lieutenant. The chief doesn't like bounty-men."

"I don't like them either," Hallac said. "Particularly since all they did was grab the perpetrator without actually finding the boy. But since you've got her, I want to talk to Tin Lizzy."

"Alleged perpetrator," Markham said.

Another bad sign. "Alleged," Hallac said. "But I still want to talk to her."

"I'll give her a call." Markham reached for his phone.

"A call?" Hallac repeated, not bothering to hide his anger this time, and Markham put the handset down again, faint color showing under the pale stubble.

"Yeah. We released her, sent her back to her hotel."

"You bailed somebody who's wanted for sex with a minor?" Hallac let disbelief creep into his voice, and was pleased to see the color darken to pink.

"We released a woman who'd been attacked by two bounty-men carrying an illegal weapon—a stun stick—and a very dubious warrant that carries no legal weight here. Their ID was really shaky—you can't miss this woman's tattoos, and they're not even mentioned on the tip sheet. So under the circumstances, we didn't feel like extending any extra courtesy toward those bozos."

Tattoos? Hallac thought. *Oh, hell. I should have guessed, once we found out about Stone.* He said, "You knew this was a Systems case. What kind of physical description did you expect? We're lucky we got the fucking gender right."

"This woman's got tattoos all up and down her left side," Markham said. "Give me a break. No way it's the same person."

Hallac took a deep breath, controlling his anger with an effort that made the muscles in his shoulders tighten, on the verge of cramping. The old man at the condos had to have known—but of course it wouldn't have occurred to him to mention them, seeing her every day. He'd have assumed they knew, and, equally of course, the people who had known Lindi Ray and Camelia Knight wouldn't have known about the tattoos. He swallowed a curse, too aware of wasted time, and shook himself back to the present. "I still want to talk to her."

"I'll call the hotel," Markham said. "She's prepared to come in and answer your questions."

"Yeah, right," Hallac said. "She's long gone, and the boy with her. You comfortable with that, Markham?"

"I trust my people," Markham answered.

"I want names," Hallac said. "I want to talk to them."

"Jack Iovanni and Francesca Vara." Markham pushed himself to his feet. Hallac copied him, slowly, allowing himself a faint sneer at the blatant attempt to intimidate. "The arresting officers. Iovanni's once of my best, as Vara is on the Systems side. They'll be glad to talk to you."

Systems. Hallac bit back the word as though it was a curse. That explained everything— *though what a Systems cop was doing on the street, making an arrest in real time, I don't know. But Systems takes care of its own. Even Corbitt was prone to that, making too many excuses for the techno-geeks like herself . . .* He shook the thought away, recognizing his own exhaustion, and made himself focus. "Then let's do it. But put in a call to Ms. Rhea's hotel. Please."

Markham touched keys on his computer. "My secretary's on it. Who you want to talk to first?"

"Vara," Hallac said. Systems was the key, always had been in this case.

"Suit yourself." Markham gestured to the door.

He led the way across the crowded squad room, dodging through a maze of desks with an ease surprising in such a big man, stopped finally in front of a desk jammed into a corner along with a computer hutch. The desk itself was crowded with miscellaneous gear, smokes and a fancy phone and a secondary keyboard and monitor, and the woman behind it looked up at them without affection.

"This is Lieutenant Hallac," Markham said. "He wants to talk to you about last night."

The faintest of smiles flickered over her face, but she stilled it and gestured to her extra chair. "Be my guest."

Markham grunted something and moved away, leaving them alone, and Hallac took the seat, focusing his attention on the woman across the desktop. Francesca Vara didn't look like a cop. In fact, he thought, if she'd been sitting on the other side of his desk, it would have been all too easy to mistake her for a perpetrator, some cracker busted in the small hours and still waiting for her late-sleeping lawyer. That was the problem with Systems: too many of its people came from the same virtual culture as the guys they were supposed to be catching, and it was too easy to cut corners, to go too easy or too hard on somebody just because you thought you understood where they were coming from. From the look in her eyes, Vara didn't like him much, either, but he thought he could live with that. He looked her over again—a chunky woman, sharply dressed, with nighttime makeup still ringing her eyes and fingernails that glittered black and silver in the office fluorescents. At a conservative guess, the suit would have cost three, maybe four hundred dollars—maybe more, in her size—and he doubted she could walk three blocks in the shoe that stretched from under the desk. But of course Systems let their fingers do the walking, never had to pound a beat—except last night in Lakeview. Vara suppressed a yawn, a delicate stretching of painted lips, and he saw that she'd left a series of lip prints on the rim of her coffee mug.

"Tin Lizzy," he said, and Vara answered instantly.

"Back at her hotel. She deserved to get some sleep, even if nobody else does."

Hallac looked at her hands, braced against the edge of the desk, and she shifted them instantly to her lap, then changed her mind and reached again for her coffee. Her nails were short, at least, but that was only because anything longer would get in the way of the keyboard.

"You let her walk," he said, and Vara spread her hands.

"We had nothing on her, and she decided not to press her complaint."

"Her complaint?"

Vara shrugged. "One of the bounty-men hit her with a stun stick. Those are illegal in town, and these guys didn't have a permit."

"So you just ignored their warrant," Hallac said.

Vara shrugged again—*not as confident as she's pretending*, Hallac thought, and wished Gerretty had left him a better story, something Systems could understand. "Come on, no offense, but a private warrant with entertainment written all over it—hell, for all we could tell, this was something for one of those reality shows, not a real beef at all."

She was good, Hallac decided. Exhaustion was slowing him, making everything feel as though he was swimming in mud. That possibility hadn't even occurred to him, and it should have, he should have had an answer up and running. He picked contempt from his range of voices, and tried again. "So you let her walk. This is a woman accused of seducing a sixteen-year-old boy she picked up on the Nets, and you let her walk—you even offered to help her file a complaint against the arresting officers."

"They're bounty-men," Vara said. "Not cops."

"The warrant's good."

Vara's eyes flickered. "I know Lizzy," she said, after a heartbeat's hesitation. "This is bullshit."

"I know who she is," Hallac said. "More to the point, I know what she was. So what if she plays the jazz now, that's just how she picked up this kid."

Vara blinked again, and Hallac guessed she was rearranging her story. "She's out of that business, has been for a long time. What do you expect a kid on the streets to do, anyway?"

"Leave kids like Seth Halford alone," Hallac answered.

Vara's black-ringed eyes narrowed slightly. "I hear a different jazz. My jazz—the main jazz, the loudest word—is that your boys lost something, and this kid found it. And now you can't find him. Doesn't make you look so hot—Lieutenant."

"That's Systems talking," Hallac said. "This is the real world. It's up to you how we play it, Detective."

Vara grimaced, and Hallac knew she'd recognized the truth of that statement. His jazz, Gerretty's jazz, would play better than hers, true or not; she'd have to take that into account, he thought, and waited for her answer.

"Lizzy's willing to talk to you," she said at last. "She just didn't want to talk to those goons. Assuming you've got all the right paper-work, of course."

"If she's innocent, she shouldn't have to worry about that," Hal-lac said, and this time Vara sneered openly.

"Yeah, right. I want to see your warrant, Lieutenant. I owe Lizzy that."

Hallac sighed, reached into his pocket for the card that held the URL for the case warrants file. Vara waved it under a scanner, leaned back slightly while the page loaded. She took her time read-ing it, careful with the small print and the authorizations, and finally looked up, her broad face without expression.

"So far it's OK. But I'll need the captain's approval."

Hallac waved to her phone. "Call him. I'll wait."

Vara's mouth tightened, but she punched buttons, waited for an answer. "Captain? You seen this guy's card?" She paused, listening, and Hallac could see the effort it took not to grimace again. "OK. Your call."

She set the headset carefully in its cradle, glanced down at an electronic address pad that lay beside her keyboard. She reached for a stylus, touched miniature keys with its narrow point, and Hallac held out his hand.

"It's just printing," Vara said, deliberately misunderstanding, and the miniature unit whirred, spitting a curl of paper. She tore it loose and Hallac accepted it, squinting at the faded print. It was leg-ible enough that he couldn't complain, though, and he tucked it into his pocket. Rhea wouldn't be there, of course, if she'd ever been there, she and the kid would be long gone, but he had to go through with this farce before he could lean on Vara and her partner.

"I assume you'll provide backup," he said, just to provoke, and enjoyed the flash of anger in her eyes before she had herself under control again.

"That's up to the captain," she said, and leaned back in her chair. "I'm just Systems."

Nice save, Hallac acknowledged silently, and turned away. Even if Gerretty had screwed up his chances to get real cooperation from the Lakeview Police, they wouldn't be able to avoid giving him the minimal help he needed. And with that. . . . Lakeview was a controlled-access town, built that way deliberately. As long as Rhea and the boy hadn't left already—and that had to be a big if, he admitted, but it was still possible—it would be easy to trap them inside the ring of highway. And then even Vara would have to help him track them down.

e l e v e n

Lizzy leaned against the checkout counter, barely able to stop herself from pounding the fake marble. The terminally adorable clerk misread the look, smiling himself, and it was all Lizzy could do to match his expression. At her side, Keyz rolled his eyes: nerves, she knew, but it would pass for generic adolescent sulkiness. She'd allowed herself to sleep—had needed desperately to sleep—after she'd gotten in from the police station, but somehow she'd misprogrammed her smoke, and had overslept. *Stupid, stupid, stupid*, a voice whispered in the back of her mind, and she suppressed it, handing her cash card to the still-smiling clerk.

"It's a real pity your plans changed, Ms. Sanders. I'm afraid you're going to lose the discount."

Lizzy swallowed a curse—the thousand she'd gotten from Murfree wasn't going to last very long, at this rate—and forced a smile that was more of a grimace. "It's—my mother's had a stroke—"

"Oh." The clerk's voice was instantly sympathetic, and Lizzy willed Keyz to close his mouth before he spoiled the jazz.

"Oh, nothing too serious, the doctors think, but she needs all the help she can get right now. So I was wondering if there were any exceptions for emergencies."

"I can't do an immediate refund, but if you wanted to, you could call the company when you got home," the clerk said. "They require a health-company certificate, anyway, so that's the easiest way to do it. I can give you the number, if you'd like."

"Oh, that's really a pain," Lizzy said. "There's no way you can do it now?"

"I'm sorry." The clerk shook his head. "I don't have the authority."

There was a note of doubt in his voice, and Lizzy quickly moderated her own tone. "Not a problem, then. It was just I'm going to be flat out once we get home. But you're right, I can get the certificate easier from there."

"I'll put the number right on your bill," the clerk said, smiling again. "And all the information they'll need to process the refund is right there, except of course for the doctor's certificate. If you'll just sign here . . ."

He swung the slip of paper toward her, and Lizzy took it, wincing inwardly at the price. She'd been counting on Vara's help to get back into her own accounts, so that she didn't have to deplete the money she'd gotten from Murfree; already she'd spent more than half of it, and she was no better off than she had been. Well, maybe a little bit better—at least they were still free, and Vara hadn't turned them down outright—but this definitely wasn't working out the way she'd planned. She signed the charge, took the proffered receipt, and slung her bag up onto her shoulder.

"Come on, kid," she said, for the benefit of the clerk. "We've got a flight to catch."

Keyz followed her willingly enough into the early-morning glare, but once they turned the corner toward the cab stand, he let his bag fall to the pavement. Lizzy turned, glaring at him over the top of her sunglasses.

"Come on," she said again. "We've got to get out of here."

"You mean you actually told them where we were staying?" Keyz achieved a sneer, and Lizzy clamped down hard on her anger.

"No, I did not. But once they find out we're not where I said, they're going to start checking all the other registers, and they're going to spot us. How many single women with teenage boys in tow do you think there are going to be on the hotel lists? That's not the usual tourist demographic here."

"Oh, great." Keyz kicked the sidewalk, looking suddenly much younger. "How the hell could you mess up setting your smoke?"

It was the question she'd been asking herself all morning. "Look, Keyz, I'm not your fucking mother. I told you when I got in that we were leaving first thing, you could have gotten yourself up in time."

"I was asleep when you told me," Keyz protested.

"How do you think I felt?" Lizzy asked. "Christ, do you think I'm doing this on purpose?"

The boy looked away, squinting against the sun. "I'm sorry. So what do we do now?"

Lizzy took a deep breath. "The same as before, only we don't get to stay in a nice hotel."

"Nobody's going to help us now," Keyz said. "Especially not a cop."

He was echoing her thoughts again, and Lizzy heard her voice rise in answer. "Chessie said she'd be there. You got a better idea?"

There was a little pause, and Keyz said, almost inaudibly, "No."

"Right." Lizzy squared her shoulders, trying to project a confidence she didn't feel. "Let's go."

They took a bus along the lakefront, where the tourists clogged the breakfast bars and queued more or less patiently for the early taxis. The party boats were almost lost in the early haze, drowned in thick air and sunlight, almost ghostly even in the sunlit brightness. The air-conditioned compartment smelled faintly of mildew, imperfectly cleaned filters, and the tourists chattered amiably to each other, discussing the best slots and where to meet for lunch. Only one woman sat apart from the others, rattling dollar coins in a plastic cup, its logo worn to near invisibility by constant handling. She got off at the end of Barron, where the row of slot parlors began, and was already feeding coins into a machine before the bus pulled away from the stop. Lizzy watched her out of the corner of her eye, a part of her mind filing the movements, the stance, for some other persona, and Keyz poked her shoulder.

"So where are we going?"

Jesus Christ, don't you know anything about being discreet? Lizzy swallowed the words, said, too brightly, "I thought we'd check out the Boardwalk, then maybe walk over to Humboldt Park."

"No, I mean really—"

Lizzy scowled at him, and, too late, he lowered his voice.

"Oh, come on, nobody's listening, all they care about is the slots—"

"Keyz," Lizzy said, and there was something in her voice that struck him silent. "Shut up."

He slumped back in his seat, arms folded over his bag, and Lizzy reached for the stop cord. They were still almost three blocks from the Boardwalk, but in Keyz' mood, they'd be better off mixing with the early-morning crowds. The bus slanted obediently in toward the curb, and Keyz swung his legs to let her out of the seat, still glaring at nothing. Lizzy glanced over her shoulder, saw no one within easy earshot, and leaned close.

"You can come or not, kid, it's up to you. But if I walk off without you, you're on your own."

For a second, she thought Keyz might take her up on it, felt the start of guilty relief, and then the boy straightened, collected his bag, and followed her meekly enough. She waited while the bus pulled off, pretending to study a bright pink poster advertising a collectors' conference, and Keyz shuffled his feet.

"Look, I'm sorry. But nobody was listening."

"You don't take that chance," Lizzy said. "It's a stupid risk, and we—I—already made enough mistakes for today." She took a breath, hoping she hadn't lost him by admitting that much, and went on. "As for what we're going to do . . . We're going to find a quiet spot, and I'm going to call Chessie. Good enough?"

"Yeah." Keyz nodded. "You really think she'll help us?"

I certainly hope so. As long as her captain doesn't rescind the agreement. Lizzy said instead, "She said she would. I trust her."

"OK." Keyz adjusted his backpack, shifting it to a more comfortable spot on his shoulder. "I'm ready, then."

They took their time walking the length of the Boardwalk, then crossed the broad street to the park at the corner of Mills and Lakeview. It was almost as crowded now as it had been the night before, though the crowd had changed, was more tourists and young mothers with babies in front packs. A few skaters walked along the edge of the fountain, boards in hand, but even as she watched, one of them dropped his board and cruised easily out into the traffic. His friends followed more flashily, vaulting the traffic bumps, and she heard Keyz sigh. She glanced back, saw him watching the skaters with what looked like envy.

"I didn't know you were into that," she said, and he shrugged one shoulder.

"Not really." He paused, gave her a sideways glance. "It's just— it'd be nice to be normal, you know?"

Lizzy nodded. "I know."

There were already a few vendors around, mostly coffee sellers, and in spite of everything, Lizzy lifted her head as the lake breeze brought the familiar smell. She ignored them with an effort and found a bench in the sun, away from the discreet smoking kiosk and the cluster of laughing mothers. Keyz flopped beside her, scowling again, but she ignored him, too, reaching into her pocket for her phone. She dialed Vara's private number, the one that should connect to her central account, and waited, listening to the pulse as the system cycled. There was no answer after half a dozen rings, and she bit back a curse, wondering what had gone wrong. Maybe she should dial again, she thought, and then, miraculously, Vara's voice sounded in her ear.

"Yeah?"

"Chessie?"

"It's you."

Vara sounded out of breath, and Lizzy frowned. "Are you all right?"

"Yeah, fine. Where are you?"

"What do you mean?"

"Where are you? We need to meet," Vara said. "Face-to-face."

"I don't know," Lizzy said, automatically—face-to-face was more likely to be a trap than anything else—and she heard Vara sigh.

"Look, I don't have time for this. I'm putting my neck on the line for you, Lizzy, and we need to talk. Where the fuck are you?"

Lizzy hesitated for a second longer, then shook away the doubt. Vara was all right, was Sandy's friend, a player herself, even if she was Systems—and besides, she'd already gone too far last night to be able to back out now. "The park at the end of Mills. The one with the pylon fountain."

"I'll be there in ten minutes," Vara said, and broke the connection.

Lizzy refolded the phone, very conscious of Keyz' stare. "Do me a favor," she said, and reached into her pocket for a cash card. "Get us both some coffee—or whatever you want."

For a second, she thought he was going to protest, demand more answers than she had, but then he took the card and slouched off toward the nearest vendor, leaving his backpack behind. Lizzy dragged it closer, her mind already on their next step. She needed access most of all, access and then more cash, but with any luck Vara could help with both. That would buy them time, let them find someplace more secure to stay, out of the reach of any more bounty-men, or RCD's cops, and maybe Vara could help them there, too, since she'd already half persuaded her bosses that she and Keyz weren't exactly desperate criminals . . . She broke that line of thought, knowing she was going too far, and forced a smile as Keyz offered the coffee.

"It's mocha," he said. "That was the special. That OK?"

"That's great," Lizzy answered, and took a sip of the scalding liquid. Tired as she was still, she could almost feel the caffeine spreading through her body, masking fatigue poisons; she'd have to be careful, she knew, not to let the false energy overwhelm her.

"Is she coming?" Keyz asked.

"Yeah." Lizzy scanned the busy streets, even knowing it was too early. "She said ten minutes."

The boy nodded, and they waited in silence, Lizzy sipping her coffee. Keyz had gotten himself an iced drink, coffee and chocolate in equal measure, and drained it quickly, rattling ice and dregs. The sound was irritating, and Lizzy barely stopped herself from telling him to get rid of the cup. She had no idea what Vara's car looked like, she realized suddenly, no way to tell her from all the other cars cruising by . . . And then a car slowed, a battered, clumsy-bodied sedan, pulling into the curb in a marked no-parking zone, and it was unmistakably Vara at the wheel. Lizzy grinned in spite of herself, lifted a hand in greeting, and got a wave in response.

"Let's go," she said, and Keyz pulled himself up after her, mumbling under his breath.

The passenger doors were unlocked and the front window was rolled down, and Lizzy leaned for a minute on the sun-warmed metal, frowning as she saw Vara's grim expression.

"Is there a problem?"

"What do you think?" Vara sighed, shook her head. "Sorry. But of course there's trouble, and it's bigger than I thought it would be."

"Can you still help us?" Lizzy asked, and Vara sighed again.

"So far. But it's nothing official, you understand? We get busted, you're on your own. This is the kid?"

Lizzy nodded. "Keyz. Seth Halford."

"Get in the car."

Keyz did as he was told, though the look on his face said he didn't like it much. Lizzy handed him her own bag and slid into the front seat next to Vara. The car was better than it had looked from the outside, with a decent satellite package, onboard navigation and phone and roving Net link all in one recently installed package, and as Vara touched the acceleration, the thump of a six-cylinder engine was unmistakable. Vara glanced sideways at her and gave the ghost of a smile.

"I've got my doubts about the air bags, and you want to watch those wires under the dash, but otherwise it's a pretty decent machine."

"It isn't yours?" Lizzy asked, and the other woman shook her head.

"Nope. I took it out of the impound lot, it shouldn't be missed anytime soon."

"How unofficial does this make you?" Lizzy said, and felt her heart sink as Vara shook her head again.

"Be real, Lizzy. The captain may not like that guy, but his warrant's legit, not like those bounty-men."

"What guy?" Keyz asked, and Vara glanced in the mirror.

"You're Seth—or would you rather go by Keyz?"

The boy shrugged one shoulder. "Whatever."

Vara's mouth tightened briefly, but she decided not to pursue it. "I'm Francesca Vara, Detective First Grade, Lakeview police, at least until they pull my badge, which is likely enough. That guy is John Hallac, who belongs to RCD's private security, which is a legitimate law-enforcement agency all the same. Any more questions?"

"Yeah," Lizzy said. "How bad is this, Chessie?"

The big woman made a face. "Not that bad, I don't think. The captain isn't going to break his ass on this one, providing we don't give him cause to hurry." She looked in the mirror again, though it was hard to tell whether she was looking at Keyz or the traffic. "There's a lot that isn't right about this whole thing, not least of which is his folks aren't as worried as they should be, if the jazz was true."

"What jazz?" Keyz asked, and Lizzy shook her head.

"Never mind."

Vara slanted her a look, and a hooded smile. "Suit yourself."

"Are you going to be able to help us?" Lizzy asked, and was startled by the effort it took to keep her own voice steady. It was just the caffeine, she told herself, and knew that was a lie.

"Oh, yeah," Vara answered, and glanced in the mirror again, smiling this time. "The captain knows what I'm doing, it's just if we get caught wrong he'll deny us. And I'll be damned if I'm going to let this bastard get away with this. Nobody pulls something like this on my turf."

And I'll take it, Lizzy thought, almost giddy with relief. *I don't care why she's doing it as long as she helps us*. She said, "Thanks. So what do you have in mind?"

"It depends," Vara said. "What do you need?"

Lizzy ticked them off on her fingers. "Access, as secure as I can get. I need a new ID on this phone, and I need to check out some information—I haven't been able to get on in three days. And I need money."

"We can do this," Vara said. "Do me a favor, flip on the satellite link, and get me a local traffic report, would you?"

Lizzy reached for the controls, moving gingerly because of the wires that dripped from under the dashboard, and found the right button on the second try, then pressed the key that copied the image to the heads-up display in the windshield. The sunlight washed out most of the color, but she could make out the shape of the ring road that surrounded Lakeview and the main roads radiating into the city. There weren't many roads that led past the ring, just the Humboldt and two other roads she couldn't identify leading off each end of Lakeview, but each of them was splotched with the flashing red X that meant a traffic jam.

"Shit," Vara said, and Lizzy gave her a wary look.

"I take it those aren't natural backups."

"No." Vara shook her head for emphasis. "Roadblocks."

Lizzy swore softly, leaning back in her seat, staring at the pattern that still flashed in the windshield. Lakeview had been designed for easy policing, the chamber of commerce pages had made no secret of it—the founders had been well aware of the temptations waiting on the boats—and it was all too easy to shut down all traffic in and out of town. Maybe we should leave the car, she thought, head out on foot, but she dismissed the idea almost at once. For one thing, they would need transportation: the car was cheaper and safer than being at the mercy of commercial schedules and tickets that could be attached to names and account cards. For another, even if they did take that risk, or found a way to buy a car later, they'd still have to cross the ring road. It would be much too easy to spot them, and then tracking them across the empty fields would be a breeze.

"Can't we get past them?" Keyz asked, and Vara shrugged.

"You're both kind of conspicuous."

"I could cut my hair," Lizzy said. "Or dye it. Or both, if you think it'd help."

"It wouldn't hurt," Vara said. "But I think we should wait until they take them down."

"How long is that going to be?" Keyz asked.

Vara shrugged again, and leaned sideways to access the police band. It was partially scrambled, of course, but the tone of the voices was clear enough: nobody was particularly happy with the job. "We've got the manpower, and they've got the authority—"

"And if the roadblocks don't work, they'll sweep the town," Lizzy said, suddenly certain. "Right, Chessie?"

"Yeah." Vara scowled at the windshield. "Shut up, Lizzy, I'm trying to think. What we need is a diversion, something to give everybody the excuse to give it up—something that needs men more urgently than this warrant."

"Like a riot," Keyz said.

"Yeah, but I'd prefer something less violent," Vara answered, and swore as a tourist swerved in front of her.

Lizzy braced herself against the dash. "Collectors," she said. She remembered the do-fer riots, back when she was seventeen. Three people had been killed in the crush at Mall America, never mind the injuries, and an entire toy company had gone out of business, just because someone had spread the jazz that one of the dolls was being retired. The stupid things were still worth thirty or forty times as much as they'd been before the riot. "I saw a poster, there's a convention in town, right?"

Vara nodded. "Yeah. A big one, too."

"Suppose we put out some jazz, told them there was something here that they hadn't expected, you'd almost have to call the cops to keep them in line." Lizzy paused. "They'd have to, nobody wants to see the do-fer riots again."

Vara drew a long breath. "It'll take time to set this up," she said. "But, yeah, it could work."

"Six hours," Lizzy said. She could feel the confidence coursing through her. It was just jazz, and she could do that, she could make this happen—

"I don't want people killed," Vara said, sharply, and Lizzy shook herself.

"No. I don't, either. I'll be careful, I promise." *And I'm good, too, I can do it.* She took a breath, controlling her excitement. "But I'll need some high-grade gear to do it right."

"I know a place," Vara said. She glanced over her shoulder, made a careful left turn, sliding easily between a pair of delivery trucks and grinned suddenly. "It's called Dogtown."

"Dogtown?" Keyz repeated.

"All the towns like this have one," Vara said. "After all, the help's got to live somewhere."

Keyz subsided into his seat, and Lizzy looked at Vara. "It's not the kid's fault."

"The hell it isn't." Vara glanced in her mirror again, grimaced. "Sorry. But it's my ass on the line, too, if we can't clear you."

"I know it's my fault," Keyz said. "I—I'm sorry."

"It's not his fault Gardner Gerretty's a lunatic," Lizzy said, and Vara gave her a hard look.

"Maybe not. But maybe he'll stay out of other people's servers from now on."

Dogtown was pretty much what Lizzy had expected, except that the buildings were relatively new-looking. But of course Lakeview itself wasn't very old; these would have been part of the original neighborhoods, where the construction crews had lived. The storefronts with their fading facades had never been meant to last longer than a few years. They were still occupied, though, and the apartments on the second and third floors were obviously equally crowded. They passed several groceries, each boasting its own mix of unfamiliar, ethnic foods, advertisements scrawled like graffiti across their windows, and Lizzy spotted a restaurant where old men sat hunched over coffee, but there were no drugstores or 24/7s any-where in sight. Vara slowed the car to a crawl, looking for a parking place, and Lizzy was suddenly glad the other woman hadn't found a better vehicle.

The cyberia matched the rest of the neighborhood, too poor to afford upkeep, and trying desperately to pretend it didn't matter. The one large window was completely covered with multicolored, multilingual posters advertising local services and bands and politi-cians and the occasional free supper and cultural fest. The adhesive had chipped away the letters painted on the glass so that the "Y" looked more like a slash and the "A" like a "4." Inside, the long room was dark and dingy, the floor faintly sticky underfoot, the kind of place that made no pretense of catering to players, but existed for people who couldn't manage full-time access, who needed it for work or school and couldn't afford to admit they didn't have it. This wasn't exactly what she'd had in mind when she'd said she needed access, and she darted a wary look at Vara, who refused to meet her eyes. Lizzy made a face, scanning the bank of terminals—one of the five machines was labeled "out of order," and the connection boxes took dollar coins as well as credit cards—and the woman downloading tax forms looked nervously back at her. The woman next to her, old and gnarled, shrunk into a wool jacket even on a warm day, ignored them both, fingers slow but sure on the keyboard as she searched what looked like a genealogical site. One of the rules of the cyberias was that you never paid attention to anyone else's work, and Lizzy looked away, embarrassed, trying to pretend she hadn't noticed anything.

Other than the two women at the consoles, and the thin, tired-looking woman behind the counter, the place was empty—no, not quite, she realized. There were a couple of kids whispering in a cor-ner by the bank of video games. The consoles were as old as the computers, heavy, ungainly things with dome-display helmets and gloves that looked like they belonged on a hockey goalie, but the lights still flashed from the displays, offering cash-back prizes for high scores. That was better than it had ever been when she was growing up, when all you could win was more playtime, but then, this was Lakeview. The casino spirit reached even here.

She followed Vara up to the counter, Keyz lagging behind them both, and leaned her elbows on the scarred wood. The tired woman moved to meet them, and Lizzy thought for a second that something—recognition, maybe, and maybe disapproval—flickered in her eyes as she looked at Vara.

"Yeah?" she said, and added something in a language Lizzy didn't recognize.

Vara answered in the same language, her voice low, almost pleading, and Lizzy looked away, weirdly embarrassed. The wall behind the counter was filled with racks of health drinks and meals-in-a-bottle, each one coded for the benefit of people doing the colors; the overhead lights struck reflections from the brass of the coffee machine. From the look of things, that was what got the real workout here, and Lizzy wondered if they ever actually sold any of the fancy drinks.

Vara stopped talking, waited, and the other woman sighed, pushed herself stiff-armed away from the counter.

"Wait here," she said, and vanished through the door that supposedly led to the rest rooms.

Vara sighed, too, and Lizzy looked at her.

"Are we all right?"

"I'll know in a minute."

Great. Lizzy looked away, seeing a plate of pastries at the far end of the bar, cookies and fruit squares and things she didn't actually recognize, and wished she didn't feel too stressed to eat. She should eat, too, and soon, the caffeine was going to wear off anyway. . . . A hand-lettered sign was propped up against the plate, proclaiming that all the profits went to the skate park's maintenance fund.

"What's going on?" Keyz said, and Vara frowned at him.

"We're waiting for someone."

Keyz shrugged, looking as though he wanted to say something more, but Lizzy shook her head, and the boy subsided. The door opened then, and the counterwoman reappeared, followed by a taller, heavier version of herself. At the same moment, the old woman who'd been searching the genealogy sites levered herself up from her terminal and came toward them, fumbling in her pocket for more cash. The counterwoman moved to intercept her, and the taller woman said, "Francesca."

"Tina," Vara answered. "Can we deal?"

The other woman shook her head; more rueful than rejecting,

and when she spoke, her voice was still strongly accented. "For old times' sake, Chessie, only. Not many cops from around here." She hesitated, then added something in the other language, and Vara's face split suddenly into a grin, almost giddy with relief.

"This way," Tina said, switching back to English. "Leja, mind the store."

The counterwoman lifted a hand in answer, and Tina tilted her head toward the door. "Come with me."

They followed her through the door marked REST ROOMS into a back hallway that smelled of disinfectant and old coffee grounds. Tina stopped in front of a door almost at the end of the hall, its hinges thick with brown industrial paint. She opened it, and stepped back to let them through, saying something in the language she and Vara shared. Vara answered, touching the other woman lightly, almost tentatively on the shoulder. Tina hesitated, then shook her head, and drew Vara into a brief embrace. Vara returned the hug with interest, and when she released the other, Lizzy could have sworn there were tears in the big woman's eyes.

Vara shook herself, hard, caught the door as it started to swing closed. "All right. Lizzy, it's time you worked some magic."

"Yeah, right." Lizzy stopped in the doorway, staring at the gear banked along the far wall. A sheet of plastic was suspended above and behind it, and ran out onto the floor beneath the tables that held the consoles—protecting everything, she guessed, from whatever had left the rust stains on the white-painted plaster—but the boxes themselves were state-of-the-art. The fat cable bundles contained at least a Grade Three commercial connection, and maybe that was a supergrade intranet spine, and the blue cable was a CC-Two, because the box it came out of definitely wasn't home service or even standard commercial, but a dedicated, high-test direct connector. There was a server, too, also top professional grade, and more than a year old, haloed in wires that linked it to a backup box that was better than anything Lizzy herself had ever owned. A Double-Vision headset sat on a chair that trailed strings as though a cat had clawed it, and the gloves were heavy servoenhanced metal.

"Where'd all this come from?" she asked, feebly, wanting to ask a dozen more questions, and Vara smiled.

"Tina and Tasha and I—that was Tina I was talking to—we all

grew up playing the jazz, and a few other things. Tina just believes you have to give something back."

"Is this a robinsnest?" Keyz asked, suspiciously, and Lizzy answered before she could stop herself.

"There's no such thing . . ." She stopped then, looking at the gear under its tent of plastic. If there were robinsnests, pirate servers that stole time and cycles from the rich and gave to the poor, this was what she'd expect one to look like. She looked at Vara. "Is there?"

Vara shook her head, and her expression was abruptly sad. "No. They're just jazz, as far as I know. Tina's a programmer, or she used to be, she retired on royalties from StarTrack. She buys time off-peak, overseas, I think, resells it in the neighborhood. All this—she got it from donors, they get good publicity, and she gets the use of it."

"Will I screw anything up if I play with it?" Lizzy asked. If this was giveaway gear, there had to be some seriously flaky bugs somewhere in the system. StarTrack was a great program, a classic in the jazz, but even that didn't guarantee that Tina could afford to keep everything in order—or that she'd even care about perfect maintenance. "I'm assuming this runs the cyberia, too."

"Yeah. But don't worry, she wouldn't have offered it if you would," Vara answered.

"Can I help?" Keyz asked, and Lizzy bit back an instant refusal. Keyz was as much a player as any of them; of course he wanted a turn with the fancy toys.

"I'll let you know," she said, and seated herself at the console.

Keyz made a face, and dropped into the sprung couch that occupied one corner. He sank too far, farther than he'd expected, releasing a cloud of off-smelling dust, and quickly moved to the arm, scowling in case anyone cared to comment. Lizzy hid a grin and reached for the gloves and helmet.

She'd never used a Double-Vision set before, blinked hard at the ghost of the room superimposed on the grey start screen—or maybe it was the other way around—and flinched as the movement changed the images' relative strength. That movement changed the image again, and she closed her tearing eyes, fighting nausea. She tried again, moving more carefully, and this time the images steadied. She blinked once, taking exaggerated care, and the display brightened enough for her to see the stabilizer button. She touched that, locking the image, and concentrated on adjusting the gloves to her longer hands. Just from the feel of them, from the arrangement of the virtual controls in the air in front of her, Tina had to be one serious hacker, which went a long way toward explaining the gear. *And if Chessie doesn't want to know that*, she thought, *I'm not going to be the one to tell her.* She stretched her hands experimentally, watching icons flash on and off in the helmet, and Vara leaned past her, start buttons dotting her cheek.

"Use this account."

"Yours?" Lizzy moved her hand out of active space to accept the slip of paper.

"Not officially. Anyway, it's disposable."

"OK." Lizzy waved her hands through active space, watching icons flare, found the right image on the second pass, and entered the string of codes. She recognized some of the numbers—routing keys, internal passwords for the various pass-through servers, interim keycodes—but the overall configuration was unfamiliar, more hacker's code than a player's. *So maybe Chessie does know about her friend*, she thought. *Maybe she's protecting us.* The idea was startling, and she put it aside, frowning as the start screen darkened. Stray codes flickered past as the system searched first for its connection and then for the proper doorways, and she blinked again to strengthen the image. The room faded around her, and a password request popped into view, a bright sphere that spun to display its active screen. She reached out and wrote the final codes on it with her finger, thrilling to the pleasure of being on-line again. The sphere twirled away, red and white segments blurring to pink, and she was thrown headfirst into the Net.

She caught her breath at the sight, the familiar planes spread in front of her, light and shadow, neon and matte dark, not daring to blink away the tears that sprang to her eyes for fear of disturbing the vision. It had been too long since she'd been able to get on-line, too long since she'd been fully part of it, and she hung there for a long moment, drinking in the vision, the well-known patterns and the soft machine cues sounding in the helmet's speakers. It was too beautiful, too perfect, too much where she'd wanted to be—*and you have too much to do to waste this time*, she told herself, sternly. She had promised Vara a diversion, and a diversion she would provide.

She clicked her gloved fingers, shifting viewpoint, and watched the planes tumble briefly through her sight until they steadied again into a local overview. A site cluster pulsed orange and red with heavy traffic, and she ran her hand though another space to call the site statistics. The response popped instantly into view, faster even than her fastest machine, and she couldn't help grinning with the sheer delight of it. *First set up the jazz*, she told herself, trying to control her excitement, then you'll have the time to create a new persona, and maybe even retrieve some of your own cash. Tina's machine certainly had enough security to make that a possibility.

She turned her attention to the local Nets, tapping back into Lakeview's civic system, looking for the collectors' sites that had to be there. They were red-hot—no surprise there, with the convention in town—and pink and red threads led off in every direction, linking them to more distant, purely Net-based sites. She picked the thickest, followed them, used the gloves to pull the distant links into closer view, laying them out in a neat line in front of her. There were two icon-collectors sites, no surprise there, but she was too well known in those circles to allow this to work. She tossed them away, concentrated on the others. One was for stamps, and she opened that site, watching the pages unfold, but wadded them up again in less than a minute. The rules of that game were too complicated, too dependent on the vagaries of actual governments, for her to be able to manipulate it. That left toys and cards, and the Lakeview convention was skewed to toy collectors. She opened those sites, the pages flowering, visual cacophony, skimming the bright images until she found one that looked maneuverable. This one dealt in UE-Girls, the latest flying toy, each with its own set of trading cards and accessories that—if anyone actually played the bizarre combat game for which they were supposed to be pieces—gave each Girl her range of superpowers. There had been some jazz about a new Girl, loud enough to reach out of their specialized world, and Lizzy brushed away the other sites, teasing this one out into its separate pages. The new Girl idea probably wouldn't work—for one thing, it wasn't subtle enough to be good jazz, and for another, it was something that could be disproved pretty quickly, but a new ZPowerCard was something else.

She reached for a catalog page, drew it into the foreground so that she could see the various images. Even translated through this system's best cleanup program, it was hard to tell the difference between first and later editions of cards, or between upgrades of the various powers, and she couldn't help grinning again. This was perfect—perfect for the collectors, too, who had to have the little differences always in mind, but perfect for her, too. She leafed slowly through the Official List, trying to absorb the differences between First-Form UE-Girl and Lucky UE-Girl and all the others, working her way into the style and feel of the PowerCards. The art was bright and cheerful, clearly derived from American anime, and easy enough to copy. She reached down and to the left, leaving the catalog open, and called a drawing program. Beetle Bette UE-Girl looked like her best deal, not the most popular doll, with her green skin and heavy, iridescent wings and hair, but the makers had rearranged her ZPowers often enough to make a new PowerCard a believable option. She pulled the Beetle Bette cards to the front of the list, tapping an intangible button to copy the images. The host protested, a copyright sniffer kicking in, but Tina's system overrode it easily. The cards were easy enough to copy—the background and the details of the character history didn't change much between editions—but she stared for a long moment at the current list of powers before deciding on a new one. Bette already had half a dozen special options, from Beetle Juice to Beetle Smoke; something called Beetle Spit was probably out of line, Lizzy thought, but maybe Beetle Wing, an enhanced flight capability, would work. She reached for the image editor, carefully shaping the new form, then added the description, trying to copy the originals' somewhat stilted English. That was jazz, too—the company that invented the dolls was purely West-Coast American—but she had to match it if this was going to work.

Finally, she had it, perfectly phrased, and reached for a tool to smudge the finished image back down to the quality of a home-scanned upload. Everything was ready, including the post to the Lakeview special bulletin board, and she glanced back at the card, checking her work for a final time. Except there was a typo, she saw suddenly, and swore under her breath, but checked herself abruptly. So what if there was a typo? There had been mistakes on other cards, and those misprints were more valuable than some standard cards. And a mistake would only add credibility to any denials from the

UE-Girls Company, once someone got around to checking with them. She checked the map of Lakeview a final time, picking her targets—the toy stores and collectors' stores as close as possible to the center of the city, where traffic would already be heavy, and any disturbance would be guaranteed to draw police attention—and then launched the first of her messages.

"How's it going?" Vara asked, and Lizzy jumped in her chair. She'd been working for two hours already, she realized, and blinked to dim the on-line image.

"I've made a start." In the helmet, she could see her message sinking into the icon of a bulletin board, watched the haze of orange absorb it. If the color darkened, she'd know she made a hit.

"How long do you think it's going to take?"

Lizzy started to shake her head, then remembered the interface and answered aloud instead. "I don't know. Once somebody notices, I can encourage it, give it some shape, but—hell, it's jazz, Chessie. It's not like it's a science."

"We don't have a lot of time," Vara said, and Lizzy took a careful breath.

"I know. I'm doing the best I can." In the helmet's vision, the board's color stayed obstinately the same, and she resisted the temptation to check it again. "I have to change my phone name, anyway, otherwise—"

She stopped, seeing Vara's nod, and apologetically lifted hands, and reached into the control space again, drawing out another storage volume. She slid quickly through its contents, familiar icons flashing in and out of sight, still trying to ignore the orange dot glowing unchanged in the center of the screen, finally found an identikit routine. It was a good one, a tested upgrade of the version she had used at home, and she launched it, touching invisible controls to check preferences. Everything was set for security—erase paths, always use secure servers, never accept trace or preference cookies, identify by most recent host only—and she called the entry screen instead to begin drafting her new identity. For a second, her mind went blank, unable to think of a name—or, rather, she had too many names, too many personas, all of them potentially known to the police—and out of the corner of her eye she saw the dot start to darken. It was starting, then, and she'd need to monitor the process, nudge it along, to make sure it went the way she wanted. *Cam Jones*, she decided. That was the name she'd use, never mind that it was two halves of names she'd already used. If everything went well, she could change it again later. She filled in the rest of the information, working as quickly as she could in the unfamiliar gloves, one eye always on the darkening icon, and released the indentikit with a sigh of relief. It could run on its own for a while, would seek out all the records that linked that phone number, that phone account, to Jaen Sanders, and replace them with the new, Cam Jones, information. She waited just long enough to be sure it had made its first connection, and turned her attention to the collectors' site.

It opened at her touch, a dozen windows popping into sight, only to converge as all the threads turned to her query. Most of the messages were dismissive, at least so far, but no one was questioning the existence of the card. Instead, the more experienced collectors were labeling it a fake, and blaming her—she'd been careful to choose a woman's name—for being taken in. That was pretty much what she'd expected—the Nets still tended to assume that women didn't play the jazz, despite plenty of evidence to the contrary—and as she watched a few of the collectors began to waver, wondering visibly if they could afford not to check it out. The jazz was spreading to other sites as well, pale link-lines springing up as people copied the message, and she reached for the second of her posts, updating the false time stamps. She launched it onto a Bimini site, adding a slightly different version of the same image, watched as it was absorbed into the discourse. Two versions of the same image—*and I'm good*, she thought, *it's going to take them a while to even think it might be the same jazz*—and the collectors were going to have to start taking it seriously, particularly now that someone had noticed the typo.

A soft chime sounded, and she glanced down to see the first fake mailbox, the woman's, Ruth's, filling with private mail. She decanted the messages into a secondary screen, called up a virtual keyboard to type one-handed while she monitored the larger picture. The second mailbox, Faroush's, was getting mail, too, and she shifted her hand to begin answering those as well. After the first answers were in the system, a lot of it was simply forwarding variations, building fragments of chat on top of each other; occasionally she had to pause and compose something new, hands darting between the virtual keyboards and the main control spaces. Someone, a guy, she thought, broke protocol by asking where Ruth had found her card. Three more people instantly reminded Ruth she didn't have to answer, and probably shouldn't, and she let Ruth dither for a bit before she said she couldn't say because she didn't think the guy had had all that many in stock. Someone else queried Faroush, and this time Lizzy let him answer, saying he'd bought two at the StarPoint Trading Post in Lakeview. A few seconds later, an icon flashed beside Ruth's mailbox, warning her of an attempted trace. She reached across, diverting it to the prepared response—a hotel account in Lakeview—and saw with amusement that at least one of the people who had told Ruth she didn't have to say where she found the toy was now trying to hack her system. Lizzy gave them time enough to see the hotel account, then shut them off, turning her attention back to the main boards. Traffic had doubled again, people logging in from all over, but there still wasn't enough local interest. She hesitated, debating mentioning another store, but decided to shut Ruth down, sending an overload message. A new message popped into the thread, the address highlighted: the manager of StarPoint Trading Post was weighing in, swearing he didn't have any new cards in his shop. Three messages appeared almost instantly, pointing out that there was a sign in his window, promising new items for the conventioneers. Lizzy held her breath, hoping this would tip the balance— already there were dozens of copies of her original image floating around the Net, each with a new set of annotations—but the traffic stayed steady. In the lower screen, a message appeared, signaling that the identikit had reached its target, but she couldn't spare it more than a glance.

A new icon popped into sight, linked to all of the threads: the Oregonia Company denied any plans to release an updated Beetle Bette PowerCard at this time. She'd been expecting that, and launched the message she'd prepared in answer, pointing out that Oregonia always tried to bury its mistakes. If the card really did have a typo, they'd be doing everything they could to keep it from getting into general circulation. She wasn't the only person to make that point, either, and the fact that Oregonia wouldn't—*probably couldn't*—deny that they had plans to upgrade Beetle Bette kept the links glowing strong. She hesitated, then mentioned the second store, hijacking its address to make it look like an official announcement; a few seconds later, the store manager logged on to deny it, but the name stayed in circulation. A new page winked into existence on the Oregonia site, begging people not to be taken in by malicious jazz; an instant counterpage claimed that Oregonia was trying to buy up all copies of the flawed card to make a profit of its own. The jazz was working, taking on a life of its own, and if her hands hadn't been encased in the heavy gloves, Lizzy would have crossed her fingers, willing it to move to the real world at last.

But still the traffic stayed steady, the collectors staying on the Net, on their smokes, not rushing to the stores in the numbers that would disrupt traffic, get the police called out to control the crowds. In the lower screen, another chime sounded, signaling a successful link with the phone company, but she couldn't spare it a glance. If her jazz didn't work soon, if people didn't break, individuals would be able to get to the stores to find out that there weren't any new cards. . . . She started to compose a new post, a new, instant persona, then curbed herself. Everything was too delicately balanced, a push now might spoil it completely. And then, quite suddenly, it happened, the traffic dropping, the jagged line skidding steeply down a graph to flatten at a minimum, and she whooped aloud, watching the links fade.

"You got it?"

Vara was at her shoulder again, and Lizzy blinked to bring back the real world. "I think so. Can I hook into the police bands?"

She reached for the controls without waiting for an answer, but Vara caught her wrist. "Too dangerous. Use the traffic satellites."

She was right, but Lizzy made a face anyway, wanting the power of the police viewpoint, the certainty of direct contact. She could hack it, too, especially with this system, could float in between the cracks and no one would know. . . . She reined herself in, a little frightened by her own high, shrank the current view, and reached for the controls to link to the satellite system. It had been a while since she'd been on the Net, sure, but that was no excuse for losing it like that.

The traffic window opened, displaying the ring road and the red bars of the roadblocks, and she reached into its control space to adjust the scale. The map expanded, shouldering out the jazz and the identikit, a roadblock almost crowding out the shrunken icons of the collectors' boards, and she saw new splotches of orange and pink in the center of town.

"Is there a monitor?" Vara asked, and Lizzy blinked again, dimming the image until she could see the stacked boxes. One of them had a display screen, and she fumbled in the control space until she found the right menu. The screen lit, displaying a smaller version of the image in her helmet, and Vara made a soft noise of satisfaction.

"It's happening." She tapped Lizzy on the shoulder. "Damn, you're good."

"I am," Lizzy said, and reached down and to her left to tug out the identikit's display. The worm had almost finished its work, and even as she thought it, the last icon vanished, was replaced with a completion message. *Now for the money*, she thought, and Vara tapped her on the shoulder again.

"Well, come on. Let's get going."

"I need cash," Lizzy said. She needed a lot more than that, needed to find out the jazz on Shida, all the jazz on Orpha-Toto—

"We don't have time," Vara said, gently. "We've got to move now."

She was right, Lizzy knew, and she shifted her hands reluctantly, starting the shutdown sequence. The chimes sounded, freezing her out of the system, and she reached for the latches of the gloves. She hadn't expected it to be so hard to leave, hadn't expected to miss the Net so much—hadn't realized how much time she'd been spending out in that world, how much of her life was measured in the split time of the Nets. *No regrets*, she told herself, and didn't know exactly what she was promising. She lifted the helmet off as the last icon vanished, and blinked to see Vara and Keyz already in the doorway, gear bags in hand.

"It's a loaner," Vara said, impatiently. "Something to work with later. Now, come on."

The relief that flooded through her was a little frightening. Lizzy nodded, still half-caught in the machine world, and made herself follow without looking back.

twelve

The car was waiting in the alley where they'd left it. Lizzy blinked for a second, thinking it was still in shadow, in deeper shadows than she remembered, then realized that it was almost dark. The jazz had taken longer than she'd thought, much longer than it had seemed, plugged into the shifting systems. But at least the dark would help, add to the confusion in town, and make it harder to spot them. Vara tossed her the starter bundle, and she caught it purely by reflex.

"They'll be expecting me to drive," Vara said.

That made sense. Lizzy nodded, sorting through the dangling tags, finally found the right box and pressed the button to unlock the doors.

"And put your hair up." Vara flipped a flat leather cap in her direction, and Lizzy nearly dropped the box catching it. The other woman had a point, though, and Lizzy jammed the box and its associated tags into her pocket so that she could wind the mass of her hair up under the cap. The leather was tight, looked stupid, at least from the reflection in the mirrored window, but it did change her looks. She hooked a stray piece behind her ear, wondering again if she should cut it. Probably, and probably she should change the color, too, but there wasn't time now, just like there hadn't been time before they got to Lakeview. She slid behind the wheel, checking the unfamiliar controls, and Keyz curled himself into the backseat, looking smaller than ever. Vara slammed the trunk closed, hiding the bags of gear, and slid into the passenger seat.

"So far, so good," she said. "Let's move."

Lizzy touched the enabled ignition. The car rumbled to life, almost as powerful as the Firefly, and she took her time backing out of the alley. Traffic throughout the city was badly snarled, and she came close to getting lost even with Vara and the computer guiding her. Twice she had to pull over, heart pounding, as police cars bulled their way through the traffic. The satellite system flashed steady warnings—AVOID City Center, AVOID Highland Street Shopping District, ALWAYS GIVE POLICE RIGHT-OF-WAY—and she couldn't suppress a nervous grin. So far, everything was working, and now the satellite system was recommending the ring road if you had to travel in Lakeview at all. That should mean the roadblocks were completely down, but she held her breath as she turned onto the access ramp.

The traffic was a little easier there, heavy but moving at a decent rate. She glanced sideways to see Vara's strained face caught briefly by reflected headlights, looked in the mirror to see Keyz shrinking in his seat, face white and scared. He looked younger than ever, and Lizzy hoped that would be to the good. It'll be all right, she wanted to say, it's just my jazz working, and then she saw a spark of blue in the rearview mirrors. At the same instant, the satellite's transponder flashed, and she heard Vara swear under her breath. A blue bar appeared across the top of the windshield, announcing a legitimate police broadcast, and an arrow tracked along the bar, steering her right. The cars to either side slowed and dropped away, clearing the lane but Lizzy hesitated for an instant. This wasn't necessarily a stop, just a warning to get out of the way; the only thing to do was to obey, but she wanted to run, wanted desperately to step down hard on the accelerator and get the hell out of there. And that would be stupid, the worst mistake she could make. She tapped the brake instead, and slid the big car neatly into a gap in the line of traffic to her right. Keyz slumped down farther in his seat, curling up as if to sleep, and in the next flash of blue, Lizzy saw Vara's hand close tightly on the edge of the door.

And then the police car was past, siren finally sounding as it cut through the cars slowing for the exit. Lizzy let out her breath with a gasp, and heard Vara mutter something in her other language. Keyz started to sit up, and Lizzy waved him back down.

"No, go on back to sleep, that was a good idea." She watched the boy subside, looked at Vara. "You think we're clear?"

"So far," she answered, and looked away.

Lizzy frowned, but the traffic was getting heavy again, forcing her to concentrate on driving. It eased as they approached the interstate connector, but enough cars were heading out of town that they were hardly conspicuous. Lizzy tucked herself in behind a car with a

Power Princess UE-Girl sticker, glanced in the mirror to see the lights of Lakeview finally behind her. It looked like something—something in a movie, like the Emerald City, except in negative, bright against a dark sky. The thought was disconcerting, and she kept looking back, watching the lights diminish as the car bored on across the endless plains.

"So where are we going?" she asked, and Vara stirred, pulling herself up so that she could reach the computer controls.

"Sorry. I didn't get a lot of sleep last night."

Neither did I, Lizzy thought, and knew her anger was at least partly exhaustion. The time on the Net had been exhilarating while it lasted, but now reaction was setting in. She kept her eyes on the road, holding in the middle lane so that the long-haul trucks could sweep past freely in the slow lane, and tried not to pay attention as Vara pulled out a smoke and linked it to the console. She puzzled over it for a while, the screen light puddling in her lap, then finally closed the lid. In the same instant, a map appeared in the windshield, the colors muted to preserve their night vision.

"We're only about ninety miles from Farmstead," Vara said, "and there's a motel there that looks cheap and quiet."

If we knew where we were going—if we actually had a plan, like I had a plan when I fucking came here, we could drive all night and get somewhere. Lizzy shook the words away, feeling the rhythm of the road dragging at her, and Vara went on as though she hadn't noticed.

"Farmstead's not real fond of Lakeview—their cops don't cooperate with anybody, come to that."

"Even Federal?" Lizzy asked, skeptical, and Vara smiled.

"Especially not private cops with Federal warrants. There's a big difference here."

"What if the Feds get involved?"

Vara shrugged. "That might be different. But if RCD was going to do that, they'd already have Federal help. Whatever is really going on here, Liz, the studio doesn't want Federal attention."

Which might help, Lizzy conceded. Keyz didn't respond, and she glanced in the mirror, to see the boy frankly asleep, head cushioned on the central armrest. "So what are we going to do?"

"What were you planning to do?" Vara asked.

"Get you to get the cops off our backs so I could figure out what was really going on," Lizzy answered, and saw Vara's wry grin in the flash of a passing headlight.

"OK, scratch that one." Vara sobered. "Any other ideas?"

Lizzy made a face. "There's some jazz that Njeri Shida knows about the program, or at least he's interested in it, but that's not much help."

"Shida," Vara repeated. "Why the hell would an ex-star be interested in this program of yours?"

"Not my program," Lizzy said, automatically, "and if I knew why he was interested, I'd have some idea why the studio's freaking."

"Point." Vara sighed. "So I guess we have to find him."

"Like that's so easy," Lizzy said, and grimaced. "Sorry."

She looked sideways, only to see Vara smiling. "My mother probably kept in touch with him—she used to be Shida's caretaker, years ago."

"Your mother worked for Njeri Shida?" Lizzy's voice rose in spite of herself, and she glanced quickly in the mirror. Keyz slept on, oblivious.

"For Antares Shida," Vara corrected. "That was Njeri's mother."

"So you know him."

"He was three," Vara said. "He might just remember me."

"Better than nothing," Lizzy said, and Vara made a face.

"I didn't see much of him, he wasn't supposed to play with the help, not that I was into kids anyway. And Mrs. Shida was a certified lunatic, which didn't make things easy. You always had to be really careful, because you never knew whether she was going to be normal or not." She stopped abruptly, mouth twisting as though she'd said more than she had intended. "Thing is, I don't know if they kept in touch, Mama and Njeri, I mean. I think they do, but I also don't know what that means, just how they get in touch. They're both deep into the jazz, you understand? I'll ask, but only when I can do it without getting my mother into this. She's in a home, she doesn't have a lot of options. All right?"

Lizzy nodded. "All right." She fixed her eyes on the road ahead, truck lights red and amber in the distance, the searchlight sweep of

headlights from an oncoming car. It was hard to imagine Njeri Shida
as a baby—as a pudgy three-year-old—even harder to picture any
child turning into the sleek perfection of the films. A sign loomed
blue in the windshield, projected by a roadside transponder,
announcing a truck stop, and she glanced at Vara. "We need gas."

Vara blinked, then nodded. "Yeah. And I could call my mother
from there. She's out on the coast, it's not too late yet."

Lizzy smiled, watching the other woman settle back against the
locked door, and turned her attention back to the road. Seven miles
to the truck stop, another sixty or so to Farmstead, unless Vara found
out something that made them change direction: not bad, everything
considered. She suppressed a yawn, hoping the adrenaline didn't
desert her, and wondered if Vara's mother really had kept in touch
with Shida. That would be almost too easy—*but I could really use
some easy right now. Particularly with Gardner Gerretty involved.*
She sighed, the momentary good humor vanishing. *You'd think that
getting to the top might mellow the guy, but he hasn't changed at all.
Anybody who'd send cops cross-country after a kid like Keyz was
still wrapped way too tight.*

Finally, the truck stop loomed at the side of the road, light rising
like columns from the floodlights at the base of every sign and building. Vara stirred in the passenger seat, pulling herself awake, and
Lizzy gave her an envious glance as she fought the car into a parking
place. She cut the engine, and sat for a moment in the sudden
silence. In the side mirror, she caught a glimpse of the highway
behind them, dotted with streaks of gold for the smudge of light that
was Lakeview. The black distance was empty: light carried a long
way on the plains, but they'd come even farther. In the backseat,
Keyz came upright, yawning, the sound resolving itself into words.

"—something to eat?"

Lizzy smiled in spite of herself, seeing her face haggard in the
light from the Burger Buddy's doorway. "If you can't sleep, you
might as well eat."

"You two go ahead," Vara said. "I'll catch up."

Lizzy nodded, respecting the other woman's privacy—and it was
probably better not to get Keyz' hopes up. "You go on. We'll eat."

"I'm starving," Keyz said, and levered himself out of the backseat. Lizzy turned toward the Burger Buddy, aware that Vara was falling behind as they moved toward the neon-framed doors.

Inside, a ceiling-mounted display cube listed the area's services; she watched it cycle as they stood in line for burgers and fries, spotting more food and bathrooms, the local cyberia—a chain service— and finally a mini 24/7. That was potentially useful, and she glanced around the almost-empty dining room. It looked safe enough—the other patrons looked like truckers, smokes plugged into routing consoles—and she swung herself out of the chair.

"I've got some things to pick up at the 24/7. I'll be right back."

Keyz nodded, barely looking up. "Do you want your fries?"

Well, at least he's not scared. Lizzy said, "No, go ahead. And wait here."

"OK." He reached for the paper package, spilling the french fries onto his own tray. Lizzy sighed, and made her way through the maze of empty tables toward the red-and-white neon that marked the store. Hair dye was the first priority, she decided, and then maybe a pair of scissors, but at least she could cover the conspicuous blond. She found a couple of shades of reddish brown that would look plausible with her skin tone, and moved toward the counter, readying her story. To her relief, however, the tired-looking man behind the counter barely gave her a glance, ringing up her purchases without comment. She wadded the bag up in her hand, and headed back to the Burger Buddy to collect Keyz. He had finished her hamburger as well as the fries, she saw, but she couldn't muster annoyance.

"I can get some more," Keyz said quickly, and Lizzy shook her head.

"I'm not that hungry. Let's find Chessie."

The cyberia was next to the the truckers' lounge, a narrow, badly lit alcove that looked more suited to video games. All the big terminals were in use, and Lizzy scanned the crowd, but couldn't spot Vara among the hunched bodies. There was a row of telephone boxes in the back, however, and she guessed that Vara would be there.

"Wait here," she said, ignoring Keyz' automatic protest, and threaded her way through the maze of terminals. They were good machines, expensive, elaborate, full-access setups, and she glanced at the sign-up sheet, wondering if this might be the best time to get the information she needed. There were half a dozen names on the list, and at least two of the truckers scowled at her as she passed, daring her to try to jump the line. The people on the system were taking their time, anyway—checking routing software, downloading new information for onboard computers, checking mail or just talking to friends and family, like the stocky man who stared avidly at the chubby, bored toddler in his screen—and she doubted she had the time to spend. She put on her most disarming smile and passed through the last row of terminals to the stand of telephone boxes.

Vara was there, all right, just closing down. Lizzy caught a glimpse of the charges before the last screen vanished, and winced at the cost, but then she saw Vara's face. "Is everything all right?"

Vara nodded, not smiling. "Yeah. I think."

"Did you talk to her?" There was something more wrong, Lizzy knew, and hoped it wouldn't interfere. *And that's selfish, but right now I can't afford anything else.*

Vara nodded again, and this time Lizzy thought she saw the hint of a tear on the older woman's face before Vara shook herself back to her usual self. "It's OK, it's just—she was having a bad day, that's all."

"Alzheimer's?" Lizzy asked, cringing inwardly, and Vara blinked in genuine surprise.

"No, bad arthritis. She's already had most of her joints replaced, and there's not much else the doctors can do for her. But when the pain's bad, she takes some pretty heavy-duty medications." She paused for a second, staring into space. "I asked her if she still stayed in touch with Njeri, and she—I think she was just having a bad day, like I said."

"What'd she say?" Lizzy asked again, and this time Vara managed an almost genuine smile.

"You're not going to like it."

"So what else is new?"

"She said Russ Conti would know better than her."

"Oh, great." Lizzy took a breath, trying to control her unreasoning—unreasonable—anger. "Look, he's long gone, there's no way we can find him—"

"Lizzy."

Lizzy fell silent, knowing she'd betrayed herself anyway.

"I'm a cop," Vara said. "A Systems cop. And Russ is the kind of guy who will have stayed legal. I can find him."

"Not from here," Lizzy said, and the other woman sighed.

"No. And probably not tonight. I say we press on to Farmstead, we can hook up the box in the morning, track him then."

"That makes sense," Lizzy said, and suppressed a sudden yawn.

"Oh, don't do that," Vara said, sounding annoyed again, and Lizzy gave her a wary glance.

"Look, are you sure everything's OK?"

Vara hesitated. "I don't know. There was something—" She shook her head, scowling. "No, it was just like I said. Mama was having a bad day, that's all."

Lizzy nodded, hoping she was right—hoping, too, that the old woman knew what she was talking about. It would be worth dealing with Conti, if only Shida could help them.

Hallac frowned into the warm gel of the display hood, then remembered that the system picked up every movement and translated it to the telepresent ghost, and quickly smoothed his expression. In the narrow display—it was like looking through the window of a tank—he saw Gardner Gerretty smile, and turned deliberately to look at the woman in the bed. For a second, he thought she was awake and aware of them, but then her eyes slid away, shadowed lids closing. She was old, he thought, the kind of crone who still made the hair stand up at the back of his neck, the ones who knew death as a friend to flirt with—and she was also one of the people who helped popularize the jazz, so he should pay attention to that, and not to any imagined supernatural powers. He made himself look away from her, wondering again how such a shrunken woman could have produced a dynamo like Francesca Vara, but of course the jazz explained it all.

"So," Gerretty said, and turned to stare directly into the telepresence sensors. "What do you think, Hallac?"

Hallac started to shrug, translated it into lifted eyebrows and a tilted head. The ghost was little more than a literal talking head, contained in a box that would fit comfortably on a tabletop; body language was only good from the neck up. "I don't think she does know. I don't think she wants to admit it, though."

Gerretty grunted, looking back at the woman in the bed, and Hallac followed his gaze unwillingly. There was a console by the bed, measuring something in units; an IV line ran from it to a vein in the old woman's elbow. Painkiller on demand, he guessed, seeing the oversize button cupped in her other hand, and winced again at the sight of the swollen fingers. They looked as though she could hardly move them—the little finger in particular looked as though it was useless, curled permanently into a tight claw, and Hallac flinched again, hoping he never ended up like her. Heart disease ran in his family, but at least that killed you quickly.

"You could be right," Gerretty said, but sounded less than convinced. "Damn, why couldn't we get a trace?"

Because Vara's good. Hallac swallowed the words, knowing he shared Gerretty's frustration. They'd come so close—it had been one of Gerretty's best ideas, staking out Vara's mother, one of the great players, one of the creators of the jazz, and sure enough Vara had tried calling, though what Shida had to do with any of this was anybody's guess. But Nina Vara had taught her daughter far too well, and the trace had failed, leaving them only with the tape of the conversation.

Beside him, the lawyer stirred, and Hallac twisted to see. The camera on top of the box rotated smoothly, presented him with the new image, but the thin man hardly seemed to notice the double scrutiny.

"I think Mr. Hallac is probably right. The last face contact they had was at Antares Shida's funeral, and we have no real record of virtual contact at any time after that."

"We don't have any virtual records," Gerretty growled. "That doesn't mean anything."

"Why would they stay in contact?" the lawyer asked. He spread his hands. "Look, no offense to the old lady, I'm sure she did her best by the kid, but Shida dumped all her old staff—fired the last of them without severance. He made a clean break right after his mother died."

"So why didn't she just say she didn't hear from him?" Gerretty asked. He glanced again at the bed. "I don't buy it. She knew we were here."

"Trying to keep status here at the home," the lawyer suggested, and Hallac saw him look uneasily toward the sleeping woman.

"I don't think so," he said, slowly. "First and foremost, she was trying to protect her daughter. And yes, sir, I think you're right, she knew we were here, and I think she knew why we were here."

"You give her too much credit," Gerretty said.

"Nina Vara helped created the jazz," Hallac said, and the lawyer frowned.

"A domestic worker?"

Hallac curbed his temper. If Francesca Vara's mother hadn't been one of the first creators, founder of something that had begun as a game, a hobby, he wouldn't be wasting time hooked up to the uncomfortable telepresence box. *God knows I don't have time to spare*, he thought. Francesca Vara was long gone—*as I knew she would be, no thanks to my so-called colleagues*—and no thanks to Gerretty, either. Fleetingly, knowledge of everything else he should be doing—checking roadblocks, tracing the jazz that had disrupted the city, getting a line on Lizzy's current transport—crowded his thoughts, and he banished them with an effort. Gerretty wanted him here, and that was something he couldn't refuse. "Remember, the jazz started as nothing," he said, and was pleased that he sounded merely detached, almost academic. "And Vara did pretty well after she retired."

"She'd have had to," Gerretty muttered, glancing at the room, and Hallac nodded again. It wasn't precisely luxurious, or even nice, but this level of care didn't come cheaply. "So you think she does know? She is in contact?"

"Shida is also a name in the jazz," Hallac said. "We have no way of knowing if they're in contact, so I don't think we can assume they're not."

"That would mean she'd rather protect Shida than her own daughter," the lawyer said, and sounded shocked.

Hallac hesitated. The suggestion didn't feel right, not from what he'd seen of either Vara, but it wasn't impossible. "I suppose that could be it."

"But you don't think so," Gerretty said.

Hallac shook his head, the scene in front of him eerily unmoving in the narrow display. "I admit it's a possibility, but it doesn't feel right."

"Then how do you read it?" Gerretty sounded relaxed, almost disinterested, but Hallac could see his hand clenched tight in the pocket of his jacket, and chose his words carefully.

"I think she cares more about her daughter than she would like us to know, and I think she cares more about her daughter than herself." He glanced at the lawyer, allowed himself a quick smile. "After all, she knows perfectly well we're not going to prosecute an old lady in a nursing home—she knows what the jazz would be on something like that, and she's better placed than most people to influence—or even create—that jazz."

He couldn't point, but he nodded toward the bedside table, the smokes and the laptop piled carelessly, along with an oversize stylus and input pad.

"So we take her off-line," Gerretty said.

The lawyer shook his head. "It wouldn't work. We'd have to get some kind of order—"

"Not necessarily," Gerretty said.

"—and someone would talk," the lawyer said. "We can't keep it a secret."

Gerretty grimaced. "All right. So what do you recommend now, Hallac?"

"We have a name," Hallac said.

"She was rambling," Gerretty said.

"It's a name," Hallac repeated. In Gerretty's present mood, he wasn't going to mention the fact that this name had come up before. "And right now, it's a solid lead."

Gerretty nodded once, abruptly. "All right, I agree. What about her?" He pointed to the bed.

Hallac turned his head again, watching the image change as the minicam pivoted, the old woman coming smoothly into view. She looked like a carved doll, the kind easterners sold to tourists, shrunken face tiny among black robes. But Nina Vara was wrapped in white, white hospital sheets and a white nightgown; a dark green robe hung on the wall behind her, and the closet door was partly open, showing real clothes. For the good days, Hallac guessed, and closed his mind to pity. There were no shoes anywhere to be seen. "I think she's hoping we'll go away—as I said, she knows she's fairly safe—and I think she's hoping her daughter will call her back, maybe get some real answers."

Gerretty nodded. "All right. I'll buy that."

"I don't think we can get anything more from her," Hallac said.

"I'll buy that, too," Gerretty said, and there was a little silence.

"So where does that leave us?" the lawyer said, tentatively.

Hallac took a careful breath, knowing just how sensitive the helmet mikes were. "We're pretty much where we were before. We have a name, now we track them by conventional means."

In the edge of the display, he saw Gerretty smile sourly, and knew the oblique rebuke had not gone unheard. "Then you're suggesting we just leave."

"Why not?" Hallac asked. "I think we've got everything we're going to get, and I doubt Vara will call back."

"But she might." Gerretty looked thoughtful. "And I don't want the old lady out on the Net. I want this connection cut."

"I don't think we can do that," the lawyer said, and Gerretty rounded on him.

"I pay you to find out how to do things, not to piss yourself panicking about them."

"I don't think we should," Hallac said.

Gerretty stopped abruptly, anger deflected but not defused. "Oh?"

"Leave her the smokes, the laptop," Hallac said. "That way, there's nothing to make anyone suspicious, nothing anyone can criticize, but we can keep an eye on her connections, and if Vara does try to make contact again, we can monitor, maybe even track, the connection."

There was a silence, not as long as it seemed, then Gerretty nodded. "All right. We'll play it your way, Hallac."

"Thank you." Hallac closed his mouth over a promise of results, too relieved not to be afraid of babbling. "Then if you don't need me anymore, I'll shut down. I can set up monitoring from here."

"Go ahead." Gerretty showed teeth in an expression that was not a smile. "Make sure this works."

"Yes, sir," Hallac said, and his view wavered, then tipped nauseatingly sideways as the lawyer picked up the ghost box. Hallac reached for his controls, groping for the shutdown switch, and the camera twirled slowly, so that he was looking directly at the woman in the bed. Her eyes were open, alert, and for an instant he hesitated, about to call to Gerretty, before his fingers closed on the switch. It was just the way the camera turned and tilted, he told himself, but couldn't make himself believe it. Nina Vara had been listening the whole time, knew exactly what they were planning. . . . But it didn't really matter: she would be watched, and she would know she was being watched, and that would surely be enough to keep her in line. He'd just make sure that Corbitt knew exactly what she was dealing with. And even if Nina Vara did find a way around the taps, the traces that would be established, there was no way he was going to turn Gardner Gerretty loose on an old woman. Besides, there wasn't much even she could do, stuck in a nursing home.

He pulled off the helmet, suffocatingly tight without the illusion of an outside view, and blinked in the sudden hotel light. Across the room, Corbitt looked up from her keyboard, her eyes red-rimmed from lack of sleep, and Hallac took a deep breath, bracing himself to meet the next emergency.

"What's up?"

"Well, I can confirm that it was Tin Lizzy who wrote that UE-Girl jazz," Corbitt began, then grimaced. "Well, I mean, I'm sure, and anybody else in Systems would be sure, but I doubt it's court-worthy."

"Not enough," Hallac said, sadly. For a second, he'd had a vision of being able to get a real warrant on Rhea, interference with commerce, maybe, but if all they had was Systems logic, it would be next to impossible to convince any court to issue a warrant. "What about transport? Any idea how they got out of the city?"

"Not air or bus," Corbitt said. "I've run the ticket profiles, there's nothing there. It's possible they split up, took different flights, so they can meet up later—"

Hallac shook his head. "I doubt it." There was too much risk, particularly for the boy; besides, if Rhea was planning to sell Orpha-Toto, she wouldn't want to let it get too far out of reach.

Corbitt nodded as though she'd read the thought. "Jae and Galen are still at headquarters, but as far as they can tell, Vara's car is still in her garage. We may have lost them."

"We've got the tape," Hallac said, with more confidence than he felt. "I want you to find this Russ Conti—but get some sleep first."

"I'll need clearances for that, if you want to keep it legal," Corbitt said.

Hallac swore under his breath. She was right, of course; if they wanted to use this trace in court, they had to have the right warrants, fill out all the right forms, so that the train of evidence that led them to Conti was perfect and unblemished. "I'll get on it," he said. "That'll give you a chance to get a couple hours rest."

Corbitt gave him a pale grin, but shook her head. "I've just got a couple of things I want to finish up—"

"No." For a second, Hallac felt like a parent again. "Do them in the morning, Cady. You look out on your feet."

"One more," Corbitt said, and Hallac sighed.

"I need you fit."

"I'll be fine," Corbitt said, absently, and Hallac shrugged.

"Suit yourself." He paused, about to turn toward his own room. "Hey, Cady, do you have any idea why Njeri Shida would be interested in Orpha-Toto?"

Corbitt's hands stilled on the keyboard as she considered the question. "No. No, I don't. I mean, it's not like he was a director, or anything like that. He was just talent—not even critically acclaimed, just popular. I don't know why he'd want it."

"Vara said something about Shida wanting it—about jazz that Shida was interested in it," Hallac said. He frowned, not wanting to jinx himself. This might be the lead they needed, the information that would let them get ahead of Rhea, instead of always following half a step behind. "Check it out, Cady. Find Russ Conti first, but then—find out why Njeri Shida's involved."

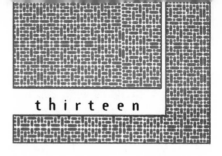

thirteen

This hotel was nothing like the last one. Lizzy rolled over in the lumpy bed, reluctantly awake in the face of the false dawn of Vara's computers. At least it was cool enough, but the air-conditioning smelled faintly of mold. And it was cheap, Lizzy reminded herself, and pushed herself upright against the wobbling headboard. Vara looked up from the screen, but Keyz rolled over on the couch, burrowing into his pillow. Lizzy smiled in spite of herself, and eased out of bed. She felt better than she'd expected, almost awake; it might not last, but she'd take what she could get. She dressed quickly— the same T-shirt she'd been wearing for days, and the same black jeans—came back into the main room to lean over Vara's shoulder. The other woman looked up at her, but didn't wave her away.

"Dot-Gov?" Lizzy asked, after a moment, and Vara nodded.

"You probably learned to hack on it."

"Yeah," Lizzy answered. The megasite was technically closed to civilians, or at least to anyone who hadn't bought the right to access it, but there were so many ways through the barriers that Conti had encouraged his after-school classes to hack it just for the practice. "Haven't they fixed it yet?"

"Probably not," Vara said, "but so far nobody's made Max change my passwords."

"Nice," Lizzy said. *Maybe we're finally getting lucky—and God knows we could use some good luck.*

"Got him," Vara said, and the screen flashed white, filled with closely spaced printing. Lizzy leaned close—Conti was still paying taxes, still registered to vote, and a Democrat, no surprise there— and Vara touched keys, transferring the address to Routefinder to create a smoke-readable map. "Now all we have to do is get there."

"Yeah." In spite of herself, Lizzy's voice was bitter, and Vara flashed her a glance.

"Look, if my mother says he's the person to ask, he's the guy we want."

"No, I know."

"The man didn't have a choice," Vara said.

"I'm not talking about the remailer," Lizzy said.

"Neither am I." Vara swung away from the keyboard. "If Gerretty pushed him hard—and I'm assuming he was pushing, if he was spending that much energy getting you put away hard, there's no reason he wouldn't be just as hard on Russ—Russ wouldn't have had any choice. He couldn't have testified for you. You know as well as I do how vulnerable remailers are."

Lizzy nodded. She did know, had thought she'd gotten over the anger years ago, was surprised to find that core of bitterness still left. Of course Conti couldn't have stood up against Gerretty even then, not when Conti was teaching would-be hackers, not when he was dodging the law to keep the remailers going, and even if he had taken the chance, one character witness wouldn't have done any good against her guilt and Gerretty's overwhelming lawyers. The fear was still with her, though, and the feeling of betrayal; she shoved that memory aside and leaned over Vara's shoulder. "I know," she said again. "Look, how vulnerable is your account?"

Vara shrugged, accepting the change of subject. "Medium, I guess. What do you need?"

"I want to check out the jazz," Lizzy answered. "I want to know about Shida, why he's interested in this program."

Vara glanced back at her screen. "Not through this account," she said. "Hang on, we'll boot something different."

"Thanks," Lizzy said.

Vara nodded, her fingers already busy on the keyboard. "So where'd you hear Shida was into this? It doesn't sound like him."

"It's common knowledge," Lizzy said. "Or at least that's what Miller told me."

"Who's Miller?"

"Just this guy—you probably know him, he does back-tech, has a semicontract with CoffeeCoffee. I know you've seen his work, seen him around. I've known him for a couple of years." It sounded thinner with every word, and Lizzy paused, frowning.

"Think you've been played?" Vara asked, and the words echoed Lizzy's thoughts too closely to be comfortable.

"No." She shook her head, hair flying, and hastily dragged it back into a loose tail. "I mean, there's no point. Somebody would have had to have been setting me up for years."

"It's Gerretty," Vara said, and Lizzy shook her head again.

"No. It still doesn't work. Look, I'm good at the tech, and I'm a mask-maker, but to go to all this trouble—there's just no point. I'm not into this. Hell, I'm just not that important."

"Or you don't know you are," Vara said.

Lizzy could almost see the thread of alt.conspiracy branching before her, a web that had caught millions of readers, jazz that didn't know it was jazz. "No," she said again. "It just doesn't work."

"You're probably right," Vara said. She frowned at her screen. "OK. You've got a couple of choices here—"

"Ms. Vara?"

That was Keyz' voice, and Lizzy turned, annoyed, to see the boy sitting bolt upright on the ugly green couch.

"Um, I'm sorry, but I just realized, I've got a problem."

There was something in his voice that sent a chill down Lizzy's spine. "What kind of problem?"

"I have to get on-line," Keyz said, as if he hadn't heard.

Vara turned to look at him, and Lizzy said, "Can't it wait? We need to track this jazz."

"No." Keyz shook his head. "I've got to—it's got to be now."

"What?" Lizzy asked, and Vara lifted a hand.

"Slow down. Start from the beginning."

Keyz took a breath. "You know I stashed it, Orpha-Toto, I mean. But there wasn't that much cash in my account, only a few days' worth, and I need to retrieve it. Today."

"You mean that thing's been sitting out there loose, just waiting for somebody to come along and hack it?" Vara's outrage was almost comical, and in spite of everything, Lizzy had to fight to repress a grin.

"You mean after all this shit, we might lose the fucking thing?" She reached for the gear bags, searching for a storage drive. "No way."

"Do we have enough room?" Keyz asked.

"It's a San-Cy cube," Lizzy answered. "If it fit on a household machine, it'll fit in there."

Keyz nodded, and Vara slid out from behind the keyboard, letting the boy take her place in front of the controls. Lizzy watched him as she unreeled a length of connector and found the right attachment port, wishing she could be the one to retrieve the program. It had been so good to be on-line the day before, to be on a real machine instead of a smoke—*but it's Keyz' program, Keyz' codes, and Keyz' money. Let it go.* She had other things to do, anyway, and she reached for the bag from the truck stop's 24/7. Vara lifted an eyebrow.

"Been meaning to ask you. What's all that?"

"Hair dye." Lizzy lifted a strand of hair off her forehead. "This is a little conspicuous."

Vara nodded slowly. "Yeah. Nobody expects a real blonde to give it up."

"They'll be expecting it this time," Lizzy said, grimly. She'd never really appreciated being blond, had heard too many jokes to enjoy it fully. "But I figured it might buy us time."

It seemed to take forever, first for the dye to process, and then to rinse the excess out of her hair, red-brown swirls like old blood sweeping down the drain, but finally she was finished. The face that looked back at her from the mirror was weirdly unfamiliar, her own, but changed, the darker color flattering her complexion. *Maybe I should cut it, too,* she thought, and lifted the scissors, but then hesitated. So much depended on being able to pass for rich, or at least better class, and nothing would betray her as quickly as a home-done cut. *Better leave it alone,* she decided, and went back out into the main room.

The download was just finished, and Keyz and Vara were breaking down the system, Keyz winding cables into a neat package, Vara folding the keyboard into its traveling configuration.

"I need to look at the jazz," she began, and Vara looked up at her.

"Yeah, I know," Vara answered. "You're going to have to do it from a smoke, Lizzy, we need to be moving on."

She was right, Lizzy knew, but it was hard to suppress a feeling of grievance as she helped carry the heavy bags back to the car. In the light of late morning, the motel looked decrepit, paint peeling from the chipped stucco, and she was glad she hadn't seen it clearly the night before.

"Are you sure we know where we're going?" Keyz asked, and Vara tapped her pocket, nails clicking on the case of her smoke through the thin fabric.

"Don't worry, Russ isn't the kind of guy to drop out completely. If any of us had looked for him off-line, he was there for the finding."

And of course nobody looked for him off-line, Lizzy thought. *I hope RCD thinks the same way we do.* But of course they didn't know about Conti, she reminded herself, and shoved the last of the gear bags into the car's narrow trunk.

They drove east through rolling farmland—back the way they'd come, Lizzy knew, and wondered if Keyz appreciated the irony. Vara kept to the middle roads, large enough for speed, small enough still to be outside the major highway control grids, stopping only for food and fuel. At each stop, Lizzy found a smoking port, and plugged herself in, trying to trace the rumors. To her surprise, Testify was still concentrating on the controversy surrounding Keyz' jazz, and the nebulous question of whether or not any help he had could be considered legitimate. "Keyz" was probably blown as a persona, she decided, but the boy would have no trouble forging something else. Opinion was still divided between whether his helper was a person or a UE program, but even the people who believed most vociferously in the possibility of a program weren't offering to buy it.

Or maybe she was just looking in the wrong places, she thought, unfolding her smoke in a truckstop somewhere along a tristate turnpike. She'd been reading the jazz sites; maybe she should check the tech sites instead. Sure enough, there were mentions on Sanborn, and the 2500, and on Friday, the biggest of the back-tech sites, but as she teased one out, followed each thread back to its source, she found someone—Miller himself, once, and a couple of other names—saying that they'd heard that Njeri Shida was interested in such a program. None of them admitted to knowing why, but seeing it was heartening, meant they weren't chasing pure jazz. If Conti had kept in touch with Shida, and if he was willing to help them, there was a chance they might get out of this without too much damage.

They reached Peterburg in the heat of late afternoon. It was a typical ex-industrial town, mill buildings converted to shops and condos in the last century, but Peterburg had embraced outlet shopping as their new industry, and the access roads were lined with flashing signs directing tourists to the mall of their choice. Most of the old-school designers were listed, plus homeware and other gear, but none of the new big names were visible: either Peterburg was going to start sliding back down the economic ladder, Lizzy thought, or they'd have to find a way to make the town hot again. From the looks of the cars, as they turned away from the malls and headed into the center of town, Peterburg's residents hadn't been doing that well to begin with.

"I thought you said he lived in, like, a trailer park," Keyz said. He sounded like he'd never encountered the concept before, and Lizzy suppressed instant anger. Just because the kid had grown up in the bosom of the EMOs, sheltered inside the whole corporate lifestyle, was no excuse for remaining this ignorant.

"That's right," Vara said, placidly. "But he works in town. And these are working hours."

Keyz slumped back in his seat, and Lizzy hid a smile of her own. It was about time Keyz developed some sense of the reality outside the Nets. *Not that I should talk, the years I spent hiding, but at least I knew what I was running from.* The town center was less crowded, a few nice cars parked in the choice spots in front of a handful of boutique galleries, the rest with the same dents and rust spots that Lizzy had noticed on the way into town. At least the church was still there, at the center of the square, and still a church, though the white paint of the steeple was streaked and stained. A handful of skater kids sat on its steps, their multicolored hair and neon-fiber shirts the brightest thing in sight, passing a smoke on a long tether. A shapeless dog lay at their feet, frankly asleep in the still heat.

Vara pulled the car to a stop outside the town cybercafe. Lizzy frowned at the bile green brickwork, wondering who had chosen the color, and then she registered the rate menu hand-painted on the wall beside the door. It was a Mabel 8's, a franchise, a chain that pretended not to be a chain, and went to great lengths to customize each outlet. It was a laudable goal, except that the range of services remained exactly the same in every store.

"I can't believe Russ is working here," she began, and stopped, shaking her head.

"It's what there is," Vara answered, shrugging. "Come on."

Inside the cafe it was cool and quiet, just a trickle of sound from the overhead speakers, mingling with the equally muted beeps of a game console in the far corner. Most of the terminals were empty; the most activity, Lizzy saw, came from a group of teenage girls who'd pushed three of the tiny tables together to make room for plates and smokes tied in to overhead junctions. From the look of the plates, they were all doing the colors, and Lizzy felt a pang of something between amusement and guilt. And then a figure moved behind the counter, still familiar after all these years, and Lizzy braced herself to be forgotten. It wasn't that Conti hadn't changed, he had gotten thinner and greyer—even his skin looked greyed, as though he was getting over some long illness—but his long horse face was still instantly recognizable. He frowned, looking from her to Vara, and the older woman stepped forward to meet him.

"Hello, Russ."

"Chessie." Conti managed a smile that was at once puzzled and welcoming, his eyes flicking to Lizzy and Keyz and then back to Lizzy. "Liz? Or is it something else now?"

Lizzy shook her head. "Still Tin Lizzy," she said, and the words came out a boast.

"You've changed," Conti said, looking at her hair, and Lizzy felt herself flush.

"So have you."

"Haven't we all?" Conti looked from her to Vara again. "No offense, but what do you want?"

"I—we need your help," Vara answered. She tilted her head sideways. "It's about the kid."

For a second, Conti seemed to shrink, as though he'd crumple in on himself, but then he straightened. "What about him?"

"He's in trouble," Vara said. "Look, I'd rather not talk about it here."

Conti pushed himself back from the counter. "Nikki! Can you cover for me?"

"Sure." A stocky, snub-nosed woman in white trousers appeared in the doorway that led to the kitchen, wiping her hands on a towel looped through her belt. "Nothing much is happening, anyway."

"Thanks," Conti said, and waved toward the door. "Why don't we step outside?"

Lizzy followed the others back through the heavy doors, wincing as the heat struck them, but she had to admit it was the safest place to talk. Vara leaned her hips on the hood of the car, and Conti leaned beside her, resting his arm on the roof. Lizzy knew she should join them, complete the picture of a group of friends just talking, but couldn't quite bring herself to do it. She folded her arms instead, and out of the corner of her eye saw Keyz looking mulish. It was a bad contrast, made them look as though they were arguing, and she jammed her hands in her pockets instead.

"So what's going on?" Conti said again, and Vara looked at Lizzy. "What's this trouble?"

"The trouble involves Keyz, here, and RCD, and maybe Njeri Shida, but mostly a program called Orpha-Toto."

"Fuck," Conti said, and Lizzy flinched again. Conti never swore, it was proverbial among his students, so to hear him curse now just brought home how potentially bad the situation was.

"Look, if you know anything—"

Conti lifted his hand. "No, I'm willing to talk, but not here. Not about that."

Lizzy drew breath to protest, but Vara just nodded. "Where and when? Bear in mind we're short on time."

Conti closed his eyes. "I have to finish work. That's five-thirty. After that . . ." He paused, opened his eyes. "There's a bar two doors down, called the Cellar—there at the blue sign. It's downstairs. I'll meet you there."

"Is that safe?" Vara asked, her voice mild, and to Lizzy's surprise, Conti grinned.

"Oh, yeah, the guy keeps it real clean. And it's quiet before the band comes in."

"Five-thirty, then," Vara said.

"You will show up this time, won't you?" Lizzy asked, and wished instantly she'd kept her mouth shut.

Conti winced. "I'll be there. Look, I've got to get back to work."

"Yeah," Vara said, and Lizzy nodded, embarrassed. Conti nodded back, not meeting her eyes, and vanished back into the cybercafe.

"Lizzy," Vara said, and the other woman lifted her hands in apology.

"I know. It was stupid. I'm sorry."

"We—you need his help," Vara said. "Don't blow it."

"Yeah," Lizzy said, knowing Vara was right. It had been a stupid comment—and she'd have to watch herself, make sure she didn't make that mistake again.

The Cellar was exactly that, the basement of one of the storefronts, clumsily converted into a bar to make the most of basically useless space. Lizzy sighed, seeing her hands pallid in the blue-toned light, and wished she was back in the custom ambiance of Testify. Vara grinned as though she'd guessed the thought, and gestured toward a table in a cone of shadow and between two neon clocks. Neither one showed the correct time, Lizzy noticed. The light didn't flatter Vara either, made the shadows under her eyes look like bruises. Lizzy let the others seat themselves, leaned against the back of a chair to consider the options. There was no menu, either electronic or on the wall, but the rack of bottles behind the bar was so brightly lit that she could read the brand names from across the room.

"What'll you have?"

Vara grimaced. "There's nothing on draft, is there?"

The bar was suspiciously empty of pump handles, just the multiple nozzle of a soft drink dispenser showing beneath the racked glasses, and Lizzy shook her head. "Doesn't look it."

"Andrews Heavy, then."

"I thought you didn't like beer," Lizzy said, and was startled by the memory.

"I don't." Vara smiled. "But it's hard to screw up opening a bottle."

She had a point. Lizzy looked at Keyz. "Same for you?"

"Light, please," the boy said, and Lizzy wondered if he'd ever been in a bar before. Nothing like this one, she guessed, and pushed herself away from the chair.

The bar was neither empty nor particularly busy. Maybe a third of the tables were occupied, mostly by twentysomethings in the brand-name clothes that marked them as store clerks with a decent discount. All people who worked in the outlets, Lizzy guessed, and after waiting on tourists all day, who could blame them for wanting a drink away from the vacation malls? She took her place in the short line, avoiding the carefully incurious looks. Strangers would be remembered here no matter what they did; better to be as normal as possible, she thought, and leaned heavily against the bar. It was the brightest spot in the entire room, with two naked overhead bulbs, and someone—the bartender, presumably, since there was no one else in sight—had dragged a chair directly under one of them. His magazine, real paper, lay facedown on the sprung seat, a dark, dangerous-looking front cover belied by the bright colors of the ad on the back pages.

"You got to get that kid out of here."

Lizzy straightened, startled, and the bartender fixed her with a stare.

"I don't serve minors. Don't even think about it."

Over his shoulder, Lizzy could see a kid who looked even younger than Keyz sitting at a table, happily cradling a bottle of beer. She took a breath, guessing it was less the age than that the man didn't recognize them, and he rattled on.

"They fine you and put you in the big register, and I don't need that kind of trouble, no way. So go on, get him out of here."

"He's not a minor," Lizzy said, and put a note of surprise in her voice. *If Russ knew this was going to happen, is trying to run out on us again, I'll fucking kill him.* The bartender was an older man, scalp shining between the strands of dirty grey hair. He looked like a caricature of a conspiracy theorist, the kind who kept his private, personally enhanced remix of the McGruder tape in the pocket of his shabby cardigan. That went with the magazine, with the ad on the back cover—Almaviva made the best countersurveillance gear available, the paranoid's choice—and she hoped she was reading him right.

"He sure as spit looks like a minor," the bartender said. "Show me some ID, or get on out of here."

Lizzy glanced over her shoulder again, relieved to see she was the only person still waiting to be served. Vara was frowning in the corner, body tensed to come and help, and Lizzy willed her to stay in her seat as she turned back to face the bartender, dropping her voice to what she hoped was a conspiratorial murmur. "No ID," she said.

The bartender stiffened, more wary than angry, and Lizzy smiled.

"The lady over there is a cop, and we're both—with her. No IDs."

The bartender's eyes flickered across the crowd. "No trouble. I don't want trouble here."

"No trouble, just drinks," Lizzy answered, and froze as the bartender's hand slid out of sight beneath the counter. *Oh, shit, I've overplayed it, and he's bound to have a gun—* The man's hand reappeared, clutching a device that Lizzy recognized as a scanner-scrambler, and she wondered if the man had tripped over the line between fanatic and paranoid. He caressed the buttons with his thumb, flipping from setting to setting, and Lizzy managed to smile again.

"So. I want two Andrews Heavies and one Andrews Light."

"You're undercover?" The bartender's voice was calmer, though his thumb still roved steadily over the buttons.

"Yeah. Undercover." *Like any cop would tell you that.* Lizzy waited, hoping this was going to work, and the man bent stiffly to pull the bottles one by one from the rack behind the bar.

"There you go, miss. And don't worry, I'll keep quiet." The bartender nodded twice, vigorously, touching the buttons again.

"Thanks." *I don't like being a cop*, Lizzy realized, startled. She'd been on the receiving end too often to feel comfortable trying those tactics herself. She took the bottles, trying not to betray her feelings, and made her way back to the table. Vara took them from her, twisted off the caps as Lizzy seated herself.

"What was that all about?"

Lizzy accepted her bottle, took a quick swallow to buy time. "He was worried about serving underage kids."

"That guy?" Keyz asked.

"Probably more worried that he doesn't know us," Vara said.

Lizzy nodded, glanced at the clock behind Vara's shoulder. "Russ is late."

"Not according to that one," Vara said, too calmly, and nodded to the one behind Lizzy.

"According to my watch," Lizzy began, and Vara frowned her down.

"According to mine, it's just five-thirty. He'll be here, Lizzy."

Lizzy subsided, knowing she was being unreasonable, and took another careful sip of the beer. Like most of the West-Coast heavies, it was almost thick enough to chew, and she wasn't sure she liked the nutty taste. This place would be a perfect setting for Testify, she thought, suddenly—Cafe Paranoia, complete with bartender and clientele who were spying on each other in the most outrageously over-the-top style. Every table would hide a trapdoor, every door would open onto a different alley—even ones that seemed to be side by side—and half the people in the backgrounds would be active wallpaper, controlled by a GM who liked to make trouble. She could do it herself, or, better yet, see if Kim Jay would be interested in the collaboration. Kim's people were all thin lines and angles, would be perfect for a place like this—and Jazzman08 would buy it, too. Assuming, of course, she was ever in a position to sell things to him again.

The thought was sobering, and she glanced at the clocks again. Four minutes past five-thirty, according to the slower of the pair: it couldn't take more than two minutes to walk from the cybercafe to the Cellar, and she suppressed a shudder. She had waited for Conti once before, with just as much at stake—she could practically smell the courtroom, antiseptic-clean and varnished until the pale wood shone, could feel the chill of the air-conditioning and the weight of the suit she'd borrowed for the trial. It had fit her well enough, censored her curves, but it hadn't convinced anyone she was an honest citizen. She remembered the fear, too, the gut-churning certainty that, without Russ—and maybe even with his testimony—she'd be convicted. And the lawyer had already told her what was waiting if they lost. She shivered, more from the remembered cold than the Cellar's damp air, and saw Vara eyeing her curiously. She sat up straighter, forcing calm—it was over, had been over for a long time, and she'd survived—and then out of the corner of her eye saw Conti coming down the stairs. In the blued light, he looked older than before, as though their sudden appearance had shaken him.

He paused for a moment in the entryway, then saw them, but detoured to the bar. The bartender said something to him, then turned away, shaking his head, to return with another brown bottle. Conti took it with a nod of thanks, and came slowly to join them, his eyes on Lizzy.

"I've—I wanted to apologize for what happened, back in the District."

Lizzy flinched. *I don't want to talk about that*, she thought, *not right now, not when I've got everything else to worry about. Just get us in touch with Shida, that's all we need from you.*

"It's maybe the worst thing I've ever done," Conti went on, his eyes fixed now on the bottle of beer resting gently on the table. "I owe you an apology."

Let it go, Lizzy thought. She tried for a mocking smile, and knew she failed. The muscles of her face felt petrified, body heavy as stone, as lead. She knew both Vara and the boy were watching her, wished they were anywhere else. "I'd rather have an explanation," she said, and the words startled her, coming out of nowhere. But it was true, she thought. *I'd rather know why, know the worst, than know he was startled.* Conti looked at her for the first time, startled himself, then looked away.

"You know what happened," he said, after a moment. "What happened was the cops were leaning on me about the remailer, and Gerretty got one of his people to talk to me—purely friendly, of course, a word to the wise—saying that if I testified for you, it would give the cops what they needed to pry the codes out of me. You know that I was friends with electronic thieves, trained them, even. I was afraid I'd lose the school contract, too."

"I stole the man's smoke," Lizzy said, and unexpectedly laughed. It was funny, in a sick way, to hear those words used against her, bigger words, bigger jazz, than she or the crime had deserved. And now Gerretty had found a new jazz to play.

"I know." Conti's eyes dropped. "I was going to go, going to testify, right up to the last minute, but by then the cops were getting nasty, and I thought—" He shrugged, eyes firmly on the beer bottle. "I thought I needed to keep the remailer secure. And keep the classes going."

"You gave them both up in the end," Lizzy said. That wasn't fair, at least not about the classes, but Conti didn't try to defend himself.

"Yeah. I know."

There was a long silence, the noise from the other tables washing over them, and Lizzy was aware again of the others' wary stares. She still thought Russ should have kept the secret, let the cops find their murderer some other way, but Vara thought he'd been right, that it was the cops' fault other people had died. And if Conti was worried about his classes . . . To know that was why, that Conti had chosen them, and the remailer, all the other people he owed, over her—it hurt both more and less, and she couldn't have said why.

"It wouldn't have made any difference," she said aloud, and knew that it was true. "Gerretty was determined I was going to the Wilson."

There was another silence, not as long, and Conti said, "Are you OK?"

Lizzy hesitated, considering the question, the air-conditioning stirring her dyed hair. What she'd said was true, something she'd known all along and hadn't wanted to face: Conti's testimony wouldn't have made any difference. *I still wish he'd been there*, she thought, *it mattered to me, that someone would stand up for me, but I guess I know why he didn't. I guess I'm OK. Maybe it's not OK, but I guess maybe I am. Russ wouldn't be Russ if he'd done anything else.* She nodded, not quite able to say the words yet, said instead, "I'm not going to let that son of a bitch do it again."

Conti dipped his head, accepting her answer.

"So," Vara said, and Conti sighed.

"So."

"What the hell do you have to do with Orpha-Toto?" It was not the question she'd meant to ask, and Lizzy made a face.

"I helped write it." Conti looked down at his hands, laced around the base of his bottle.

"Give," Vara said, but her voice was more gentle than the word.

Conti sighed again. "RCD commissioned Paul Orfanos to write them a program—using his supralinguistic theories, which everybody knew about in those days—that could pick a hit, a hit film, hit song, hit interactive, whatever, on the basis of its structure. I was Paul's senior research student, I think the only one left at the time."

"But the program works," Keyz said, and Conti gave him a startled look.

"Who said it doesn't?"

"But—" Keyz stopped, shook his head. "If it works, why don't they admit it? Why aren't they selling copies of it? Hell, why didn't they keep it somewhere a lot safer than where I found it?"

"If it works," Lizzy said slowly, "and if nobody else knows about it, then they have a huge advantage. They know how to make their stuff hits and nobody else can make that guess. Once it's loose, once it's known to exist and to work, then they have to sell it, otherwise they'll be spending all their energy fending off serious hackers. So what they want is to tell everybody it doesn't exist—"

"Except their board of directors," Vara interjected, nodding.

"—and work it as hard as they can until the other studios find out." Lizzy stopped, blinking. "No wonder RCD's done so well under Gerretty."

"It works," Conti said again, and this time there was no mistaking the bitterness in his voice. "It does what it's advertised to do. It just isn't what we were trying to build. Or what I was trying to build, anyway. I don't know about Paul anymore."

"What do you mean?" Vara asked, with more patience than Lizzy could have managed, and the younger woman made herself take a sip of her beer, forcing silence.

"It's how it works that's the problem," Conti said. "See, it was supposed to be a supralinguistic engine, but that whole theory had bogged down a couple of years earlier—Paul had made some big advances, but he'd taken them about as far as they would go, and it was starting to look like maybe he'd taken the wrong approach altogether, except he was too stubborn to admit it. RCD was about the only employer left who'd take a chance on the idea, so of course Paul jumped at it."

Conti's voice trailed off, as though he was remembering better days. Lizzy stared at him, unable to imagine him working for a studio—unable to imagine him in the bright sun and beautiful bodies that always formed a studio setting. But that was jazz, she told herself, and Conti shook his head.

"Anyway. We couldn't make it work the way we wanted to, and the studio was breathing down his neck. The guy who hired him had been fired, you see, and the new guy didn't believe in the project, not like Anders did, so Paul wrote a—he called it a mock-up of what was going to be the real Toto, and gave them that. My grant was up anyway, and they weren't going to hire me back, so I left. And about a year later Paul had his heart attack and died."

"When did all this happen, Russ?" Vara asked.

"You were just at the academy," Conti answered. "That's when I met your mother—in the real world, that is. I knew her in the jazz before that."

And when you met Shida, Lizzy thought. She frowned, trying to remember what she'd learned of RCD's history. This would have been during Richard Kullen's tenure as president, and Gerretty had come in right after he'd lost Krakau and Shida—come in with a string of hits, she remembered, or, more precisely, he'd come in and released a string of hits. Nothing spectacular, nothing innovative, but solid, hard-core moneymakers, exactly the kind of thing RCD was doing today. "Did you know Gerretty then?"

Conti frowned. "By name, sure. He was getting a name, but when Kullen took over from Anders, they kicked him out to R&D. I was shocked when I heard they'd made him president—" He stopped abruptly, eyes widening, and Lizzy nodded.

"He must have had the program then. His formula. The jazz that everybody thinks doesn't exist. But it does exist, right? And that's how he took over."

"He'd have had to convince the board of directors," Keyz said, sounding dubious.

"Easy enough," Conti said. "Look, the program was pretty fool-proof, you just gave it a large enough sample of the style you'd like to duplicate, and Toto would tell you whether your script was going to make it. It would have been better to work with finished films, of course, but that was too expensive. We just used them for the data-base."

"Are we talking blockbusters or just moneymakers?" Vara asked.

"Either. Whatever you sampled, put in the database, Toto would work toward."

"And it suggested changes?" Lizzy asked.

Conti nodded.

"Directors must have loved that," Keyz said, eyes wide again.

"They weren't wild about it," Conti said.

"So what's the rest of it?" Vara asked.

"What?" Conti looked startled, as though he'd been a million miles away, and Vara frowned.

"You said you wrote a mock-up, and it works. So why isn't it the real thing?"

"It's the way it works," Conti said. He made a face, no longer even pretending to taste his beer. "It's supposed to analyze supralan-guages, right? And it uses some of the techniques that Paul worked out, some clever algorithms, some smart code to break down what you give it, it figures out their common structure, things like that. But what it doesn't do is fit those common structures into a larger grammatical framework. All it does is tell you how to make what you gave it more like all the other things you gave it." He leaned back in his chair as though that explained everything.

"I'm lost," Vara said, after a moment. "Isn't that what it's supposed to do?"

"Yes, but," Conti said. "Toto was originally intended to connect all this to something bigger—something outside the group of sources you gave it. A real deep structure. Not only that, it doesn't recognize when sources are completely dissimilar. You can give it any random grouping of texts, and Toto'll come up with a grammar for it. It'll be nonsense, but it'll produce nonsense in the same pattern." He shook his head. "So it can tell you how to make a film like a bunch of other films—which is what RCD wanted—but it can't give you any insight into why those films were hits. Which was the other part they wanted. And, of course, it can't predict the next breakout success."

"No *Kanze Angel*," Lizzy said. And RCD hadn't had a breakout hit since Gerretty took over, she realized, just more and better versions of about five film standards.

Conti nodded. "Yeah. Exactly. And if we'd done it the way I wanted to—the way we said we were doing it—it could have done that, too."

"RCD must've been pissed," Keyz said.

"Do they know what they have?" Lizzy asked. "What they didn't get?"

"I don't think it matters," Conti said.

Probably not, Lizzy thought, *but I bet it matters to the poor bastards who have to change their ideas to fit the formula.* Not that that hadn't been going on forever, but now, with Orpha-Toto in place, there was nothing to argue against, just a set of numbers that no one could ever challenge because they didn't know it existed. If that was ever turned on the jazz . . . She shivered at the thought. Nobody was going to go that far, she told herself. The jazz depended on being untamed, on allowing for the quirky thoughts that turned into unexpected hits—except that Orpha-Toto had done its job all too well with Keyz' jazz. Testify, Jazzman08, had jumped to take it on.

"What I wish I did know," Conti went on, "is exactly what RCD did with Toto after Paul died. What kinds of testing, whether there were any revisions, stuff like that."

"We could try hacking the system again," Keyz said.

"I don't think that would be smart," Lizzy answered automatically, and saw the boy grin.

"So. I've told you about Orpha-Toto," Conti said. "What's this trouble you're in?"

"We need your help," Vara said. "Keyz here managed to get hold of a copy of a program called Orpha-Toto—I assume it's your program?"

"If you got it from RCD, it is," Conti said. In the blued light, he looked positively ill.

"And RCD's been trying to bust him ever since," Vara went on. "They're put a live team out after him, and they're so touchy about saying that they lost something that they've put out a private warrant on Lizzy for child abuse."

"You've got to be kidding." Conti said up straighter, angry now, and Lizzy sighed. That was Conti, too, the unwillingness to face reality.

"They've got my juvenile record," she said. "And time in the Wilson. Plus he's a nice suburban kid. That jazz will play."

"It's not right." Conti shook his head. "Oh, I know, it'll play. Go on."

"They said they'd put me in jail," Keyz said. "The studio cops, I mean. And fire my parents, too, and they didn't have anything to do with this. It isn't their fault at all. So I ran."

"So what do you want from me?" Conti asked, warily, and Vara leaned forward, resting her elbows heavily on the table.

"The jazz is, Njeri Shida's interested in this program."

Lizzy nodded. "Interested enough that every time you find a reference to the program or something like it, you find a shadow thread leading somewhere that there's an offer saying Shida wants it."

"I talked to Mama the other night," Vara said. "She says you've stayed in touch with him."

Conti hesitated. "I used to know where Njeri was living, but that was a while ago. He may have moved on."

Lizzy swallowed her accusation, but Vara had no such inhibitions. "Bullshit," she said, conversationally, and even in the dim light Lizzy could see his blush.

"Look, this—let's go back to my place. It'll be easier to talk there."

The place was filling up, and a back door had opened, admitting a trio of black-clad teenagers dragging amplifiers. Lizzy winced, imagining the volume in the confined space, even as part of her mind added them to wallpaper at Cafe Paranoia. Sketch them taller, give them the fangs and glowing eyes these kids were trying to simulate with contacts and dental prosthetics—and set the band to eat anyone who screwed up egregiously—and they'd be perfect. *Assuming I ever get to build it, that is.* She shook herself back to reality, saw Vara looking at the band.

"Maybe you're right. OK, let's go."

There was something strange about Conti's trailer. Lizzy seated herself on the arm of the couch, not wanting to meet the cold glare of Conti's wife Shirle, and glanced cautiously around the long room. It was comfortable, certainly, and better kept than any of the trailers she'd lived in as a child—there was even a freestanding fireplace, tucked into the corner of the room closest to the little kitchen. It was unlit, of course, and emptied of ash, but there was wood and a handful of pinecones piled in a basket beside its open door, ready for the return of cold weather. There was a big media center, screen and controller and playback deck with good-sized speakers, in the opposite corner, and she had a sudden image of Russ and Shirle sitting in the center of the floor, turning from fire to screen and back again. There were books, too, stacked in shelves, and a rack of disczines—and that was what was missing, she realized. There were plenty of zines, but not a smoke in sight. No larger gear, either, she'd expected that, had known there wouldn't be because she couldn't picture Conti owning the equipment and not making his presence felt again, but it was very strange not to see any smokes. He had to own one, surely, she couldn't imagine him reading his zines on the coarse-grained media-center screen—but there were cables running into the kitchen, the flatwire that linked to a secondary monitor, and another one running along the ceiling into what had to be the bedroom. So maybe he was using the cheapest tech, Lizzy thought, playing the zines through a main box instead of a smoke, but the media center's shelves were in shadow, and she couldn't identify the smaller components.

Someone said her name, and she jumped, all too aware of Shirle's lifted eyebrow, then relaxed as the voice went on: Conti explaining what had happened, nothing more. He told the story fairly, Lizzy admitted silently, as far as he knew it, and it was a relief to see Shirle's expression change from hostility to acceptance.

"So what are you going to do?" she asked, and Conti hesitated.

"I—" He stopped, shook his head. "Shida's on the Isle Rialto."

"The Isle Rialto," Lizzy repeated. It made sense, when she thought about it: the casino/resort had been built mid-sea on a platform that had been an oceangoing oil refinery, which made it extraterritorial, answering only to the government where its holding company was registered.

"They value their celebrities there," Vara said. "Management would certainly help keep the vidirazzi away. And anybody else he didn't want to deal with."

"Like us, maybe," Keyz muttered. "Where is the Isle Rialto, anyway?"

"Off Gulfport—the Gulf of Mexico," Vara answered. She smiled, wryly. "We get a certain amount of cross traffic in Lakeview. If we'd known—well, there's usually at least three flights a day down to the Isle."

"Will he talk to us?" Lizzy asked, and Conti shrugged.

"He's pretty careful about what he says on-line. I'll help you contact him, but I think, if he's going to help you, you're going to have to go there."

Lizzy shook her head, but there was nothing to be gained worrying about the wasted time. "It's a hell of a long drive," she said. "Does RCD know he's there?"

The phone rang in the kitchen, interrupting Conti's response. Shirle turned on her heel and vanished through the doorway, her voice an indistinct murmur as she answered.

"They'd have to know," Conti said, and Lizzy sighed. If the studio hadn't been keeping track of Shida's whereabouts, it might have been worth it to risk a commercial flight, or even a bus, but as it was, every flight's passenger list would autoroute to a studio surveillance program.

Vara nodded. "I don't think we dare fly," she said. "But it'll only take three days to get there—or four, depending on how much we sleep."

Too long, Lizzy thought, but she couldn't think of a better option.

"Once we get there," Keyz said, "is there, like, a ferry or something? And that place is supposed to be expensive, too."

"The main thing," Lizzy said, and looked at Conti, "is whether you'll introduce us. Set up contact for us."

He started to nod, but he was interrupted by a flurry of movement in the kitchen.

"Russ." Shirle was standing in the doorway, and there was something in her voice that raised the hairs on the back of Lizzy's neck. "The cops are coming. You've got to clear out."

"Shit," Vara said, already reaching for her bag, and Lizzy copied her, swallowing fear that tasted of bile.

"Me?" Conti asked, and for a second Shirle looked as though she wanted to shake him.

"You, them, all of you." She took a breath. "That was Jean, at Dispatch—you remember, we used to do Game Night with them?"

Conti nodded, white as a ghost, and Shirle hurried on, the words tumbling over each other. "So she says, there's a warrant out on you, as some kind of accessory, and out-of-jurisdiction cops coming in to make sure they don't just walk over here and ask what's going on, and she doesn't like it any better than anybody else, but there isn't anything they can do. So you'd better get the hell out of here."

"She's right," Vara said, gently, and Lizzy tried to match her tone. "Come on, Russ."

Conti shook himself, looked once around the trailer. "I can't—I haven't got time—"

"Here," Shirle said, and held out a smoke. "Grab your jacket and a pair of jeans. And go."

Conti took the smoke, but made no move toward the bedroom. "What about you?"

"I'll be fine," Shirle said, and her voice softened. "You know I will. Just go."

"Come on," Lizzy said again. The trailer seemed claustrophobically small, the comfortable furniture looming like barriers in her way. She could see Keyz shaking, caught in the same vortex of fear, and forced a calmer voice. "Did the woman say how long?"

"About twenty minutes," Shirle said. "Less with the sirens." She was moving as she spoke, brushed past them into the bedroom, came out a minute later with a rough bundle of clothes, jeans and jacket and shirt crumpled into a wad of fabric. "Go, Russ."

"But—" Conti took them as though he was caught in a trance.

"If you stay," Vara said, "they'll bust you regardless. And that's no help to Njeri."

Conti nodded, his face tragic, shook himself into motion like a machine coming slowly on-line. In the doorway, he hesitated again, looked back to meet Shirle's eyes.

"I'll be fine," Shirle said. "I've got the union, and Jean and Tilyer know me. Nobody'll expect me to know or tell."

Lizzy looked over her shoulder, wondering if she really believed it, wondering, too, if she really thought she could stand up to RCD's police. She was union, of course, assuming she was still working construction, and heavy-machinery operators were still hard to find, so all that might help, but still. . . . Vara tapped her arm, and she headed for the car. Vara was already fumbling with the remote, popping the doors, and gestured for them to get in. "No, Lizzy, in front with me."

Lizzy did as she was told, swapping places with Conti, who slid into the backseat with Keyz. Vara gunned the engine, scattered gravel, and pulled the car out of the narrow drive between the two buildings. Lizzy clung to the door, looked back to see Shirle still outlined against the faded curtains.

"Get the onboard systems on-line," Vara ordered, and Lizzy bent to the task, touching the keypad to tune the machine to the nearest stations.

"Anyone in particular you want?" she asked, and rocked sideways as Vara took another corner too fast.

"Take it easy, Chessie," Conti said, and Vara's head lifted.

"You want to get trapped in here, with just the one road in or out?"

Conti subsided, and she touched the gas again, sending the car sliding onto one of the larger access roads. "Anything with traffic reports, Lizzy. See what they're saying."

Lizzy braced herself against the dashboard, wishing she could see better in the fading light, touched the keypad to cycle through the source menu. Two locations promised local traffic, and she punched them in one after the other, watching the colored lights appear and disappear along the base of the windshield. Both showed the pattern of the park's roads, a series of concentric loops that all fed into a single entrance, and she made a face at the sight. No roadblocks yet, or even traffic problems, but it would be almost too easy to catch them here.

"Nothing yet," she said, and lifted her head to check their

progress. They had reached the central street, and she could see the gates ahead, lights glowing warmly in the gatehouse windows, and from the trailers to either side. This was an old development, old enough to have proper streets and aboveground cable connections stranding from the trailers to overhead lines: not the sort of place that usually saw the police, and she wondered what they'd make of this.

"What about LoneStar?" Vara asked, and Lizzy hesitated, trying to remember the codes.

"What's the access number?"

"Channel 17," Conti answered, and Lizzy keyed it in.

The lights in the windshield ran and shifted, resettled to show a smaller-scale map of the town, the main roads outlined in glowing purple, smaller roads sketched in blue. The main traffic icons all glowed green, and she shook her head even as she punched in the specific query. The miniscreen lit, telling her there were **no significant delays**, and she flipped the screen away.

"Nothing."

"Damn." Vara slammed a hand against the steering wheel, swore again as a light turned red ahead of them.

"Take it easy," Conti said, and Lizzy saw the other woman swallow hard.

"Look, Russ, we've got a serious problem here."

"I know."

Lizzy twisted in her seat, looking past Conti's pale face to see the road empty behind them. "Cop channels?" she asked, and Vara touched the gas, accelerating decorously through the intersection. There were no police cars in sight on either road, just ordinary cars and trucks caught in the neon from the storefronts, she crossed her fingers. If Shirle's friend had warned them in time. . . .

"If the numbers are the same," Vara said, "try Channel 2."

Lizzy touched keys. "Nothing."

"Fourteen."

"Something." Lizzy frowned at the hash of static. "Well, there's something on the channel, but it's either too far off, or it's scrambled."

Vara took her eyes off the road long enough to glance at the little screen. "Scrambled. Give them my general password—the one I gave you."

Lizzy nodded, fumbling for the scrap of paper, then punched the codes into the machine. For a second, nothing happened, and she held her breath, hoping no one had deleted Vara's access. They'd been lucky so far that way, somebody was bound to notice sometime. . . . Then the screen cleared, offering a menu. "Map, general ops, locator, communications," she read, and Vara nodded.

"General ops. If they offer interpretation, say yes."

"Right."

Lizzy selected the subchannel, watching the map in the windshield shimmer and shift, tracing out a new pattern. This one showed more of the side streets, a fine blue web covering the lower part of the screen, and this time there were red dots moving along the major streets.

"That looks," Conti began, leaning against the back of the seat. "Of course, that's got to be the cops."

Lizzy touched the keypad again, recalling the menu, opened a second screen for the locator and punched in Conti's address. Sure enough, the red dots were converging on the yellow cross that marked the target.

"Can you get audio?" Vara asked, and grimaced at the distant sound of a siren.

Lizzy touched keys again, shook her head. "No audio." She slid through the menu again, checking the submenus. "Wait, here's the general alert." The words filled the little screen, scrolling past at a steady pace, and she read the important bits aloud. "Two adult females, juvenile male, last seen driving—shit, they've got a description of the car."

"Plates, too?" Vara asked.

Lizzy shook her head again, realized the other woman wouldn't see her. "No. They don't have phone numbers, either."

"Well, that's something," Vara said. "Hell, we can't risk it—trying to get out of here now that they know the car. Russ, is there anyplace around here that would take us in? Friends, family, crooks, anything?"

Lizzy sat up carefully, aware of the faces in the cars to either side. They had reached the main shopping street, running between the downtown and the linked series of discount malls, and Vara kept strictly to the middle lane, trying to avoid the worst of the traffic. No

one seemed to be paying attention to them, didn't seem to be looking at anything except their own heads-up channels or the narrow-
casts from the stores, and she hoped that they just looked like
another quarreling family, cranky from too much shopping. Conti
didn't answer for a long moment, and Lizzy looked back to see his
head bowed against his chest.

"Yes," he said at last, "there's a place. I can call in a promise."

"Where?" Vara demanded, and Lizzy caught her breath, hearing
the blat of a siren. Keyz slumped down in his seat as brake lights
flared, and an armored carrier swept through the intersection ahead
of them, warning lights sweeping across the line of cars.

"That was this one," Vara said, nodding to the display. "Come
on, Russ, there's not much time left."

"Keep going straight," Conti answered. "They're just past the
last outlet."

Vara nodded again, put the car into gear as the light changed.

"Who is?" Keyz demanded. "Where are we going?"

"Stormhafen," Conti answered, and Lizzy frowned. The name
sounded familiar, was something she should know but couldn't
place, and Vara gave the man a sharp glance over her shoulder.

"I thought—"

"They moved," Conti said, and belatedly Lizzy remembered.
That was the name of the covenanted community, the one where the
murders had been.

"They'll let us in?" she asked, and Conti glared.

"They felt they owed me—well, Silent William said they owed
me, and he's one of the lords, his word goes for all of them. They felt
it was as much their fault as mine that someone died."

"Where?" Vara said again, and Conti leaned forward, resting one
arm on the back of the front seat as he pointed with the other.

"Just keep going straight. They're about two blocks past the last
outlet—they have a shop and a bar, I heard."

"You haven't been there?" Lizzy asked, and in the windshield
saw Conti's reflection shake his head.

"No."

"Were they here when you came?" Vara asked, and shook her
head. "Sorry. None of my business."

"It's OK." Conti eased back in the seat, his face once again in shadow. "No, they weren't. The town voted them in overwhelmingly."

And I bet you wouldn't have come if they had been here, Lizzy thought. *I wonder why you didn't move.* But of course Shirle had her job, there was that to consider, and maybe Conti was finally getting tired of running. She put the thought aside, glanced at the map again. Most of the police patrols were past, converging on the trailer park, and she looked at Vara.

"Can't we make a run for it?"

"Hit Function-3, #6," Vara answered, and Lizzy did as she was told. A new set of lights appeared, paler yellow, lurking on the roads that led toward the main highways. There was one less than a mile ahead.

"They'll expect it," Vara said, unnecessarily. "And they know the car. Now . . . Now we've got to ditch it and hope for the best."

They left the car in an alley and walked the last three blocks to the wall that closed Stormhafen off from the outside world, gear hastily concealed in shopping bags. They were still carrying way too much, Lizzy thought, looked more like refugees than tourists, but no one seemed to be paying much attention to them. There weren't as many shoppers here as in the main malls, but there were still people around, a crowd to blend in with, and Lizzy tried to match them, look as though she had nothing in her mind except another expensive skirt. Vara looked impossibly calm, a reassuring presence in her jacket and jeans, one hand touching Keyz' shoulder as though to keep him close. Her eyes narrowed at the sound of a siren in the distance, but her stride never varied. Lizzy tried to match her calm, cringed inwardly at the blast of a second siren, this one less than a block away. She looked over her shoulder, seeing an armored car moving slowly down the middle of the street, the cars pulling left and right to make way for it. It didn't have to be for them—the malls had to be heavily patrolled as a matter of course—but it was hard to keep from ducking as the heavy car slid past, the camera's light playing over the crowd. Vara kept walking, giving it a single disinterested glance, and Lizzy deliberately joined a group of tourists gawking after it, hoping to look as though she was with them rather than Vara. And then at last the car was past, turning the corner toward the parking lots.

"You think they've figured out we're not at Russ's?" she asked, stretching her legs to keep up with Vara, and the other woman shrugged.

"Could be. We can't worry about that now."

"Another block," Conti said, voice tight, and Lizzy nodded, shifting her bags on her shoulder.

They passed the last store, the crowd thinning out around them, and the main entrance to Stormhafen loomed ahead of them, heavy carved-stone pillars punctuating a smooth concrete wall. The top of the wall was strung with glitterwire, itself a defense as well as a warning system, and Lizzy wondered how a medieval-lifestyle community could justify the anachronism. But they'd have to come to some kind of compromise with the present if they were going to create their vision of the past. The gate itself was guarded by men in long shirts of soft-looking metal and each wore a helmet that looked like the tip of a bullet. They stayed punctiliously on their side of the gate, and a yawning man in the grey-green uniform of a private security firm stayed equally carefully on his. Beyond the men in armor, she got a brief glimpse of a woman in a red dress moving toward the lights of the tavern, caught momentarily in the swing of light from a passing car, but the rest of the compound was in darkness.

Silent William's tavern lay around the corner from the main gate, not hidden, but not advertised, either. On this side of the compound, the wall was set well back from the street, leaving a few yards of straggling lawn between the sidewalk and the compound's wall. The tavern jutted out into that space, the stones of its wall fading seamlessly into the pale poured concrete. It was a long, low-slung building, with a tiled roof and a carved and painted bush hanging over the door.

"That used to be a real bush," Conti said suddenly, "and they had a thatched roof. But the fire code stopped all that."

Lizzy nodded, not knowing what to say, looked at the light spilling onto the sidewalk—another compromise, she guessed, electricity instead of torchlight. The sound of voices came with it, the murmur of half a dozen lazy conversations. Conti seemed to brace himself and stepped across the narrow threshold.

The voices ebbed slightly at their entrance, faces turning to see who was there, and Conti managed a polite smile. Lizzy copied him, hanging back uneasily by the door. Most of the people in the room were wearing herb-dyed homespun, dresses and tunics and trousers that looked a little like earth-hippie clothes, but there were a few people in street clothes, too. They weren't unfriendly, but the place wasn't welcoming, either. It was too alien even under the ordinary electric lights, with its central hearth and no bar or serving wenches anywhere in sight, nothing like the Faires and Manors that were all she knew of the period. Conti glanced around as though he was looking for something, and a stocky, round-figured woman seemed to materialized out of the shadows at his elbow. She was wearing the same shapeless dress as all the other women, but with a pair of huge gold pins fastening the straps of an equally shapeless jumper.

"Is William here?" Conti asked, and the woman's frown deepened.

"He's here," she said, drawing the words out, and Lizzy heard the sound of a siren from somewhere in the nearby streets.

"I'd like—I need to talk to him," Conti said.

"Russ?" The voice was muted, a practiced half bellow that sounded as though it had been honed by years of shouting over storms and fighting. "By the Thunderer and his goats, I never thought I'd see you again."

Conti wasn't a particularly small man, but he had to look up to meet the big man's eyes, very blue in their web of wrinkles. Conti submitted to the big man's embrace, the big man's belly like a small barrel between them, and from the look on his face, the handclasp was a test of strength.

"What in the name of all the gods brings you here?" the big man—he had to be Silent William, though the name seemed particularly inappropriate—demanded. "I heard you'd dropped out—dropped off the face of the invisible, and maybe more."

"I gave up the invisible," Conti answered. The siren sounded again, closer this time, and another answered it. Lizzy edged away from the door again, wondering if they'd found the car already.

William's mobile face sobered abruptly. "Understandable. What you did—it's not forgotten."

"Don't speak too soon," Conti said.

Lizzy heard the distant thump of a helicopter. William looked up as it came rapidly closer, peering past the smoke-stained beams.

Following his gaze, Lizzy saw a gap in the roof directly over the central hearth. "That for you?"

Conti nodded. "I'm in trouble, William—we're in trouble, me and my friend. This was the only place left to run."

A spotlight swept the street, flashed once through the smoke hole and on into the compound, then swung back to cover the street. The sirens—there were at least three of them—were definitely closer. William looked from Conti to the others and back again, teeth showing in an enormous grin. "You're family, Russ, you always were. Come on in the back room, all of you, and we can talk."

At least one of the sirens had stopped, not a good sign at all from the look on Vara's face, and Lizzy followed the big man toward a door that stood all but invisible in the sidewall.

"Come on," William said again, and waved them through. He shut the door behind them and slid home an iron bolt as thick as his index finger. This was obviously William's private workroom, complete with desk and rough-hewn table piled with papers, and shuttered windows that gave onto the street. There was a second door in the wall beside the kitchen, and William jerked it open, revealing a white-tiled corridor that ended in an open-platform lift.

"That's a service tunnel?" Lizzy said, doubtfully, and William brushed past her.

"Not that way. Quick, help me with the fireplace."

Lizzy stared, not understanding, and William made an impatient noise, stooped to the edge of the hearth. "Help me, some of you, this thing's heavy."

He lifted as he spoke, and Lizzy saw a crack widen at the edge of the raised bricks. Lizzy crouched to help, and a second later Conti and Vara had joined them, levering up the mass of stone to reveal a dirt-floored hole easily tall enough for a man to stand upright. Several men, Lizzy thought, light-headed with fear and exertion, deep enough and wide enough to hide all of us.

"The ladder's there," William said, and nodded to the log basket. Keyz stooped, found it instantly, a rolled bundle of rope and wood, and hooked it without being told over the brackets set into the edge of the hole.

"In you get," William said. The stone was suddenly lighter in

Lizzy's grasp as a counterweight engaged. "I'll tell them you went out the back, let them chase themselves through the service tunnels."

"What about all those other people out there?" Vara asked, and crouched beside the ladder. "What are they going to say?"

William smiled. "Only my household knows about this hidey-hole, and they say what I tell them to."

"Not everybody out there's your family," Lizzy said, and William gave her an unfriendly stare.

"And anyone who isn't, all they know is you went in here with me. Do it or don't, but you don't have much time left to make this work."

"Right," Vara said, and swung herself down into the hole. "Come on, Keyz."

He followed, and Lizzy lowered herself reluctantly after him. Conti lowered the gear bags to her, and she caught them, let them slither down to Vara and the boy. The space was smaller than it had looked from above, and the bags crowded it; it was only big enough for them to sit if they didn't mind tangling legs. Conti hesitated at the top of the ladder.

"William—"

"Later," the big man said, firmly, and Conti let himself down the rest of the way. William lowered the slab until the counterweight released, and the stone slammed down, cutting off the light. Lizzy caught her breath, an old irrational panic flooding through her, and reached behind her until her fingers touched the wall. She flattened herself against, telling herself there was plenty of air, plenty of room, felt her heart racing anyway, her body with a mind of its own. There was a rustling sound, and finally a weak glow diffused into the room. Vara held up a glowstick the size of her little finger, turned slowly so that she could see their faces.

"Is everybody OK?"

"Yes," Keyz said, and Conti nodded.

"Lizzy?" Vara swung the light, catching the younger woman in its pale gleam. She scowled, folding her arms tight across her chest because she was sure her hands were shaking.

"I'm fine."

"You sure?" Vara kept the light on her, and Lizzy suppressed a curse.

"Yeah, positive." She glared at Conti, wishing Vara would turn the light away. "Look, is this guy really going to help us?"

"He gave his word," Conti answered.

"Shut up," Vara hissed. "Both of you."

Footsteps sounded overhead, dulled but distinct, and Lizzy looked up in spite of herself. Vara cupped her hand over the glow-stick, then tucked it under the edge of her jacket, and they dropped back into darkness. Lizzy tilted her head to one side, all but blind, heard first a mumble overhead, and then William's distinctive voice.

"—left them here, I tell you."

Another indistinct mutter, a question, this time, from the tone, and William's answer came through clearly. "That's the service area. There's a dumbwaiter and a tunnel instead of a loading dock."

"Where does it lead?" This time, the lighter voice was perfectly distinct, and Lizzy guessed the man was standing almost on top of the trapdoor.

"I told you, to the service tunnels," William answered.

"Where do they go?"

"Across the street," William said, and Lizzy imagined him waving his arms in vague direction. "We share access with the stores on the other side. I think the dock's behind Santana's."

"Get on it," the other voice said, and faded as he moved away from the trapdoor. Lizzy cocked her head again, tracking the footsteps—some, maybe most of them moving toward the tunnel, and the rest back toward the door—and then a door slammed. In the darkness, someone—Keyz? Lizzy thought—stirred, and Vara lifted her hand, letting just a little more light seep into the chamber.

"Wait." Her voice was barely a whisper, just a breath of sound. Lizzy flattened her back against the wall—not the dirt it appeared, or at least dirt covered with some kind of polymer, made herself focus on that touch so that she wouldn't have to think about how small the room was, how deep underground. It was funny, she thought, she'd spent the last eight years in Crystal City, and for part of that she'd rarely left CC Underground, but that had been different, bright lights and space, a refuge rather than a trap. And this was a refuge, too, she told herself, but the words rang hollow.

"You asked if we could trust him," Conti said, suddenly. He kept his voice down, only a hair stronger than Vara's whisper, but the passion was unmistakable. "William will keep his word. That's part of the point of this community—here a man, or a woman, is only as good as their given word, and William would never betray that. If he says we count as household, then the rest of the community will protect us as though we're part of the clan. I wouldn't have brought you here if I didn't think that—if I didn't know it."

"I believe you," Lizzy answered.

"The police don't understand what they're dealing with here," Conti went on, as if she hadn't spoken. "They never have, not really. They'll think what everybody does, that nobody takes this kind of risk for a stranger, they'll search the service tunnels before they'll even think of searching the compound—if they even get that far. We'll be safe here."

"We believe you," Vara said, soothingly, and Conti dipped his head.

"Sorry."

Lizzy pressed her shoulders harder against the wall, wondering how long they'd been there. Probably not very long, maybe, ten, fifteen minutes at the outside, but she could feel her heart racing, wished she could get her breathing under control. There had to be air coming in—first, William wouldn't have built the place if it was going to suffocate anybody he stashed there, and second, they'd probably already have noticed if air was going to be a problem—but she kept looking up as though she could find the invisible vents. Besides, suppose William hadn't planned on keeping them there for very long—suppose he'd just meant people to hide there for a few minutes—hell, suppose he'd never really meant anyone to hide there at all, and hadn't ever thought about air. It would have been better to take their chances in the service tunnels, she thought, and shook her head. That was just stupid—maybe the lack of oxygen was starting to get to her. She looked up longingly toward the trapdoor, hidden in the shadows above her head. At least they had some light, even if the little sticks were only good for an hour or so. And at least they'd have some idea how long they'd been here once it went out, she thought, and suppressed a laugh that had too much of hysteria in it.

Footsteps sounded overhead again, and she reached for the ladder, hand closing tight over the heavy ropes. If it was William, if it was only William, then the trapdoor would open, and they could all climb up into the light. . . . The footsteps stopped, and she held her breath, willing the trap to open. Out of the corner of her eye, she could see Vara listening, too, equally intent, shading the little light with one hand. Then the footsteps sounded again, moving away, and she swore under her breath, fighting down another surge of fear. Maybe William had decided they were too hot, that it was too dangerous to help them, maybe he was just going to leave them trapped, forget they'd ever been there. The covenanted communities genuinely had their own laws, managed their own affairs; the police weren't supposed to interfere except in certain rare cases. *Russ says this guy's all right,* she told herself, firmly. *You don't have to worry about that.*

Something touched her face, a crumb of dust or soot drifting down from the underside of the hearth, and she jumped, brushing at it. The ladder jerked, slapping against the dirt wall, and she steadied it, making a face.

"Careful," Vara whispered. "Sit down, Lizzy, it may be a while."

She sat herself, still shielding the light, so that it sank like water draining, barely reaching Lizzy's waist. Conti copied her, stiffly, balancing himself between two bags, and Lizzy made herself let go of the ladder. The dark closed in on her, enclosing her, so that all she could see were vague shapes of the people crouched at her feet. If she sat, she could be in that light, too, but the walls would be even taller, the dirt higher over her head. *It's not dirt*, she told herself, and reached back to touch the wall, feeling the polymer cool and smooth under her palm. *It's sealed, it can't collapse. You were deeper underground in Crystal City*. She didn't quite believe it, but made herself bend first one knee and then the other, lowering herself to the ground. The floor was polymer, too, smooth and slightly rubbery, and she spread her hands against it, trying to convince herself that nothing was going to collapse. There would be air, plenty of air, and nothing was going to fall on her. She reached for the ladder again, wrapped her fingers around the rope. If the worst happened, if the light went, at least she'd know where the ladder was, where to get out. She had a brief, too-vivid image of her skeletal body, bony fingers still tangled in the rope, shook it away with a gasp.

The light was starting to fade, she noticed, tried to tell herself it was just the way Vara was holding the little stick. The other woman was frowning, though, and that hope died. She closed her eyes, searching her memory for some setting, some image, that would distract her, but she couldn't seem to concentrate. She was too aware of the light fading, imagined she could see it fail even with her eyes closed, and opened them with a gasp to find that it had dimmed even further. Vara shook the stick; it flared, but began to fade almost at once.

"Do you have another one?" she asked, and Vara shook her head.

"I was lucky to have this one."

And then, miraculously, there was the sound of stone grating on stone, and light poured in as the trap lifted. Lizzy shot to her feet, still gripping the ladder, and saw the big man grinning down at them.

"All gone," he said, in what passed for a quiet voice. "You can come up now."

Lizzy didn't wait for a second invitation, pulled herself up the ladder and out onto the cold hearth.

"Don't like tight spaces, eh?" William asked, and Lizzy saw that there were two more men from the community with him. They were both young, both disapproving, and Lizzy drew herself up, forcing calm.

"Not particularly," she said, and turned to help Keyz, caught his hand as he reached the top of the ladder and steadied him onto the hearth. Vara called her name then, and she turned to help lever the first bag of gear up into the light.

"It's all taken care of," William said, as Lizzy reached for the next bag. "They think you got out through the service tunnels."

"Did they search the community buildings?" Vara asked, and dragged herself awkwardly up onto the hearth.

William nodded. "Quick but thorough, if I do say so. They didn't find anything—since, of course, there wasn't anything to find."

"Will they be back?" Keyz asked, and William looked at Vara.

"I think the lady's in a better position to answer that than I am—am I right?"

Vara nodded. "Yeah, I'm a cop. It depends on how seriously they take the idea we went out through the tunnels. But I think we're safe for now."

"You're safe for as long as you stay here," William cried. "The Jarl has spoken. You're under his protection."

But how much good does that do against local cops? Lizzy wondered. The covenanted communities were their own jurisdictions, independent townships with their own rules and laws, although she wasn't sure how that applied to nonmembers, but from the look on Vara's face, they should be able to hide here after all.

"Thank you," Conti said, sounding out of breath from his climb up the ladder. "And we thank the Jarl, too."

"You'll have your own chance to do that," William answered. "He wants to talk to you."

"Ah." Conti's mouth twisted into a rueful smile, and William burst into laughter.

"No, no, it's not so bad. But the Jarl wants to hear the story for himself, and offer what aid we can. He hasn't forgotten either, Russ, don't worry."

"That wasn't—" Conti stopped, shook his head. "Who's Jarl now?"

"Ingvar Boneless."

Lizzy blinked at the name, and Conti laughed, sounding suddenly years younger. "Just the man I'd like to see dealing with all this."

"Exactly so," William agreed. "You'll want to talk to him." He beckoned to the younger men behind him, who held out heavy capes. "Put these on, and we'll take you to the Hall."

Lizzy took one, gingerly, grateful that it smelled only of wool and soap, and slung it awkwardly around her shoulders. Keyz did the same, and she saw his face contort as he suppressed a giggle. They did look pretty silly, she admitted, not at all like the hafeners, who wore the ungainly garments as though they were born to them—or at least, she told herself, as though they wore them every day.

"Thank you," Conti said again, and Vara echoed him.

Outside the tavern, the compound itself was unlit except for a handful of candles and lanterns that showed at the windows of the low-slung buildings. One of the young men had a lantern, too, and Lizzy followed close, trying to keep in the circle of faint light. The cape was warm against the evening chill, but the folds were bulky, and it took concentration to keep from tripping over the heavy length of it.

The Hall was at the center of the compound, the largest of the low-slung buildings, its heavy roof finished in timbers carved with animal heads. There were more carved heads topping the doorposts, and lean bodies coiled around their lengths; in the flickering lamp-light, it seemed as though the twining bodies breathed and shifted. The Hall itself was crowded, men and women and the occasional older child clustered around a long fire pit, and Lizzy saw Conti frown.

"A lot of people up," he said, and William glanced over his shoulder, showing teeth.

"The police woke them. I told you, they searched the village."

Was this the entire membership? Lizzy wondered. It was hard to count in the shifting light, and hard to keep track of who she'd already counted, but she thought there were at least thirty-five adults present.

"Lord Jarl!" William called. "I've brought our guests."

"Thank you."

The crowd parted, as well trained as extras in a film, and for the first time Lizzy saw the man in the carved chair. He was smaller than William—smaller than most of the men by half a head—and lightly built, his long grey hair held back by a band of metal that was not quite a crown. Lizzy knew she was staring, tried to look politely away, and Keyz elbowed her.

"I thought these guys picked their kings by combat. That guy couldn't beat anybody."

"Quiet," Vara said.

"Gentlemen," the Jarl said. "And ladies. I bid you welcome to Stormhafen. Russ is known to us these many years, and more than welcome; these others are welcome, too, in his name. As we've all seen tonight, they are sought by the mundane police—so much so that the police were willing to violate our covenant in order to search for them. For that reason, and for the friendship we've had for Russ, I offer them the freedom of the community, and its sanctuary. By my order, no one may speak of their presence, or in any way betray that we have seen them. I charge you all to relay that word to anyone who isn't here, and to obey it utterly."

There was a rumble of response, and a ripple of bows and curt-sies. Lizzy knew her mouth was open, closed it firmly.

"In the meantime," the Jarl went on, "return to your beds. If the police return, the guards will give us warning."

"Lord Jarl!"

Lizzy couldn't see who had spoken, but then a bearded man in a red tunic and baggy trousers stepped free of the crowd.

"Sturla," the Jarl said, and the bearded man dipped his head.

"Lord Jarl, the town has violated the covenant in this. Will we sue?"

"That's a possibility," the Jarl answered, "but I think the wiser course would be to wait for daylight and have a word or two with the sheriff."

"They've no right to come in here." That was a woman's voice, but Lizzy couldn't spot the speaker.

The Jarl lifted his hands. "Gentles, let's leave it 'til morning. We can't make any intelligent decisions tonight."

There was another murmur at that, not all agreeing, but the peo-ple on the fringes of the group began to move away. The Jarl pushed himself up out of his chair.

"William, bring our guests to my chambers."

The big man bowed. "As the Jarl commands."

Lizzy followed him down the length of the hall, passing hafeners in various states of undress, all with heavy cloaks thrown on against the chill. From a distance, she guessed she and the others could pass for one of them, and hoped it wouldn't come to that. It was all very well for the Jarl to give orders that nobody was to say anything about them, but she'd never yet been part of a group that didn't have one member who was willing to sell out. They stopped in front of another door covered with carvings of intertwined animals, and William set his hand on the latch.

"Wait here," he said, and the door closed behind him.

Lizzy wrapped the cloak tighter around her shoulders—it was genuinely cold in the hall, as though the central fire pit was the only heat—and realized she was standing next to Conti. The man looked tired, but less afraid than before, and Lizzy hoped he was right.

"Russ."

"Hm?" Conti blinked, then focused. "What?"

"Ingvar Boneless?"

Conti grinned. "He's a lawyer."

"Oh."

The door opened again, cutting off any further comment—and probably just as well, Lizzy thought, stepping into new warmth. Anything she could have said would just have been anticlimactic.

This room was much smaller than the others, and smelled of pine smoke. Ingvar Boneless—Ingvar Boneless, *Esquire*, Lizzy thought, and suppressed a giggle—was sitting at a worn table, his coronet discarded on top of a pile of papers. Another man—no, a woman in man's clothes, Lizzy realized, and wondered which she was supposed to notice—stood at his shoulders, and William perched uncomfortably on a too-small stool. There were more papers under his elbow, standard computer printouts, just like the ones under the Jarl's crown.

"Have a seat," the Jarl said, and waved vaguely toward a line of stools standing empty against the far wall. "This sounds like a real mess, Russ."

"It's exactly that," Conti answered. "I wouldn't have gotten you involved, Ingvar, if I'd had any other choice."

"We've been hearing a lot of jazz," the woman in drag said.

The Jarl lifted an eyebrow. "This is Sigurd Longlegs," he said. "My shield and sword."

Conti managed something like a bow. "Honored."

"As am I." Longlegs gave a jerky nod. "You're a friend of the household, no one questions that, but I'm concerned about the risk." She looked at the Jarl as she spoke, and he dipped his head.

"Sigurd is usually right about things like this. What the hell is going on?"

"You don't want the details," Conti said, and the Jarl grinned.

"No, I don't. Just the high points, please."

Conti spread his hands. "I've come into this late, but I know Chessie—that's Chessie Vara—and I've known Tin Lizzy for years. I trust them completely."

Lizzy blinked once, feeling faintly ashamed. That was the last thing she had expected to hear from Conti, especially after the way she'd been hassling him.

"They're trying to help Keyz here—what is your real name?"

"Seth. Seth Halford." Keyz sounded definitely subdued.

"They're trying to help Keyz, who managed to get hold of a program that I worked on that belonged to RCD Studios." Conti stopped as the Jarl held up his hand.

"Don't tell me there was a theft involved."

"I won't," Conti answered promptly, and the Jarl gave a weary grin.

"Go on."

"Since then," Vara said, "RCD has been trying to arrest Keyz—Seth—and has threatened to fire his parents if they don't give him up. Besides putting Seth in jail, I mean. They've put a lot more time and effort into this than would make any sense unless this program is a hell of a lot more important than they say it is."

The Jarl made a face. "Have you considered going to the police—a different jurisdiction, of course?"

"I tried," Lizzy said, before she could stop herself. "That was why I took Keyz to Chessie, I thought she could help us. Only her superiors decided to honor the warrants after all."

"They were private warrants," Vara said.

"You're a police officer," the Jarl said, and she nodded.

"That's right."

"And you went along with this?"

Vara took a deep breath. "Sir, I was convinced that unless I took this kid physically out of town, RCD was going to lose him so well that there wouldn't be any point in appeals or protests. Not to mention the trouble Lizzy was in."

"Which I don't need to know about in detail," the Jarl said. He leaned back in his chair, steepling his fingers. "If that's true—and I believe you, ladies—then I don't know how much help I can be."

"There's a chance that someone in the industry can help us," Conti said. "Someone who knows something about the program, and why it's so important."

"Do you mean to tell me you don't know what it is?" the Jarl asked, and Conti shook his head.

"I'm not telling you any such thing. What I am saying is that I know who can help us, I just need time to get in touch with him."

"That shouldn't be a problem." The Jarl leaned forward again, setting his elbows on the table. "We maintain a virtual village as well as the community here, and we've got a pretty heavy system to run it all."

"The graphics are intense," Longlegs said.

"And we maintain full security. Gold Standard." A flicker of something, almost pain, crossed his face, and he managed a smile. "You see, we learned something from our tragedy."

Conti dipped his head again. "If we could use your system—"

"Of course," the Jarl said. "But not, I think, tonight."

"And not tomorrow, either," Longlegs said. "They'll be monitoring for at least forty-eight hours. Especially if they're being as paranoid as you say."

"So what do we do?" Lizzy asked, and looked at Conti. "Do you know how to contact him?"

Conti nodded. "That," he said, with a tired smile, "will be the easy part."

And the hard part will be convincing him that we're worth the risk. Lizzy nodded in her turn, then hesitated, looking back at the Jarl. "Sir, may I ask a question?"

The Jarl spread his hands. "Ask, lady."

"How—I thought you people didn't do modern technology. Not that I'm not grateful, but—" She made a face as William laughed. "Sorry. None of my business."

"Technology has its place," Ingvar Boneless said. "We respect and honor the past, but we know we can't completely re-create it, nor do we want to do so. The goal of our household, our community, is to live with honor in this world, and to do so we've surrounded ourselves with the trappings of this community, its symbols of honor and purpose, to remind ourselves and to make it easier to keep our faith. But we can't give up everything of the present, neither the Nets nor, for example, modern medicine, not if we're to honor ourselves by taking proper care of our families and our children. We're creating a should-have-been, not what actually was." He paused, the lamplight gleaming on his grey hair. "Does that answer your question?"

Lizzy dipped her head, copying Conti, for the moment wholly believing in the gesture. "Yes, sir."

"I thought you'd understand," the Jarl said, unsmiling. "You've kept faith yourself, and in the most difficult times."

Lizzy blinked. *I suppose we have*, she thought, *though some of it was just I couldn't think of anything else to do. Well, I could always have turned him in, but that wouldn't have been right—which I guess is what he means. I never thought of it that way.*

"In the meantime," the Jarl said again, "William, take them to a guesthouse, make them comfortable, and tomorrow we'll see how it looks for access."

"Thank you, Ingvar," Conti said. "Any debt between us is surely paid. I probably owe you now."

The Jarl shook his head. "What we owed you—that debt is not yet paid. But even when it is, I hope you'll remember you're still a friend."

Conti closed his eyes, but not before Lizzy thought she saw the starting tears.

William pushed himself stiffly to his feet. "Come on," he said. "Let's get you settled."

Lizzy followed him from the room back into the cold shadows of the hall, drawing the cloak around herself in a gesture that was already starting to feel normal. *Maybe this will work,* she thought, *maybe they will be able to hide us long enough for Russ to talk to Shida, and maybe we'll get out of this after all.*

fifteen

The town was depressing even for the rust belt, Hallac thought, leaning against the window frame of the room opposite the interrogation room. It was probably an interrogation room itself, though it lacked the amenities of the other, had neither a one-way mirror or the full recording suite, but the Peterburg police had offered it to them as a break room. And maybe it wasn't an interrogation room, Hallac thought, since it had a window. The only escape would be suicide, through the glass and a straight drop of five stories to the employee parking lot, but in this place, you'd have to think about it. He tapped the glass, heard the familiar clunk of plastic. Probably it was safe enough, but still, it wasn't a risk he'd like to take. There were probably a few people whose only remaining pleasure was to dent an officer's car.

In the middle distance, he could see the dark outline of the Hammond Industries sign, black against the distant sea of neon that marked the tourist malls. A steady line of cars, white lights paralleled by red, ran between the malls and the resort complex just outside the downtown. They were staying there themselves, crammed into a single suite because the end-of-summer shopping season was just beginning, and he'd been all too aware of the contempt of the girl on the front desk. He hoped she didn't try that attitude with Gerretty when he arrived; she didn't deserve to be fired, not after what he'd seen of the tourists. Not that they were evil, just thoughtless, here for the bargains, and wanting a bargain in everything. On the way into town, they'd passed a straggle of galleries offering local crafts and the occasional fine-art piece, and he felt sorry for the owners, at the mercy of the bargain-hunters' whims. Better to be selling "antiques"—at least there you could have the satisfaction of cheating the customers.

The door opened, and he turned to see King close it again behind her. She held out a box of coffee, and he took it gratefully.

"Any progress?"

King shook her head. "Not a thing. And frankly I don't think we're going to get anywhere."

Hallac nodded morose agreement. Shirley Conti was not the kind of person who could be intimidated, at least not easily. She'd asked for her phone call, and kept asking until she got it—and the local cops obviously knew and liked her, so there'd been no excuse for putting her off—then called her union and said nothing more until their lawyer arrived. Well, nothing except thanks for the coffee, Hallac amended, and allowed himself a wry smile. You couldn't fault the woman's manners. "Nothing in the tunnels, then?"

"Nope." King sighed. "You don't think they got into the compound, do you? I mean, Conti did know that big guy, the bartender."

"Silent William," Hallac said. "Born Harris Batchelder." *Ten years a Navy SEAL, too, with half a dozen police actions. European and Asian, to his credit: you had to wonder what made a guy like that retreat into the nonreality of a covenanted community.* He tipped his head to the side, putting aside that question, made himself concentrate on the more important one. The cars streamed past in the distance, a river of light. "I doubt it," he said at last. "First, we searched the place. They weren't there. Second, I don't think Conti could still get that kind of support from them. It was his server DiAngelo was using to get at the community members."

"Seemed to me that William was still fond of him," King said.

"He's only the outside liaison," Hallac answered. "Not the— whatever their leader's called."

"Fucking weird," King muttered, and Hallac sighed, not wanting to admit he agreed.

"What about the trailer?"

"They're still working on it, Galen says." King shook her head. "Did you notice anything funny about that place?"

"You mean besides there being no computers in a place that belongs to a famous expert?" In the distance, some of the lights had stopped, had been stopped for a while, and now a series of emergency lights, blue flashers and then red, were forcing their way up alongside the line of light.

"That struck me as kind of odd, yeah," King answered, with

irony. "According to the neighbors, they're living on her salary, he just works part-time at some local cafe.

"From what Cady said, he could make a lot more than any construction jockey," King said. "Even one with seniority."

King nodded. "But he doesn't. And she doesn't complain."

"So?" Hallac's voice was mild.

King shrugged. "So nothing. Except maybe we can push her a little. She does a lot of caretaking with him."

Hallac nodded. "It's a thought. That lawyer of hers won't like it."

"So we have to be subtle," King said.

Subtlety was not her strong point, and Hallac suppressed a sigh. "Let's see what turns up at the trailer first."

"You're the boss," King said, with suspicious equanimity, and Hallac looked at her.

"I mean it, Jae."

"I'm listening."

"Do that." Hallac looked out the window again, seeing the flashing lights now clustered, the traffic moving slowly around them, like water through a partially blocked tube. "All right. Back to work."

King made a sweeping bow, gesturing for him to pass ahead of her. Hallac ignored it and crossed the broad hall to the other interrogation room. Shirley Conti looked up at his approach, her face carefully expressionless, but he thought there was a flicker of concern in her eyes. The lawyer, sharp-eyed and stocky, impeccably suited in spite of being called out at ten o'clock at night, turned away from the one-way mirror.

"Mr. Hallac. I have to ask you again if you're charging my client."

She had the hint of a Hispanic accent, to match her brown skin and dark hair. Hallac shook his head. "There's been no decision, Ms. Rubeo. We still have a number of questions we need to ask Ms. Conti."

"You should be asking those questions of her husband," Rubeo answered. "My client has no knowledge of any of these issues."

"We'd be happy to talk to her husband instead," Hallac answered. "And your client is in a position to help us find him."

"She is not," Rubeo said. "As we've told you more than once, she does not know what her husband planned to do after he left their house, and—obviously—she's had no chance to hear from him since."

Hallac stared at the woman without answering. At her shoulder, Shirley Conti sat quietly, hands folded on the tabletop, a crumpled coffee box a little to their left. She had big hands, Hallac noted, absently, big hands and big wrists to match her rawboned frame, but then, you'd need both size and strength to handle the big construction machines. Her expression was calm, even a little withdrawn, and for an instant he wondered if she really was as worried as he hoped. But she had to be, he told himself. She wasn't stupid; she knew what was at stake. She would be worried, even if she didn't dare admit it. He watched her for a moment longer, letting the silence carry his skepticism, saw her eyes slide away, focusing again on the crushed box.

"Excuse me, John."

Hallac turned, knowing his team wouldn't interrupt him with irrelevancies, and lifted his eyebrows to see Lapenna peering in through the half-open door.

"Can I talk to you for a minute?"

Hallac nodded, looked over his shoulder at the lawyer. "Excuse me. We'll be back."

Rubeo inclined her head, unspeaking, and Hallac followed his partner across the hall and into the break room.

"What's up?" He didn't have to ask if it was good.

"Cady's still checking some things," Lapenna said, "but we thought you should see this."

He held out a faded slip of paper, and Hallac took it, blinked twice at the familiar logo. It was a pay stub from RCD, in Conti's name—but old, more than ten years old at least, and maybe more, if he was misreading the fuzzy date stamp. "So he worked for us," he said, slowly. "So what?"

"He worked in R&D," Lapenna answered. "In fact, he worked for Paul Orfanos."

"So he knows the program," Hallac said. He could feel a cold dread settling over him. Keyz was taking—had taken—the program to the one person who could tell them exactly what it did, and why it was worth more than he was authorized to spend on its recovery.

"Hell, he wrote the program," Lapenna said.

"But he's off-line," Hallac said, and knew he was clutching at straws. "He wouldn't know where to go." *But Lizzy would: and with the maker to tell her exactly what she had, she would know just where to go, what to do; she would have more options than he would ever be able to track—And why the hell didn't Gerretty mention that one of the authors was still alive, back when this whole thing started? If he'd told me Conti was one of the makers, I'd've started looking for him then, got all the warrants I needed for the trace, not had to waste time now. Then the minute his name turned up—back in Crystal City, for Christ's sake, that was the first time someone mentioned Russ Conti—I could've had him staked out. I could have had them.*

Lapenna was shaking his head. "There's more."

"Great," Hallac said, savagely, and Lapenna shook his head again.

"It's Shida, boss, that's the connection. Vara's mother took care of Shida, Conti knew Shida—Cady's checking it out, but it looks like they're planning to sell this thing to him."

"Shida," Hallac repeated. He let his head fall back, rotating his skull on his shoulders, working out the tension. Shida had plenty of connections himself, throughout the industry; Orpha-Toto would be just the thing to persuade another studio to employ him, and the hell with RCD's contracts. Considered dispassionately, it wasn't a bad idea of Lizzy's, either: Shida would have cause to be grateful, plus there was a personal connection to keep him honest. It was probably safer under the circumstances to deal with Shida, even if they might make more money dealing directly with another studio. "Where is Shida these days?"

"The Isle Rialto," Lapenna answered promptly, and Hallac guessed he'd already looked it up. "Cady's checking some stuff, but this looks like the best lead we've had yet."

Hallac nodded, and his smoke buzzed. He made a face, fished it out of his pocket, sliding back the cover to activate the pure communications mode.

"Gerretty's here. Just in the parking lot." It was King, speaking without preamble, and she cut the connection before he could ask any questions.

"Goddammit—" He broke off, shook his head again. "Gerretty's here. We'd better get back in there."

They were there ahead of Gerretty, but not by much. Hallac just had time to tell one of the local cadets to clear away the coffee boxes and to inform Conti's lawyer that one of the owners of the missing property wanted to speak to her client.

Rubeo frowned. "I'm not really sure that's appropriate."

Before she could go any further, the door of the interrogation room slammed open, and Gerretty shoved his way into the room, towing his own lawyer and a stressed-looking Corbitt in his wake. Hallac frowned at her, annoyed that she'd been dragged off the most promising lead they'd had in days, and she mimed apology and powerlessness. He felt his frown deepen—it wasn't Corbitt's job to be dancing to Gerretty's wishes—and smoothed his expression as Gerretty turned on him.

"So. She is—"

"Shirley Conti. Wife of Russ Conti, who has apparently gone into hiding with Halford, Rhea, and Vara."

"There's no reason to assume that," Rubeo said, sharply. "For all we know, Mr. Conti could have been coerced into joining them."

"Shut up," Gerretty said, swiveling his heavy head to look once at her, then looked back at Hallac. He moved like a buffalo, the other man thought, irrelevantly, and braced himself to meet the charge. "Does she know anything?"

"She says not." Hallac kept his voice neutral, not wanting to trigger Gerretty's temper, but the bigger man snorted anyway.

"Of course she says not. I'm asking you what you think. And you—" He glared at Rubeo again. "Keep quiet."

Out of the corner of his eye, Hallac saw the lawyer lift an eyebrow, but she was smart enough to let Gerretty hang himself if he wanted to. Shirley Conti sat very still, her hands still folded on the tabletop, only the pallor of her knuckles, the fingers locked against each other, to betray her tension.

"Well?" Gerretty demanded, and Hallac took a careful breath.

"I think she knows what they were planning, at least in general terms. She certainly knew both Rhea and Vara before this, if only as acquaintances of Mr. Conti's. Anything more specific, no, I don't think she knows."

"Right."

Gerretty turned to face Conti. She lifted her eyes to meet his glare, but nothing else moved in her frozen face.

"You. Listen to me. I'm sick of playing games with you people, so I'm only going to say this once. Tell me what you know—what they said, what they were planning, anything you know—and I won't prosecute you for conspiracy."

Rubeo drew herself up to her full height. "I beg your pardon, Mr.—Gerretty?—but you have neither the authority nor any legal basis to make such a claim."

"And who are you?" Gerretty's eyes narrowed.

"Ms. Conti's lawyer—" Rubeo began, and the big man cut her off.

"Unlikely. You're her union's lawyer, and that's a different matter."

"My job is to represent Ms. Conti's interests," Rubeo said.

"Her best interest is to cooperate with me," Gerretty said. "I mean what I say. Unless I get full cooperation, right now, I will prosecute to the full extent of the law. Ms. Conti is part of this criminal conspiracy, and I can make that stick."

"Pure jazz," Rubeo said.

"And the jazz is my business," Gerretty said. "I do this every day, for bigger and better than you. You think I can't make this happen?"

"The union will stand behind Ms. Conti," Rubeo said.

"Hah." Gerretty showed teeth in something like a grin. "The hell they will. She's more trouble than any union has been willing to take in decades—and you'd better believe that, Ms. Conti. They'll pull you, or make a deal. They can't afford to do anything else."

"My job," Rubeo said, stubbornly, "my contract, is to protect Ms. Conti's interests—"

"And if the union is stupid enough to back you," Gerretty went on, as if she hadn't spoken, "I will personally see that they pay dearly for it. There's plenty of jazz about the unions, some of it has to be true."

Rubeo's eyebrows rose at that, and Hallac grimaced. Gerretty was going way too far with this one. This wasn't the right union, to begin with, though the right jazz would smear all of them. And even if most of the studios would love an excuse to break the union hold on certain jobs, there was no guarantee that the other heads would back him. Except they probably would, if the jazz were good enough, and Rubeo's face reflected that knowledge. Conti still sat frozen, her pale eyes not moving from the men in front of her.

"Sir," Hallac said, and Gerretty swung to face him.

"Well?"

"We have another lead. It may not be necessary to pursue this matter."

They all heard, very clearly, Conti's sudden intake of breath, expression for the first time coming into her face, and Gerretty's smile widened.

"Talk to me."

Hallac held out the pay stub. "Apparently Mr. Conti once worked for RCD, as an associate in R&D."

"Orfanos," Gerretty said, and Hallac nodded.

"And he was friends with Shida."

"That son of a bitch. I didn't think he had it in him. She always had the balls, not him."

Well, I suppose that explains why he didn't tell me about Conti, Hallac thought. *I wish to hell he had.*

Gerretty turned back to the table. "Lawyer, you'd be smart to advise your client to answer my questions. Is it Shida? Are they going to the Isle Rialto?"

Conti's eyes strayed to her lawyer. "Do I have to answer?"

Rubeo hesitated, and Hallac could almost read her thoughts. On the one hand, she needed to protect her client, but on the other, Gerretty was right, he did have the power to make life extremely difficult not just for Conti, but for the union that was trying to defend her. "Yes," she said slowly, and Conti's mouth tightened.

"Well?" Gerretty asked.

"They mentioned Shida," Conti said, reluctantly.

Gerretty snorted. "And?"

"I don't know. They didn't say anything else."

Gerretty's eyes narrowed, and Hallac said, "I don't know that it matters, sir. We can assume that they're in touch with Shida, or Shida's in touch with them, and that means we can guess where they're headed."

"Go on."

Some of the anger had faded from Gerretty's eyes—he turned it on and off, the explosive temper, Hallac thought, but it was still real and dangerous. "If Shida is involved in this, then I think we should let them contact him. Let them make their deal. And then we can arrest Shida as well."

Gerretty's head lifted, and for a second Hallac thought he would paw the ground. "That's only good if it works. If you fuck up, we lose—" He stopped, remembering Conti. "Everything."

Hallac nodded, dry-mouthed. "That's the risk, yes. Against the possibility of removing a major thorn from the studio's side."

"You don't need to tell me that." Gerretty stopped, took a deep breath. "All right, let's discuss it. Elsewhere. How long can you hold her?"

Hallac shrugged. "We can't really charge her—"

"Find a way," Gerretty ordered. "I want her out of circulation until this is over."

"Sir," Hallac began, and Gerretty shook his head again.

"Do it." He shoved through the door without waiting for an answer, his lawyer scrambling to keep up.

There was a heartbeat's silence after the door closed—not quite slamming, the mechanism was too good for that, but harder than it should—and then Rubeo took a slow breath.

"You can't do it. You have no cause, and there are no charges you can file."

"You've got guts," Hallac said. "I'll give you that." He rubbed his neck, suddenly aware of his own tiredness, wished he could spend an hour in a hot tub, or, failing that, just take the time to stretch. "And, frankly, I don't want to hassle your client when her husband's already in some serious trouble. I'll make a deal."

"Such as?" Rubeo's voice was wary.

"Permit the local police to hold Ms. Conti in protective custody—that's a term that can cut several ways, and it's pretty comfortable—for the next seventy-two to a hundred and twenty hours. That way, Mr. Gerretty gets what he wants, and your client is also protected from any further accusations of involvement."

Rubeo shook her head. "I don't know—"

"I'll do it," Shirley Conti said.

"Are you sure?" Rubeo looked back at Hallac. "Look, I think my client and I should have some time to talk this over."

"Absolutely," Hallac agreed, and Conti shook her head.

"No, that's not necessary. I agree. I want to do it, Gina."

"All right," Rubeo said, sounding dubious, and Hallac beckoned to Corbitt.

"Call Jae, will you, Cady? She can set this up."

King appeared almost at once, and he explained what was needed, laying emphasis on comfort and protection. King nodded, saying nothing, her eyes moving from Hallac to Conti and her lawyer and back again, and Hallac wondered how much of Gerretty's tirade had been heard beyond the interrogation room. They were supposed to be soundproofed, but Gerretty's voice carried all too well. Conti and Rubeo followed her from the room, and Hallac finally allowed himself to stretch.

"Uh, John?"

Hallac relaxed, slowly, met Corbitt's worried frown. "What?"

"Wasn't that just a little over the top?"

Hell, yes. He said, "Mr. Gerretty's taking this theft personally."

"He's a flake."

"Cady." Hallac put all the warning he could muster into the word. "I wouldn't repeat that."

She made a face. "Sorry." She paused. "Do you think he'd've done what he said? About the unions, I mean?"

"I doubt it," Hallac began, and knew he didn't sound convincing.

"Don't do that," Corbitt said. "Damn it, John, don't lie to me. You think he would have, and I think he would have, and we both think he would have gotten away with it."

"I think they were both bluffing," Hallac said, and willed himself to believe it. "He was bluffing about the studio hassling the union, and the lawyer was bluffing about the union going to bat for Conti. He was just better at it, that's all."

"Do you really believe that?" Corbitt asked, and Hallac made himself meet her gaze squarely.

"Yes. I do." *But all the same*, he thought, *we'd better be right about Shida.*

• • •

Lizzy drifted into the main bar at Testify, a translucent ghost among the crowd. The borrowed system was one of Stormhafen's best, and the colors were clean and perfect, with none of the fuzz or greying that betrayed inadequate hardware struggling to keep up with demand. It was good to be back on-line, good to be back in the system again, and she took the long way in, drifting between stream-lined deco pillars and through the wallpaper crowd rather than dropping directly into the main scene. The band was a grainy lift from an ancient film, not her work, and the carefully applied color couldn't quite hide the lower resolution of the source material. As she stepped "down" onto the dance floor, an icon popped up at her elbow, a big-headed caricature bowing and holding a tape measure, and a message spilled across the helmet's viewplate.

Conform personal image to setting?
Unconformed images will be greyed.

"Conform," she said, but the voice pickup didn't seem to be working, and she reached into the control space instead to agree.

Thank you. One moment, please.

The icon and the message vanished together, were replaced by a second caricature, this one a uniformed maid holding a mirror. Lizzy glanced at the image it displayed—a lay figure, draped in generic beauty, looking like a fashion sketch in the floor-length gown—and accepted it, too, knowing that the gown would look better in real life. Whoever had done the dress-up hadn't really understood bias-cut and the fabric clung and swirled like something out of anime. Against the setting—*my setting*, she thought, with pride—the failure was more obvious than ever, and she guessed she might still have a job, if she ever got out of this.

She shifted her fingers, letting the lay figure rotate so that she could scan the crowd, the false fabric billowing improbably at her feet. Most of the dancers were wallpaper, except for a few, probably long-distance lovers or possibly rehab candidates testing new move-ment options, and she skimmed past them and the wallpaper band, concentrating instead on the figures in the tiered banquettes that formed a horseshoe around the ballroom. About a quarter of them were greyed, people so attached to a particular self-icon that they refused to change, even to match a space like this. Or maybe they were just unwilling to concede to its image, though if that was the case, she couldn't understand what they were doing here. She clicked her fingers, calling up Testify's whois function, and watched names appear beside each of the figures that represented an actual user. To her surprise, some of the greyed figures were nameless, and she eyed them thoughtfully, wondering which of her rivals had added that touch. It was also possible that they were evading whois, but most people who wanted to remain anonymous just offered an unrecognizable package. Her own system was showing just that kind of package, a name and an open profile that only Shida would have cause to contact—assuming, of course, that he had received Conti's message.

She shook that thought away, moved back toward the lowest ring of tables. At first, they were all filled, but as she let herself drift closer, an empty one appeared, white linen and crystal gleaming under the chandeliers. A bottle of champagne was waiting as well, the ballroom's default, dewy in a silver bucket, but she dismissed it, replaced it with a cocktail in a thin-stemmed glass. A caricature waiter appeared, motioning toward the table, and a new message appeared in the viewplate.

View company menu?

She dismissed it, not wanting a wallpaper date, and let herself "sit," enjoying the smooth transition in the world around her. The table decoration, a single long-stemmed rose, vivid red in a tall silver vase, was maybe a little out of scale, and she made a note to edit that later if she had the chance. She mimed sipping the cocktail, wishing it was real—not that she could afford to drink and surf, not until all this was over—and let the music wash over her, settling herself to wait. She couldn't make her presence much more obvious; she would just have to wait, and see how Shida chose to make his approach. She tilted her head, trying to see the band, and several tables slid smoothly out of her way, clearing the sight line. The lead singer, slim and black in an incredibly oversize suit and a goofy grin, danced in a tight circle to the horn solo, then grabbed the microphone again for the next verse.

#Miss?#

The vocal simulation was good, even on the difficult silibants, and she glanced back to see another caricature, this one a boy in a bright red uniform trimmed with gold. The pillbox hat was vaguely familiar, and she frowned, then dredged up the costume: a telegraph boy, and he was holding something out to her on a silver tray.

#Telegram, miss.#

It wasn't a telegram at all, of course, just a pale grey rectangle, and she hesitated for an instant before accepting it, thinking of traces and viruses and other nastiness. Her fingertips tingled as she "touched" it, and a stream of text popped into view as her filters took over the translation.

Analysis: keycode access one-use. Connect unity privacy gold-5, prior payment received, capture refused.

In other words, she thought, *someone's offering me a key to a private meeting, a sealed no-records room somewhere off this volume. The only trick is finding the door—assuming I go, of course.*

But it was bound to be Shida, and she smiled, miming emotions she knew could not be conveyed by the figure's blankly pretty face. The telegram vanished, purpose achieved, and she said, "Thank you," but the telegraph boy had already disappeared. She glanced around the room, wondering how conspicuous it would be for her to leave immediately, then laughed behind her helmet. It would be more conspicuous if she didn't: anyone who'd noticed that exchange was bound to assume she was meeting a lover; not to hurry would be to invite attention.

The only problem now was to find the door. She rose to her feet, pleased again with the smooth transition—the underlying code was the major reason she had always liked working for Testify—and began moving away from her table, tracing a spiral pattern through the crowd. There were more people now in the room as the West Coast came into peak hours, and she had to pay attention to keep from impinging on other users' spaces. Then at last the room froze, and a doorway, translucent side posts and lintel and a multipaneled door, all perfectly in period, loomed suddenly between two tables. The privacy field had already captured her, she knew, would simply show her image winking out as though she'd dropped off-line, but she still glanced over her shoulder as she opened the door.

The volume within was disappointingly plain after the richness of Testify's ballroom, just a plain grey sphere, empty of setting or iconage. She hesitated, seeing her own image redrawn, reduced to a simple disk, and a new message winked into existence in her helmet.

Meet me at ChildWorld.org.

Beneath the message was the bright blue sphere of a dewdrop. It made a certain amount of sense—the security at ChildWorld was strict enough that neither she nor Shida would have to worry about eavesdroppers, and it all came from the host site, wouldn't attract attention—but she hesitated again, wondering if this really was Shida. She'd followed Conti's instructions, but she'd received no confirmation of any of it. For all she knew for certain, this could be RCD's jazz, designed to lead her into some kind of trap. She shook herself. Anything was possible on the Nets, but sometimes you had to just accept the jazz you were given, and assume your own security was good enough to handle any problems. She reached for the dewdrop before she could change her mind.

The holding sphere vanished in a swirl of grey, and there was an instant of darkness before the site menu appeared, its screen growing downward before her eyes. As always, the place made her vaguely uncomfortable: it was a free site, all its mods and subs freeware, designed to give kids who couldn't leave their homes a virtual playground. Some of the users were sick kids, permanently paralyzed, or bedridden, or undergoing treatments that confined them to a room or two or left them too weak to play. They were the designers' original intended audience, but more and more the kids on the site were the urban semipoor, the just-working-class families who wanted to keep their kids safe from the streets. She couldn't enter the play areas without giving her name and an instantly verifiable phone number—ChildWorld knew it was a target for pedophiles—but the parents' area was less strict, protecting them as well. She reached out to the icon that gave access, feeling nothing as her finger passed through the image, but the site menu dissolved, and she was suddenly in a pink-walled room scattered with blue-and-yellow flowers crude as a child's drawing. A sign appeared at the bottom of her display, spelling out its message in bold letters.

TODAY'S SETTING FOR PARENT-SPACE CREATED BY . . .
OTTAVIA MONRO, AGE 8.

The name was in the child's own writing, bold rainbow letters, the i dotted with a butterfly and a bigger butterfly clinging to the final o. She hoped that Ottavia's family had seen it, would be proud, and looked around for Shida. At this hour, dinnertime or after bedtime almost everywhere, the parent-space was almost empty, just a single stick figure waiting at the spot where the wall became translucent. As she moved closer, she could see a few child-shapes moving in the playground, and another menu bar appeared, offering a view of the other rooms. She ignored it, looked at the stick figure.

"Shida?"

"Tin Lizzy," the stick figure answered, and Lizzy blinked, recognizing the pleasant tenor from any dozen of Shida's films. "Russ tells me I should talk to you."

"He tells me the same thing," Lizzy answered.

There was a little pause, and when he spoke again, Shida's voice was tinged with laughter. "We're fortunate to share such a friend."

Lizzy took a deep breath. This was serious, prison or worse for her and for Keyz, not just elegant jazz, a game to pass the time. "He also said you were reliable."

There was another little pause, and the laughter vanished from Shida's voice. "Then let's cut the jazz. Is it true you have a copy of RCD's formulary program?"

That was cutting the jazz with a vengeance, and Lizzy couldn't help glancing at her own security telltales. They all still glowed green, no traces, no lurking listener, and she said, "Yes. It's called Orpha-Toto."

"Russ—" Shida began, and stopped himself abruptly.

"Was working on it when you knew him," Lizzy said. "It's finished, and it works, and RCD is using it to pick their hits."

"Fantastic," Shida said.

"So why do you want it?"

"Does it matter?" The amusement was back in Shida's voice, and Lizzy ground her teeth in frustration.

"Up to a point, yes. First, it matters because we need to know you can keep your end of any bargain—"

"We?" Shida asked.

Lizzy ignored him. "And second because I like to know what kind of jazz I'm dealing with."

"It's not jazz," Shida said. "I—it's known among my circles, film people, that RCD has something that acts as a formula. I know someone who is interested in using it to break RCD. He wants it, and he's promised money and protection if I provide it."

"And can this person deliver?" Lizzy asked.

"Yes."

Lizzy waited, and heard Shida sigh.

"His name's Sharkadi, Peter Sharkadi—you remember FireFish?"

"Yes." All too well, in fact, Lizzy thought, and she remembered Sharkadi, too. FireFish had been his baby, an independent studio that had somehow scraped up enough capital to try making films on its own. Unfortunately, although the talent was unmistakable, a combination of budget and distribution problems had destroyed the company, and Sharkadi had finally been forced to sell out to RCD in order to keep anything going. "Does he still have enough clout to do anything?"

"If he brings them the formula—brings them Orpha-Toto," Shida answered, "he can do anything he wants."

"Who's they?" Lizzy asked.

"Who's your 'we'?" Shida countered.

Lizzy hesitated. "A kid named Keyz, myself, Chessie Vara, and Russ. We've all stuck our necks way out for this, we need help before we can do anything."

"Peter's got an in with another studio," Shida answered. "I don't know which one—and I don't want to know right now—but it's a major. I think they can do what you need."

There was a moment of silence. Through the wall, over the Shida-icon's shoulder, Lizzy could just see three hazy children pushing a virtual merry-go-round. A fourth child-icon played solemnly with an icon that might have been a toy or another child. "I need assurances that you can shortcut some criminal charges. Erase them without record."

"I don't know," Shida began. "Drop the charges, sure."

"I don't have time to bargain," Lizzy said. "The kid deserves to have this whole thing erased, and I already have a two-strikes conviction. Can you do that?"

Shida paused, and Lizzy imagined him rearranging his assumptions about her, about all of them. "It can be done," he said at last. "I'll make sure of it."

"Agreed," Lizzy said.

"Will you bring the program here?" Shida asked.

"You're on the Isle Rialto?" Lizzy asked in turn.

"Yes." Shida paused, obviously calculating. "I'll reserve rooms for you here, pay for them and all that, under whatever names you want. When can you arrive?"

"Ah." Lizzy smiled, the expression behind the helmet wry. "We have a slight problem there."

"Go on."

"We're staying in a covenanted community," Lizzy said. "And we can't leave until I can put together some convincing jazz that will take the cops someplace else. I told you RCD was being serious about this."

"This isn't Russ's Vikings," Shida said, and Lizzy hesitated, wondering if she should tell the truth.

"Yeah."

"Then we don't need jazz," Shida said, "or, more precisely, we don't need your jazz. You know what films at Frenchman Bay?"

Lizzy shook her head inside the heavy helmet. "No. I don't even know where Frenchman Bay is."

"It's on the coast opposite the Isle," Shida said. "Maybe two hours away. Look, *Yorvick: The Settlement* films there, Andrea X likes to spend time on the Isle. They've just started shooting again."

Yorvick was RCD's turgid, Viking-era soap, loudly despised and widely watched throughout the community. Lizzy said, "Are you suggesting—?"

"If this is the same group," Shida said, "I know they used to do extra work. I can get them work, I know the guy who's directing *Yorvick*. And you can fly in with them. You do it right, nobody will know what happened."

"If they're willing," Lizzy said. "Wait." She triggered a hold without waiting for Shida's answer, and lifted the helmet's faceplate, blinking in the sudden light. "Russ?"

There was no answer, and she started to roll her chair back from the console, but had to stop and free the trailing skirt from the wheels. The hafeners had been more than generous with the loan of clothes, but she was still having trouble maneuvering in the clumsy garment. "Russ, are you there?"

"Here," Conti answered, reappearing in the doorway. He looked almost as incongruous as she felt in his loose tunic and trousers, the stubble of a beard slowly spreading across his cheeks. "Is everything set?"

"Not quite." Lizzy freed her skirt again, pulled herself back to the console. "Shida asked if the hafeners still do extra work— apparently *Yorvick* films on the coast near the Isle, and he thinks he can get the director to bring them in to work on the new season."

"It would only improve things," Conti muttered, and shook himself. "Sorry. But it would work, wouldn't it?"

"Assuming the hafeners were willing," Lizzy said. "Well?"

"I think they would be," Conti said. "William used to broker for them, I can get his number—or he's listed in the register under his real name, Harris Batchelder."

"All right," Lizzy said, and lowered the faceplate again.

"I think they'll do it," Conti said, his voice muffled now. "They may complain about the show, but it's the only thing everybody here obsesses about."

Lizzy lifted a hand in acknowledgment, grimacing as the flowered walls of parent-space came rushing back to surround her.

Shida's stick figure still waited patiently by the observation wall, and she moved to join him, drifting down over the imaginary tiles. "They'll probably do it," she said. "They have a broker on-site, a guy named Silent William—Harris Batchelder is the name he goes by, the name he's listed under."

"OK," Shida said. "I can do this."

There was a pause, as though he, too, was listening to something off-line, and Lizzy said, "I hope so. Because otherwise you'll have to wait for us to figure out some other way to get there."

"Unless something goes wrong," Shida said, "you'll hear from the director in a couple of days."

"All right," Lizzy said, and knew she sounded dubious.

"Don't worry," Shida said, and vanished from the parent-space.

Lizzy triggered her own release, and didn't stay to watch the shutdown, relying on the automated systems to warn her of anything problematic. She lifted off the helmet, squinting again in the change of light, and Conti pushed himself away from the doorframe where he had been leaning.

"Well?"

"He says the director will be in touch," Lizzy answered.

"Then I guess we're set," Conti said. "Assuming William goes along with this."

But he will, Lizzy thought. It was just the kind of thing the hafeners loved. And it would get them to the Isle Rialto.

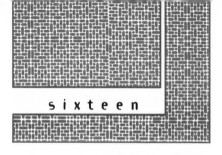

Yorvick's director contacted Silent William two days later, offering transport, meals, and lodging—cheap enough, Lizzy thought, since they'd be living on the set itself—and a stipend that was well within the SAG/SEG margins. The debate, and there was plenty of it, was mostly pro forma: everyone in Stormhafen wanted to be part of the group, either to try and improve a show or to participate in something they genuinely enjoyed, and the contract was accepted by an overwhelming margin. It was the perfect escape for them, Lizzy knew, the perfect way for them to slip out of Peterburg, but after everything else she'd been through, Shida's plan seemed entirely unreal. And that, she told herself sternly, was exactly the kind of attitude that would get her into serious trouble. Shida's jazz had worked; all she, all they, Conti, and Vara, and Keyz, had to do was to play it out.

Lizzy shifted the heavy bag on her shoulder, careful not to let its strap catch on the silver brooch that fastened her outer dress. This was the strangest role she'd ever played, in a lifetime of playing strange parts, creating new personas, and she was still having trouble figuring out what made Jorunn Ornsdottir tick. She glanced at her reflection in the nearest window, and for a second couldn't find herself in the line of would-be Vikings. Partly it was that she still hadn't gotten used to the darker hair, but mostly . . . Mostly it was the way the clothes, the role, changed her—diminished her, though that was not how the hafeners chose to read it. The dark grey dress with its long tight sleeves and the paler aprons with their twin silver brooches hid her curves, turned her body into something irrelevant, masked by the messages of status and wealth carried in the clothes themselves. Not that she didn't look good, she decided, and the hafener women had been more than generous, pulling from their own best and second-best stock to provide for her and for Vara, but it was not a persona she could recognize. In the reflection, she could see Conti giving her a wary glance, and she met his eyes with a smile.

The borrowed clothes suited him a little better, softened the worried lines, the wary stance, but he still didn't look much like anyone's idea of a Viking. Of course, the Vikings weren't just raiders and pirates, she reminded herself, as she'd been reminded repeatedly over the last week, but even knowing that Conti still didn't quite look as though he belonged. Keyz looked better, indistinguishable among the pack of kids at the middle of the line, dressed like all the other boys in loose trousers and tunic and shapeless bright-colored shoes, a cap tipped with a plastic boar's tooth hiding his hair. Vara, on the other hand, looked as though she belonged, just another tired, out-of-temper matron with bags to watch and a household to move, and Lizzy caught herself envying the other woman. For once, it was Vara who was getting into the situation, not herself.

She gave her reflection a final glance, resisting the impulse to tug at her sleeves. The tattoos were well hidden; unless the cops had enough information, evidence, to justify a body search, she should get through all right. But that, of course, was the crucial issue. The cops knew exactly who and what they were looking for, and the jazz for a week had been the thoroughness of the search of Peterburg. People were saying there hadn't been anything like it since the big drug crackdown of '22, and the ACLU had sent a SWAT team to monitor the proceedings. There were still random checks on the roads and on outgoing planes, and she hoped their faked ID would be good enough to pass. She'd done them herself, hours of careful work in databases and then with the community's printers, all with Longlegs looking over her shoulder, trying to absorb as much as possible. The links had worked last night in Stormhafen; she would have to trust that nothing had changed since then.

The line moved forward again, and she shuffled forward, closing the gap. The bag was heavier than ever, and she set it gently between her feet. At least they'd started boarding; maybe they would get by without have to test her IDs against police scanners. The airline was boarding them first, maybe because they'd had experience with reenactor groups, and Silent William stood beside the boarding stewardess, helping match the community names to the real names on her list. More than half the hafeners refused to answer to their legal names—a few had managed to forget that identity entirely, were genuinely startled by their old names—and Lizzy looked at her feet, hiding a grin at the stewardess's increasingly harassed expression. William saw her looking, and gave her a conspiratorial smile, but then the expression faded, his eyes going to something in the middle distance. Lizzy controlled the urge to turn and look, glanced instead into the nearest darkened window, and caught her breath, swallowing a curse. There were cops coming, an armored TAC squad, or at least the Peterburg equivalent, the crowds parting for them as they marched toward the gate. Her IDs would be tested after all.

"Holy shit," the man in front of her said, turning, and translated automatically, "I mean, blood of Odin."

Lizzy turned, too, and shuffled sideways with the rest of the line, letting the squad sweep past them to the gate. Four of the team took up positions on either side of the tunnel, two on each side, while a fifth man set up a portable scanner, and the sixth—presumably their officer—lifted off his helmet to talk to the stewardess and Silent William. He kept his voice low, but William's boomed out over the nervous muttering.

"Lieutenant, I don't know why you should pick on us, and I'm not happy—"

The lieutenant lifted his hand, and William stopped instantly. The lieutenant said something more, and William shook his head, exasperated, but nodded.

"All right." His voice was quieter, but still loud enough to carry to most of the hafeners. "We'll cooperate."

"Thank you." The lieutenant waved to the man with the scanner, who had already unfolded the legs and was just untangling the nest of input cords. "All right, everyone, this is a routine spot check of all passengers for Atlanta. You have a right to refuse the search, but if you do so, you will not be allowed to board the plane. You may be able to leave on a later flight, and the airline has agreed to honor your tickets for exchange, if there are seats available. Is that clear?"

Someone at the front of the line—one of the other women, Lizzy thought, with a tunic-clad toddler balanced on her hip—said something in a voice too soft to hear.

"We are aware that some passengers are making connections," the lieutenant answered, "and we will do our best to keep from delaying takeoff. Of course, the more cooperative you are, the faster we can get through with this."

Right, Lizzy thought. By putting it like that, the lieutenant was getting the majority of the passengers on his side—he would know that the hafeners, who might have protested on principle, were trying to make connections in Atlanta just like everybody else. The scanner looked efficient, too, a bulbous projector like an oversize hair dryer, and her hands tightened momentarily on the strap of her carryall. She made herself relax, trying to look calm, and shuffled forward again as the TAC team passed the first family through the gate. *Jorunn Ornsdottir*, she repeated, still clumsy with the unfamiliar words, *Jorunn Ornsdottir who's really Toni Inglis. Only that's not how she would see it. For Jorunn, it's the other way round.*

The line lurched forward again as the TAC team released another entire family, mother, father, two kids. Keyz was ahead of her, with Vara, plausible enough as aunt and nephew, and she held her breath as they stepped up to the scanner. The lieutenant said something, voice too soft to hear, and then waved them through. The first IDs had worked, Lizzy thought, with relief, and moved up behind the pair of young men who'd qualified as stunt techs. They went through without trouble, too, and she dared to let herself hope the cops might be getting a little lax.

And then she was at the gate, the scanner looming large on her left, the TAC team lieutenant on her right, flanked by William and the silent gate stewardess.

"OK, miss," the scannerman said. "Bag on the plate, please."

Lizzy lifted her bag onto the table, and the lieutenant said, "Name?"

"Jorunn Ornsdottir." The name came out easily, believably, but the lieutenant sighed.

"Real name, lady, don't waste my time."

"Toni Inglis." She was on easier ground here, knew that Toni was a computer tech, one of the people responsible for maintaining the community's remote site while they were on location, and she met the lieutenant's stare easily.

"Hey, Lieutenant," the scannerman said. "There's a lot of gear here."

"Yeah?" The lieutenant came around to study the display. "OK. What is all this, ma'am?"

"Household computer," Lizzy answered. "Plus tools, mine and Lord Karl's. We're setting up a site once we get there, so the people back home can see what's going on."

The scannerman was working as she talked, plugging in cables and checking the results on a secondary screen. "Your smoke, too, please."

Lizzy curbed the desire to reach for a nonexistent pocket, opened the pouch that hung at her waist, and produced the smoke. The scannerman took it, plugged in a length of minicable.

"OK. That's clean."

Lizzy took it back, closing the case and restoring it to her pouch, and the scannerman kept talking.

"She's got all the tools, plus some games and shit, and what looks like a bunch of templates."

The lieutenant nodded, slowly, still staring at the screen. "What's that?"

Lizzy gave a blank smile, knowing it was Orpha-Toto. She'd compressed it as much as they dared, but it was still too large to fit into anything Keyz could plausibly carry, not when he was playing at being a mere extra.

The scannerman frowned, did something to his keyboard. "Don't know. Ma'am, you want to ID this program?"

Lizzy looked where he pointed. "That's one of Lord Karl's templates. The master copy for the setting."

The scannerman nodded, accepting the explanation, but the lieutenant frowned more deeply.

"Where's this Lord Karl? Is he here?"

"He's coming in tomorrow night," William interposed. "He couldn't get away from a project he was working on for his mundane job."

The lieutenant hesitated, glanced at his scannerman. "You OK with it, Chip?"

The scannerman nodded again.

"All right, let it pass. You said everything else is clean?"

"Yes, sir," the scannerman, said, tugging cables free.

"Then go on through."

Lizzy swept her bag off the table without bothering to close it, slung it over her shoulder, and started toward the tunnel that led to the plane. Once she was out of sight, around the gentle curve that brought the tunnel into perfect alignment, she stopped to rearrange things, sliding the components back into their optimum configuration. Something wasn't right—*not that I'm complaining*, she added instantly. *But it doesn't feel right.* She lifted the bag back to her shoulder as Conti came down the tunnel toward her.

"Are we OK?" she asked, and he shrugged.

"So far." He was frowning, too, the same unease gripping him. "I don't know, this is awfully easy."

"Don't say that yet," Lizzy said, and Conti shook his head.

"No, these guys are pros."

"Or they're supposed to be," Lizzy said. "Maybe they're just dumb—or tired."

Conti shook his head again, and she sighed.

"All right, I don't believe it, either. But frankly, I don't know what to do about it."

"Me neither," Lizzy said. She shook her head in turn. "Go through with it, I guess. But we may have to do something different when we get to Gulfport."

Frenchman Bay was a bleak stretch of paradise, palm trees, planted at fifty-year intervals along the beachfront road, the signs that directed the summer tourists to the 'gator farms and the cover where they could watch the filming of *Yorvick* starting to peel in the humidity. The hotel was just as tired, and Hallac rested one hand against the window frame, wishing he was home. He hadn't spoken to his wife in three days, and that had been a snatched conversation, barely more than *I'm OK* and *I love you*; it had been more than a week since they'd been able to talk properly, and he was beginning to feel the ache of it, one more dull misery to match the grey sky. From the suite's main window, he could just see the roofline of the *Yorvick* set, poking over the edge of the dune. He was fairly sure there was no such thing in northern England, where the show was supposed to take place, but that didn't seem to matter to anyone. In any case, the reenactors were settling in, and his fugitives with them.

Once they made contact with Shida, once he had the proof he'd promised Gerretty, he could bust them, and finally get home. He closed his eyes, hoping it would be soon, and heard the suite door open and close behind him.

"What a dump," Corbitt said, not cheerfully, and he took a deep breath, turned to face her. It was impossible to tell if she was talking about the suite or the town.

"What've you got?"

"Not much." She dropped her bag on the sofa, reaching for her smoke as she talked. "They're here, all right, made it safe through the transfer in Atlanta, and presumably they're going to start looking for ferry service soon enough. Everybody on the set is scrambling around trying to make room for them, they're not going to notice if a couple of them go missing."

Hallac nodded. He had worked on a couple of shoots, could imagine the chaos well enough, and that chaos had to be increased by the presence of the reenactors. He wondered if the set's houses were sturdy enough to live in, or if RCD's on-site director had had to have something built.

"Peterburg is still pissed at us," Corbitt went on, staring at her smoke. "Jae's been trying to calm them down, but they're not happy."

"You can't blame them," Hallac said, and Corbitt grimaced.

"I can. They're being idiots."

Hallac made a face himself, thinking of the mail he'd gotten that morning—a formal complaint from the Peterburg police, pointing out that they'd asked for their cooperation with several outstanding warrants of questionable provenance, and then turned around and told them to let the suspects through, spoiling Peterburg's chance for a capture credit—and shoved the thought aside. It didn't help that this was his idea, he still felt guilty, both for spoiling Peterburg's record and for getting them mixed up in this mess.

"At least they're still willing to hold Ms. Conti," Corbitt went on. "They could've made a real stink about that."

Could have but didn't, Hallac thought, and guessed that Shirley Conti had friends on the force. They would think she was safer with them, and they were probably right. Which was one more reason to play things this way, he told himself, and glanced back at the window. It was early evening already, and the sun was low in the sky, the palms' shadows stretching halfway down the beach. "When's Gerretty getting in?"

Corbitt glanced at her smoke. "Tonight. John—"

"Who's watching the suspects?" Hallac cut her off without compunction, not wanting to hear her doubts.

"Galen. With a local crew for backup."

"Local?" Hallac asked.

Corbitt made a face. "Well, not local cops. RCD security assigned to the shoot. The site director was perfectly happy to detach a couple of them to help."

"Good enough."

"At least they shouldn't get pissy about the credit," Corbitt answered.

"I wouldn't bet on it," Hallac said, and suppressed a sigh. "Any sign of movement?"

"Not when I left. We've got a tap on the Isle, if they try to contact Shida that way, but I'm betting they'll try to get there in person."

Hallac nodded. "And Galen's covering."

"There was a lot of movement and craziness," Corbitt said, "but I think they've got it tapped. He'll give us a buzz if any of them tries anything."

Hallac nodded again, his eyes turning to to the window. You couldn't see the Isle Rialto from here, at least not on a hazy day like this one, but it was out there, somewhere on the horizon line. Shida was there, had been there since he'd fought his case to a standstill; it was about time someone resolved that situation. The words felt hollow, and he grimaced, wishing he'd figured out a better way to distract Gerretty. "What about the ferries, or whatever? We got them tapped?"

"Yep," Corbitt answered. "There are two commercial sea ferry lines, plus a helicopter ferry, and then of course just about any of the fishermen will run you out there for a price. But I'm tapped into all the commercial lines' computers—yes, we have a good warrant for that."

"Sorry," Hallac said. "Go on."

"As for the fishermen, there's no way in hell we can watch them all, which is why Galen's concentrating on the targets. He figured—

and Jae and I agreed—that we're better off letting them take the lead, take us to where they wanted to go." Corbitt looked down at her smoke. "Since we're not arresting them until they've contacted Shida."

There was a note of distaste in her voice, too strong to be ignored, and Hallac turned away from the window. "Problem, Cady?"

"Yeah." She met his stare unflinching, her mouth twisted down into a scowl. "I don't like it. If we're going to bust them, let's do it. Whatever this kid took, the longer he has it out, the more likely he is to make a copy or to find a seller, or just to lose it out there on the Net somewhere. And, personally, I'm not looking forward to trying to convince Mr. Gerretty that there aren't any copies running around loose."

She had a point, too, and Hallac sighed, made his voice as winning as he could, hoping to convince himself as well. "Look, you know perfectly well what's going on. Shida's been a very vocal pain in the ass ever since he got that settlement. Do you blame Gerretty for wanting to take him down a few pegs?"

"Yes."

"Christ, Cady!"

Corbitt's shoulders twitched, but she said, stubbornly, "Well, I do. We ought to fucking leave it alone."

"You'd be smart to let that go," Hallac said.

She met his stare for a second longer, then looked away. "Whatever. So we're still going to try to drag him into this?"

"He's already involved," Hallac said.

"We don't have any proof of that," Corbitt said. "Nothing that wouldn't get us laughed out of court."

"We'll get proof," Hallac said. "Let it go." He glanced toward the ocean, the calm, almost waveless sea, so different from the heavy surf of the Pacific. Somebody was wading in the shallows, almost fifty yards out and still not much more than knee deep in the pale green water. Farther still he could see the white line of a sand reef, the waves barely kicking against it, and he hoped Corbitt would listen.

"All I'm saying—" Corbitt's smoke beeped twice, cutting off whatever else she would have said, and she turned to it without apology, tapping her stylus against the screen. She worked for a couple of minutes, then straightened again. "Results from the Isle. Shida's trying to get in touch with them."

"Have they responded?"

"Not yet," Corbitt answered, still working her stylus, and Hallac's eyes narrowed.

"Is this a legal tap, Cady?"

"No." Corbitt shook her head. "We're going to have to slide over this if it gets to court."

Hallac sighed, accepting the necessity. "So what did he say?"

"He's got a fisherman they should go to." Corbitt gave a feral smile. "All we have to do is keep on eye on him."

Assuming this wasn't jazz, Hallac thought. Shida was a master of that game. "Yeah, put a watch on the fisherman," he said, "but tell Galen to stay on the group at the set. We don't want to take any chances."

L izzy sat on a bench at the edge of the camp, on the rising ground that divided the *Yorvick* set from the hotel where the stars and the technical staff lived. This was technically state land, once a park, but the film company's lease had proved too lucrative to refuse. Half the beach was now closed, to give room for the occasional longboat landing, and the hotel had no rooms left at any time of year. Not that that seemed to make much difference, she added, smiling to herself. Even now, well past tourist season, at least a dozen cars had stopped at the observation point while they were moving the hafeners into the village set, and even from a distance, she'd been able to see the sun on the camera lenses. Free publicity, the site director called it, and a junior publicist had made sure she offered all of them info-disks before they got away. Most of them had taken the little buttons, and then a cameraman had slipped round afterward to retrieve the ones that had been discarded. Tomorrow there would be a fan-club visit, or at least that was the current jazz. At the very least, the hafeners would be on full display, and Silent William had gone around the little huts twice already, checking for anachronisms. Smokes and phones were all stored away in the hafeners' hotel suite, along with the computer gear, and Lizzy glanced over her shoulder, looking down at the fake town. There were no lights visible, but the air was touched with woodsmoke from the cooking fires. Vara was down there somewhere, still caught up in her borrowed persona, and Lizzy wondered how long it would take the other woman to free herself from those obligations. She herself had slipped away as soon as it was practical, first volunteering to help get the computers back to the hotel, and then sliding out of that group so that she could change into normal clothes. In an oversize shirt and jeans, she blended perfectly with the technical staff, knew she could always claim to be part of the publicity team if anyone questioned her presence.

She turned sideways, letting the wind catch her, blowing unfamiliar dark strands of hair back out of her face. Beyond the beach and the soft glimmer of the breaking waves, light glowed on the horizon, a bright spot, like a cloud: the Isle Rialto. Supposedly there were telescopes on the hotel's observation deck, and on a clear day you could see the platforms, but at night any details would be drowned in the haze of light. Shida had promised to send word, instructions on how to get there, but so far she'd heard nothing. She sighed then, feeling the hard weight of her smoke in her jeans pocket. She'd heard nothing because she hadn't looked for a message yet, hadn't checked either of the accounts she'd given Shida, and it was more than time for her to do so.

And yet it still didn't feel right. She shook her head, no longer seeing the soft surf and the pale distant lights. They shouldn't have made it through the checkpoint, not if the TAC team was halfway competent—Vara had muttered about it throughout the flight, torn between relief and outrage at their incompetence, sure that RCD had made the TAC team let them through. If she was right, then they should ignore Shida, fade quietly, and find some other option, someone else who would be willing to protect them from RCD in exchange for Orpha-Toto—except that Shida was the only person she could think of who had any incentive to treat them well. It wasn't much, but she did know the other buyers: it was better than nothing. This was all Gerretty's doing, she thought. If it wasn't for Gerretty, they could have made a deal with RCD, particularly when Keyz hadn't known what he was getting into, and didn't want anything to do with it once he found out. But Gerretty was never willing to deal.

Something crunched on the path behind her, and she swung around on the bench, a part of her poised to run. It was Conti, of course, flashlight looped around his wrist, and Lizzy allowed herself a sigh of relief.

"What's up?"

"I was going to ask you the same question," Conti said. "Have you heard from Shida yet?"

Lizzy rubbed her wrist, pushing the sleeve back so that the tattoos showed black and silver in the reflected light. "Not yet."

"Have you checked?"

Lizzy looked away, feeling suddenly like a child again, like the student she had been. "I haven't had the chance—" she began, and stopped herself. She wasn't Conti's student anymore. "No. I haven't done it. I've been sitting here wondering if the whole thing's RCD's jazz."

To her surprise, Conti nodded in agreement. "I've been thinking about that myself."

"Any conclusions?"

Conti shook his head, smiling ruefully. "I just keep going around in circles."

"Yeah." Lizzy circled her wrist again, thumb and forefinger meeting above the bone, watching a spark of light flare in one strand of holofiber. "We've got to do it," she said at last, and pushed herself to her feet before she could change her mind.

The hotel lobby was very bright, and comfortably busy, knots of film crew occupying the bar and restaurant staff, their voices loud and cheerful over the ubiquitous music. The outer edge of the bar had been set up as a smoking area, and Lizzy settled herself at one of the little tables, tapping the surface over the blinking button to ignite the menu. It lit without hesitation, offering an assortment of services and a blank connection at a nominal charge. Lizzy picked the latter, writing in her phone number to pay for it, and Conti settled himself opposite her. The jack opened, and she plugged the minicable into the socket, waiting while the system made connections. Then the screen lit, and she touched the preset that would collect her mail from the first of her accounts. The message was waiting: a man's name, the name of a boat, and an address.

She killed the connection, and looked up at Conti. "Rice New-man, of the *Starcatcher*. It's at 47 Archer."

"The main beach road?" Conti asked, and Lizzy touched her screen, calling up a local map.

"Just off that. It looks like it's where all the charter docks are."

"So what's the word?" Vara loomed suddenly over the table, and it was all Lizzy could do to keep from jumping.

"We have the message," Conti said, and the older woman scowled as she pulled out her chair. She had abandoned the hafener dress for jeans and T-shirt, looked more herself again.

"So what does he say?"

"He gave us the name of a boat and a person," Lizzy said, and swung the screen to face her. "I assume he's got everything set up."

"Yeah," Vara said, and sounded unconvinced.

"Where's Keyz?" Conti said.

"Upstairs," Vara answered. "I left him in the web suite. Last I saw, he was helping set up the site links."

"That should keep him out of trouble for a while," Conti said, and Vara showed teeth in a strained smile.

"I hope to hell. I don't know, guys, I've got a bad feeling about this." "You and me both," Lizzy said. "But I don't know what else to do."

"We could back out," Vara said. "Find somebody else to help us."

"Any suggestions?" Conti asked, sourly, and Vara shook her head. "Not offhand."

"Besides," Conti said, "we know Njeri."

And that matters. Lizzy looked down at her smoke again, not really seeing the map. "The real key's Gerretty," she said. "He's the one who's pushing this, he's the one who can stop it. But I don't know how the hell we can get at him." *What I do know is that he's hard to get at—look at what he was willing to go through just to get back at me. But there's got to be a way, assuming, of course, I'm willing to take that kind of risk again.*

"Again, that's what Njeri may know," Conti said, and Vara made a face.

"Or may not. He's looking to get something out of this, too, Russ."

"I don't think we have any choice," Lizzy said, and closed her smoke. "But I think I should go alone. If there's something wrong, one person has a better chance of getting away."

"Or if you get caught, it's just you," Vara said. "I agree."

Lizzy sighed, wishing the other woman hadn't been so quick to go along with the idea. "Tomorrow morning, then," she said, and the others nodded. "Then we'll know."

Lizzy made her way along the beachfront road, grateful for the breeze that floated in off the water. The waves were smaller than ever, barely lapping the pristine sand, and she watched them idly. The beach itself was almost empty, diminished by the high tide, just a couple of families wading with ridiculous solemnity through the edge of the waves. A pair of children ran shrieking, their voices high as gulls', the taller one kicking up a bright fan of spray, but they were called to heel almost at once. Back at the set, the Viking kids were doing the same thing, the girls with their ridiculous dresses hiked over their knees, and she wondered if the director had had the sense to get a camera out there.

She put the thought aside, grateful for the palm trees' shadow as the beach and the road curved north again. It was less than a mile from the set to the town proper, where Archer Road split off from the beach loop, leading along the fishing piers, and already she could make out the tangle of radar masts, dark against the white sky. Most of the day fishers were already at sea, but a few still remained, Nets hanging bunched while crewmen hustled at incomprehensible tasks. Even as she watched, one backed slowly out of the crowd, Nets folded like wings, and started for open water.

There were more tourists on Archer, a long line at the ferry office, buying tickets to the Isle or one of the half dozen island picnic tours, clusters at each of the boats that advertised sport fishing. The fence that lined the pier was dotted with brightly painted boards, mermaids and skindivers and leaping swordfish almost crowding out the day and half-day charter rates. There were numbers, too, addresses, usually crowded into the last corner, and she kept an eye on them as she moved along the dock, trying to blend in with the other tourists. Number 47 turned out to be a little beyond the fish hall, where anybody could go in the evening to buy fresh-off-the-boat; she pretended to study the notice board—hall opens to the public at seven, Frenchman Bay expressly makes no warrant of

freshness or value, buy at your own risk—and let her eyes slide sideways to study the boats tied up at the pier. There was only one at 47,
a neat-looking motorboat with a high bow and a comfortable-looking
cabin, and she turned toward it as casually as she could manage, trying to spot a name. There was no charter board, just the numbers
wired into the fence, and she hoped she was looking at the right one.
The wind brought the smells from the fish hall, salt and seaweed at
first, not fish at all, until she came around the far side where a stand-
pipe dropped the melted ice directly into the harbor. She wrinkled
her nose, and a man appeared in the boat's hatchway, hauled himself
easily onto the tidy deck.

"Looking for a boat, miss?"

"I was told I had a charter," Lizzy answered, cautiously. "A boat
called *Starcatcher*?"

The man nodded, waving his hand to encompass the boat's tidy,
unscarred deck. "That's me. You the lady who wants to go to the
Isle?"

"That's right," Lizzy answered. Something moved in the shadows by the fish hall, and she glanced toward it, only to blink as the
sun dazzled her again. Had there been someone there, and if there
was, did it matter? She turned slightly, trying to watch without being
too conspicuous. "How much?"

Something moved again, and this time Lizzy was sure she saw
someone crouching behind the trash bins that crowded the narrow
catwalk running alongside the hall. It could be an ordinary thief, a
pickpocket waiting for easy pickings among the tourists, but it was
too early to make that likely. No, the odds were it was the police, and
she took a deep breath, the sense of doom that had followed her ever
since Peterburg crashing down on her at last. *I knew it was too easy,
getting out of the airport, I knew they let us go. . . .* She killed the
panic, made herself focus on the boat below her. "Sorry, what was
that?"

"I asked how many people. Will it be just you?"

Lizzy shook her head, dry-mouthed. "Four of us, all told. And
luggage."

"You know there's a public ferry," the man said, and she forced a
smile.

"The schedule's not convenient."

"OK." The man's tone made it clear he thought she was crazy, a verbal shrug of the shoulders. "It's fifty each—the ferry's cheaper."

"That's OK." If it was Hallac watching, she thought, then he'd let them get this far on purpose, and he was likely to let them get all the way to the Isle before he moved in. The only question was why.

"When do you want to go?"

"As soon as possible," Lizzy answered, and glanced at her watch. "What's the earliest you can leave?"

"Lady, that's your call." This time the man did shrug. "As soon as the rest of you get here, I guess."

"Yeah." She reached for her phone, watching out of the corner of her eye. She couldn't see the man on the catwalk anymore, couldn't see any movement at all, and she turned slowly, scanning the street to either side. Nothing but tourists there, no one who looked like a cop or who even seemed to be paying attention to her at all, just one more woman gossiping with a good-looking sailor. "How long does it take to get there?"

"Let's see." The man squinted up at her. "The tide's just turned, so, say, around an hour. If you wait too long, the tide'll be against us, that'll make it a little over an hour."

"Right," Lizzy said, and touched the key to complete the call. She switched on the scrambler as well, knowing it probably wouldn't do more than delay the police, listened as it rang twice, then a third time, before Conti picked up.

"Yeah?"

His voice sounded ragged, as though he'd been shouting, and she heard him clear his throat.

"It's me," Lizzy said, and the sigh of relief was audible.

"Are we set?"

"I think so." Lizzy hesitated. "We may have watchers."

"We expected that," Conti said, nervously, and Lizzy squinted down at the boat, dazzling white in the strengthening sunlight.

"Hang on a minute," she said, and touched the hold button. "Hey, Newman?"

The man looked up, shading his eyes. "Yeah?"

"Any chance we could pick up the rest of my party?" That would tell for sure whether or not the cops were waiting for them on the Isle, she thought. If they let her go, let the boat leave without stopping it, then they were expecting this move, expecting them to try for the Isle—and probably they knew about Shida, too. If they didn't, if they weren't sure what was happening, then they'd bust her, or at the best she'd see them scrambling to keep up.

"Depends," Newman answered. "Where're they at?"

"The hotel," Lizzy said. "It's got a dock."

Newman grinned, and she felt instantly stupid. "Yeah, I can do that. No charge. We can be there in ten minutes."

"Fair enough," Lizzy said, and opened the channel again. "Russ? We'll pick you up there."

"When?" Conti asked, and she shaded her eyes, scanning the street again. Still no sign of watchers, no sign of movement, official panic, and she wondered if that was good or bad.

"Ten minutes."

"We'll be there," Conti answered, and she cut the connection.

"All set, Mr. Newman," she said, and he pointed to a gate in the fence.

"Then come on aboard."

Lizzy worked the stiff latch, and stepped through the fence, balancing carefully on the narrow stone as she closed the gate behind her. There was still no sign of pursuit—no sign of anything, even the watcher she had seen before seemed to have vanished—and she stepped down carefully onto the unsteady deck. Newman started the engines, a soft purr of sound, and cast off easily, edging the boat away from the pier. Lizzy leaned against the roof of the wheelhouse, staring back at the shore, not sure what she was looking for. Nothing moved among the tourists, no one seemed out of place, and she guessed whatever was going down was going to happen on the Isle. This was the endgame, and they, both sides, had already set up their final moves days ago. All they could do now was play them out, and hope their planning was good enough.

The others were waiting at the hotel dock, her own bag packed and ready with theirs. Under Newman's direction, she threw her full weight against a mooring rope, holding the boat against the dock, and the others scrambled awkwardly aboard. Lizzy scanned the shore again as they cast off, but there were still no signs of any watchers. *Not that I'd expected any*, she added silently, *but it just confirms my fears*. She saw Conti watching as well, first the shore and then her, but the noise of the engines and the rushing water made conversation difficult. She was grateful for that as she settled herself on the comfortably padded bench in front of the wheelhouse, blinking as the occasional flick of spray struck her face. They all knew what they were up against; there was no point in discussing it any further.

The Isle Rialto swelled on the horizon, first just a reddish smudge, and then the platforms showed more clearly, the towers becoming distinct, rising from the bay's calm on their spindly legs. Keyz moved to the bow to watch it, oblivious to the spray, and Lizzy shaded her eyes to see better, wishing she had binoculars. It looked exactly like what it was, an oil refinery converted to a resort, the hard lines barely softened by the removal of the biggest machines, and she couldn't help feeling vaguely disappointed. Somehow, from all the jazz about the place, she'd expected something more spectacular. This—this was just workaday, pretty ordinary, even with the long pennant streaming off the central tower. It looked black against the hazy sky, but she knew from the jazz that it was really dark red, tipped in sunlit gold. At the height of the winter season, it was white, both to stand out against the clear sky, and to remind its visitors of the snow they were avoiding. A spark of light caught her eye, something moving beyond the tower, and she squinted, watched it resolve into a helicopter. It hovered for a few minutes, then sank gently down among the mid-height towers. That was the way you were supposed to arrive on the Isle Rialto, the way the stars did it, and she couldn't help wishing they were coming in like that.

Of course, a helicopter would be even more conspicuous than the rented boat, but if she'd guessed right, it wouldn't have mattered. The cops wouldn't want to touch them until they'd contacted Shida. She took a careful breath as the first of the massive pylons loomed up from the seabed. Tourists in bright, comfortable clothes leaned over the lower deck railing to watch the boat in—wondering maybe if they were somebody important—and she wondered in turn which of them were spotting for the cops.

The light vanished as the boat slid under the edge of the main platform, and its motion changed, sliding sideways now as well as up and down. She braced herself against the seat as the boat threaded its way between the pylons, its engine suddenly loud in the relatively confined space. The boat slowed even further, gliding between two of the biggest pylons, their sides fringed with seaweed and shells. Ahead, she could see a platform built around the central shaft, a low, wooden thing that looked remarkably fragile against the massive tower. It seemed to be floating, and she guessed it had to move with the tides. A group of the Isle's staff was already waiting, two with ropes and heavy fenders, two more in jeans and blue Isle T-shirts hanging back, ready to take the luggage, and Newman gunned the engine again. The boat staggered, and one of the staff caught a trailing line, ran forward to loop it around a bollard, and the boat settled comfortably against the dock. A good-looking young man in a blue T-shirt snapped a mock-salute in their general direction.

"Coming ashore, ladies? Gentlemen? Need a hand with the bags?"

Vara and Conti exchanged glances, then Conti nodded. "Yes. We're visiting friends, so is there someplace we can store these until later?"

"Absolutely," the young man answered, "and only a nominal charge. We'll put them in the red lockers for you."

The other blue T-shirt was already scribbling claim checks, and Keyz took a tighter hold on his carryall, heavy with the storage block.

"This stays with me."

"Not a problem," the first blue T-shirt answered, without suspicion, and Lizzy allowed herself a sigh of relief. Keyz gave her a wary look.

"And what do we do now?"

"Go up—" She'd almost said upstairs, knew that was wrong, and compensated quickly. "—up there, and see if we can figure out a way to find Shida."

"So you really think we're going to get that far?" Keyz demanded.

Lizzy shrugged, lifting her own carryall to her shoulder. "I figure there's a good chance of it, since if we're right, we're going to have to get in touch with Shida before they'll want to do anything."

"Come on, guys," Conti called, a fair imitation of a vacationing parent. "We're wasting time."

The second blue T-shirt offered a hand, and Lizzy accepted it, letting him steady her as she stepped over the rail. The platform was almost as mobile as the boat, and she was grateful to be able to step into the elevator that filled the pylon's core. The whole thing had once been the well shaft, she remembered from the Isle's Web site; the pylon's hollow core extended to the sea floor and met up with another hole that went thousands of feet into the ground—or at least that was the jazz. Not that it mattered, there had to be plenty of solid steel between the elevator's base and the open shaft, but from the way Keyz shifted at her side, she guessed he'd seen the same information.

The elevator door opened onto the main deck, letting them off into soft, warmer air that smelled faintly of flowers. Lizzy glanced around, expecting to see potted gardens, but then realized that the smell had to come from some kind of expensive aerosol system. A nice one, though, she thought, not like the usual deodorants, not just masking the chemicals underneath. The plaza itself was busy without being crowded, a row of pushcarts selling cold drinks and trinkets lined up along its center, but Lizzy was aware of more than a few glances, people still looking to see if they were somebody. None of them felt like a cop, though, and she let her eyes travel upward, to the catwalk strung along the side of the nearest building. It wasn't a catwalk, really, was a lot wider, wide enough to hold a single row of tables with bright umbrellas over them, and it looked a little more crowded than the plaza, more people leaning on the rails between the tables enjoying the mild excitement of a new arrival. One of them was very beautiful, a striking man, actor-thin and lightly muscled, dark skin well displayed by a cream-colored shirt and trousers. His close-cut hair flattered his rather bony face, and Lizzy couldn't help shaking her head in admiration. Ahead of her, she saw Keyz elbow Conti, not daring to point.

"Up there. Up there, on the next level. Between the pink umbrellas. It's *him*."

Conti tipped his head to look, letting his gaze sweep ostentatiously along the entire length of the rail before he looked back at Keyz. "Yes. You're right."

Lizzy saw the first movement out of the corner of her eye, fell back instinctively, letting a trio of backslapping tourists screen her from view. Surely the cops wouldn't do anything yet, would wait until they tried to contact Shida—assuming that was Shida and not some studio double. And then a young man in a red Isle T-shirt, a contact mike clipped to his shirt collar, seemed to materialize at Conti's shoulder.

"Russ Conti?" he asked, politely enough, and in the same instant a tall woman, tourist shirt flapping off her skinny shoulder, moved purposefully toward them, scowling. Lizzy didn't wait for more, took a single step backward, putting more tourists between herself and the others, looking for a way out. A tangle of the Isle's security in white trousers and dark red T-shirts surrounded Vara now, and Lizzy took the first set of stairs, climbing up quickly, out of sight. She heard shouts behind her—cops' voices, and a startled shriek from a civilian—and she kept climbing, past the catwalk toward the observation deck at the top. Under other circumstances, she might have gone down, toward the service levels, but the Isle was small enough that the staff would know each other. She would do better on the upper decks, passing for rich, where the questions would have to be a little more discreet.

She ran out of stairs about four levels up, where a curved platform that had probably held a crane had been converted into an outdoor bar. It had been crowded, too, most of the tables holding drinks, or a jacket thrown casually over a chair, but everyone had crowded to the rails, leaning over to gawk at the scene on the plaza below. Lizzy hesitated for an instant, then slipped a half-empty drink from a table and moved to join the gawkers, craning her neck to see.

"What's going on?" she asked, and the woman next to her turned, spreading her hands.

"Police action—I ask you, on the Isle?"

"I heard it was terrorists," the stocky man beside her volunteered. His voice was faintly, definitely European. "Out to blow up the Isle."

The woman rolled her eyes. "I don't think so, Franz, really. Oh, look, isn't that Shida, down there?"

Half a dozen people craned farther, one man nearly dropping his drink, and Lizzy said, "Maybe it was vidirazzi, then."

She could hear footsteps on the stairs behind her, focused on the crowd below, not daring to turn.

"Oh, I hope not," the woman said, turning fully to face her. In that instant, Lizzy was fully part of the group, completely included, and she could have kissed the other woman. "Or maybe I do, at that. At least if they've been stopped. Though where there's one, there's usually a pack."

"Someone should make a proper law against it," Franz said, and the woman sighed. Behind them, the footsteps stopped, retreated, clattering back down the staircase.

"Franz is sweet," the woman said, confidentially, "but he's not American. He doesn't *understand*."

"And glad of it, sometimes," the man answered, without rancor, and gave Lizzy a smile that transformed his rather homely face. "Though I can't say honestly this is one of them."

The woman smiled, dazzling, and Lizzy guessed she had been a star in her day. "I said he was sweet. And gracious, too."

Lizzy smiled back, letting the other woman extricate herself gracefully, and stretched over the rail again to see what was happening. The first frantic search seemed to be over, and the cops had gathered in a knot, Conti and Keyz and Vara at the center of it. They looked very small, and for the first time, Lizzy shivered at the enormity of the situation. It was down to her to salvage things, find Shida and somehow make this vague deal that the jazz said he wanted. And what if it was just jazz—maybe even created by RCD, the cops who'd been chasing them? Shida wouldn't give a shit, would be perfectly happy to turn her in, and she'd be back where she started, or worse. No, she told herself, it didn't make sense that way. The jazz she'd seen was real, she'd checked it out, and there was no way RCD could have made it all. But the question now was what she could do, what she would do next.

She took a deep breath, knowing she'd have to move soon, before a waiter came around offering more drinks. On the plaza below, one of the cops pointed upward, and she flinched, then realized they were pointing at the spot where Shida had been standing. It looked as though Conti shook his head, denying, but the angle was bad, and it was hard to read the gesture. And what the hell could she do, without even a copy of the program? Shida wasn't likely to stick his neck out without some immediate payoff, but without Orpha-Toto, all she had was promises. Maybe it would be better just to fade, save herself if she could. She'd done everything she could possibly be expected to do, risked everything to try and help Keyz, and it wasn't working. If she kept it up, she was bound to go down in flames; maybe it would be wiser to back out, slide back into the shadows, build a new name, a new identity, and start over again. RCD wouldn't want her, now that they had Keyz and the program—and Conti and Vara, for that matter. They'd be watching the ferries, of course, but there were bound to be other private boats. She could get back to Frenchman Bay that way, catch a bus to Chicago or anywhere. Nobody would be looking for her anymore.

She shook her head slowly. No, that wouldn't work—well, it would work, would save her ass, but it wasn't right. She shied away from the word, and couldn't find another. OK, it wasn't right, then, not right to leave when there was still something she could do to help Keyz, because she'd promised, and she knew what it was like when someone broke that kind of promise. And, who knows, maybe Shida would still help them, might still be able to do something after all.

She pushed herself away from the rail, and practically ran into a big man in a denim jacket, silk tie blowing back in the strengthening breeze. "Sorry," she said, and started to turn past him, but the stranger caught her arm.

"Hang on a minute. You were with those folks down there."

"I don't know what you're talking about," Lizzy said. Her mouth was suddenly dry again, and she set the empty glass on the nearest bus tray. "Let—"

"Don't give me that." The big man kept his voice down. "I saw you. What are you, viddies?"

"What's it to you?" Lizzy asked. *If he wants vidirazzi*, she thought, *I'll give him vidirazzi, just don't let him call the cops.*

The big man grinned, showing too-perfect teeth. "Thought that'd get your attention. Who're you after?"

Lizzy gave him a look, and he nodded.

"Right, OK, sure, we can't talk here. Where do you want to talk, missy?"

"Someplace public," Lizzy answered, and the big man grinned again.

"What about up top? It's a nice view, not too many people up there this time of day."

"Fine," Lizzy said, and the big man shifted his grip on her arm, produced a passable imitation of polite guidance. She let herself be drawn around the curve of the bar, where a white-painted spiral staircase led up another level to the roof of the bar.

"After you," the big man said, and Lizzy climbed, squinting in the heat and light. Once on the roof, she could see why nobody was up there. The view was spectacular, all right, but the sunlight reflected painfully off the roof, so that it almost felt as though she was standing in a lake of steam. She could feel the sweat pearling on her back, licked her lips and tasted her own salt.

"All right," she said, turning to face the big man as he pulled himself up the last step, "what's in this for you?"

"A share of the story," the big man answered. "A credit line."

"Not likely," Lizzy said. This was a part she could play, not like the Viking woman. She turned away, shading her eyes from the glare. "Look, I appreciate your not yelling for the cops, but at this point, there's nothing they can do about me. I'm clean, and it's your word against mine that I was ever with those guys."

"This is the Isle," the big man said. "Give me a break. They can kick you off for looking cross-eyed."

"Fine," Lizzy said, "we've established that you can hurt me, but what can you do for me? Because right now, they've got all my gear, and that doesn't leave me much to make a story with."

The big man sneered. "Don't give me that. You've got at least a smoke on you, probably a minicam."

Lizzy paused. "Maybe. I repeat, what have you got for me, that I should give you a credit?"

"I can get you to Shida," the big man said.

Lizzy stifled a laugh, unable to believe her luck, and the big man scowled, misinterpreting.

"Hey, I know what I'm doing. I may be freelance, but I've been here for eight months, I've made connections. I can get you to him."

"Face-to-face?" Lizzy asked.

"Are you crazy?" The big man stared. "He'll have the cops down on you so fast you'll think they had jet packs."

"We have a deal."

"You and Shida?" The big man's eyes were wider than ever. "I don't believe you."

"Whatever," Lizzy said, and shrugged. "But do you think we'd have showed up like this if we hadn't had an agreement?"

The big man paused, considering. "All right. I'll buy that. But I want cash up front."

"No credit?"

"Like you'll ever get a story like that aired," the big man said. "Because if it wasn't Shida who got you busted, then it was his old studio, and they don't let shit like this get by them."

It was close enough to the truth that Lizzy sighed. "How much?"

"A thousand. Cold."

"I've got five hundred in cards," Lizzy answered. "Take it or leave it, the rest of my stash is with my producer. I can pay you the rest later."

The big man hesitated. "And the credit."

"Assistance credit," Lizzy said.

"No. Full reporter's line, or the deal's off."

Lizzy sighed. "All right. It's a deal."

The big man held out his hand, and she reached into her pocket, fanned the last of her cash cards.

"Half now, half when we get there."

"You don't trust me," the big man said, and Lizzy didn't dignify that with an answer. Apparently none was expected, because the big man waved her toward the staircase. "Downstairs and into the bar."

Lizzy did as she was told, grateful for the interior air-conditioning. The big man bought himself a drink and consulted his smoke, then left the drink untouched on the bar, motioning her toward the door. They came out into a broad interior corridor, also air-conditioned, Lizzy was pleased to notice, and the big man turned left, toward the center of the Isle. All the corridors were designed to be cool and pleasantly dim, after the brilliance of the decking, and in spite of herself she thought she could enjoy herself here. The big man paused in another plaza, this one smelling faintly of rain and grass, checking his smoke again, and then led the way down a corridor marked TOWER GUESTS ONLY. Lizzy knew better than to look around for the security, but spotted at least two cameras tucked into corners.

"We're getting close," the big man said, softly. "Just so you know, he's got a reputation for hitting first."

Who would blame him? Lizzy thought, and rolled her sleeves back, the tattoos showing black against her pale skin. They were the only token she had, the only password, that might get Shida's attention before he yelled for cops just to protect himself.

"Hurry," the big man said, and broke into a half jog. Lizzy copied him, and they turned a corner just in time to see Shida push through a door from the outside. His eyes narrowed, seeing the big man, who quickly lifted his hands, palms out and empty.

"She says you want to see her."

"Really." Shida's voice was uncannily familiar from his films, a light, pleasing tenor, well taught enough to hide its expensive education.

"You were expecting me," Lizzy said, and stepped forward herself, holding her own hands out so that he could see the tattoos. Shida blinked once, looked at the big man.

"My God, this must be a first. You weren't lying." He looked back at Lizzy. "Tin Lizzy, I presume?"

"That's right."

"Then we do need to talk. Go away, Jones."

"Sorry." The big man held out his hand to Lizzy. "Payday first."

Lizzy reached into her pocket, came up with the last of her cash cards. The big man snatched them from her, turned quickly away, counting them while Shida watched with ostentatious patience.

"Go away," he said again, and this time the big man obeyed, striding away down the corridor without looking back. Shida looked at Lizzy, his striking face expressionless. "I guess you'd better come in."

After the improvised working spaces of the last weeks, the Isle Rialto's security suite was almost unbearably luxurious. Hallac ran his finger along the edge of a keyboard, idly admiring the expensive system, glanced sidelong to see the three prisoners—suspects, he corrected himself, at least according to the warrants they were using—sitting silent in the holding room, their faces dimmed by the one-way glass. Not that it was likely to deceive any of them, particularly with Vara there to warn them, but it was a technique that had to be tried. Especially since nothing else seemed to be going right. He frowned at the memory, the Isle's security crew moving in too soon, so that they'd had to act before contact was made, and winced at the thought of Gerretty's response.

"Cady," he said aloud, and Corbitt looked up from her screen. "Any luck?"

Corbitt shook her head, brushed wisps of hair out of her eyes. "Nothing so far. Look, John, this is Gold Standard, I'm not likely to break this kind of lock without a couple of weeks and a little luck. Maybe not at all, if he's bought SOTA. Or got it from the cypherpunks."

Hallac grimaced—this was not what he wanted to hear—and moved to stand behind her, peering over her shoulder at the moving display filling her screen. It meant nothing to him, just strings of multicolored numbers that formed a wavering curtain of light, the northern lights seen sideways. "I thought you people knew how to break the cypherpunks' stuff."

Corbitt gave him an exasperated look. "Every time somebody figures out one of their algorithms, one of them writes a new one. And they've talked some of the best and the brightest into working for them. Not that I blame them, sometimes."

That was a warning, and Hallac lifted his hands in apology. "Sorry. You know why I'm asking."

Corbitt's frown softened. "Yeah. I'm doing the best I can, John. It's in there, I can confirm that much, but I can't get to it."

The suite door opened, admitting the Isle's head of security, and Hallac straightened quickly. "Keep trying," he said, and moved to intercept the stranger. "Mr. Chen."

"Lieutenant," Chen answered. There was a note of something in his voice, irony maybe, that made Hallac frown. Joe Chen was tall and elegant in an expensively cut grey suit several shades darker than his hair. "May I have a few minutes?"

"Absolutely," Hallac said, and waved him toward the single inner office. He left the door open, so that he could watch the prisoners through the one-way glass, and Chen allowed himself a thin smile.

"Any progress?"

"Some," Hallac answered. "What can I do for you?"

"It's these warrants." Chen did his best to look apologetic, and almost succeeded. "While we are of course delighted to help RCD Studios in recovering its missing property, and to cooperate in holding the fugitives who had it in their possession, there is nothing in these warrants to link Mr. Shida to this—a blackmail scheme, you said it was?"

"Apparently," Hallac said, stiffly. He hadn't expected anything else, was fairly sure that Chen's people had acted prematurely in order to protect one of the Isle's more prominent residents, but it was galling to have the limits of his cooperation spelled out so clearly. "We're confident of getting the details."

"And when you have them, of course we'll be more than willing to provide assistance," Chen said. Over his shoulder, Hallac saw the main door open again, and Gerretty came in, trailed by a lawyer carrying an expensive databoard. He moved toward them as Chen continued smoothly, "But until then, I'm afraid we can't offer further support."

"No, of course not," Gerretty said, savagely, and Hallac saw Chen's face tighten for a second before he controlled himself and turned to look up at the newcomer.

"President Gerretty, how nice to see you. I trust you've been made comfortable."

"Cut the bullshit," Gerretty said. He filled the doorway, one hand braced on each side of the frame, hands white-knuckled on the painted metal. "Hallac, I want to talk to you."

Chen rose easily to his feet. He was as tall as Gerretty, but slighter, moved like a dancer in his grey silk. "If you'll excuse me, then?"

"I'll want to talk to you later," Hallac said, and Chen managed a blank smile.

"Of course."

Gerretty's eyes narrowed, but for once he controlled his temper, just lifted one hand from the frame and straightened slightly, so that Chen had to brush past him, his slim body dwarfed by the other man's bulk. Hallac came to his feet as well, bracing for possible explosions.

"So," Gerretty said, and didn't bother to wait until Chen was out of earshot. "What's the word?"

Hallac hesitated, but the main door was closing, and he

shrugged. "Mixed. The prisoners aren't talking yet, but I think they will. Cady's identified that Orpha-Toto is present on the datablock we took from the Halford boy, but she hasn't been able to crack the lock, or to persuade the boy to give us the key."

"What about Tin Lizzy?"

"Still at large." Hallac took a careful breath. "Chen's people are looking for her, of course, and I've got Galen and Jae covering the docking points and the helipad. She can't get off the Isle without them spotting her."

Gerretty grunted. "You think Chen's trying to find her?"

"Yes." Hallac controlled his eager nod, knowing he was too glad to have something positive to say. "He's got no reason not to."

"Did he fuck up the arrest on purpose?"

Hallac took a breath, said carefully, "Shida's an important resident."

"Fuck that." Gerretty waved his hand, waved the words away. "How soon can you crack the datablock? That's the key. Once that's open, there's plenty of evidence Shida was looking for it."

Yeah, right, Hallac thought. *Pure jazz, all of it, nothing that'll stand up in court.* He said, "Uh, that evidence—"

"Is out there," Gerretty said. He glanced at the lawyer. "Right, Jean?"

The woman shook her head. There were huge circles under her eyes, imperfectly blotted by rings of concealer. "Sir, while there is circumstantial evidence—"

"All right, fine, we'll get more," Gerretty said. "What the hell do they want, a signed confession?"

"That would be acceptable," the lawyer said. "Provided, of course, it was legally obtained."

"Then you'd better get on with it," Gerretty said, and looked at Hallac. "May I suggest you start with the boy?" His tone was savage, the implication clear: *if you can't get information out of a sixteen-year-old boy, you're not worth what I'm paying you.*

"We were planning on it," Hallac said, with dignity, knowing it sounded weak, and Gerretty snorted again.

"I'll sit in, if you don't mind."

Hell, yes, I mind. Hallac shook his head. "I'm not sure that would be wise—"

Gerretty showed teeth in something like a smile. "Oh, don't worry, John, we'll have Jeannie here along to make sure we both stay in line. Right, Jean?"

"If you insist," the lawyer said, her voice pallid with exhaustion. "I would advise against it, however."

Gerretty waved the words away. "Get the boy in here."

Hallac reached for the intercom, knowing better than to argue. "Kevin? Bring Halford in here, please."

"Sir," the lawyer said, "this is ill-advised."

"Oh, shut up," Gerretty said, and the woman went quiet, folding her arms over the databoard.

"Have a seat," Hallac said, motioning them to the chairs placed on his side of the desk, and flipped on his own recorder. The little video camera whirred once, performing its self-check, and the screen faded on, showing the empty chair that waited for the suspect. Hallac touched keys, bringing up the time/date stamps and the antitampering codes, and Halford appeared in the doorway, escorted by one of the Isle's security men. He kept his hand firmly on the boy's shoulder, for all that he showed no signs of wanting to bolt, and Hallac nodded. "Thanks, Kevin. Seth, please sit down."

The boy sat, folding his hands carefully in his lap. He looked if anything younger than his years, thin and frightened behind any attempt at street toughness, and Hallac felt a stirring of sympathy. The kid's parents were perfectly ordinary, nice, middle-class, middle-of-the-road educators who had obviously raised their child to be pretty much like them. It seemed a shame to have to treat him like this—though if he'd kept his fingers out of spaces where he didn't belong, none of this would be happening. *I bet he knows that now*, Hallac thought, and nodded to the security man.

"Close the door, please, Kevin."

The security man backed away, closing the door behind him, and through the narrow panel that was the room's only window, Hallac saw him take up a Marine's stance outside. "Interview number two, subject Seth Halford, 1302 hours. Present are the subject, John Hallac, investigating officer, Gardner Gerretty, interested party, and Jean—"

"Thibeaudy."

"—Thibeaudy, attorney for the interested party." Hallac paused, flipped open his smoke, and reached for his stylus to call up the list of questions.

"Let's cut the crap," Gerretty said. At his side, the lawyer stiffened, but he waved her to silence. "Look, kid, Halford, you understand that you're in some real serious trouble. Right?"

There was a moment of silence, and then the boy nodded, warily. "Yes."

"You also understand that this trouble of yours is going to get your parents fired, and that nobody in the EMOs—in private education anywhere—is going to hire them again after what you've done."

Halford didn't answer, but Hallac thought his face paled even further.

"I don't intend to make a deal with you," Gerretty went on, "because I don't deal with thieves, and I especially don't like bargaining with people who steal from me. You stole Orpha-Toto, and you're going to pay for it. I'm going to get you tried in the postjuvenile system, and I'm going to see you get the maximum sentence possible. Orpha-Toto is worth over five million, plus it's a development product—if you don't know what that means, you can ask your cop friend out there, but you can take it from me you won't see daylight unsupervised until you're older than I am now. Do you understand that?"

Halford didn't answer, and Gerretty frowned. "Do you understand?"

"Yes."

Hallac glanced at the display, wishing he hadn't turned it on. So far, it was just—barely—legal, the threats explicable as statements of fact, and he hoped Gerretty would leave it at that. In the monitor, Halford's face looked even more drawn than in reality, and he winced at the thought of what a good defense lawyer could make of it.

"Now," Gerretty said. "Much as I hate to admit it, you have something I can use, and, like I said, I'm not going to give you any crap. You can do this my way, and I'll leave your parents out of it."

Halford's head lifted, only the slightest movement, but Gerretty saw, and lifted his hand in response.

"Don't say anything yet, you worthless punk. What I want is a conviction that includes Shida, and to get that, I want two things from you. First, I want the key to that box out there." He jerked his head toward the window. "Second, I want your testimony that Shida planned this entire thing, that he's the person behind this."

"But he isn't," Halford said, almost in spite of himself.

"I told you not to say anything." Gerretty glared at him. "If you give me that, those two things, I'll see that your parents' involvement is minimized. They won't work for an EMO again, except maybe public-sector, but they will work. If you don't . . ."

He let his voice trail off, and in the monitor Hallac saw the boy's hands tighten on each other.

"What about Lizzy?" Halford asked. "And the others."

"What about them?" Gerretty's eyes narrowed, as though he was assessing the likelihood of the boy's agreeing to cooperate.

"What happens to them? You help my folks, OK, that's great, but what about Lizzy?"

Hallac suppressed a sigh. The loyalty was admirable, but it wasn't likely to impress Gerretty.

"I don't deal with trash," Gerretty said.

Halford shook his head, pale face determined. "Then I can't help you."

"If you don't," Gerretty said, "I will make personally sure that both your parents are convicted on the same set of charges, as well as for contributing to your delinquency. They will be convicted as accessories, and they will be convicted under the parental-responsibility laws, and this level of theft ranks up there with murder, so they won't be fined, they'll get jail time. And that's on top of the minimum five-to-seven for helping you with the theft."

"They weren't involved," Halford said, through clenched teeth. "You've no right—"

"You don't have any rights left," Gerretty said. "You should've thought of that before you broke into my computers." He leaned forward, only slightly, but seemed to tower over the boy. "I told you, we are beyond the crap. It doesn't matter whether or not your parents did anything, I can make it seem like they did. You think you know the jazz, boy, but it's nothing compared to what I can do. And what I will do, if you don't do what I want. And don't give me any bullshit about 'it's not right,' because I don't give a damn. You're going to do it, or take your parents down with you."

He stopped, looked over his shoulder at his lawyer, who sat pale and silent, and gave a grunt of laughter. "Right. I've said what I wanted to say."

He rose to his feet, the lawyer imitating him, and Hallac looked away from her imploring gaze. This recording was pure dynamite, would absolutely destroy any case Gerretty tried to make; even within RCD, it would be enough to damn him completely. Then Gerretty leaned across the desk, punched buttons to stop the machine and eject the palm-sized cassette. Halford flinched away as Gerretty waved it in his face.

"And don't get any idea that this will help." He dropped the cassette to the floor, stamped hard on it, crushing it under his heel. Hallac heard the plastic shatter, swallowed the pointless protest. There was nothing he could do to stop Gerretty now.

"You've got six hours," Gerretty said, and slammed the door open, almost hitting the waiting guard. The lawyer hesitated, then closed her mouth, and followed him. Hallac sighed, and after a moment, went around the desk to pick up the shattered cassette. Even a casual glance was enough to tell him it was beyond repair, beyond even Corbitt's salvage. He set it on the desk anyway, not knowing what he wanted to do with it, and looked at the boy, still sitting motionless in the chair.

"Look, Seth," he began, groping for something that might comfort, and Halford looked away. "Look, if you give us the key, give us Orpha-Toto back, maybe we can make a deal on the rest of it. Keep your folks out of it. Maybe do something for Rhea—for Lizzy."

Halford looked up quickly, but there was no hope in his eyes. "Do you think you can do that?" he asked, and dredged a bitter, adult laugh from somewhere. "I don't think you can."

He was right, too, and it stung, and Hallac's eyes narrowed. "Suit yourself, kid," he said, and gestured for the guard. "Kevin, take him back with the others." He hesitated, wishing there were something he could do, some way of helping—but the kid had put himself beyond help when he crossed Gerretty. "He'll be back in six hours," he said, his voice without inflection, and the boy nodded.

"I know," he said, and let the security guy lead him from the room.

Hallac stared after him, swore under his breath. He felt guilty as hell, as though he could or should have done something different— *but Halford shouldn't have been hacking*, he told himself. *It may not be real, but it's still stealing, and it's never without consequences. Even ones like these.*

Lizzy sat in the corner of Shida's living room, keeping well back from the window and the narrow sweep of the phone camera's focus-finder. Shida busied himself at the bar, pouring drinks Lizzy suspected neither of them really wanted. He was younger than she had realized, younger than she was herself, and every bit as handsome as his image in the films, even without the perfectly cut suits to emphasize the breadth of shoulders and lean length of muscle. He turned away from the bar holding the elaborate drinks, dark pink nectar cut with rum, moved as gracefully as a dancer to set Lizzy's on the table beside her, then reached for the room remote, lowering shutters across the main window.

"So you're Tin Lizzy," he said, and perched comfortably on the arm of the sofa. "I've seen your work."

Lizzy shook her hair out of her eyes, feeling drab and ugly—worse, overdone and fat and ugly, the tattoos gaudy even in the room lights. "That's me."

"And you've found a copy of Orpha-Toto." He sounded more depressed than pleased, and Lizzy stiffened. She'd been counting on him, needed desperately for him to be able to help. "Things have changed. You know RCD's already been onto me about this. Joe Chen—he's Isle security—as well."

"You got us here," Lizzy said. "I don't know what they've told you, what they say we have, but we had a deal."

"Things have changed," Shida said again.

Lizzy nodded, stuffing down a rising feeling of panic. If Shida backed out, couldn't help them, wouldn't help them, there was nothing she could do. "What I'm looking for is a way to get RCD off our backs—I'm perfectly willing to give them back their damn program, there weren't any copies made, but I want us to be left strictly alone."

"What about this Keyz?" Shida asked, and Lizzy managed a tired smile.

"I think he wishes he'd never seen the thing. Yeah, he'll give it back."

"What does Russ say?"

"Russ?" Lizzy blinked, startled—she had forgotten Shida's connection with the older man, had been expecting him to ask about Vara—and Shida sighed.

"Oh, come on, Lizzy, he wrote the thing. What does he think we ought to do with it?"

Lizzy paused. Shida was a lot younger than she'd imagined, a lot less sure of himself, not what she'd wanted to see at all. "I don't think I care what Russ wants. Look, RCD—Gardner Gerretty—is trying to come down way too hard on a sixteen-year-old kid, it's something he's done before, and I want to stop him. That's the main thing—the only thing."

Shida looked away, the rest of his body unmoving, poised like a statue against the pale yellow wall of his suite. The stance was calculated, showed off his lean figure, though to be fair he'd probably been doing it so long that he'd forgotten how not to pose. "I don't know if I can help."

"What do you mean?" Lizzy heard her voice scale up, the careful vowels blurring. "You've been putting out the jazz that this matters to you, that you're willing to pay ridiculous amounts for it—you've even come this far, helped us get here. We've got the program—"

"RCD has the program," Shida corrected.

"We can get it back," Lizzy said. *How I don't know yet, but there's got to be a way.* "But I'll need your help, your protection."

"I'm telling you, I don't know if I can do that." Shida slid abruptly off the arm of the sofa, landing like a child in the overstuffed cushions. He started to draw his knees up toward his chin, and stopped, scowling, as though he was afraid he'd betrayed something. "Look, I told you about Sharkadi. He was the one who wanted Orpha-Toto, wanted a copy so he could get what was left of FireFish out from under RCD's control, right? He promised if I helped, he'd get me out of the noncompete clause of my settlement. I think he was going to use it to blackmail Gerretty, or sell it to one of the other studios, whichever seemed likelier to work."

"Neither," Lizzy said. "Not with Gerretty involved."

"He wasn't this crazy when I was working," Shida said, and, in spite of herself, Lizzy laughed.

"Oh, yeah, he was. You just didn't piss him off bad enough."

Shida lifted an eyebrow. "I suppose you could be right. He didn't put that much stake in action-adventure. I suppose I should be grateful, even—if he managed to kill my career and my chances of ever working again just because he was mildly annoyed, what would he have done if he actually cared about it?"

"He'd have found something," Lizzy said. "Look, I'm serious. Maybe he didn't give a shit about losing you, or your income, because I can tell you what he does when he does care. About ten years ago—"

She knew to the day, if she'd cared to work it out, but she couldn't afford to think about it that closely, not now. "About ten years ago, I was working as a body." She saw Shida's eyes narrow, assessing her body, the tattoos, and managed a smile that she knew was bitter. "Yeah, I was younger then, and thinner, and, no, I hadn't acquired the body art. But you know, or maybe you don't know, that bodies tend to double as hookers, because you don't get paid that much unless they use your face, so one night I picked up a guy after filming, and it was Gardner Gerretty. And I didn't like the way he treated me, which I guess is pretty presumptuous, from a hooker, but he was worse than your average customer, so I thought I'd get a little of my own back, and I stole his smoke." For a second, she could almost see the case again, plain, shiny, cheap black plastic, not even monogrammed. "And he got me arrested, made sure I got convicted, and then made sure I got sent to a Wilson center—you know about them?"

Shida nodded, his face very still.

"Then you know that's a little out of line for what I did."

Shida nodded again, almost reluctantly, no other muscles moving in his body.

Lizzy took a breath. "Look, I'm not saying this is about me. I'm out, I'm clean, I got a real job—I'd be clear if it hadn't been for Keyz. But it looks to me like Gerretty's fixing to do the same thing to him that he did to me, and I'll be damned if I'm going to stand by and see it happen. That's why I'm here."

"I know." Shida's voice was almost inaudible. "I checked you out."

And you let me make my speech anyway. Lizzy said, with all the dignity she could muster, "If Gardner Gerretty would go to those lengths to bust a body and part-time prostitute, what do you think he's going to do with this kid?"

"I know," Shida said again. He took a breath. "I already talked to Pete—Sharkadi, I mean. Or he's already talked to me. Discreetly, but he made himself clear. He doesn't want anything to do with any of this. Not anymore."

Lizzy swore under her breath, not caring anymore if she sounded like white trash. *What the hell am I going to do now? I've got to get Keyz out of this shit, and Russ and Chessie, too, I got them into it . . . If Shida can't help—what if I said it was all my idea, that I'd talked the kid into it? I could maybe go underground, get a new identity, let Tin Lizzy take the blame.* She rejected the thought even as it was formed. Gerretty wouldn't believe it—more precisely, he wouldn't accept it unless it came with her arrest, and even then he was more likely to use that jazz to get stiffer sentences on all concerned, without keeping his part of any bargain.

"I don't know how much we could have done anyway," Shida said, and for the first time his voice lost the star's careful timbre. "I don't know if Pete could've sold the formula anyway, if his connections were good enough to protect him." He shook his head. "When it was jazz, I could manage it, I've got my own connections there, and I'm good."

He glared at Lizzy, daring her to contradict him, and she nodded slowly. Shida was good, no question, but the jazz had been, he was as good off-line.

"But now that it's real . . ." Shida's voice trailed off, defeated. "I'm nobody, not in that world. I'm not even rich, compared to them. I can't even buy results. I'm sorry."

Lizzy took a slow breath, the anger fading as quickly as it had appeared. This was just her luck, the way things always worked, the one person she'd counted on, gambled on, failing at the last minute. Even when you thought you had it taped, everything worked out, there was always a weak link you hadn't counted on. You couldn't expect to go up against somebody like Gerretty, like RCD, and survive. She shook herself then, knowing there was nothing that she could do, and that at the same time that she had to try, and Shida went on, almost as though he was talking to himself.

"I don't think Pete could have done that much anyway. I don't know if he could have sold the formula—Orpha-Toto, I mean—without proving that it worked, and the minute he tried to prove it, RCD would have moved in. Nobody would have been able to touch it, no matter how much they wanted it."

Without proving that it worked. The words struck a faint spark of memory, something Conti had said hovering on the brink of a connection. Lizzy frowned, drink forgotten, trying to tease out the hidden thought. Russ had said there was something wrong about the way Orpha-Toto worked—not that it didn't work, because it did, but the way that it worked. And that was the real reason RCD had to keep it secret, she realized suddenly. Not just because they didn't want the competition, but because if any of their competitors used Orpha-Toto, or anything built like it, the sample from which the program drew its grammar would be irrevocably tainted. If it really had read deep structure, the way Orfanos claimed it did, it wouldn't have mattered, the program would have been seeking something real that would have showed up even in the homogenized product of a dozen similar programs. But because it didn't, because it derived structure only from the samples it was given, the more similar the samples the more narrow its grammar and the less useful its suggestions would be. *And the more likely that audiences would get bored with films that play just like every other film,* she thought. *I bet they're already spiking the mix with other studios' films, and using mostly old films of their own, from before the formula. Suppose I managed to bust loose another copy, threatened to give it for free to every studio there is?* She shook her head again, rejecting the idea. No, that would take too long; by the time she'd proved she could do it, Keyz and the others would be under indictment, and if she had to go through with the threat, they'd have been convicted before she could spread the program widely enough to do any good.

"How the hell did Gerretty get away with it?" she asked, and Shida frowned, puzzled. "I mean, with this formula thing. Didn't the site director kick up a fuss?"

"I thought everybody knew that," Shida said. "The jazz was everywhere. When the shareholders elected him, it was a provisional thing. Gerretty said he'd raise the profit margin by thirty percent in the first two years, or they could fire him, and he'd pay back half his salary. He did it, too."

"I was in the Wilson then," Lizzy said. She blinked, a new idea spreading before her, unfolding like the best, the nastiest jazz she'd ever seen. "So his whole career is now built on Orpha-Toto. What if it didn't work?"

"But it does work," Shida began, and shook his head again. "I don't see how that helps us, it's worked well enough so far."

"But suppose it didn't," Lizzy said again. "Suppose it was all jazz, something Gerretty concocted to get control of RCD. Suppose it was him picking the hits all this time, not a program."

"They'd still be hits," Shida said. "And RCD's got a great record under his tenure, that's the problem."

"But if the shareholders—if the board of directors thought he'd lied?" Lizzy asked, and, slowly, Shida nodded.

"If they've put everything into assuming it was foolproof, a program that can't miss, can't have a bad day, can't make a mistake. . . . It might work. They wouldn't keep him on—they couldn't. People are fallible. Programs aren't."

"And if Gerretty goes down," Lizzy said, "nobody else is going to prosecute Keyz. Oh, maybe in Juvenile where it belongs, but not like this. And there are a bunch of possible self-defense claims he, all of us, can make along the way."

"You're talking some major jazz," Shida said, and Lizzy nodded.

"It'll work." She could almost taste it, not the biggest jazz that had ever been played, there were more outrageous visions, but solid, workable, playing on expectations the way the best jazz always did. Nobody outside a very narrow circle really believed that RCD's formula was a program, not even a superexpert; it had just been an easy way to make light of the studio's undeniable successes. Inside that circle, though, nobody wanted it to be a person, infinitely fallible, capable of prejudice and opinion and ultimately almost guaranteed to make an expensive mistake. Put those two assumptions together, and she could bring down Gerretty.

"And it's jazz," she said, smiling now. "It's what we do best. We'll be fighting him on our terms."

Shida rose in one fluid motion. "You want my help?"

"I need it," Lizzy said, and the younger man nodded. "I'll set up my gear."

Lizzy floated in nonspace, buoyed by Shida's expensive rig, the helmet and gloves both so light she could almost believe they weren't there. She had the best of Shida's gear, and the fastest connection, while the actor worked on a system scraped together from older components, but she didn't have time to savor that acknowledgment of her skill. An array of network nodes hung in front of her, bright dots that formed the edges of a net that stretched to an unreal horizon. They flared in turn, pulsing with messages that popped into the array of windows propped in front of her eyes, a vertical curtain between her and the horizontal spread of the schematic Net. So far, everything was going just the way she'd planned, the whisper that she'd dropped into the E-Net central node spreading at the speed of light, bouncing from site to site because even if it wasn't true, it was too good not to repeat. She fed it, judiciously, reinforcing the story, mentioning Orpha-Toto and Orfanos in one place, the supralanguages in another, intending to go back and link the two, but before she could make the connection, someone else had made it for her, tying Orpha-Toto and RCD into a neat package. It wasn't Shida, either, and she was grinning as she grabbed her prepared jazz before it could launch. She adjusted the text, and set it loose to confirm the story, as far as anything could be confirmed in the jazz. In one corner of her vision, a window tracked RCD's stock: nothing yet, nothing that she could be sure could be attributed to the jazz, but there were a few flickers, deviations in the offshore markets, that looked promising. RCD had issued a denial, something of a surprise, since they usually ignored the jazz, and that provoked a wave of response, including a community of film fans and critics who popped up a site that traced the possibility of the story's being true. Possible, they concluded, not probable, but more than just jazz, and Lizzy judged it was time to launch the second phase.

This was the tricky part, the point where everything turned round one more time and caught Gerretty firmly in its coils. She'd already prepared the package, threading it through a cheap, fee-mail site, the kind of place that catered to users without good access of their own: just a brief note, claiming to be from Conti, acknowledging Orpha-Toto as his own. She released that, watching it spread as people who'd known Conti picked up the word that he was back and repeated the message for that fact or lie as much as for the RCD connection. The RCD debate picked it up as well. The makeshift forum dissected it in passing, agreeing it was a fraud, and Lizzy launched a second message. This one purported to be from Conti, too, but it was better made, came through a plausible node, the one that hosted the cybercafe where he had worked. It admitted Orpha-Toto, admitted he'd worked on it, said, reluctantly, it didn't quite work the way they'd planned, and warned people away from using it. It wouldn't give the answers they wanted, he said, and that was all.

That was something people wanted to hear, and this one, too, was picked up and repeated, spreading along the RCD threads even faster than the original message. Shida put his name behind it, first in private, and then, with feigned reluctance, in public. Opinion stayed divided as to whether it was really Conti, but most people seemed to think it was—*and well they should*, Lizzy thought, watching a message pulse blue and green along one section of a major entertainment tree. *We know him pretty well, between us.* In any case, it didn't matter, as long as some of them believed and repeated it, and anyway there was a good chance that at least a few people who didn't believe it would still pass the word along, because the possibilities were so deliciously nasty.

She had another message prepared, a series of them, dropped them one by one into the debate: someone claiming expertise in supralanguages, agreeing with "Conti"; someone else saying they'd never believed it was a program; a third voice asking plaintively who was making the decisions, then, if the formula didn't work. The last one seemed to sink like a stone, drew only a handful of responses, but she knew it had been seen. She hesitated, hands poised to launch another question, and decided to wait a little longer. Already there was enough interest, too much interest, and a light flashed once in the distant Net, signaling the first uptake of the crucial question. She worked her fingers, drawing the section closer. It was in the right place, too, the heart of the professional lists, the ones that were supposedly restricted to people who actually worked in films, and she reached into the control space, groping for the tap Shida had set for her. He still had low-level access to RCD's phone space; she wouldn't be able to read the messages, but she could track the patterns of traffic.

The new design popped into a new window, branched like a nerve, and she drew it close, watching the nodes light up as word passed from level to level. There were half a dozen conference calls in the Halliday Tower, mid-executive level, according to Shida's key, and then a light flared in Studio Central, an upper-level call, linking five local and two outside numbers. The board of directors, convening to discuss the matter, she thought—hoped—and glanced at the stock window. The price was fluctuating, dropping in the main indices, rising wildly in the Asian markets, and she would have crossed her fingers if her hands hadn't been busy. Instead, she reached for YENN's main node, pulled its headlines into full view: *RCD board calls special meeting, denies rumors of Gerretty firing.* That, of course, meant pretty much the opposite, and Lizzy slowly extricated herself from the web of light. It was over, pretty much, just the last moves to be played out, the BoD's decision and Gerretty's inevitable resignation. *Though I suppose he might wait to be fired,* Lizzy thought, and lifted off her helmet. *That would be Gerretty's style.*

It was chilly in the suite, too much air-conditioning without the incoming sun to balance it, and she rubbed her hands together, dragging her sleeves back down in a futile gesture. She stretched, and shivered, and Shida said, "You did it."

She looked at him, hoping he was right, the certainty she had felt on the Net fading as she dropped back into the real world, and Shida nodded.

"I've been off for a while, been watching the E-channels. They're slow, but they generally get the message."

Lizzy looked past him to the media screen, divided now into four separate sections with headlines playing across their tops. RUMORS OF TROUBLE. STOCK PRICES DROP. RCD BOARD HOLDS EMERGENCY MEETING? GERRETTY IN HOT WATER: so she'd made it real, she thought, taken it from pure jazz and made it so real that the studio had responded almost as quickly off-line as on.

"You did it," Shida said again, and sounded very young.

"What's happening here?" she asked.

Shida worked the remote. "Nothing on the local, so far—but of course it didn't happen here. Gerretty knows, you can bet on that. I saw the calls come in."

"Yeah," Lizzy said. This was the part she hadn't been sure about, hadn't been sure she liked, except that there was a part of her that savored a chance to gloat. "But does he know what it means?"

Shida lifted an eyebrow and muted the headlines, which were replaced by a babble of voices. "What are you talking about?"

"Somebody has to tell him he's lost," Lizzy said.

"He knows," Shida said. "And if he doesn't, his people do."

"He can still do damage," Lizzy said. "And I want this as neat and clean as we can make it."

"That's crazy," Shida said. "Everything you said—he could hurt you."

"I doubt it," Lizzy answered. "He's still got something to lose."

"I don't know about that," Shida said, somberly, and gave himself a little shake. "You may be right, at that. Somebody has to tell him, or he'll never believe it."

"And that somebody is going to be me," Lizzy said.

She made it almost all the way across the platform before Security noticed her, walking easily through the lavender twilight, watching the moon rise across the bay. It was an almost unnerving spectacle, the perfect disk turning the headland and its lighthouse black, drowning the light itself, and Lizzy caught her breath, trying to fix it in memory. The moon's reflection was like a strip of crumpled silver, the sky around it almost blue, stars banished, even the evening star obscured, lost in the staggering whiteness, and she knew she'd try to re-create it in at least one of her settings. And probably fail, too, it was almost impossible to create *space*, never mind the heavy, natural colors, all at their extremes of tone, but it was a thing to think about, a promise to hold her up through the next hours. At the foot of the next stairway, a security man touched her shoulder, and she turned, smiling.

"I think you were looking for me."

They brought her to the security office on the platform's lowest level, watching her closely, never, after that first moment, touching her. Lizzy let herself be shepherded through the dimly lit corridors and then into brightness, from the tourist areas with their carefully planned night-lighting to the working areas where atmosphere didn't matter. She didn't bother memorizing the route or look for a way to run, and she knew from the way her escorts looked at each other that they were worried about her docility. They brought her finally into a large inner room where a pretty, tired-looking blonde was working at a console, and told her to wait while one of them went to inform Mr. Hallac and Mr. Gerretty. The blonde looked up at that, blank expression sharpening to interest, and Lizzy guessed she had to be the on-line cop. She would have asked, putting off the moment a second longer, but then the door to the inner office opened, and the security man beckoned them inside.

They were all there ahead of her, she realized instantly, not just Hallac and Gerretty, but the black woman who'd arrested Conti, and Conti and Keyz and Vara. Vara had one arm wrapped awkwardly, protectively, around the boy's shoulders. Gerretty had a closed phone in his hand, but turned like a bull at their entrance.

"About fucking time."

The security men glanced at each other, and Hallac frowned. "Where'd you find her?"

The guards exchanged another glance, and Lizzy drew herself up, ready to answer herself if they lied. But the first one cleared his throat and said, nervously, "She was on the plaza. Heading this way."

"No trouble?" Hallac asked.

"No, sir."

Hallac sighed, looking down at his desktop. "OK. You can go."

The security men backed away, almost tripping over each other in their eagerness to get out the door, but then they were gone, the door closed behind them.

"All right, Ms. Rhea," Hallac said. "What's your jazz?"

"You set this up," Gerretty said. He shook the phone in her face, the short antenna almost hitting her in the eye. Lizzy held her position, with an effort, every muscle tensing again. "It's not going to do you a damn bit of good. That little bastard still stole from us, and he's caused serious damage to our system. Even if I go down, the board's going to make him pay for that."

"They're going to get you first," Lizzy said. She looked at Hallac. "I'm assuming you know what's been going on. Mr. Gerretty has some questions to answer back at the studio."

"Bullshit," Gerretty began, and Hallac's eyes dropped to his desktop. "Hallac, they're still under arrest, and I expect you to keep them under arrest, bring them to trial."

Hallac said, expressionless, "It's up to the board, of course."

"God damn it," Gerretty said. "God damn you all."

He slid the phone back into his pocket, breathing hard, and it was all Lizzy could do to control her nervous grin. She'd done it, she'd brought him down, paid him back for the two years she'd spent in the Wilson—more than that, she'd saved Keyz, because there was no way the board was going to bother with them when they had Gerretty to deal with. And then Gerretty brought his hand back out of his pocket, and the phone was gone, replaced by a gun. Lizzy froze, staring—it had to be tiny, was dwarfed in the big man's hand, but the open muzzle looked enormous—and Hallac said, "Hold on, now . . ."

His voice was soothing, designed to get people out of hostage situations alive, but Gerretty ignored him, took a step and then another, arm at full stretch, until the muzzle was practically touching Lizzy's hair. She swallowed hard, knew she was shaking, and tightened her fists to deny him at least that satisfaction.

"I wouldn't," Gerretty said. "Nobody gets the better of me. Nobody."

"Mr. Gerretty," Hallac said. Lizzy could see him take a breath, his voice suddenly firm. "Put the gun down. You can—if you fire, you will be charged appropriately. I promise you that."

Great, Lizzy thought, *he still won't call it murder. But it's going to be murder if he doesn't stop him—*

"I don't care," Gerretty said.

Lizzy turned her head, carefully, trying to see the man's face. Dark eyes glared back at her out of a red face, but it was the gun that drew her eyes, irresistibly, chrome steel-bright in the working lights.

"You thought you'd just walk in here and tell me I'd lost," Gerretty said. "Walk in here and gloat. You thought you could win. Well, I'll tell you something, girl. You're not crazy enough to beat me. Call it off—kill that jazz, or I will kill you where you stand. One shot in the head, right through the eye—not nice."

Lizzy closed her eyes, made herself open them again, not wanting to die blind. And she was going to die, she was certain of it, as sure as she'd ever been of anything. Gerretty had no idea who she was, no idea that they'd ever met before, she was sure of that, too, sure that she was just another obstacle, impossible to get rid of this time. She'd known what Gerretty was like when he didn't get his way—she should have listened to Shida, stayed clear, and let Hallac handle things. But she hadn't known, then, that Hallac would act, and he might not have done it if she wasn't there. *Be careful what you wish for*, she thought, breath catching in her throat. She'd gotten Keyz out of it, but it didn't seem to matter as much as it had.

"I'm waiting," Gerretty said, and Lizzy hunched her shoulders in spite of herself, as though that would somehow help. He was almost close enough that she could think of grabbing the gun, but he was bigger and heavier, rich enough that he was probably in better shape, too: she had no real chance of wrestling the gun away. Out of the corner of her eye, she saw Hallac tense, weight shifting imperceptibly onto the balls of his feet. She would duck, she decided, down and to her own left, go out trying.

"It can't be stopped," she said, and licked her lips. "You lose."

Keyz cried out, and there was a sudden movement to her right, Vara drawing the boy's face against her chest.

"Gerretty!" Hallac shouted, and there was a shot, louder and longer than she'd expected, and exploding pain.

She woke, unexpectedly, to sunlight and salt air, blinked unhappily, recognizing a distant ache. That probably meant she wasn't dead, but at the moment, she wasn't sure she was grateful. Her head throbbed, two distinct and angry pains layered one on top of the other, and she cringed at the thought of a bullet in the brain. She moved her fingers, quick and furtive, was relieved when they responded. Her toes answered, too, and she cut her eyes sideways, not wanting to move her head.

"You're awake," a cool voice said, and she blinked again, swallowing to get her voice back.

"Shida?"

"I hope you don't mind. Chessie thought you'd get better treatment if I took an interest."

"No." Lizzy blinked again, trying to feel her entire body at once, terrified of what might be wrong. "What—how bad?"

Shida smiled, cool as ever, and Vara leaned forward into her line of vision.

"Don't worry, he mostly missed."

"Mostly?" Lizzy's voice cracked, throat burning, and Shida's smile became an open grin. "John Hallac—RCD's boss cop on the job—shot him just as he shot you. And you were ducking, too, they think. So you've got a fractured skull where the bullet grazed you, but no permanent damage."

"It was a little gun," Vara said. "You were lucky. The bullet caught you just about here." She touched her own head, just below the crown and above her left ear. "I guess there were some fragments, but the surgeons just took them out, put in a plate instead. How are you feeling?"

"Like somebody shot me," Lizzy said.

Vara laughed, loudly enough to make the younger woman's head hurt even more, and Shida said quickly, "They're going to kick us out when they see you're awake, but is there anything else you want to know?"

"Gerretty?" Lizzy asked.

"Busted," Vara said, with satisfaction. "Attempted murder. No way he'll get out of that one. Plus a batch of false-arrest charges, and probably fraud on top of that, once the criminal stuff's taken care of."

"I trust you'll testify, when you feel up to it?" Shida asked.

"Oh, yes," Lizzy said, and the others exchanged satisfied glances.

"Seth is back with his parents," Vara said, and Lizzy blinked, confused again, before she remembered Keyz' real name. "And the studio has agreed to drop all charges against you and Russ and Shirle. And Njeri, too. I gather there will be some charges against Seth, but they'll be suspended in exchange for his testimony and a general agreement to keep things quiet."

"What about you?" Lizzy asked, and the big woman grinned.

"Well, I'm not quite flavor of the month back home—there are a few little issues my bosses aren't completely happy with—but the commissioner in Lakeview is taking full credit for my being involved. It's great publicity for him."

"So you keep your badge?" Lizzy pressed, wanting to hear it said, and Vara nodded, the crazy grin fading a little.

"Yeah. I keep my badge."

"Russ isn't doing too badly, either," Shida said. "There are at least four or five studios who want to hire him to rebuild Orpha-Toto."

"That doesn't sound like Russ."

"I didn't say he took the job." This time it was Shida's turn to grin. "People are listening to him again—like it or not, he's back, and there are a lot of small co-ops and indies that want him to work for them. Not building formulas, but tearing them down. I think he's going to take one of them."

There was something about Shida's grin that suggested he'd brokered that deal, and Lizzy wondered what the actor was going to get out of it. *Probably more than I will—except I didn't really expect to survive.* That definitely counted for something. And at least Keyz was all right, and Russ and Vara. *And maybe I'm all right, too.* The thought was startling, not least because she hadn't known before how much she'd feared Gerretty and everything he stood for. *But I won, this time—more than that, I saved the kid. I did—well enough.* She started to nod, realized she couldn't, and managed a smile instead. It would do, she thought, and let herself drift back to sleep.